DEADLY TRESPASS

SANDRA NEILY

This is a work of fiction. While some Maine place names are real locations, some are fictionalized. All characters, businesses, and incidents are products of the author's imagination and are used in a fictitious manner. Any resemblance to actual persons, living or dead, or actual events is purely coincidental.

However, the clear cutting of forests, the use of poisons and predator derbies to kill wild animals, wolves as a constant controversy, and corporations' ability to degrade public interest agencies and some organizations...these events and trends are not fiction. (See author's notes.)

Published by Kwill Books 2017 First Paperback Edition

ISBN-13: 978-84-946149-5-8

http://www.kwillbooks.com/

To Bob, my white knight in jeans.

Without you, your faith, love, and sacrifices, there was no opportunity to grow my voice into Deadly Trespass. *I am grateful beyond words.*

TABLE OF CONTENTS

AUTHOR'S NOTES

As of 2017, here's what's fact, not fiction.

1080 poison: The USDA (United States Department of Agriculture) "Animal Services" office continues to use the lethal poison 1080 to kill predators. In 2015 it claims to have killed 3.2 million animals (including coyotes, bobcats, bears, wolves, and mountain lions) with various methods. The illegal black market use of 1080 also continues.

Predator derbies: Contests to kill predators (complete with prizes) are held in some western states.

Incidental take: Under the Endangered Species Act, The U.S. Department of the Interior dispenses permits that allow the injury or killing of a listed species, within the permit's guidelines and limits.

Clear cutting: In Maine, and the U.S., and throughout the world, harvesting most or all the trees on a site is still an established or permitted practice, defended by industry as a viable forestry management tool.

CHAPTER 1

I wasn't really breaking the law. Maine's a practical state. My ancestors knew they couldn't slap a deed on something that slithers through fingers, so they made rivers and trout public property and left it vague how we'd get to them.

Last week my biologist boss thumped his coffee-stained map and complained about a billionaire buying up lands he used to fish on. I leaned over his shoulder, memorized Carla Monson's streams, and, on my day off, drove north.

I parked next to a pile of naked logs that dwarfed my car and stared at Monson's gate. Behind the wire she'd grown a green oasis where "No Harvesting" and "No Trespassing" signs swarmed the fence: signs that exclude people from large chunks of wild terrain are special invitations to me. I was a trespasser as soon as I could crawl away from my house toward woods and waters the wealthy used a few weeks a year. Behind Carla Monson's gate, spawning trout had to be flinging themselves upstream under fall leaves as orange as their cold, swollen bellies. They were my kind of invitation.

Pock jumped out the window and crawled under the gate where his nose vacuumed the ground, and his wagging tail telegraphed urgent discovery. I slid my bike, pack, and fly rod under the gate, lay on my back, and skidded below nasty razor wire. Up on my knees, I rubbed my lumpy fingers, aware that arthritis was punishment for living past fifty, but strangely cheered that cold streams were my choice of painkiller. I saw serrated ATV tire tracks and muddy prints that didn't fit my dog. Maybe a coyote—a large coyote. I groaned, stood, and yelled Pock's favorite ice-cream invitation. "Let's go, baby. Yip, yip. Zip, zip."

No dog. I whistled and yelled again, annoyed I'd have to retrieve a Labrador retriever. When a rising breeze rained pine needles onto my shoulders and blew Pock's frantic howls at me, I shoved loose hairs into my ponytail, shouldered my pack, and pedaled up Monson's rutted road. Navigating an unfamiliar track I didn't want to travel after dark, I crushed late-blooming goldenrod and bent low as the old road tunneled through birches twisted low by last winter's heavy ice.

Behind a cedar swamp, Pock's yowling rose to a frantic pitch, and he sounded squeezed for space. What could corner a ninety-pound dog? Officially, we'd killed off cougars and wolves years ago, but that hadn't stopped rumors of them roaming the woods. I didn't want to arrive home with a half-chewed dog—or not arrive home at all.

I dropped my bike and waded into the swamp. Muck oozed down my boots and glued my toes together before I found him, belly down in the dirt, ears flattened toward his back. Between howls he pushed his nose under a fallen white pine, its roots limp and naked over a dirty hole. Ancient mold stung my nose and eyes as I picked my way through amputated branches and pulled my dog away from the body.

Shannon Angeles lay under the massive tree. I knew her shocking red hair, her Flash Fire nail polish, even the smiling moon sticker on her left hiking boot. She wore the same pitch-stained clothes she'd worn days ago when she returned my battery charger and played tug-of-war with Pock. I saw only one collapsed cheek, but I knew my best friend was dead.

I knelt and slid damp hair off her nose and squeezed my eyes shut. I'd had my hands on dead people I didn't know, but never a dead friend. I couldn't smell death—couldn't smell blood or bowels let go. Shannon smelled like rain and white pine. My head pounded as if I were underwater without air. *Breathe*, I thought. *Breathe through it. Open your eyes and do this for Shannon. See this for Shannon. She'd want a full report.*

I gulped pine-charged air, opened my eyes, and reached for her left side where I pulled broken branches from her face. Gray, pink-tinged fluid dripped from one ear, and one green eye stared at me the way she always stared at me when I didn't have answers. I liked answers but I loved Shannon.

A tree limb had pierced her neck in a near-perfect impalement, and I had a bizarre moment remembering a line in a first aid manual, "object stuck in flesh, protruding from flesh." When I saw bark glowing green under the wound's stretched tissue, instant sweat glued my shirt to my back.

The cheek I could see was whole, raked raw into purple bruises, and the cheek I couldn't see seemed propped on a metal box and jagged strap that didn't look like her tools. I leaned toward her outstretched arm and my stomach heaved as I saw it all. Dirt lifted her nails—nails that had clawed the ground around her into a frenzied semicircle. How long had she known she was dying?

"Oh, Shannon honey. What happened? What went wrong?" I sobbed and rocked and stroked her hand. "Don't go. Don't go. Please don't go." Pock crawled to me and licked Shannon's fingers each time my rocking brought them to his nose.

I don't know how long I held her hand trying to rub warmth into it. Shivers rattled my teeth, we'd lost the sun, and I wanted help on the scene before animals grew restless in the dark. Thinking about hungry wildlife, I pulled an emergency blanket from my pack and covered the parts of her I could reach. The blanket wasn't big enough to discourage visitors. I needed a language animals respected—a language one large coyote might understand.

"Pock," I ordered, "pee here."

We'd lived in suburbs and cities, so my dog knew how to urinate on the tiniest blade of grass. He wetted the edge of the cloth and backed off, ears cocked at the strangled sound of my voice.

My turn. I bent toward Shannon's ear. "You'd understand why I'm doing this, sweetie." I dropped my pants and squatted near her face, pouring a perfect puddle. "Pock and I are marking our territory. *Our* territory," I whispered, zipping up my fly.

Then I yelled. "Listen up! This is *my* friend. Anyone who touches her answers to *me*." I grabbed a large branch, and when I broke it over my knee, the snap sent Pock between my legs. I piled broken pieces over the cloth and raised my voice until it was more screech than sound. "I mean it. Don't mess with me."

I thought about leaving Pock on guard, but I knew he'd flee anything that howled in the dark. I tugged his collar and waded back to my bike.

I don't remember much of the return ride over the woods road unless it involved pain. I crashed into a frost-heaved rock and somersaulted over my handlebars, landing on my pack and exploding my water bottle so it soaked my back. Then I picked up my bike and pulled out my headlamp. Its ribbon of light narrowed the forest's gloom into a path I could follow. I didn't bother to load the bike.

In the car, Pock leaned from the passenger seat into my lap, and I gripped his fur as if it were the last firm rock on a collapsing wall.

I drove east, away from the gate where hours ago I'd registered my travel plans and entered Great Nations Forests' timberlands, lying to the gatekeeper, Sam, about my destination. I always lied to him and encouraged others to lie too. Before she could wear a bra, my daughter Kate had leaned away from the window when Sam leered in. "Let's call him Sketchy Sam," she'd said, "so we never forget what he really is."

As Great Nations' gatekeeper, Sketchy Sam had control of millions of acres under his twitching thumbs, and he liked to think he knew everything. His pickled, beet-red face vibrated under sharp hawk eyes. He knew more than he had a right to know. I didn't want him to know about Shannon.

I headed toward the nearest north woods phone booth—a tree limb wedged into a pothole with flagging tape and a battered cell phone case advertising a working signal. I dialed 911 and said I'd found a friend dead in the woods. Under a tree.

The dispatcher asked me if I was safe, and then he surprised me. "Do you have any reason to consider her death suspicious?" Were 911 folks supposed to ask that?

"Why would you ask me that? I don't know. She's under a tree."

"I need to contact the appropriate first aid and investigative response teams," he said. "Do you know if there were witnesses to this event?" I knew what that meant. No witnesses to an unexplained death meant he'd call it in as a suspicious death, but I didn't want to play.

"Trees," I said. "Maybe some squirrels. You going to send the cavalry, or what?"

"Please give me your GPS coordinates."

"I don't do GPS," I snapped. "I'm parked in a *phone booth* east of Bluffer Brook and any game warden on any road in Maine will know where I am."

The dispatcher's voice slowed to the drawl emergency personnel use for people who are not quite right. He told me to lock the car doors and wait.

I was passed out in restless sleep when Pock growled, but I wasn't worried. The blinding light held high over my car and the strong stride said Maine game warden—and I knew him. After I unlocked the door, Robert Atkins lifted me into a hug. His crisp, forest-green uniform creaked leather from belt to gun holster to citation books. Authority poured off his shoulders and greased his black boots. I'd never hugged him before. He was too mythic, too foreign, and too much my ex-husband's friend. He smelled like fresh wood. "What is wrong?" he asked.

Wrong? Wrong? I could feel anger crawl up my chest into my mouth, but I swallowed it into a thought. *I'll tell you what's wrong. My best friend, the one who knows more about trees than anyone up here, just got killed by one. Explain that one.*

"What is wrong?" he said.

"Robert." The name came out as a croak. I'd never called him Robert or even heard his whole name said out loud. "Moz," I said. I cleared my throat, pressed two hands on his chest, and pushed for space. "Evan never did tell me what Moz means. Secret Penobscot word? Tribal thing?"

"Your husband never asked me," he said. "Moz is Abenaki for moose." He slowly swept the light from my head to my feet, stepped behind me to repeat his examination, and then flashed the beam through my car. Pock's eyes glowed red, but he wagged his whole body in gleeful recognition.

I could barely see his intent black eyes lock onto me, but I knew Moz assessed my chatter. Shock? Disorientation? Some other emotion he'd have to navigate? Hell, I didn't know and I was the one chattering. "Yeah. OK," I said. "But that doesn't explain anything."

With his free hand, he walked me backward and leaned me up against the side of my car. "Will you be able to tell me about your emergency if I explain why I am compared to a moose?"

I don't remember the entire explanation. I think he dragged it out to settle my adrenaline jitters, but it was clear he'd earned his nickname methodically pursuing poachers through brush and streams. Apparently, he chased criminals in a straight line that ignored ground conditions—the way long-legged moose plow through woods without swerving for much. While other wardens searched for easy routes, Moz must have been a quarter mile ahead of them, his hands already on someone's collar. He lifted the light to study my face. In the dark, all I could see were cheekbones and teeth. "Alright," I said. "But let's do this in the dark. Turn off the light."

CHAPTER 2

The next day, despite nightmares where Shannon's one eye lit me like a green searchlight and my throat felt worse than a bad case of strep, I went to work. Near town, three TV vans blew by me. At that speed, branches overhanging my driveway would decapitate the crews' antennas before the reporters reached my camp. I smiled a small smile. My face didn't feel ready for anything more.

I was tempted to go to ground, to crawl some place low where I could pull ferns over my head and sleep on moss. I wasn't ten years old any more. I needed a hiding place that was happy to see me. My suit-wearing friends in the legislature had wondered why I'd abandoned them to handle dead animals, but I found working the game registration station comforting. I liked the camaraderie of moose, the hunters who killed them, and the scientists who made sense of it all. I needed a place where death was routine—maybe even celebrated by those who'd done the killing—and the wool-clad crew had seemed pleased when I showed up. They'd tested me though, spearing deer droppings onto toothpicks and leaving them next to the chips and nuts. On my first day, a pellet made it past my lips before they rolled their eyes to warn me off.

Inside the airplane hangar that doubled as a registration station, moose season had started without me. Trucks and carcasses were lined up outside the open bay doors, wind rattled the building's metal siding, and across the lake an early snow line dusted Spencer Mountain's rocks. In the cove, geese enforced social order, honking and rushing at less desirable flock mates. I could relate.

Ken Douglas, my biologist boss, removed my name tag, dropped an ancient fedora on my head, and briefed the crew. "Let's treat reporters to the usual guts-and-maggots discussion that moves them out the door. None of us is going to know this woman today, and while we're hiding her, let's work her hard so she stays busy."

He studied me with steady brown eyes that peered from under brows so bushy they collected leaves and twigs. He knew about furtive animal behavior, knew I'd moved north to hibernate and lick fresh wounds.

I saw his eyes roll just before I saw the reporter hipping her way through the garage, cameraman tethered to her by cables. In three-inch heels, she teetered on a concrete floor slick with moose parts—a beginner sent to the hinterland on a minor story. Her thin leather jacket barely covered a skimpy camisole too short to cover her navel. Raised bumps speckled her cold bare legs.

She clutched a white-haired man's arm and charged into an interview. "This is Dory Perkins from station WABW in Bangor, Maine. I'm talking with a hunter at the Greenwood check station." She pressed her microphone into his beard. "The wardens found a dead woman alone in the woods. Did you know her?"

"No, ma'am." He fumbled in his camouflage vest and raised a small camera. "Just that she was alone."

"Do folks up here think it was foul play?" she asked.

With one finger, he lowered her microphone. "Excuse me, young lady. Grandson's big day. I promised I'd get a shot of the weigh-in."

The reporter scanned the crowd looking for her story. Hunters in brown-green camouflage jumpsuits bumped up against fathers lifting children for a better view. Tourists waved cameras over their heads and snapped unexpected local color. While everyone shuffled cold feet and pointed at the scales, I ducked behind an arriving truck just pulling into line. I wasn't going to help the press sensationalize Shannon's death, and I wasn't going to give up a good hiding place.

Dory Perkins wandered outside, tugging at her captive cameraman like he was leashed for a walk. The crowd pressed against the truck as Ken climbed the carcass. He looked more like a short, squat wrestler pinning a hairy opponent than a wildlife biologist. Grunting as he stretched his arms over the bull's butchered belly, he strained to connect two sides of a slippery strap.

Soft moose muzzle brushed my lips when I leaned into the truck's cab. I pressed my weight into the animal's neck, closed my eyes, and imagined him alive. Four hours ago, he'd been knee deep in Tomhegan Bog, flesh rippling with urgency, nostrils squeezed back to suck in female-scented air. He must have heard the hunters stop and open their doors, but maybe a cow grazed upwind. While he swung his nose toward her, men stepped into the road and raised their rifles.

Overhead machinery coughed into life as I whispered to deaf moose ears. *Tonight, I will see you back in the swamp.* I'd had trouble falling asleep, replaying divorce drama alone in the dark. And how could I sleep anyway if Shannon's cracked nails were behind my lids when I closed my eyes? Last year my therapist suggested visualizing a serene location, maybe a warm beach. I visualized moose easing their hairy bulk down into leaves. I conjured up dark thickets and crushed grass—willed myself to a stillness that heard teeth grind twigs into food. I didn't tell my therapist that large herbivores put me to sleep.

I certainly didn't tell her about my imaginary animal conversations.

I whispered again. *Tonight, I will see you back in the swamp.*

Tonight, I will be ground into burger.

Not when I close my eyes. I can see you alive.

Can you see the other swamp, and your friend alive in it?

Sometimes imaginary conversations don't go where I want them to go.

Ken hit the switch and webs of cable tightened bloody straps under the animal's belly. As the bull's head rose from my hands into the air, its final breath warmed my fingers.

“Nine hundred and eighty-two pounds,” said Ken. I reached for my clipboard and bent to enter the bull’s weight as the reporter marched up to the far side of the truck.

“Are you in charge?” Dory asked, reaching up to tweak Ken’s pant cuff. “I’m looking for Cassandra Patton Conover. I’m told she works here and she found a dead woman in the woods. No one wearing a uniform will speak to me. Not cops. Not state police. Not game wardens. All I get is ‘ongoing investigation.’ I need to find this Conover.”

Ken tilted his head sideways and squinted like he was having trouble understanding her question. “You’re not looking for a job are you, miss, because although we can’t see how we’d ever replace her, we seem to have misplaced Ms. Conover.”

“I’m not done here,” she said. “Something’s not right. Too many cops and game wardens crawling all over the story for this to be an act of God. When a forester for big timber gets killed by a big tree and the uniforms close ranks—it’s a story that smells.”

As she huffed away from the truck, men stared at her smooth belly and smooth face. I thought she was just about the age of Evan’s new wife, a woman so young I could have delivered, diapered, and presented her to my husband on our first wedding anniversary.

I considered the eviscerated moose. Yes. I might know what it felt like to be gutted and strung up.

"Patton? Patton? You still hiding? Screwdriver. Need the screwdriver," Ken said. His gloved hands pried open teeth still green from a pond weed breakfast.

I ducked low and wiggled the tool above my head, suddenly aware I hadn't spoken all day and that no one seemed to mind. I'd given up on mirrors but would have liked a quick peek to see what the crew saw. Was I leaking tears I couldn't feel? Had I forgotten essential clothing? I patted down my men's overalls and layered-on flannel shirts and—thanks to the Baptist thrift store—discovered I was fully covered. "Down here," I said.

Ken sighed. "Just pass it up to Moz, de-ah," he said. "He's come looking for something to do." Moz clenched the screwdriver handle between his teeth, keeping his hands free to pull a Buck knife from his belt.

Straddling the moose, Sergeant Robert Atkins looked every inch an epic hero. A dark hero. Straight black hair, black brows, black eyes, and, if he was angry, a black glare that disarmed the lawless like a drawn gun. He seemed impossibly tall even though he was just over six feet, his height rising from an erect posture that straightened his back, lifted his shoulders, and squared his jaw. He looked both sculpted and alive at the same time.

I'd never considered him an animal specimen until that moment when I almost smelled the hangar fill with pulsating pheromones. I wondered if Moz could scent women's interest the same way a bull moose sniffed the air for mates.

Shannon saw it. "How can you miss that man?" she'd asked. "Is he invisible because he's your ex-husband's pal? I never saw that man match up. I think he's some kind of backwoods angel who guards you. Not 'cause you need it, though—something else going on."

Moz sliced his knife down the side of one canine tooth. He wedged the screwdriver under the gum line, popped the tooth from its socket, and handed it, dripping, to me. I slid it into a vial of preservative where it would yield up its secrets to biologists. Moz knocked drops off the wet screwdriver and left it balanced on the edge of the cab where I could reach it.

"De-ah," Ken said, "Moz needs the combs."

I handed them miniature combs that called up scary memories of lice checks in elementary school. In two months, ticks could suck ten gallons of blood from a moose calf and tilt its fate toward death. The men crouched back to back to comb the hide and count ticks. I scribbled infestation numbers called out to me and tried to feel grateful for all species—even lowlife species like reporters and ticks.

Investigating a tick-ravaged carcass near Bluffer Brook, Moz was the warden who'd caught my emergency call, and next to Ken, he was the only other man I trusted.

CHAPTER 3

Moz jumped from the truck, landed lightly next to me, and turned me toward the doors. "We believe you should walk to the dock and deeply breathe air," he said.

Ken reached for my clipboard. "The moose under me looks more alert than you do. Take a break."

Goose droppings made travel to the town dock tricky, like navigating a field of cigar-sized land mines. Geese screeched and complained. *Our turf! Our turf!*

I know. I got it. Everyone thinks they've got turf.

Go 'round! Go 'round! Our turf! Our turf!

I stomped my way through the flock, thinking geese were spunky but naive. *Listen. You need to know our species can take your turf and evict you anytime we want. I mean, I wouldn't do that, but—but get used to the rest of the world.*

Stripped of its masts and motor, a naked-looking boat bumped against the dock. I climbed aboard and lay flat on splintered wood, hoping the heaving deck would rock me to sleep. I was beyond tired, when eyes feel like they're closing over sandpaper and skin feels nauseous. I pressed the broken sides of my phone together and pulled up my daughter's last message. She'd sent a picture of her roommate holding a newspaper that said, “Trespasser Finds Crushed Forester.” I groaned.

I was dialing Kate when I felt the boat sink under the weight of something heavier than geese. Off-duty, Moz had traded his black boots for soft moccasins. He crouched on his heels and slid pack straps off his shoulders.

I clutched the phone to my chest. “Thank you for calling someone to drive me home. And for my car and bike. They got home, too.” I watched him watch me and then I looked at the hemline where his green pants brushed against his moccasin beads. Was the law investigating me or was I in a large, quiet Penobscot space, the kind of space my tribe avoids? “Is this official?” I asked.

He kept his crouch. My knees would have been screaming.

“Are you investigating me?” I said, sitting up. “Is this official?”

It was almost a whisper. “Officially me,” he said.

“That clears it up nicely. You mean there’s more questions? Shannon died under a tree. I saw her.” I was too tired to slap my mouth closed. “You must have figured out why Shannon was behind Monson’s gate. I bet you and your search team fingered every frigging rock behind the gate,” I said. Moz was a calm but fearless investigator of the world. I should have known something was up when he looked away, but my eyes burned and my throat closed with questions. Tears dripped down my chin and soaked my collar.

He handed me an ironed bandana. "You will want to know about Shannon and the tree." The tree looked healthy to me. Did I miss a rogue tornado that shredded only a slice of swamp? How could someone who thought of trees as friends end up under one? Moz's black eyes returned to me, softer this time. "After a logging crew cut the tree into sections, they cut the branch near her throat. Only an inch of bark was visible as she went to the ambulance."

He pressed one finger on the toe of my boot. One finger was OK with me because I had private fortifications like Monson had gates. Last month when Shannon treated me to a massage and the masseuse had tried to knead tension from my shoulders, I'd slid off the table, dressed, and fled. Who knew the fear of never being touched again could be found by fingers?

Moz shifted his crouch toward the lake and adjusted his jaw so its bones tightened his skin. He chose a cool, flat voice. "Ms. Monson insists that Shannon be autopsied. It was a suspicious death occasioned by criminal trespass, so she will be obliged. For some unexplained reason, she is not filing trespass charges against you."

I didn't want to think about Shannon stripped on a table. "Carla Monson," I said. "I thought she was in Florida."

"That appears to be true," he said. "Do you know her?"

"No," I said, "but she looks like an ancient refugee—set face, crossed arms, overly long braid tucked into a raggedy skirt. In the paper she doesn't look like the millions she's got."

"Her manager, Gordon Samuels, is camped inside the gate trying to block our investigation. Do you know him?" Moz asked.

"No." I looked toward the lake where wind tilted waves into swells. Geese bobbed behind us, arched white necks stretched toward us like eavesdroppers, and then they were airborne, squawking and flapping their wings.

Dory Perkins shoved her cameraman down the ramp to the dock, yelling questions without waiting for answers. "Hey, Conover! Since you quit lobbying you're hard to find. Any truth to the rumors you were run out of town?"

I don't know how Moz rose to his feet on a tilting boat, but he made it look easy. We were both headed toward our late fifties, but he was limber. I swayed to my knees and flopped over sideways like a beetle struggling to right itself.

Dory clutched her crew as if he were solid ground, ignoring his frantic efforts to skate upright on wet planks. "Can you explain how in nine million acres of woods, you just happened to be on the same patch as your dead friend?" she called.

One foot braced on the boat, the other on the dock, Moz wrote something in his citation book, ripped the page, and stuffed it into the cameraman's coat pocket. Dory gasped as Moz pulled his knife and let it hang in the air for long seconds before he severed the ropes holding us to the dock. Dory wasn't done. "So, Conover, how could you identify someone who was pressed flat by a tree?

And you're guarded by that guy in green because you know something we don't?"

We blew away while she yelled at her cameraman. "Hey, hey. Get that shot. It's mine. Game warden and dead woman's friend ... adrift in investigation. Hey, hey. Do it!" He fiddled with his camera and smiled at Moz.

"What did you give him?" I asked.

"An offer," Moz said.

"Offer of what?"

"Trout flies in exchange for invisibility."

"You bought him off with fishing gear? How did you know his currency?"

"His hat has collected many seasons of misdirected flies." Moz sat and crossed his legs, leaning against the outer wall of the boat's small cabin. He smiled. "Much like your hats."

My fly-casting skills weren't something to brag about, so I crawled over to sit beside him. "No motor," I said. "No oars. No paddles."

He raised one arm into the wind and sampled each direction with his open hand. "But privacy for perhaps ten minutes when the wind returns us to town."

I looked up the length of Moosehead Lake and wished for miles of angry water to shove us north where no one lived. Between what Moz knew and I knew, we'd be fine for days. I liked that option better than town and Dory Perkins.

Moz nudged me. "How would you answer that woman if you spoke truth?"

I couldn't remember when someone had asked me for truth. I was used to lobbying for the forest's future and spewing out stuff with an imaginary gag over my mouth, the don't-be-shrill requirements of the job, but I'd quit the fight to save deer some forest. It wasn't personal. Legislators don't want some lobbyist dishing them bad news about a sentimental industry rooted in their constituents' families. Logging and papermaking were Maine history. I got that. I understood why the elected and the elect essentially clapped hands over their ears—even when I wore lipstick.

What could the truth sound like? *Do it, corporate captains who own too much forest. Slash it like you're mowing down pick-up sticks. Raze the next generation before it grows up to be logs. Cut it so hard your Wall Street bean counters do happy somersaults. I hope I'm alive to witness your fall if someone finds out you've stripped, stolen, and sold our forest. I'll be cheering from someplace you haven't cut if I can find one.*

I thought I could do truth out loud, so I took a ragged breath. "The reporter had three questions, right? OK. No one kicked me out of Augusta. I kicked myself out of town, and I don't think anyone noticed enough to raise a leg and add another kick. Two. Shannon and I probably ended up on Monson's land because it's the only uncut woods left near town, and we prefer woods to stumps." My voice croaked on the last answers. "Three. Tree or no tree, I'd know Shannon from a boot lace or a fingertip. And, and ... I don't know what happened, but after I get some sleep, I might want some answers."

I picked at deck splinters and tried to ignore the fresh soap smell of Moz's neck. I had no idea what I smelled like, but it wasn't soap. "What did you and the boys make of the strap and box under Shannon's cheek?" I asked.

Moz uncrossed his arms and reached for his pen. "Strap? Box? Describe, please."

"Under her head I saw a piece of brown strap with a small, chunky metal box riveted onto it. About the size of a child's juice box, but I didn't want to pull on it and disturb her," I said.

"You urinated next to her. That was not a disturbance?"

I picked more splinters from my fingers. "I don't want to know how you know that."

A hint of a grin lifted the corners of his mouth. "A respectful gesture is revealed in its intent. In the future, if you find it necessary to mark my territory, I trust you will also exercise similar respect."

I couldn't think of a snappy reply. I felt the ground shifting between us even though the nearest dirt was underwater. Why had I pushed Moz away when he'd answered my 911 call? I liked hugs. I could have used a hug.

We were on a collision course with a long dock. Moz slid down the wall we shared and extended his legs to shove us off. "I found nothing under her head. I was not, however, the first person on the scene."

I could have cared less about drifting to town, so I reached for a floating rope tied to the dock and hauled us toward shore. "Who was there first?" I asked.

Moz pulled his knife, cut us free, and shoved us clear of the dock without making a fuss over my resistance. "A Great Nations logging crew. When I arrived, they had installed a generator and lights. No one mentioned any items found under or near her." Back up against the cabin's wall, Moz inspected me—long seconds at my eyes, my mouth—at my fingers picking soggy wood. "You are certain of the strap?" he asked.

I wanted to be in bed, smothered under quilts, wood stove roaring, and Shannon's one green eye forgotten in sleep. "Yes," I said.

"I have questions," he said. "I have questions about the tree."

"Trees fall," I said.

His black brows narrowed into a single dark line, a bank of threatening weather. "The pine was old, but its roots were strong." He raised his hand for silence. "Most troubling is sound. She would hear roots give up ground. She had time to move."

Yes, that was the question. Why hadn't Shannon gotten out of the way? My brain felt heavy like I'd funneled molasses into it through my ears.

I returned his soggy bandana. "OK, I need to know. Are you a cop on this?"

He tucked loose, straight black hair behind his ears, hair worn longer than law enforcement liked. The warden brass avoided *Moz*, not sure how to supervise an American Indian who spoke Oxford English. I knew his grandmother had used an English exchange student to lift her grandson's failing grades, because Evan complained the tutor's influence made Moz pike-up-the-ass annoying. I heard each Moz word as a tightly-wrapped package.

His eyes constricted to chilly pieces of coal and I found something to do with my boots. I knew better than to call him a cop. If I cut up *Reader's Digest* stories of resourceful men—and a few women—and blended them together with beer and insect repellant, I might get the right game warden brew. They were rescuers of lost children and confused adults, and usually the first to sort out backcountry scenes we humans made messy. Most only wanted a job defending vulnerable animals, so they used a private code that offered poachers no mercy. They had bad-boy behaviors too, but Moz wasn't a womanizer.

I was about to apologize when he jumped into water up to his knees and shoved the boat onto a pebble beach below the hangar. "I have something to give you," Moz said, waving a group of watchers back toward the check station. He reached for his pack and then tilted his head, leaning one ear into the wind to hear the yelling it blew at us.

Ken's voice rose above the noise of slamming truck doors. "Cool it down now, boys."

CHAPTER 4

As Moz steered me toward the garage, geese and feathers fluttered away before us. A white pickup truck with the Great Nations Forest logo of endless trees in front of endless skies blocked the driveway. Like rigid retrievers on point over birds, GNF's crew bosses, Ridge Dumais and John Tario, stood stiffly by their truck. Just as stiffened up, a much younger man—maybe an older boy—held his camera and long lens to one side. His sunglasses, useless in fading light, looked useful in a staring contest.

Moz disappeared when a crowd of more green uniforms arrived to stand with Ken and supervise the scene. Despite the cold, Ridge's exposed arms were veined muscle ropes, tight from years of disobedient chainsaws. The onset of a soft beer cushion pushed his belt as he leaned toward the younger man's wired energy. The young man had biceps so explosive they strained his shirt into tight, twitching cloth. He had a few inches on the logger, but Ridge radiated an angrier force field, so it seemed like an equal match.

Friendly-feeling hands pulled me up against a soft down jacket. I felt I'd landed with geese. "Patton, let the boys sort it out," rasped a growling voice. I turned to find Peter Markes buried in a puffy parka that made him look like a blueberry balloon.

"We've been looking for you," he said, holding me at arm's length. "You look better than the last time I saw you. You're eating again. I like a woman with curves." He tugged at my overall straps. "Conover, you're an attractive woman wearing unattractive clothes that suit you."

When I squeezed Peter, parka feathers escaped into the wind. "We? You and who are looking for me?" I asked.

"My intern. Ian." Peter pointed at the young man who'd raised his free hand into an I'm-not-armed position. "We have a proposition."

Peter didn't look as good as the last time I'd dropped by the *Bangor Weekly*. His skin was stretched over outsized cheekbones and his Mount Rushmore–sized nose loomed larger over pale lips. Even a coat meant for arctic travel couldn't hide his diminished bulk. I leaned into his padding. "How'd you find me?"

"Moz."

"You know Moz?"

"We help each other. He directs the state's search and rescue team. I direct the state's largest paper. You know. The one with your name on the front page today." He tucked my arm in his arm and walked me toward the parking lot. "You working?"

"Nothing steady, but I have firewood, and I'm current with the vet," I said. "I'm done with rooms that don't have windows; I'm exploring seasonal work, and—you'll appreciate this—I'm not talking much."

Peter put his mouth next to my ear. "Yesterday. Tough day for you. I am sorry about your friend. Keep your head down. The vulture press is circling, looking for something dark and sinister—but I'm not here about yesterday."

I tightened my grip on his arm, an arm too lean for someone who liked to keep himself on the heavy side, like a bear that adds fat to get through lean times. When the intern removed his dark glasses and grinned at Ridge, the wall of uniforms leaning outside the hangar nudged each other and headed inside toward waiting trucks. One of them had his hands on a very wet Dory Perkins. Wrapped in a wool blanket, she looked like she'd interviewed the lake, so I smiled and wiggled a few fingers.

Ridge waved the boy forward. "Taking pictures of my truck? What for?"

Lifting one sneaker missing its laces, Ian thumped a sticker on the truck's bumper. A gray wolf head with oversized teeth leered at us. Lips dripped bright blood that pooled around the lower corners of the frame, and two wide diagonal black lines—like tire treads on roadkill—slashed the wolf's image from top to bottom. "What's the deal?" he asked.

"No wolves," said John Tario, tugging at jeans that had nowhere to settle on his skeletal frame. With his free hand, he pressed one flopping corner of the sticker back in place and grunted. "It means no wolves."

I saw Ian's shoulders lift and tense before he grinned again and clipped a cap on his camera lens. "Thanks. Just doing some research on what matters up here."

Ridge glared at me as if I were the source of all evil and stalked over to stand a pebble away from my toes. "Ask *her* why we've got to protect what we've got. She could care crap about our paychecks. Ask *her* about the government plot to force wolves back on us." I knew Peter had my back but he was lost in a parka. Ridge threw a head toss at Ian. "You know MAST?"

Ian shook his head.

"MAST made a law to stop wolf lovers. Maine Association of Sportsmen and Trappers." He patted his jeans pockets, looking for his keys. "No wolves. Not unless politicians vote for 'em in Augusta. As if *that's* going to happen."

When trucks in line gunned their engines, Ken appeared, shouting and tapping his watch, but I held up five fingers asking for more time.

Ridge snarled at Ian. "You part of her bad news press party? Yesterday was just her *latest* shit show. For all I know she dropped a tree on that woman just so I'd have more shit to wade through. Now I have to drop every goddamn thing I'm doing and tap-dance around whatever guano pile she's made."

Ridge's snarl made sense. I'd earned his venom and I had no regrets.

Ian pushed his sunglasses up over his forehead so his hair stood up in unruly spikes. "What'd she do last time?" he asked.

Ridge worked his tongue around a plug of chew in his cheek, chomped for a few seconds, and then spit at my boots. He pulled a package from his shirt pocket and wedged more chew in the other cheek and smiled. I smiled. There was always a chance chew slime conditioned leather.

"OK. What'd you do?" Ian asked me.

Ridge smirked and his partner pushed parking lot pebbles with his boots.

I shrugged. "Someone left a stack of 'cease and desist' letters and emails in my car," I said, "all addressed to Great Nations Forest LLC's home office in Idaho, all official communications asking Ridge's employers to stop cutting deer habitat. I saw no return GNF mail directed to the Maine Department of Game and Wildlife, who'd sent the messages, so I assumed there was a black hole somewhere in the company's Idaho office. I alerted reporters to the deer-with-no-homes problem."

Ridge snorted. "*You* are the pain-in-the-ass problem."

"Well, there was some pain, but probably not in *my* ass. I let the press know Maine's voluntary guidelines set up for its corporate forest friends weren't working," I said. "I showed them proof that biologists' appeals to stop cutting deer habitat were ignored." I raised my hands, framed a picture, and made clicking noises. "And I took pictures of slashed deer yards. Ridge, I think you and John were featured in coverage about the deer herd crashing." I felt

Peter's hand on my elbow, ready to pull me from the scene if it blew up.

"Drama, drama, drama," said Ridge. "Trees grow back. What is it with you people?"

Ian stepped between us and with a bit of shoulder twitching made room for Ridge to back up. "Deer? Crashing? They hit some kind of wall?"

"That's pretty much it," I said. "A snow wall. Without old trees with wide branches that keep snow off the forest floor, deer starve and die. They can't fight through deep drifts to find food or stay warm so they die."

"You don't know squat about forestry or deer, Conover," Ridge said. "It's not like deer are nailed to the ground. They can move, ya know." He trotted fingers from his right hand up over his left arm, but his fingers looked peppier than starving deer. John Tario laughed and hitched up his pants.

"Move where?" I asked, shaking slime off my boots. "Florida? You cut most all the old trees on *all* the land you own."

"OK, I'm done," said Ridge. "She sounds the same out here as she does in print. Same crap." He jerked open the driver's side door and waited for John. "We own the land. All she owns is her mouth."

Ian waited until the truck disappeared before sauntering over to us. Strutted maybe. He dropped his sunglasses down to his nose and ran a hand over light brown hair cut to look artfully scruffy.

His free hand rubbed square jaw bones that held up a crooked, cocky grin. "Ian Glenburn," said Peter, shoving me forward. "Meet Cassandra Patton Conover. Patton."

Ian crushed my hand and ignored my gasp of pain. "You've got seven pages on Google. I've got two, but I've got time," he said. I considered the boy and the older man. What could they possibly have in common? Ian looked at Peter expectantly.

I looked at Peter expectantly. "You said you had a proposition?"

Peter looked down his nose at Ian and then at me. I felt paired with someone I wouldn't have chosen for any team I'd ever played on. "Wolves, Patton. Help my boy find the wolves he thinks are here."

CHAPTER 5

I chewed on French bread that was real French bread—crusty, yeast-perfumed, and very far from France. "I'm not available, Peter. Bad time for me. I need to take care of some Shannon stuff, and besides ... there are no wolves," I said. We were squeezed into a booth at the Road Kill Cantina facing Ian, who seemed to prefer windows looking out at truck bumpers. On the wall, tiny white lights illuminated the antlers of deer, moose, and one moth-eaten extinct caribou. The heads always made me feel good about Kate. "I can't call those things *mounts*," she said. "Too sex-icky. We'll call them dead heads."

I slathered more butter on my bread, thinking I could get a free meal and then duck out to Shannon's apartment. For what, I didn't know. Maybe I just needed to breathe her air and ask *why?* "No wolves in Maine," I said. "Except for occasional loners on vacation from Canada."

"You might not be as smart as we both think you are, Patton," said Peter. Ian grinned, but Peter lifted a long finger at him. "Don't misunderstand me, young man. She's good. Of course, at the beginning of our adventure together, she was a loose cannon sent to besiege the paper mill in my home town. She assumed I didn't know the river went into the mill clean and came out green. She assumed a lot of things she needed to un-assume."

Ian reached for the bread, but I grabbed the basket and snatched the last piece. "OK, OK. Peter sent me into the mill to follow his engineer brother around," I said. "And it turned out I met the real folks—the ones with mortgages they couldn't pay during shutdowns. The ones who got burnt or cut up and were refused insurance. People just trying to get by."

Peter raised his water glass in a mock toast.

Ian licked his fingers and pressed bread crumbs off the table and into his mouth. "Must have been a comedown," he said.

"Depends," I said. "I never understood the town's rabid loyalty and now I do. If my great-grandparents hacked away a swampy wilderness and built a mill that paid more than most Maine jobs, and generations of Conovers lived and died in the shadow of the mill and its largess, I might be OK with killing a river, too."

"But you're not," said Ian.

"I'm not OK with a false choice—the jobs or river choice. The Penobscot River—healthy—is a multi-billion-dollar soup of jobs and assets whether the cash comes from rafting and paddling companies, gawking tourists, fishermen, irrigated blueberries, or shellfish harvested at the mouth of the river."

"So," said Peter, swiping away crumbs with his napkin, "this is the part where you pay attention, young man. After I educated Patton and she calmed down, I offered her a spot on the paper to air her ideas about how the outdoors makes money. Her column—"

"You get my ValueNature column for less than pennies," I said. My legs felt twitchy under the table. Sometimes they started to leave before the rest of me figured out I wanted to leave.

"I promised I'd help you get national exposure, and we'll get there," Peter said. "First I need some national exposure of my own, and that's where Ian comes in. And you come in."

He leaned on his rolled-up parka, eased himself against the wall, and looked more ancient than his seventy-five years. "Ian's come north to propose an exposé and is highly recommended. He broke a story on septic crime that no one else in Stamford had pieced together."

"Septic crime in Connecticut? That must fill up police notes in the paper. Who recommended him?" I asked.

"He did." Peter smiled at his own joke. "When he came north to clean out his mother's basement, he read through years of my paper and came to sit outside my door. *He's* the kind of puppy you have to take in because it sits on your porch and won't leave."

"What does that have to do with wolves?" I asked. My wolf experience was limited to endangered species battles that somehow always involved the big bad wolf. Last year, I'd hoped for a tame public hearing to stop the sale of wild turtles to pet stores. We sat through a parade of frantic witnesses who all sounded like the first person who left spit on the microphone. "Put the goddamn turtle on a special list where it's a crime to touch it, and next time the feds will add the murdering wolf. Our kids, they'll get savaged at the bus stop and our dogs chewed off their chains. And for damned sure, deer get slaughtered in blood orgies." The box turtle didn't make the list.

The Road Kill Cantina's owner marched toward us, balancing plates in one hand, a full coffeepot in the other. No one should describe the French as laid just back because they stretch a meal into four hours and five bottles of wine.

"No more wolf talk," she said. "No talk of animals we cannot prepare. Eat while flavors talk to each other. Bien. Mangez." She bent and planted a soft kiss on my ear. "Quel dommage," she whispered. "A shame—chère Shannon." She left another kiss and stomped off to conduct surveillance on assistants who might substitute lard for butter. The kissed ear felt warmer than the rest of me.

Francoise ran her business like a petite officer ordering folks to eat French versions of diner food. Her uniform was a purple leotard fused onto a lithe body missing hips and breasts. "No drunk grabbing places," she said. Her road kill theme camouflaged haute cuisine, and her tequila night earned the town's devotion. Over seductive food and drink they blabbed about everything they weren't supposed to blab about and Francoise heard it all.

I leaned low to inhale my grilled cheese—what the menu called "Flattened Before Grilled, Ham Hits Cheese." All my fat cells moaned and leaned toward the plate before my mouth could get there. "Lobster Rolled Over" dripped into Ian's lap as he used one hand to forage though a gym bag. "Don't care what she calls 'em," he said. "Best crêpes ever." He pulled a folder onto the table and dumped news articles between us.

I shuffled through them and pushed them back. "This is what you've got? Some iffy-sounding folks called the Howlers who howl at what isn't there, a plague of too many beavers, and a coyote shortage?"

"Patience," muttered Peter. Oh, right, advice from a man famous for refusing to give youthful writers—any writers— slack.

Ian slapped a page from the Maine Department of Game and Wildlife's website on the pile and crowed, "Last year a wolf was shot inside Maine's northern border." He almost bounced in his chair. "Your wildlife commissioner—the one that wears lizard ties—he funded this wolf-tracking survey. Something's going on. Don't tell me they're spending money looking for what's not there."

I read the first lines. "Wildlife Lottery Pays for Wolf Hunt. This month, Ken Douglas, District 10 wildlife biologist, completes a full year of field research into the possible presence of wolves in Maine. His department hopes to reduce controversial speculation about the existence of this federally listed species."

I sat up straighter and leaned the page into the light. Everyone trusted Ken. I'd talk to him before I'd listen to the kid wannabe reporter. A woman across the pub wanted in on our conversation, nodding at her table companion but tilting her bobbed blond hair in our direction. I moved my hand to Ian's articles and turned them over.

Peter poked his grilled cheese around his plate. "Piece it together for her, Ian," he said. "And no *smaaart* phones."

Ian slid his phone back into his pocket and frowned. "The Maine accent cuts into the smart part."

"That's the idea," said Peter.

I applauded Peter's goal to take down the smartphone. Kate's efforts to slide my fingers across her screen made me feel prehistoric. I could see it was going to be a long day. I'd been up before dawn going through old photos, searching for one that captured Shannon's smile. "Can you do this quickly?" I asked. "I'm fried. My dog's at home, paws crossed, praying for headlights. My plants know the woodstove's cooling."

Ian made a tent of his arms over his paperwork. "There are wolves in Maine. More than one. Maybe a pack. They did what the experts said they couldn't do. Cross the river. Cross from Canada."

"You're a city boy, right?" I asked.

Ian sniffed and rearranged his papers.

I reached my fork across the table and poked his arm. "Never been in the Maine woods, right?"

He rolled his eyes. "That has nothing—"

I rapped the table with my fist. Our silverware and the couple next to us jumped a bit. “And despite the biologists trying to find them and the timber companies’ alertness—I mean their paranoia—to rare animals that bring regulatory plagues down on them, *and* despite people who howl—despite this motley crew overturning every log in the forest, *you’ve* found them?” Through melted cheese my voice sounded slurred. “Tell me how you’ve done that. I’m confused.” I wasn’t, but in front of Peter I wouldn’t totally dismiss the kid.

Ian snorted. “I doubt it.” He looked right at me, gray eyes wide and insolent. Late-day Mel Gibson stubble crawled across his chin and cheeks. “You’re not confused. Peter says you’re sharp. ‘Wicked sharp,’ he says. Says he trusts you to get it right before others do. *And* he says you listen better than you used to.”

That sounded like vintage Peter, who slid a cooling half-sandwich to my plate and said, “Our boy has dug up some interesting leads.” He pointed his coffee mug at Ian. “Connect what dots you have for her.”

Ian bent so low his shirt buttons swam through cream sauce. “There’s kind of a Bermuda Triangle of weirdness south and west of that big park you have up here. Too many beavers are jammed together in one place. And another thing ... most of Maine has exploding coyote numbers, but in this one area, they’ve almost disappeared.” Satisfied, he sat back and crossed his arms. “Wolves love chowing down on beavers. They’re wolf caviar. On the other hand, wolves hate coyotes. When Yellowstone National Park imported wolves, they killed or chased off the coyotes."

I sighed into my best slow-student voice. "That was a huge government program. Imported wolf packs carefully introduced to new terrain. Yellowstone National Park was a big, orchestrated, planned wolf reintroduction."

A chair scraped the cantina's wood floor. The blonde woman aimed for us. Thin and agile, she dodged low-hanging lights. Ian herded his papers back into his duffle.

Peter used his feet to push a chair toward her. "Vicki, do join us. You're just in time."

Ian angled the chair toward our guest. "Ms. Brinkman, thank you for fitting us in today. I spoke with you two days ago. I'm Ian. Ian Glenburn."

The woman pushed the chair back under the table and stood behind it. Clearly, a grilled sandwich ripe with imported cheese was bait for an arranged meeting, and I was easy prey after too many Cheerios eaten over the sink.

Like an announcer squaring off boxers, Peter made introductions. "Patton, this is Victoria Brinkman, energetic and relentless interim director of the Maine Forest Trust. She's grown it from a dipshit outfit to a multimillion-dollar conservation game changer. Vicki, this is Cassandra Patton Conover, infamous environmental gadfly and crusader for the disappearing Maine when she's not counting moose teeth."

Vicki raised regimentally tweezed eyebrows over eyes outlined in strong black eyeliner. No smudges. No wayward strokes. Her makeup sent a serious message. She had pale, otherworldly blue eyes. Wrinkle-free around her mouth and probably in her mid-forties, she'd arranged her hair to sweep over a determined jaw. The rest of her bones outlined her sweater and pants with lean sophistication. In *my* forties, I'd camouflaged my bones with leftover pregnancy.

I answered her brows' question. "Moose teeth are just a sideline. I think we've been in the same hearing rooms, but as you were sitting with the other side, I don't think we've been properly introduced." I offered my hand over the table. She leaned forward and pumped it with precision, then rearranged bracelets up the arm of her black cashmere sweater. The sweater disappeared into even blacker pants that disappeared into fur-lined suede boots. Vicki didn't patronize the thrift store like I did.

"Call me Vicki. I *am* delighted to finally meet you. I took up the reins at the trust just as you retired from public life. I understand from Peter that we are both passionate about forest issues, and that we might even agree on how little time is left before it's too late. I must really apologize to you all. Peter. Ian. And Patton. May I call you Patton?" She breezed on. "I only have a moment to show you where to find my land manager, Engunn. For your interview. I'm due at Munsungun Camps for a planning retreat."

Ian pulled crumpled maps from his duffle. I nibbled Peter's rejected grilled cheese and doubted Vicki and I would agree on the "too late" thing. Most large landowners cut trees faster than new ones could sprout up to be toothpicks. It was probably already too late.

I didn't trust the trust and its much-advertised partnerships with the timber industry. Vicki's group had a mission to preserve commercial forest lands—what it called the "working forest." I was OK with the tree business if it wasn't greedy. I liked toilet paper and birthday cards, but I was sure whacking down too many trees wasn't a threatened enterprise. What kind of upside-down environmental mission was that?

Vicki's silver bands slid down her arm and clinked on the map. A sharp spice scent I couldn't name overpowered Francoise's cheeses. I pushed my plate away.

She tapped the map with her bracelets. "Engunn's here surveying a new easement we're partnering with Great Nations just north of Grants Farm Inn. He'll be camped at Canada Falls. Because I will be tied up and Peter says you are on deadline for this column, Engunn will brief you on the economics of what we do."

Her black-rimmed eyes narrowed on me. "The columns you publish are so overdue. If the public knew how much money was locked up in the forest, I'd be able to convince the Ford Foundation to free up more millions."

Vicki liked my work. Most people didn't bother with it, so I leaned back in my chair and nodded helpfully.

She forced jewelry back up her arm, lifted the chair she leaned on, and tapped it more tightly under the table. "Contact me should you need more background. Engunn's a whiz with maps but less adept at staying on message with reporters. I emailed your paper several quotes I'd appreciate your considering. No pressure. Use or don't use as you decide."

She waved, walked back to her chair—high heeled boots sharp on worn floors—and slipped into a purple jacket decorated with fluttering ski passes I couldn't afford. She called out to her companion, and when she breezed out the door, it banged against the outside wall and failed to close. *No pressure, my ass*, I thought, grateful for the air.

"Peter." I pointed at my chest. "Reporter?"

"Better pay than moose teeth. I'm hiring you to continue your columns, but that's just your cover. Ian will file some of your ValueNature pieces as blogs so I can make nice with the digital death squad gunning for the paper. You know this country and its natives. I'm engaging you to help my boy here find wolves. I want a national story. One that looks impressive in real print. I need something big to buy time with my board."

I shook my head.

He slid one arm around my shoulders. "I know you, Cassandra Patton Conover. It will do you good to be out in the woods where the press can't pick at you and make a big deal out of ... whatever it is. Out where you and Shannon were your best selves. Out where you're more at home than anywhere I've seen you park yourself, so you need to get out of town. And when it all hits you, wouldn't you rather be there than here?"

I felt my mouth behaving very fishlike, gaping open and shut as I tried to breathe and swim away from the hook at the same time.

"You'll make good money," Peter said. "I'm using my own funds, but you'll work under the protection of the *Bangor Weekly*. If you're officially talking about money and jobs, you should be able to investigate the backcountry without speaking the dreaded 'w' word. Ian's working for free. I assume he'll stay at your camp. I'll make it right with your boss so you'll work next season."

"I seeeee," I said. "We need to investigate wolves without mentioning them. Is that everything?"

"No." He squinted at the shadowed parking lot. "Someone's in your car."

CHAPTER 6

Someone's always doing something to my car. Sometimes it's angry folks who think I'm an environmental thug out to seize their land. That group probably used a shotgun on my car, pockmarking it so the backside reads like the word *ouch*. My tires have been slashed; my kayak's been snatched off the roof rack and run over by something with deep grooves.

Sometimes anonymous donors leave me compromising material they hope I'll expose to daylight, sure they'll be fired for leaks to the press. And sometimes it's Moz, leaving me paper-bag puzzles. Tangles of multicolored hair, chewed sticks, bark streaked with suspicious stains, or—his favorite—scat with food clues. My assignment? Recognize half-digested body parts hiding in feces—discover what the diner had dined on.

The dome light clicked off. Either there was something new to find, or someone had stolen dog blankets and emergency toilet paper. "Let's move this over to camp," I said.

I let Peter pay the check. Last week I'd left a filled grocery cart in the cereal aisle, impressed by what I couldn't afford. Peter's offer would feed me while I waited for snow, and Shannon's apartment could wait. There wouldn't be answers there anyway, and her overfed tropical fish could stand a diet for a day or two. I had three months before my diplomas would help me drive grooming machines up ski slopes into blizzards, and my bank account wouldn't stretch until it snowed. I started the car and contemplated the brown paper bag of lumpy something on the passenger seat. The bag didn't squirm, rattle, or hiss so I thought it could wait awhile.

Twenty minutes and ten miles east of town, I parked below moss-covered racks where Conover hunters hung game off the ground. I don't hunt, but I could have. Was it a secret that I could see one leaf overturned by a hoof or snort like an angry buck and entice him close enough to know I wasn't an available mate? I hoped to change male traditions by calling myself Patton, but each fall the "Bring Your Rifle Leave Your Woman" sign hung on Antler Camp's door.

Each fall, my mother and I sharpened knives and cut butcher paper into squares until my father's Jeep, groaning under deer tied on the hood and jammed-together uncles, pulled into our yard. Grinning like royalty, my brother, Giffy, rode a pile of guns in the backseat. I decided hunting had to be overrated if it hurt so much to be left out.

I was supposed to be George Patton Conover, a son named after the general who had commanded my father's North African tank unit and brought half the division home alive. When I arrived female, my father held onto *Patton* and my mother chose *Cassandra*, hoping liquid syllables would drown the general's name.

My father and I inhabited different worlds. His real estate business sold the woods around our house and the shores in front of it. He waved in gravel trucks and filled sea caves where we played pirate, selling filled clam flats as "recovered" real estate. Then he sold the rest of the neighborhood. Beaten by rising taxes and mansions mushrooming on tiny lots, my friends' fathers sold their houses and wharves and retreated to landlocked neighborhoods and scraggly backyards where their lobster boats sagged on blocks waiting out the winter.

I hated working in my father's office. Surly and silent, I mailed brochures to people who had Maine fantasies and out-of-state money, my wounds always fresh as condos covered the beach where I'd discovered shy hermit crabs and barnacles' feathery arms.

After building up the coast, realtors and developers wanted the forest, a vast vista of potential house lots. Trespassing was probably just an excuse—cover for my mission to know Bluffer Brook places before they sprouted driveways and septic systems. Before someone like my father destroyed them.

Antler Camp looked ancient because it was ancient. Generations of Conovers embraced our outpost with a passion that surpassed black flies, spring snows, and barn doors shredded by carnivores. The bear-proof pen inside the barn was a message that we'd staked out territory at the edge of wild.

Around the sagging camp walls, wood smoke fingers drifted into the arms of low-hanging limbs. Inside, wool coats hung on antlers. Baskets of boots, waders, and snowshoes smelling of leather and long use were nailed to the wall. A giant pine table tattooed by restless children glowed under suspended gas lamps, and around the woodstove, chipped rocking chairs competed for space with a couch that sighed when we sat on it. Behind the stove, mildewed *National Geographics*, worn-out nature guides, and children's books crowded tall shelves.

I'd dragged a bed from the sleeping porch into the kitchen and squeezed it under the eaves so the Garland cook stove could warm my sheets. I didn't know camp was the safest place on earth until I arrived shipwrecked from my own life.

Survival meant avoiding, if possible, all men. I imagined their voices echoing from a rowboat marooning me on an island for the crime of aging. Their voices grew faint as they rowed away and left me in a country of mostly invisible old and older women. I promised Kate I'd get my hair cut and colored, tweeze my eyebrows, and go to the gym. Privately, I decided to breathe deeply, practice acceptance, and explore my new location outside a country of men where my visa had been revoked.

On the day Evan smiled his way through our court date, I charged three years of deodorant, brown rice, canned fruit, and other essentials to his credit card and drove north.

I covered mirrors with towels so I wouldn't see myself with his eyes, wouldn't see the woman who'd "let herself go." Wouldn't see gray hairs invading blond hairs or sad blue eyes I didn't recognize. Who was that woman anyway?

"What will you do?" wailed my mother off the answering machine as I dragged three years of supplies over the sill and Pock unloaded squeaky toys. I heard the nursing-home food cart rattle into her room. Silverware clattered near her phone. "Did Evan give you money?" she asked. "Well, I wouldn't worry on that, dear. God's divine love meets every human need."

Oh, right. Divine love. Divine love hadn't put much energy into my address. As real estate boomed, my father only left his office when he needed sleep and clean shirts, and my mother memorized the Bible but never noticed our daily exodus. Giffy and I swallowed great gulps of unpreached air as we vaulted the porch railing toward a woods escape. Stairs were too slow.

Before I could punch the delete button, my mother asked, "Will anyone know where you are when you're off alone?" I replayed the message, tears leaking into table grooves as I melted onto my arms.

Her question didn't seem important until I fell through soft spring ice. Pock dove into my hole, happy to join me for a frigid swim. With numb hands, I shoved him up to solid ice and then slid up behind him. Lying on my back to spread my weight, I inched toward shore.

Clearly I could count on my dog for company but not rescue. I stripped, wrung out my clothes, redressed, and jogged to the car on snowshoes that resembled small icebergs. Kate lectured me, and we created a *flight plan* strategy, pledging ourselves to report attempted destinations and modes of travel to family or friends and then report our successful return.

Of course, I couldn't call Pock to file a flight plan about grilled cheese. When I opened the front door, ninety pounds of brown distress lifted his leg in midair and aimed at the nearest tree. I stacked wood in a delicate pyramid over the fire's remains and cracked the stove door to fan flames into the bark.

I placed the paper bag in a circle of light on the table and found Moz's formal lettering: "Found Bluffer Brook. Use sterile gloves. Return to bag. Leave in boathouse." I rummaged through my paddling gear for a first aid kit, snapped on gloves, and pulled a notebook from the bag. Next to the Great Nations Forest company logo of endless forests and endless skies, Shannon Angeles had printed her initials and "FOD"—our private code for whatever overwhelmed us, whatever threatened the natural world. FOD. Forces of Darkness.

Shannon was an evangelist for wild places, but she'd joined GNF for the salary and a fast exit from her Yale loans. "Forest health is a lengthy, cyclical enterprise," she'd said, tossing a match into company newsletters she stuffed in my woodstove. "Not suited for cut-and-run management and quick profits. Three more years and I'm paid up. Free."

Free, I thought. *Is dead free?* I leaned my cheek on the notebook's cover and breathed its pine scent. When a sheet of paper drifted to the floor, I bent to retrieve a photocopied chart that stopped my breath. Under its title, "Diagnostic Analysis: Comparison of Coyote, Wolf, Dog," neat columns separated track size, hair, scat, stride, and something called intergroup spacing. Shannon's margin notes looked scrawled and hurried.

Four-inch track. Large dog or wolf?

Straight line of travel. Wolf.

Hind foot placed inside front print. Usually wolf.

In less than twenty-four hours the wolf was—literally—at my door.

I heard Pock's fevered barking and cold dirt crunch in the driveway as someone sprinted into my shed.

Ian's voice was muffled behind the wall. "Is he friendly?"

"Depends," I said. "What'd you do to him?"

"Nothing!"

"Not so. That's his up-to-something bark. Did you use the smartphone thing coming down the hill?"

I waited. Pock barked at Ian.

"Yes."

"And what else?"

"I was listening to some stuff."

"What stuff?"

Logs rolled and thumped. "Let me in. I'll show you."

"Hang on." I slipped the notebook under a pile of maps and opened the shed door to find Ian balanced on my woodpile. Below him Pock chewed bark into a soggy gift he hoped to share. "Bring wood with you," I said. "Where's Peter?"

Ian lifted his pack and two skimpy sticks to join me by the stove, wiping his phone with his shirt. "Peter sent apologies 'cause he had to get back to Bangor. Dropped me at the top of the hill and said to keep an open mind on Vicki, to think of her as a younger version of you before he brought you up." He hooked his grin sideways at me. "No. His exact words were *visionary*, *edgy*, *driven*. He thinks Vicki's got good intentions."

"Anything else?"

"He gave me blog ideas, names of people to interview, and something for you."

Ian handed me a note, shrugged off his jacket, and backed up to the glowing red stove. Pock nosed his food bowl into the living room, an urgent message banged off chairs and walls. Peter's note was brief: "I will pay you five dollars more per hour than the most you've ever been paid. I expect you to earn it. PM."

"So, welcome. I suppose." I felt invaded. "What were you listening to?"

With a pained sigh, Ian swiped commands into his phone. "No signal." He waved the phone at my ceiling. "No signal?"

"There's a landline that works sometimes. Cell signals are back up the hill or on the roof." I felt strangely satisfied. "Just tell me."

"Minnesota has a Wolf Center site that howls. I had the volume cranked. I couldn't know you had a dog that would freak."

"Pock. His name is Pock." Dog ears twitched as I lifted the food bowl. "He's usually calm about coyote noise."

"Well, he freaked. Crawled downhill on his tail after the first wolf howl."

I filled the battered bowl with kibble and set it on the floor while Ian turned to roast his colder side next to the stove. "You should lock your car. Peter says it's just an undercover mailbox. What'd you get this time? And what's with the doctor gloves?"

I filled the teakettle. The chart might explain Shannon's trespassing at Bluffer Brook. I didn't trust Ian, but I trusted Peter and he'd dropped Ian into my life. Most of all, I trusted Shannon, and she thought she'd found surprising tracks. Dog? Wolf?

I lifted her notebook and Ian grabbed for it.

CHAPTER 7

"Gloves first," I said, pulling a second pair from my kit. I pointed to the sink. "Wash your face. You're sweating from too much stove. You'll ruin pages." Moz didn't want fingerprints. Until I knew more, I'd have to manage Ian.

I slapped gloves into his hands. "There are times to ask and times not to ask. This is a no-ask time," I said. He scowled and lunged for the sink.

I let Pock out into the night and looked left and right for skunks feeling perky before hibernation. My dog dove off the dock to retrieve a buoy anchored in the cove.

Ian rubbed his face with his all-purpose T-shirt. "There's no hot water."

"There's tea." I dropped tea bags in mugs and placed a jar of honey on the table.

Dry and gloved, Ian opened Shannon's chart and whistled. I heard the click in a reporter's brain that screams, *Yes! I am so on to something*.

He almost panted with anticipation. "You found this in your friend's notebook?"

"Yes, but don't get all hot over the chart. Read the footnotes," I said, closing the stove door before it ignited my walls. "Great Danes, Saint Bernards, and bloodhounds. All leave tracks over four inches."

Ian flipped through pages, turning the notebook sideways and upside down to squint at Shannon's notes. I already knew about the logbook. Last summer Shannon dropped it on us like a grenade with a pulled pin.

Shannon and I always saved an August week for our annual "no balls" canoe trip, a reunion that celebrated the year four of us survived a Maine Guide training course. I was the oldest, Shannon was the youngest, and Molly and Judith were in their forties. We'd explained the obvious to boyfriends, husbands, brothers, and sons. No balls. No men.

We'd shed weighty life issues by the campfire, and then naked in a sweat lodge—a leaky tent filled with hot rocks—we burned ourselves down to simple sensation. We spit mouthfuls of water and wine onto broiling rocks. An hour in the sweat lodge blurred vision and erased the line between dark lake and dark night. We used our toes to find cool water.

Water fingers slid up our bodies faster than shivers could follow and animal noises swam around us. A beaver's tail slap marked us as intruders. Cow moose exhaled two-note moans toward calves hidden deep in a backwater marsh. Bull moose surfaced from underwater meals, antlers gushing water. My favorite night noise was almost too intimate—the short, soft "hoot" of parent loons seeking their chicks' hiding places.

We all shared the same water. The same small currents eddied between us and floated our weight away from earth. It was as weightless and complete as I've ever felt or ever hoped to be.

In August, camped where two rivers emptied into Seboomook Lake, we waited for rocks to heat. Three pairs of eyes turned toward me with silent questions. *You wanna go first? Didn't you have the shittiest year?* I shook my head until tears splashed into my bowl. Molly squeezed my shoulder and Judith swiped a bandana across my cheek.

Shannon tugged my ponytail. "Tougher bark grows over the scar," she said. She put her plate of peanut noodles on the ground and licked her chopsticks. Then she opened a plastic bag, removed her Great Nations' notebook, and held up its neat calculations.

"My harvesting plans," she said. "I make it possible for the company to cut most all the real trees on a site. I work the numbers so, on paper, the scrawny trees and brush we leave behind add up to a phantom forest. Our paper forest allows us to look like we're practicing forestry—when we're not."

I didn't need proof. A few hundred yards behind our campsite, giant tree-eating tornadoes might have touched down in the middle of nowhere. Except for a green fringe by the river, the forest looked sucked away.

Shannon stalked circles around us, thumping the ground with her hiking boots. "You know they spray, right? Poison species that have no future as toilet paper or magazines? And don't get me started on reforestation bullshit. They don't replant, but they'll be back to cut young trees. Even if I bought it all, I'd need a few hundred years to fix this forest."

She slumped on the bottom of an overturned canoe. "And our *so-called* asset manager sucks. I plan small roads for clean streams. Anderson Barter has them bulldozed into highways and ignores fines for gravel in the water. It's just a business expense." She sighed. "In Idaho he made GNF a fortune turning woods into getaway mansions. Well, why not? He was a hot local realtor they passed off as a planner."

Shannon's waving hands fanned the fire. "He's a relentless citizen. EMT calls in the middle of the night, part-time deputy, scouts on weekends. Anderson believes everything he does makes Greenwood better. Says the resort will bring jobs." She shut her mouth so hard we heard snapping teeth. "Damn." She slammed her notebook.

"No!" we begged. "More!"

She turned her head to contemplate smoke the wind swirled at us. Her hair's red highlights grabbed the fire's crackling light and she looked dangerous. Coyotes started up an edgy chorus, yipping in overlapping waves of sound until, in mid-howl, the chorus quit. Under my ponytail, tiny hairs stiffened involuntarily.

Shannon's mouth tightened into a grim line. She dumped the last driftwood on our fire. "On Anderson's computer I found a screen with a sketch of Wild Pines Resort. Plans for a gated community, two thousand condos, and two golf courses. I'm partial to the two-mile paved golf cart path that allows fishermen to commute through *wilderness*." She wiggled airy finger quotes and slipped into singsong shopping-channel narration. "This one-of-a-kind resort amenity allows adventurers to motor to pristine streams, wilderness ponds, and rushing rivers before it joins the Bogside Bar. Have that second martini overlooking our moose watering hole."

I stared at sparks burning pinholes in my pants.

Shannon grabbed her flashlight and waved it across the river where pink bits of flagging tape whipped back and forth in the rising wind. "Maine's forests have survived generations of greed. Not likely they'll survive this. Ladies, I give you Wild Pines Resort!"

Forty-five miles from the nearest paved road, Great Nations Forest LLC was flagging the driveways, septic systems, and house lots of Wild Pines Resort. Shannon unzipped her pack and yanked out her raincoat.

"Maine's woods aren't African scrub or Malaysian rain forest," she said. "It grows back if we leave it alone. No forest recovers from golf courses, condominiums, and parking lots. At Yale, they call it 'hard deforestation.' In Idaho, Great Nations mowed down aspen valleys for ranchettes. In Utah, it bulldozed pinyon pine canyons for condos.

"In Maine, Great Nations will carve up the last real forest east of the Mississippi, cut it heavy, build permanent roads all over it, and sell it to developers. The developers will sell it to people who'd rather park golf carts in three-car garages than hike grandchildren into ponds to find frogs. Wild Pines. Wild Pines! Good Christ! The bulldozer boys are blind, deaf, dumb, *and* stupid. How could anyone name a place after what they've just killed? Wild Pines will be a phony address in some slick brochure."

Coyotes yipped again. Across the lake, irregular squalls ripped the surface into dark waves, and the rain hit us like a wall of wet, stinging bees. Blown backward, we struggled toward our tents as rocks hissed in the drowning fire.

CHAPTER 8

"Earth to Conover." Ian waved Shannon's notebook in front of my eyes. He pulled folded maps from the back cover and mashed out wrinkles with his fist. "I want to know about the colored lines, the green shaded stuff, and your friend's question marks. You got anything to eat?"

Ian inhaled a loaf of banana bread as I talked colors. Active logging roads were brown. Red diagonal slashes were gates blocking roads. Blue lines marked discontinued logging roads that could rest until trees returned. Chunks of light green territory marked conservation lands logging crews were supposed to avoid. Shannon's question marks floated over a concentration of red gates and blue closed roads that ringed the green northern edges of Monson's conservation lands.

"Shannon was curious about the closed roads," I said. "Carla Monson owns her own private preserve—the green territory under Shannon's question marks. About a hundred thousand acres or so." I moved my finger around the green edges of Monson's land, over the red slashes of her gates, and then along the faint wavy line marking Bluffer Brook—amazed that a map could squeeze my heart. Hurt that Shannon had tracked an unshared mystery.

Ian snorted. "So? Some roads aren't open."

I swiped my fingers over the map. "Three weeks ago I was up north posting hunting regulations," I said. "Most of these roads were open, crews hauling wood fourteen hours a day. Now most every road near Monson's land is off-limits."

As Ian picked up the bag and tipped it to read Moz's writing, something hard smacked the floor. He reached for the skull and lifted it into the light. Neck bones dangled from a stake. The teeth were so obvious even Ian guessed.

He touched the small chain and it clinked like delicate jewelry. "Beaver. Why chain him up? There's teeth marks on the chain. He was tied up alive?"

I reached for the skull and poked my fingers through eye sockets into grooves where scavengers had gnawed the beaver's last meal from its teeth. The skull felt licked clean. Weightless but heavy with messages. When I leaned my nose on the beaver's jaw, it smelled like a dried wound left too long under dirty bandages—but familiar. Last summer, working the souvenir counter at a nature center, I'd gathered skulls, antlers, hooves, and body parts around me. I imagined animals backward from body parts into life. First flesh on the bones, then blood humming in pursuit or escape.

I guessed the beaver's last minutes. Desperate, he circled the stake, tightening the chain until he chewed links near his neck. Gnawing the chain, he didn't hear the dog, coyote, fisher, or—

perhaps, this time—wolf. Feeling a chill shadow, he turned toward his hungry fate.

I opened my eyes into Ian's frown. "Beaver as wolf caviar, Ian. Food. Convenient, captive caviar," I said. I reached for the stained topographic map I used as a place mat. "Find me your 'plague of beavers' article and let me map what we know while you bring in more wood. The heavy logs for an all-night fire are on top. Wear the green jacket so you won't get covered with shavings."

Ian lifted his dark glasses from his head and placed them on the table. He swiped both hands back through his hair and massaged his neck. "I'm going to assume the skull séance sent you somewhere we needed to go and that beds here are *not* free." He grabbed the green jacket and stomped into the shed.

I sighed and pulled Ian's files from his duffle, spreading the beaver article, GNF's road map, and my larger topographic map down the center of the table next to a neat row of pencils and yellow highlighters. The beaver article was a downloaded news bulletin from the Maine Association of Sportsmen and Trappers. Apparently, its director, Mike Leavitt, had endless grievances against wildlife biologists who refused to open a special season on beavers north of Seboomook Lake. "I grew up trapping beaver as a kid and it was a barrel of fun," said Leavitt. "But I think it's a hell of a lot more fun to catch brook trout. Trout can't breathe in warm, shallow water so when there's too many beavers and too many dams, some beavers gotta go."

Game wardens had deputized volunteers from the Levesque family to clear streams in the affected area. A photograph showed men yanking apart a complicated log structure, mud up to their armpits. "We couldn't figure out why so many beavers are parked here," Barry Levesque said.

Barry might have been confused, but Moz had deciphered the beavers. The skull meant he wanted me to know what he knew—that someone had opened a beaver restaurant in our part of the world. Were wolves the invited guests?

Shannon's Great Nations road maps were simple survey maps. My ancient topographic map half-filled the table with the world around Antler Camp. On it my camp and the town of Greenwood hugged the southern shore of Moosehead Lake. Except for small islands of private lands, tribal reserves, and some scattered protected state lands, most of the map's terrain was Great Nations forest: brown mountains, creased ridges, blue meandering streaks of streams, and dark green smudges of unbroken forest lands. My brain updated the map, thinking in silent stump fields and bulldozed roads that weren't on any tourist's map.

I transferred each Shannon question mark that hovered over her closed roads to my topo map and highlighted them into bold yellow lines. Like the spokes of a bright carriage wheel, they circled Carla Monson's boundaries. Then I traced black outlines around the streams listed in Ian's beaver article. A loop of over-beavered territory lay like a large beret against Monson's northern boundary.

The missing center of the yellow wheel and whatever lay under the hat shape of beavered streams belonged to her.

Ian stomped back and forth, logs stacked up his arms, hair glued white and flat with spider webs. "Conover, isn't there an easy way to heat this place? A knob? A switch?"

It felt good to have a complaining kid around. I missed Kate and hoped she had a November holiday so she'd bake me chocolate chip cookies and challenge me at Scrabble. I'd learned tons of obscure animal body parts at the nature center.

When Ian shrugged off my jacket and leaned over the topo map, wood chips drifted down onto Mount Katahdin. "You forgot something," he said. "I'm gonna put her inside the gate. Tracking a wolf." Inside the gate at Bluffer Brook, up the dotted line marking the old logging road where I'd bicycled, he scrawled a heavy black question mark.

If he hadn't put one there, I would have.

"Excuse me," said a voice behind the open shed door. Ian and I leaned toward each other to hide the table. Anderson Barter's badge glinted in dim light. "The shed door was open so I came through. That OK?"

CHAPTER 9

I walked toward Anderson and reached for the papers he passed through the door. "The sheriff sent me out so you could sign your statement. I hope you know that wasn't by the book—doing it over the phone." He bowed his head, replaced his deputy cap on a recent buzz cut, and leaned around me, eyes straining toward the table. The wide Boy Scout grin I'd seen running errands in town narrowed into a stretched line across his teeth. Ian sat on the table and maps, swinging his legs as he peeled an orange.

I'd never noticed how pale and pudgy Anderson was. His khaki shirt strained against a belt almost hidden behind a combination of belly fat, pagers, radios, and phones. His skin looked like a just-hatched salamander—ghostly white and translucently smooth. Either his Great Nations duties were accomplished in an underground office, or he needed a dermatologist.

I stepped sideways to block his momentum and waved my hand toward Ian. "Peter Markes at the *Bangor Weekly* has an intern helping me research an assignment." Ian mumbled a greeting around a mouthful of orange. I reached for Anderson's elbow. "Let's go outside for privacy. I'm not into sharing yesterday's news."

Deputy Barter planted his feet a few inches closer to the table—almost on top of me. I pushed. His tummy gave limp, Play-Doh resistance, but he didn't move. "You were discussing Shannon Angeles," he said. "Need to amend your statement? Add more? Know something we don't?"

Anderson was about my height, just under five feet seven inches. I thought I could grow an inch taller if I used my guide voice and flexed my gym muscles. He flinched as I pinched slack skin against his forearm. "Outside. Please," I said. *And no more Shannon talk. We'll have none of that.*

Grabbing my down vest and headlamp from a nail near the shed, I jogged to his truck and slammed its door. It was jacked so high off the ground I could have run over short people without seeing them in the road. Seconds later Anderson hoisted himself into the cab. "Deputy," I said as he panted to shut the door, "when you're in uniform aren't you supposed to drive a county cruiser? Why the Great Nations truck?" Red colored his ear lobes in my headlamp's beam. I turned away.

"Headed home and just doing a favor for the sheriff. Won't help you to get huffy with *me*," he said. I was quite sure real police didn't threaten people about getting *huffy*. I shook out the wrinkled statement and held it under my light. In uniform to drop off a few papers on his way home from the office? Driving a company truck? Would it matter, his mixing up a part-time enforcement career with his Great Nations loyalties? Of course. It already mattered.

Anderson handed me a coffee-smelling pen. I signed both copies and placed one between us. The cab of a truck is normally an intimate place. In my youth, I said and did things I regret, seduced by trucks' companionable spaces, country music, and sweaty baseball caps. Anderson's truck was a hard, cold shell lit by an imposing GPS unit. In the rear seat, silver toolboxes blinked back reflections of dash readouts. I smelled citrus cologne and gun cleaning oil, and thought he might be armed for both seduction and resistance.

I grabbed for the door, but he grabbed me first, ripping my vest. Feathers flew at him like geese flapping inside a cage. For a moment, I mourned the vest, a thrift shop favorite I'd have to mend it with duct tape. I should have known facing Anderson down in front of an audience—even a lowly intern—had consequences. I wasn't prepared for the threat.

"You've been a big player down in Augusta." He panted and shifted his grip on me. "Acting like landowners can't do what they want with their own property. Our country was founded on the sanctity of property. Sacred. Property is sacred. We—we own over a million acres of sacred property. And that's just in Maine. Not your land. *Our* land. Our *land*." His eyes were gone to the dark woods above my head. Oil on his fingers greased my nose. His whisper hissed in my ear.

"You and the reporter think you know something. You shouldn't feel so special. On our land, you're nothing but a woman alone in a beat-up station wagon driving on deserted roads."

Light thumped down on the truck, and Anderson's words ended in a strangled expletive. "Shifruggahhh." Shadows snapped into stark, black outlines of trees, barn, house, and fence. Anderson covered his eyes and howled while I tumbled out of the truck and crawled away.

Something rolled and crunched down the hill into the driveway. No motor noise, just intense light trying to penetrate fingers I'd crammed into my eyes. I heard a grinding hand brake and single pebbles pinched as tires rolled to a stop near my head. Ticking metal parts announced something large and official. The voice, when it came, was not a surprise.

"I now see the directions say I should not use the full search capacity of this light unless I need to illuminate a target at least a quarter of a mile distant," Moz called out. I heard a dial click, and behind my lids the light faded into murky fog. Instinctively I'd tucked myself into a balled-up, fetal lump—standard bear attack posture.

He crouched beside me and patted my shoulder. "You may sit in my vehicle, please. The seat is wet from Pock's swim. Drink the tea and place the tea bag on your eyes. I will be talking to the deputy."

I heard Anderson's truck door close softly as I felt my way from gravel to the seat of the search and rescue van and leaned against my wet, wagging dog. I rubbed his fur, squeezing hairy drops into my face and eyes, feeling the rounded edges of what was clamped in his teeth. I squinted at the remains of a white mooring buoy. Either he or Moz had finally pulled it from the cove. I smelled bitter tea, fished out a strange tea bag from the mug on the dash, and slapped it on my eyes. Anderson's truck roared into sound, and its headlights flashed over me as it cut across the lawn and flattened late-blooming mums my mother had planted in defiance of early frost.

Moz opened the driver's door, whistled Pock out of the van, and tossed the slippery buoy and its trailing rope after him. Darkness dropped mercifully on us when Moz turned off the searchlight. He lifted the tea bag from my eyes, emptied its contents on the ground, and draped it over his mirror.

"Moose intestine sewed into a pouch. Reusable. You need not look offended. It is more sanitary than anything a waitress might serve you." He chuckled and pulled my crumpled statement from his pocket. "You left this in Anderson's truck."

The banter about tea and intestines was a prelude to genuine conversation. Wardens use chat time to assess the mental status of folks under stress. Gives them time to create control strategies. The Penobscot part of Moz probably considered abrupt questioning rude.

I never operate that way. I like to find the vulnerability in people and go after them before they have time to regroup, so I went after

Moz. "The message you left on the paper bag had me thinking you planned a quiet retrieval, not a spectacular entrance. I'll be picking gravel out of my neck for weeks. Forgive me if I think the searchlight was overkill. I'm used to you being more of a myth than something real anyway." I couldn't stop. "So why are you all of sudden so *real*?"

Moz spread his calloused hands wide across the steering wheel until veins lifted over his skin. We'd always had a "don't ask" relationship. I never asked why his wife had left him even as I routinely collected his young children and added them to our summer household while he searched for hikers who'd left the trail, children who'd left picnics, or Alzheimer's patients who'd left home. Often I wasn't awake to see him gather his boys off the couch.

When I moved permanently into Antler Camp, he didn't ask about my missing marriage. He shoveled my mailbox after feverish snows and he chain-sawed downed trees from my road. I had no reason to be rude. Hunched in my seat, I shivered with cold and regret.

Moz inhaled a deep breath and exhaled a patient list I should have thanked him for. "As a myth I couldn't have sorted out the substantial mess here tonight. I was in the sheriff's office when Anderson suggested he deliver your statement. I came to sit on your dock and watch your house after I saw Anderson change into his uniform when I knew he was not on duty. I went into the water to help Pock because he was struggling with a rope in the cove. I went for the van when Anderson went for you. I used the searchlight because he had a gun and it is complicated for one lawman to wrestle another to the ground."

"A gun? He had a gun? I couldn't see it. Too much of him was hanging below his belt." I stuffed loose feathers into my vest and pulled the ripped zipper over my chest. Anderson had lied. The sheriff hadn't asked him to deliver my statement. He'd arranged the camp visit and dressed for it. "What did you say to him?" I asked.

"That I will keep private." Moz turned toward the lake, where shards of pale moonlight cut their way through treetops onto the beach. "I regret giving you Shannon's notebook. I regret involving you," he said.

"We're already involved if wolves have anything to do with it, but you already know that, don't you?" I snapped. "You must have the same suspicions Shannon had. You sent the beaver skull, so you must think it's connected, and you probably know about Peter's covert research project. What I don't understand is why you'd leave me something that might be evidence. You had me wear gloves to handle it. Why risk your job?"

Except for drops sliding off his wet hair onto his pants, Moz might have been stone.

I pushed harder. "You have all kinds of biologists and wardens who'd be foaming at the mouth just to guess at what we *think* we know. I've enjoyed our nonverbal guessing games over animal remains, but I'm no biologist. Why *me*?"

If I'd kept up with yoga, I could have bent double in the van and kicked myself. What did Peter call my car? The undercover post office. Moz didn't trust his office, the state, his boss—whoever—to do the right thing. He trusted me.

He fingered the deer embroidered on his sleeve's insignia. "I thought I could carry them together. Warden and woods, but all is changed."

"What's changed?" I snorted. "Seems like the same good-old-boys club of timber executives and sucking-up state officials still in charge. Bureaucratic copy machines still spurting out meaningless agreements about *vol-un-ta-ry* wildlife management." I shifted in my seat so I could face his profile. "Last month Great Nations went to Washington to stop the U.S. Fish and Wildlife Service from mapping lynx habitat on company lands. *Your* boss—*our* wildlife commissioner—tagged along to explain how voluntary agreements—optional, of course—work better than requiring owners to save some terrain for the natives. Natives who were here first ... even before your folks."

I couldn't stop the edgy sarcasm I spewed. "Oh ... and right on time Governor Lord called a press conference to complain that endangered species regulations were 'counterproductive to the future of Maine's fishing and forestry industries.' Seems he's another cheerleader for wildlife volunteerism. The state capitol is still as corrupt as it's always been. As long as you stay far out in the bush, tracking poachers and rescuing children, you can avoid these people and their politics. What's changed?"

I'd always wanted to give that speech in public but hadn't been ready for unemployment. Moz nodded once, like someone standing aside to watch a flash flood crest and recede. Then he switched on the van's headlights. On the camp roof Ian bent over his phone wearing my father's Russian fur hat. From where we sat, he appeared to be hosting a small animal on his head. Without looking up, he popped a thumbs-up into the air. Moz's face creased into movement. "Wolves. Wolves are the change. The governor and his business friends. The governor and his hunting friends. They will not tolerate wolves. Their ancestors exterminated wolves from Maine and they prefer it that way. No animal is so pursued and tortured. So hated." He dropped into a reverent whisper. "No other animal carries such magic."

We watched Ian inch toward the ladder he'd propped against the roof, still working his phone as he lowered himself with one hand. Pock jumped up against the van window and pressed his slobbery buoy on the glass.

Moz reached across to open my door. "There are people who suspect wolves. Anderson and Great Nations suspect. By closing roads and limiting access, they hope to create time and space to find them. There are people who believe because they have found signs they trust. Shannon found tracks and believed. The person who chained the beaver as food probably knows more than all of us."

Moz pulled a corner of my sagging vest up to my shoulder before he turned and climbed out into my driveway. "The wolf is a dangerous endangered species not because of what it does but because of the fear that follows it. Anderson thinks you suspect wolves. If he thinks you believe, that you have proof, he and his people will be dangerous."

I couldn't think of anything to add. I already knew Shannon believed in the wolves, and I'd used up enough airtime in anger anyway. We leaned on the outside of the van and watched the moon paint silver paths up the lake. I felt the cold drop down on us, falling temperatures squeezing frost from the air, coating rocks with a glycerin sheen.

Moz cleared his throat. "I think Shannon believed *and* I think she knew." In pale light his face was liquid granite. His chiseled features, strong slanting nose, and square jaw seemed to melt backward into his cheeks. His voice was hard. "On the other hand, Maine's game wardens are now ordered not to know. Behind closed doors, at headquarters, people suspect. Officially we continue to have 'insufficient information.'"

He reached for the typed pages I carried and turned them over, drawing a quick map with a pen pulled from his breast pocket. "When you head north, find the Mahoneys camped on a stream above Seboomook Lake. They should have sufficient information. Ignore those who ridicule them as Howlers."

Stalking to the van, Moz dragged the buoy's rope in a grim tug-of-war with Pock, who lived for ropes that behaved like escaping snakes. Then he drove without headlights up the hill and into the night.

I'd survived a brutally long day, starting early when the last loon left my cove and flew south toward water that wouldn't freeze. From my bed, I'd heard its cry, short and strangled from the effort to call and fly at the same time. After that lonely echo, migrating seemed more appealing than hibernating at camp—everything too cold without Shannon. *Hours and hours ago,* I thought. I folded Moz's map and stuffed it in my overalls pocket. Wolves might be easier to track in snow. Maybe I'd be migrating north, not south.

CHAPTER 10

I tossed a sleeping bag on the porch couch and told Ian to wear the fur hat all night. Then I showed him how to flush the toilet with a bucket of water and pointed to the outhouse alternative. He was mumbling about primitive waste disposal when I sank onto my bed.

Too tired to undress, I kicked off my boots, flipped a quilt over my legs, and thought Shannon a message: *If you tracked wolves, I'll track wolves. I forgive you for that secret and probably whatever else is secret because someone took that thing I saw under your head and I want to know what it was and what slimy person took it. So. So, I promise to pick up your trail. I am a bit pissed you left me out. Miss you more than chocolate.* The last sound I heard was Pock's breath rasping over the buoy in his teeth as he turned three times and settled on my feet.

The next morning, Tuesday, I was up early, my cooler packed with food, dog kibble in animal-proof tins, camping gear in my car, and canoe strapped to its roof. I wedged a grinning Shannon picture into the first aid kit.

Stuffed with logs, the wood stove was surrounded by house plants shrouded in sheets that would give them three warm days.

Ian's cold weather wardrobe, saved from the ski area's lost and found bin, covered the dining room table: rain pants, parka, long underwear, fleece sweatshirt, wool socks, and a hat that didn't look like a bear.

On the dock, I ate yogurt mixed with apples I pulled from the nearest tree, and gripped my bowl with mittens that folded open to free useful fingers. My friends considered me woefully underemployed, but I felt rich. Very rich. At my desk overlooking the capitol's dome, I'd have missed the beaver swimming a sapling across the cove and the woodpecker hammering insects from rotten pilings. I'd have missed the buck blowing angry air at me as I lugged the canoe past the compost pile. *You should toss out more apple cores and lettuce. It's getting thin out here.*

Anything else?

Across the cove they leave us grain and corn.

Don't trust people in general and especially don't trust people who put out food for you. You never know what they're after. I mean it.

He tossed his antlers and trotted up the trail, weaving between rusted cars toward the last green grass. My mother called our neighbor Motor Mark, grateful my brother could never actually repair the wrecks that littered his field. Last week he'd escaped to Arizona, leaving me a message scrawled on a carton of spoiled sour cream. "See ya when it thaws."

I used Peter's message to list people we'd interview, planned a three-day itinerary, and was exceptionally ready to go. Snores from the porch told me Ian was not, so I snatched the buoy from Pock's mouth and slid it into his sleeping bag. Soon he was up and mumbling. The outhouse seat was ice on his ass. I didn't own coffee. He wouldn't be caught dead in discarded clothes. In ratty jeans and T-shirt, he glared at me.

"It's brand-name gear doctors and lawyers leave behind," I said, stuffing a duffle. "There's a thousand dollars in here."

"I'm not a kid and I don't need a mother," barked Ian. He used his fingers to comb his hair. "No mirrors? That fits the pioneer motif." He put both hands on the dining table and leaned toward me, narrowing his snapping eyes. "Look—I need to know everything you know, and I need to know what happened outside with the deputy and the warden last night. I don't need to be sent to the shed while you do the thinking."

I winced at the direct hit. "The skull," I said. "The beaver was staked as a free dinner. The deputy was feeling out how much we know. The warden thinks wolves are the most dangerous endangered species because threatened humans might be more of a threat than wolves, and he's got the humans divided into three camps. People who suspect wolves. Anderson and Great Nations are probably in that camp. People who believe because they've found some proof—probably Shannon. And finally, people who know for sure. That group, if it is a group, includes the beaver-staker."

He looked around. "Where can I brush my teeth?"

I pointed to the kitchen sink, picked up the rejected clothes, and went to wait in the car.

His silence didn't melt for miles. The unfolded topo map cocooned him in the passenger seat, erecting a wall between us. I didn't expect him to savor that magic moment when frost undresses trees. Before dawn, I'd rolled over in bed and opened the window to hear each leaf scratch bark and slither from branch to branch to land on mates below. Blown into the road, they regrouped as bright leaf tornadoes that funneled down the road behind us.

Ian sulked but I ignored the silence. "Here's the rest of it. Moz says Great Nations is closing roads to control possible wolf access. He thinks humans get dangerous when they appear, and along those lines, people with questionable agendas will soon join us in the woods."

Pock crawled up on the duffels and tried to scratch a bed into the top of them.

"What do you think of the topo map?" I asked.

Ian tilted the map until I could see his eyes. "The beaver dam areas overlap the closed roads you transferred from your friend's map. She died in this same area, but she was just inside the Monson woman's land." He raised the map and disappeared behind it. "I'm OK with organizing what we find on a map if we get to wolves before the questionable agenda people do."

"What were you doing on the roof last night?" I asked.

"Working." He wiped his sunglasses on his dirty shirt. A hefty truck bore down on us, chains glinting over tall mounds of cinched logs. Bits of bark slapped my windshield as it passed us and careened away. Inside the car, dust hung in a gritty haze.

Ian sighed and cleaned his glasses again. "I got a lot done last night. Some on the roof. More later going through your stuff in the shed after you'd checked out."

"*My* files?" I asked. "That's bold."

"It's not like they were taped up. When I went out to sample outhouse living I saw files in coolers. Coolers?"

I reached for gum. Chewing multiple pieces organized the dust in my mouth and sent it on its way. Calmly, I said, "Coolers are my storage system. Weather and rodent proof, easy to stack and free. Lazy campers leave them behind."

Ian raised the map up over his face again.

"Let's organize," I said. "You tell me what you were working on. I'll suggest interviews and a schedule. I think we need to talk to people who work outdoors near wildlife—for whatever we find at this point. We'll be at Six Rivers Timber's operations by ten. I left a message for Phil Bryan, their wildlife biologist, but I think we'll need to use the blog cover with him. Six Rivers has the only wildlife professional working for any Maine timber company, and he's been in the woods for years, probably meeting up with everything that breathes out here."

I didn't share my private agenda to know what Shannon knew and go where she'd gone, and I didn't tell Ian that Shannon was a volunteer supervising Phil's graduate student assistants and she thought he was grooming her to replace him. Some days she loved Phil and other days she dismissed him as a spineless sellout. That seemed like important information, but only to me.

Ian pulled his laptop onto his knees. "Did you know your neighbor has an open wireless connection?"

I shrugged my shoulders. "Motor Mark? He's only here when it's warm and he can grow his car collection."

Ian snorted. "Well, his signal hits your roof, and he didn't create a password to keep you out, so I downloaded more wolf stuff. And Peter emailed me some of your columns to fix and said he'd publish while we're on the road."

I swerved to avoid rocks aimed at my car's exhaust system. If a log truck claimed the only lane, I'd find a ditch. Like floaplane pilots who scan water for emergency landings, I scanned roadsides for alternate parking. Mostly I thought about turning around so I could spare my car and evict Ian. "I met you yesterday and now you're publishing *my* writing?" I said.

"Peter didn't tell you the deal? Some of the blogs will be short versions of what you've already given him." Ian lowered his shades and looked directly at me for the first time that day. "I didn't do much ... just split 'Wetlands Worth Billions' into two posts and pumped up the entertaining parts."

He slipped out of his sneakers and propped his bare feet on my dash. I wondered when he'd beg for socks. "Why are you hiding up here?" he asked, waving one of my files. "Connect money to this and you make news. Most people avoid environmental blah-blah-blah like the plague, or Al Gore, or the sniveling scientist that's last on the news. But you've got something hot. Cash. Everyone loves cash, and some of this is weird enough to snag people. A hummingbird festival drops six million dollars into an Arizona town no one's heard of? Grizzlies rip salmon out of rivers to entertain tourists and that's worth ten million to another no-name Alaska town? And this one. Wild bees in Maine. Really? Seventy-five million for making blueberries blue?" As he lifted a thick report, the file's other contents slipped to the floor.

"Pick it up," I said. "It's *my* research."

The edge was back was in Ian's voice. "I don't get what you're doing living under layers of scavenged clothing, counting moose parts, listening to tree noise, huddled around your stove. That cabin's cold. What you have to say could be very hot." He slumped in his seat and shoved his glasses more firmly over his eyes.

Perhaps he'd failed to notice that he wasn't being paid for our wolf adventure, that he was sleeping on my couch, and that he was eating my food. "I can't live on *hot*, Ian," I said. "Can you?"

CHAPTER 11

Without summer tourism, Greenwood was a hardscrabble edge-of-the-woods town. Road Kill's parking lot was filled with idling trucks, mud-splattered log trucks, trucks towing trailers of dead moose, and trucks with children strapped in booster seats.

Ian scuffed his way toward the cantina's front door. "Doesn't anyone up here drive something that gets over five miles to the gallon?"

"I called ahead and ordered you coffee and a breakfast sandwich," I called. "We're on Peter's expense account, so bring a receipt. Donut for me, please."

Francoise staggered around the back of the restaurant dragging two large white buckets. Looking left and right, she lifted one bucket, dumped its contents over the wharf into a sloppy splash, and put a finger to her lips as she dragged the second bucket to use as a stool outside my car door. "I dump old shells as bait for my crayfish traps. If you won't tell the code enforcement man I treat you to my Crayfish Crawl." She sat and leaned toward me, sharing a cloud of shellfish perfume. "Are you coming to Shannon's party?" she asked.

"Party?" My neck flushed warm against my raised collar. I'd planned on helping Shannon's parents clean her apartment but felt sure I had a few days until the autopsy process was complete.

"Her parents ship her home this week but pay me to create a Friday party. They are too sad to come but want friends to remember with fun." She scowled at my canoe. "Cold for the boat. I made your sandwich with extra bacon the way you like."

"Great! Extra bacon," I said. She'd charge for it and Ian would eat it all.

She poked my arm. "Why do my truckers and loggers stop work? Is it Shannon? They sit too long and buy only coffee."

On a good day, Francoise's restaurant had better gossip than a hair salon. If loggers at her counter knew about wolf activity, Francoise would know about wolf activity. "Are they talking?" I asked.

"Not much, but angry at not normal things. They say boss men that never leave offices drive roads and kick them off." She jumped from her bucket, grunted with the effort to lift it, and dragged it to the back of my car. "Where is room for this?" she demanded, lifting my rear door. "Old grease for bear guides at Grants."

Ian dropped a donut without a napkin on my side of the dash. The hot smell inflated my sinuses. "Like we need more grease," he said.

"Not to worry. Tight top. Guides buy grease and donuts to trick bears to traps," she said. "They like chocolate donuts."

"The bears or the guides?" I asked, swallowing my own donut. Apparently, I shared the bears' passion for chocolate pastry.

She slammed the door and raised her empty bucket toward us in farewell. Her pigtails rotated like directional antennas when she was in a hurry, springing all over the place as she trotted back to the restaurant.

Ian stuffed the last bite of bacon and croissant into his mouth. "Done with that? Let's hit it."

I accelerated onto a dirt road so coffee could spill in his lap and clarify the trip's chain of command. Pock crawled over gear piles to safety on the floor, and I slid Aretha Franklin into the CD player. "Chain of Fools" and a powerful odor of French fries wafted through the car.

Wiping drops off his shirt, Ian tossed his cup into the ditch, so I pulled over. We sat and listened to Aretha, but I ejected the CD when she started feeling like *a natural woman*. Nothing felt natural about camping with Ian. I waited for him to figure out the car wouldn't start until he reclaimed his trash.

Inside the car, dust hung in a gritty haze. Ian wiped his sunglasses on his dirty shirt, opened his door, leaned low to retrieve his cup, and returned to slump in this seat. I turned on the wipers to clear dust and then turned north onto the Twenty Mile Road.

"I'm guessing twenty more miles of dust," Ian said. He rummaged through his duffel, flipping through more of my files.

"Let's get to the land trust guy today. Get him interviewed and get back on wolves. Vicki Brinkman told me he's mapping out a deal between the trust and something called Great Nations." He uncapped a yellow highlighter and swiped it over a Maine Forest Trust newsletter. "There's money in it. The timber company sells easement deals without selling land. Don't get that, but sounds like a slick trick."

I tried to peel the foil wrapper off a tiny tub of peach yogurt while negotiating a stream that had jumped its culvert and swallowed the road. "It's complicated. Last time I tried to explain easements to a legislative committee, most of them left for smokes." I pointed my spoon at our topo map. "On the other hand, we might pump this man Engunn for useful information. See if he's got wildlife info on his maps or find out if the trust's done any field research."

Ian lifted his shades and scowled at dark clouds. "When we get back to town, let's find your boss and ask him what he found tracking wolves last year. And Peter told me to find someone named Anita Stockdale. She had a government job dealing with wolves and now sells what she knows to something called the New England Wildlife Consortium." Ian lifted his phone out his window.

"What makes you think you'll get a signal?" I asked.

"I have an app that locates hot spots. How far is the timber office? I've got a weak signal."

We gained ground on a slowing log truck—the dust cloud we'd followed for the last half hour. I thought it might be the same truck that spit bark at us earlier, but all dust clouds look alike. I couldn't manage the yogurt and drive, so I leaned back and offered it to Pock. He couldn't get his whole muzzle inside the container, but I knew somehow he'd get it all.

Slowing my speed to avoid the truck's dust, I realized there was no speed I could drive to avoid the cloud unless I turned and drove away as if pursued by bandits. I thumped my brakes and violated a north woods edict: I stopped in the middle of the road. Never, never stop in the middle of a logging road. I punched my emergency flashing lights. The cloud swelled, inhaling more dirt and dust from the sides of the road. An angry weather system of grit rained on my car.

Trapped between ruts, I couldn't turn around. I slammed into reverse, swerving and backing blindly into the dust cloud hanging in the road behind us. Suddenly the road ahead and the road behind vanished. I turned the wheel toward the last ditch I'd seen and let the car drift toward it. Wheels left packed dirt and sank into soft, collapsing shoulder. In slow motion, we tilted down, balanced between road and ditch.

"What the hell's going on?" shouted Ian.

"Out," I yelled. "Out of the car. Truck's backing at us! Run for it."

“Pock,” I called, shoving my door. “Out. Out!” He lunged forward and pinned me to my seat. Claws digging my thighs, he gathered front legs to spring. My fingers strained for his collar. I hung on as he dragged me from car to ditch.

Brakes squealed. I crawled over Pock, pressed him into the dirt, and slapped my arms over my head. Loose chains clanged and banged. More brakes screamed, and then—low rumbling thunder that I knew belonged in a mill—loose logs looking for a place to land. Face down in Pock’s fur I felt the ditch vibrate as the truck accelerated away from us. *Please, please*, I prayed. *Have bad aim. Have bad timing*. I lifted my elbow to check on Ian and saw two massive trees catapult end over end into the ditch across the road. Saplings and brush snapped and splintered. I ducked and winced. Snapped bones have the same crisp sound right before someone starts screaming. Pock shrugged me sideways and raced for the woods.

Crouching in the bushes above my ditch, Ian sank to the ground with a weak smile and raised a few fingers in salute. “Good choice of ditch.”

An hour later, as I held a growling dog, a nervous Québécois log truck driver towed my car from the ditch, shoved the loose-hanging canoe back onto the roof racks, and warned Ian about “les femmes dangereuses.” Ian’s bare feet, grease fumes, and a Subaru that looked like a failed safari produced lots of head shaking and

French curses as our rescuer showered us with more dust and peeled away.

As I drove, chewing too much gum and gripping the wheel so hard my hands looked bloodless, Ian held his sunglasses out the window and poured our drinking water over them. I wondered if he'd ever been camping. "Someone just tried to flatten us," he said.

I turned into a rutted driveway and parked by Six Rivers' double-wide silver trailer. Ian stared at full gun racks mounted in each battered truck as he tied his sneakers. "The natives look insanely equipped," he said. "You ever been threatened before? I saw the pile of slashed tires in your shed."

"Oh, those," I replied. "I keep them to remind me I have appreciative audiences in unlikely places."

"Seriously."

"Seriously? After a few hot campaigns aimed at improving harvesting standards, I got hate email, hate snail mail, hate voice mail, and, one morning, slashed tires. The police investigated, but nothing came of it. I don't think large—very large—corporate landowners are threatened by our efforts." I opened a can of baby wipes and scrubbed my face free of dirt until I smelled newly diapered. "They usually have a lock on the politics and the politicians, so there's no need to behave desperately. But if you really mean *seriously*, I've never had anyone deliver such an in-your-face message. For what it's worth, if someone meant to do us in, I don't think he'd use a log truck on a traveled road. It's not a precise method." I offered Ian the baby wipes but he sneered and waved them away.

"Message? A berserk truck firing logs at us was a *message*? What message?"

I remembered Moz's hard, moonlit face and Anderson's grip on my ripped vest. "I'm in and out of here all the time," I said. "For years I've come and gone working the environmental cause. Woods crews change my flat tires, bring me gas when I screw up, and they're gracious about showing me their operations. Never a hint of ill will on these back roads. Maybe—"

"Maybe we're in the land of the most dangerous species and right now it's a toss-up who gets that award." Ian opened his door, grabbed the roof rack, and pulled himself out and into a stretch. "Someone still tried to flatten us."

I half lowered windows so Pock would enjoy air but not freedom. "Please lose the sunglasses, Ian," I said. "Folks will just snigger behind your back."

There were no folks to be found, but the trailer shook with heavy machinery we couldn't see. Up on the covered porch we studied posters and maps.

Ian tapped a map with his glasses. "What's a DWA?"

"Deer Wintering Area. The state biologists map them and hope landowners won't cut them. Voluntary guidelines only." I wiped my hand over the map. "This is an old map. Half of these are cut now. In the winter deer need shelter trees to be about 10 percent of their woods. Up here now—and this old map won't show it—most owners manage less than 1 percent of their lands for shelter."

Ian shrugged. "Leave a few trees. What's the big deal?"

"It's a tough call for owners. Old trees aren't worth much to the bottom line, but tall, old pines and spruce that hold snow off the ground mean life or death to deer and other species. Six Rivers is one of the few owners trying to keep shelter, but their bean counters are screaming about wasted wood. It's a struggle."

Ian leaned into a large map cut by bold black lines under an even blacker heading: "Endangered Species Act Alert. Critical Habitat for Threatened Canada Lynx." He rose on his toes, inspecting red graffiti spray painted on the trailer wall. "ESA. Essentially Stupid Animalrightswingnuts." What looked like a cluster of red grapes was probably wing-nut testicles.

Ian grinned and lifted his notebook. "What's Critical Habitat?"

I sighed, thinking of endless legislative debates on the habitat needs of insects, amphibians, birds, and unpopular mammals. I could almost taste the tasteless granola bars I'd eaten on the sly behind my upended briefcase. I couldn't risk a sprint to the cafeteria or I'd miss the one comment guaranteed to swing a committee into a "no" vote on even the most timid protections. Three years ago, when I had the flu and leaned too long against a cool marble bathroom wall, my favorite legislator killed protections for stressed mayflies.

His pithy comment made national news. "There's already way too many goddamn flies. I can't barbecue a steak without them falling into it and gumming it up. I say we turn up the flame, kill them all quickly, and be done with it."

I nudged Ian toward a photograph, an alert lynx crouched in a birch tree, black tufted ears barely visible against snow and bark. "OK, here's lynx: large cats listed as a federal threatened species and entitled to mapped territory with special protections. That's their critical habitat. Lynx are picky eaters, so this mapping is all about protecting their food as well as their homes and travel routes. Lynx need forests that grow snowshoe hares."

"Wolves. Have they got some territory mapped?" Ian asked.

"I don't think there's been much detailed mapping in Maine. Just a general stab at outlining wolf-livable lands."

"Why not get it cleared up? Map what they need."

Out of habit, I dropped my voice. "It can get very hot. Habitat mapping can trigger some kind of government interaction with you, your land, and sometimes how you make money off your land. Generally, the more land you own and the bigger the plans you have for your land, the more adjustments you might have to make." I pointed to a large patch of green wetlands on the nearest map. "Sometimes it's simple. Don't build wide roads and slime them with chemicals where salamanders crawl across to a breeding pool. Sometimes the requirements are tough. Out west, the spotted owl stopped cutting on federal lands so sawmills that depended on cheap government logging contracts failed. Lots of very angry people."

Staring too long at a map that should have shown recently closed roads but didn't, I lost Ian. He was around the corner wearing a Six Rivers hard hat and leaning in Phil's truck window, both staring at a growling skidder. Skidders are a combination bulldozer and tow truck on steroids. Trees bounced and thrashed, towed behind gigantic tires, and, of course, Ian's hard hat was tilted over a boyish grin.

Phil reached out a hand and grasped mine. Wearing a blue flannel shirt and lime green vest, Phil looked almost sporty. Deep in a wind-sculpted face, his mischievous brown eyes glowed under a wool hat heavy with patches—faded badges for Trout Unlimited, Ducks Unlimited, and the Ruffed Grouse Society.

"Patton. Always good to see you. I'm explaining to this intern fella that I'm more of a wildlife mediator than a wildlife biologist," Phil said. He pushed his hat back on his head and snorted. "And yes, I guess what I do is about money. I manage wildlife so it reduces the company's cost of doing business. So we don't tangle with regulators. Pay fines and such. Got some things for ya."

Phil handed me a large picture of Shannon standing in the middle of a shaggy group of university students—all of them raising peace signs for the camera. He coughed. "What can I say, Patton? I'm so sorry. I don't understand why anything like this happens."

I swallowed an audible gulp and held up the picture so Phil couldn't see my eyes.

"I wish she was here to shove you in my face," he said. "She told me to listen to you and come up with a plan to deal honestly with lynx. Now the feds have gone and mapped good Christly thousands of acres and everyone's all nerved up about an animal that's not going to be a problem. Generally, if we don't run over lynx, we won't upset them. Lynx like what we do because snowshoe hares like what we do. The bunnies breed like bunnies in the stands we've thinned out and the lynx eat the bunnies. Works well."

Phil eased out of his truck and walked back toward its cargo space. "Now don't quote me complimenting you. I get to retire next year, and I plan to be in and out of these woods on friendly terms with everyone. I'm walking the straight and narrow until then. If I don't get my pension, I'll be a Walmart greeter 'til I croak."

He passed Ian a stained brochure. "This the kind of information you're looking for, young 'un? Everything the Maine Forest Business Foundation wants you to know about money, jobs, and trees. Take it. I got no use for fluff."

Ian pried apart the booklet's waterlogged pages. "Is what's in here essentially correct?"

"As far as it goes, yes," Phil said. "One of every fifteen Maine jobs comes from some kind of forest activity, from the cutting to the making of things. Of course, they don't say they cut, load, and haul with a fraction of the hires they once had, but it's true—we are sitting on an eleven-million-acre gold mine.

"Here's what's not in there. Last year this country spent eighty-five billion dollars buying cars, but it spent a hundred fifteen billion getting out to connect with wild animals. Hunt, fish, trap, and just watch 'em." He pointed a gnarled finger at me. "I assume, Patton, you'll get that to the thing you write for the paper?"

I nodded. "Probably next week. So, Phil, what's on your radar screen for interesting wildlife these days?"

He rooted around in the truck some more. "Funny you should mention radar, though I know you didn't mean it literally. The strange thing about my job is that we're going to need more technology to keep what's wild—wild. Glad I'm retiring before they come up with more gadgets." His face disappeared behind coils of rope and broken antennas. "The New England Wildlife Consortium buys me six-thousand-dollar collars to track lynx, so I guess lynx are on my radar screen. The collars talk to satellites. The satellites talk to computers. Computers talk to our map programs. We know lynx like we camped with them. A screen tells us if they're eating, sleeping, or dead."

He opened a box and lifted a gray strap that looked dive-suit-rubber strong. A black box was riveted into its center seams. Instantly, Shannon's sightless eye blurred my vision and a sharp spasm stabbed my chest. Lying neatly in white tissue paper, but without blood, was an exact copy of the strap I'd seen under Shannon's bruised cheek.

CHAPTER 12

While I stared, Ian grabbed his notebook and Phil and headed uphill toward the machines. I was still working on breathing, not walking, so I yelled after them, "Do these ever just come off?"

Without turning, Phil yelled, "We can release them by remote control, but one falling off on its own? No."

My knees felt seasick but I leaned into the truck and grabbed the collar's instructions. The Lottflex GPS 7000 Tracking System promised a "revolutionary system to track wildlife subjects and record accurate data on movements, locations, and mortality."

At my car, I rubbed Pock's nose through the window and stashed the instructions in my pack. I could imagine Shannon on her hands and knees inside Monson's gate. She was a traditional tracker, pushing me down to notice snapped twigs while she sniffed fur snagged on bark. She was traditional, but she'd know what this kind of collar could do that she couldn't do. My brain went black trying to imagine a bloody hand lifting a bloody collar away from her cheek.

Moz needed to know I'd identified the missing strap. Even if I avoided warden communications we couldn't trust, the woods hosted a primitive bush system where information crossed rivers and jumped mountains, so I hoped he'd just appear. I settled Pock with a granola bar and followed the rutted track toward noise.

Phil was perched high on a stump and he leaned down on my shoulder. "I've heard you've got a healthy interest in deer, Patton. Me too. I've managed to bring in methods that don't mow down the whole crop. Now we pick and choose as we work through what we own. Leave more forest for animals. More stockholder cash later on because we let trees get grown up."

He pointed at the slash pile of quivering limbs. "We'll haul those limbs into the deer yard across the road for winter food, and when we're done, seed this yard with tasty grass that's up by spring." He removed his hard hat and unfolded its fuzzy earflaps. "I hoped Shannon would continue my work. She was wasted on Great Nations—knew more about trees and wild critters than I ever will."

Cold explored my uncovered places—the gap between my socks and jeans, the back of my neck, the tips of my ears. Phil replaced his hat, pressing its flaps over his ears. We watched Ian scratch in his notebook, his eyes never leaving the growling machines.

"Phil," I asked, "why is Great Nations closing roads where it planned harvesting this fall?"

I saw Ian's fingers freeze over the paper and Phil's white brows arch toward each other in disapproval. "You don't waste time getting to what's prickly. Probably why folks' panties are twisted in a knot over you."

He wiped his hands down faded canvas pants. "Here's what I know. Last time Shannon came to work with my grad students—

July, I think it was—I asked her if she'd ordered the closings. She was spitting angry after Anderson Barter closed a whole bunch of roads and told her to back off. Told her she'd be reassigned this fall."

I hoped my face looked friendly because the rest of me sank toward my toes. Shannon hadn't said a word to me about a transfer.

He rubbed both hands over his face, smoothing his deepest lines. "I asked her—again—to think about replacing me next year. She asked me what I got paid and said she'd think about it. Got in her truck and blew me a kiss. That's the last time I saw her."

"Was she acting normal? I mean, anything outside of her normal I-can-change-the-world attitude?" I asked.

Phil smiled. "I bet given enough time and money she could. She could do that. No. She was all Shannon, but on the other hand, who turns down a job that beats their old job hands down? What was up with that?"

To change the subject, I scraped mud off my boots onto the ragged stumps around us. "We're headed up to interview someone named Engunn who's working for the Maine Forest Trust up at Canada Falls. Any advice?"

Phil snorted. "You going to talk money? Ask that fella how much Great Nations gets from the deal he's working. Vicki and her crew? Not your normal land trust where people get off their asses, raise money, and buy someplace before it's bulldozed. She's working an experiment—kind of a partnership with skidders. I like the idea of protecting forest as a cash crop. The trust's out front with that mission, but Vicki raises millions from people who think she's protecting something else besides loggers' paychecks.

"Because I get around, I get to see her little experiment not working most every day when one of her 'partners' rams a skidder through a stream or flattens a deer yard and the trust is missing in action." He laughed and raised his fist into an obscene plunging gesture that surprised me. "She's in bed with the people who wrecked the stream and cut the yard. You can't climb into bed with the business end of the woods and police the brothel at the same time. It's a conflict of interest, pure and simple."

My heart leaped into hopeful thumps. I thought I was the only one who didn't trust the trust. Phil waggled a finger at me. "And I *do* mean brothel. This isn't just consensual bedding by two groups using each other. Serious money changes hands. I think the trust might agree to most anything to get what it wants."

"What does it want?" I asked.

"Not sure. The deal making's behind closed doors, but I'm guessing it must be mighty impossible to force good forestry on the company that gives you cash to run your organization." He slowly lowered one leg off the stump and then the other. "I'm glad I'll be gone when the sludge trucks roll."

I turned to see Ian's reaction to something septic. Shirtless and struggling, Ian pointed at me with his free arm. His other arm was attached to the rolled-up shirt he'd tied around the neck of my squirming dog.

Pock cowered and flattened his ears in Lab apology, but I yanked a leash from my pocket and pulled him to the parking lot. Ian passed me at a trot, trying to crawl into his T-shirt and sidestep stumps at the same time. I found him shivering his way through my duffle of lost-and-found clothes, frantically piling items on the car hood.

Phil pulled up next to us in his truck. "I'm late for something, but it's not your fault." He tossed a hard hat to Ian. "You dropped this. Keep it. Might come in handy if you hang out with Patton."

He pulled away but quickly shifted into reverse and backed up the driveway to pass Ian a long, sturdy bone. Ian held it grimly between two fingers and dropped it into the back seat.

Phil laughed and slapped his steering wheel. "It won't bite. It's not from the mouth end. I'm guessing you're headed toward Bart and Marta Mahoney. Ask them to compare that moose femur I just gave you to the one they've got." With a jaunty wave and more cackling laughter, he disappeared in dust.

Ian struggled to pull wind pants over his jeans. "Again, tell me why we're working this money cover thing? Add Phil to the list of people who suspect or know or ... *whatever*." He stopped dressing and glared at me, bare feet balanced on top of his sneakers so his toes wouldn't touch the ground. "Where's the socks?"

I felt he'd learned his clothing lesson. "Rolled up in the hat," I said. "And you're welcome."

Huddled in the front seat of the car, Ian looked like a refugee determined to wear the contents of his suitcase rather than carry it. "Who let the dog out?" he called.

"Was the door open when you got here?"

Ian shook his head as he tried to haul a narrow neck gaiter over one swollen sleeve.

"That goes over your head and down around your neck." I leaned into the back seat to inspect the car's contents. "Did you unzip my pack?"

"I pawed around to get to mine. Don't think I opened anything." He held out his arms, lumpy with multiple layers of clothes. "Isn't this enough? This is more shit than I own."

"My bag's open." My most favorite piece of clothing was missing. Some people cling to worn teddy bears, but I hoarded my threadbare guide jacket. Like Phil's wool hat, it was an informal résumé—my first Maine Guide patches unevenly sewn on the front pocket.

I considered the possibility I hadn't packed the jacket, grabbed some baby wipes, and swiped at raspberry seeds and black smudges smeared on Pock's shoulder. My best friend had a difficult time deciding whether to eat scat or roll in it, but either way he'd enjoyed himself. "From a bear," I said.

"I don't want to know how you know that," Ian said from the front seat.

I didn't expect people to understand how fiercely I loved my dog. He didn't start out as *my* dog, because my cousin Liz Anne kidnapped him. Liz Anne was in the habit of visiting dogs chained on four inches of chain or dogs with emaciated eyes looking out of tiny pens. When she'd seen enough, she skipped past animal control officers and animal shelters, stole desperate canines, and found them new homes, swearing new owners to secrecy. Pock came to me as a puppy so covered with sores I thought he was pink until the antibiotics kicked in. Evan hoped he'd mature into a duck hunting tool, but his new wife was allergic to pet hair, and, anyway, giving me Pock helped Evan erase all traces of his former married life.

My first night at camp, sunk in tears by the woodstove, I pushed him away. The harder I shoved, the more he butted himself into my lap, so I let him lick my hands and then I buried my face in his fur. After dark, he jumped on my bed, circled three times, and collapsed on my feet.

Leaning into the car, I fluffed up his dog bed and shut him in next to the grease bucket. First thing at Grants: find the bear guides. Francoise owed me. My car would smell like a diner for years.

Ian bent over his phone and laptop.

"Not curious about my coat mystery?" I said.

"I don't know the next time I'll find civilization and a signal." He rubbed his cheeks. "I can't feel my face. I need coffee."

"Lunch on the road," I said.

"Oh, yeah. A restaurant ... or maybe up here just a shack and outhouse."

"Nope. Just the cooler." I thought I heard a small moan as I started the car.

Ian snapped off his phone and dropped his sunglasses over his eyes. "How long would you have searched for the dog?" he asked. Pock raised his head as if he knew we discussed his worth.

"Until I found him," I said.

Ian groaned.

I thought I'd try praise. Praise was important for improving behavior. "Extra credit for catching Pock," I said. "Way beyond the call of reporter duty. When he's on a scent he disappears, and there's usually something unpleasant on the other end of his adventures."

The words were out before I could inhale them back. The air in the car felt heavy, like air weighed down by a threatening storm. I should have been in the morgue's waiting room or at the funeral home keeping Shannon company. Ian bent over his notebook, his attempt to give me space in a car so small our elbows touched between the seats.

"Ian, the first aid kit's under your seat. May I have it?"

Before I could pull it into my lap, he had it open and was lifting Shannon's picture to his window. "Those are eyes. Hot," he said. "Your friend's hot."

I propped the photo over the speedometer display and braked hard for multiple partridges flapping up from a dust bath in the road. Ian clutched for everything in his lap that slid toward the floor. In true partridge family form, the chicks scattered all over the road and the hen dropped one wing to feign injury, decoying us away from her fleeing children.

"Zoo," Ian said, fiercely. "Zoos have it locked down. Animals on one side of the fence. Humans on the other side with the vending machines."

In the rearview mirror, I saw the mother partridge charge my tail lights. *You driving to a fire?*

Well, are you trying to reduce the size of your family?

You couldn't know how good a roll in dust feels.

Is that an invitation? I'm tempted because it sounds better than what I'm up to right now.

I saw her hop off the road to find her family as Ian thumped his computer onto his lap.

"You won't find a signal," I said.

"Don't need it. I saved stuff."

"We'll be at Great Nations' gate in about forty minutes. Sandwiches are on top in the cooler. How about you increase my wolf education as we eat?"

Ian sighed, turned, and reached into the cooler. He sniffed the lunch bag. "Peanut butter and fluff! Raspberry fluff! Oh, man! Raspberry fluff." He inhaled one sandwich and slowed halfway into his second. “Is this a ‘no ask’ moment or are you going to tell me what you did at Phil’s truck after we left?”

CHAPTER 13

I could see why Peter liked Ian. For a youngster, he seemed to have solid peripheral vision—seeing what he was and was not supposed to see—and he was nervy and bold. I could imagine Peter, feet up on his desk, enjoying our partnership as revenge for my nervy years of stomping into his office.

When I told Ian that Shannon's missing strap matched Phil's tracking collar, he yelped and pumped raspberry fist prints onto the car's ceiling. "Yes! She found them."

If the collar put Shannon under the wrong tree at the wrong time, I couldn't celebrate. "Calm down. We don't know if she found anything but a smashed collar. I need to find Moz and put him on the trail of what's missing, because taking the collar was a sneaky move—maybe even illegal if the wardens think it's evidence," I said.

Ian licked his fingers and wiped them on his shirt. "Aren't we trying to avoid official people who might be crowding us?"

"We are," I said. "But I think Moz is trying to avoid them, too." Ian looked up from his computer and raised one hand into a 'what gives?' gesture. "Warden Atkins may be walking a thin line between his warden boots and his moccasins," I said. "He trusted us with evidence because he doesn't trust his department to do the right thing by wolves." I paused. "*If* wolves are here."

Ian needed a quick course on the collusion and inbreeding of state wildlife officials, legislators, and landowning corporations. I ran through last summer's D.C. lobbying trip that had Maine's Game and Wildlife officials partnered with the Maine Forest Business Foundation on a mission to stop mapping lynx habitat on corporate property. Through habit, I softened my summary to a discussion of "inappropriate influence"—the timber industry's control over *our* wild animals. I was used to thinking of the arrangement as the *corrupt* and the *corrupted,* but I was new to saying it out loud.

"Whoa, whoa, whoa," Ian said, grabbing a third sandwich that I thought might be mine. "Back up. Your official Maine wildlife people went to our nation's capital to meet up with the tree cutting people so they could all lobby the federal wildlife people to stop some kind of protection process some animal needs? Don't our *wildlife* people get paid to take care of ... *wild life*? And don't we pay the salaries of the *wildlife* people so they will take care of ... *wild life*?"

"It's complicated," I said. "The forest business has pretty much owned Maine's movers and shakers since the gold dome rose over the capitol. They own the land, the mills, the obvious jobs, *and* the Augusta lobbyists on their payroll. On the other hand, shy wild things avoid Augusta, sports bars, and golf courses where they're much discussed."

Ian stared out the window, his eyes not focused on the gathering bank of heavy clouds. I wondered how he'd like paddling in rain and swallowed a last bite of sandwich, my stomach rumbling for what had already disappeared into Ian.

"The selling out is done in Augusta and D.C.," I said. "I don't indict our biologists in the field. They'll try practical arrangements with landowners rather than wait out the nasty politics of the Endangered Species Act."

Ian tapped his keyboard. "ESA. ESA. Peter sent me a predigested Endangered Species Act clip put up by wolf activists in Washington—state, not D.C." He mumbled and scrolled. "Can you concentrate *and* keep us on the road?"

"I've dodged a log truck and partridges. My record's good."

Ian's fingers were a blur on the keys. "According to the Washington wolf lovers, if something shows up that behaves like a wolf, it's protected by the Department of the Interior's bureaucrats in the U.S. Fish and Wildlife Service."

I pulled into a side road behind a pond fringed with dense grass and climbed from the car. "I need to do my back," I said. I reached for a high limb and collapsed my knees so my arms could hang me upright. Each snap along my spine delivered a better kind of pain.

Ian squinted at his screen. "The Endangered Species Act gets serious with people when they do something called a *taking*. That's 'transporting, harassing, harming, pursuing, shooting, wounding, killing or trapping a listed species.'" His voice droned into a monotone I couldn't hear, but I already knew the mumbo jumbo.

"Deadly language," said Ian.

"OK. Here's the heart of it," I called. "It's against the law to do anything to a wolf except watch it from a distance. If one or more of them returns to parts of Maine where their ancestors lived, anything that bothers them is off-limits. That's road building, house building, tree cutting, hunting, trapping, and—just a guess—humans burning up backcountry trails on rowdy machines." I found my feet and did a little happy dance. "What's not to like about wolves coming home?"

"Pretty unlikely one wolf could roadblock all that stuff," Ian said. "Bet it's kind of a no-brainer choice for most people: choose all that popular stuff or one unpopular wild dog that's probably hiding out."

I bent over and stuck my fingers under the toes of my boots. "Some history, Ian. If we hadn't been so selfish, narcissistic, careless, and ignorant as we conquered the planet—exterminating species we're supposed to share the place with—we wouldn't need an endangered species anything. Yes, it's sacrifice, effort, dislocation, energy, money, creativity, courage—don't get me started on the list. It's too long, but it's the right thing to do. Who knows? Some obscure chemical in some lizard's brain could unlock a cure for youthful impatience."

Ian snapped his computer closed. "Let's get out of here. Pleeeeease."

I stood to windmill my arms and unkink more body parts. Years hunched over computers left pinched nerves in my back and tendonitis in my elbows. Black armbands pressing my tendons were such permanent jewelry most people assumed I was mourning something.

Looking like planes hooked up and refueling in midair, dragon flies mated in free-fall spins above the pond's surface. By the water raccoons had stacked a neat pile of pale orange crayfish shells. Pencil-thin turkey tracks crossed and re-crossed each other, mapping the usual turkey dithering common to a relaxed outing, and at the water's edge dinner plate-sized tracks seeped water.

Ian slammed the car door. "Hello out there? You alive?"

I bent through a wall of bulrushes and waved him toward me. "Want to see a moose wallow? Just don't let Pock out."

Ian tiptoed from dry patch to dry patch. "Argggh. Smells like a barn in here. One moose do that?"

"One horny bull advertising his virility by rolling and peeing in mud," I said. Floating like an oil slick, a yellow film followed the hoof prints into a mud hole that could eat my car.

Ian scowled at dripping poplars hanging over the wallow. "Muck's in the trees, Patton. In the trees."

"We must have just missed the action."

Ian groaned and snapped his fingers. "Aw, shucks." He turned toward the car, shouting, "I don't understand why you and your buddies are so jacked up on fluids and body parts. Your woods is a graveyard or a toilet. Get a life, for Christ's sake."

I went after him and reached for his arm. "Don't. Move." I nodded toward the trees on the far side of the pond. They swayed violently. The breeze wrinkling the water toward us carried crisp cracking sounds as if someone whacked a bat on wooden bleachers.

Snorting short, powerful bursts of air, a bull moose crashed toward the pond. He tossed brush and moss over his head, paused at the water's edge, and bent low to rip his reflection from the pond."

"Holy shit," Ian cried. "He's the size of a house!"

The moose thrust his vast head into the wind, lifted his long muzzle, and rolled his lips back and forth over his teeth, tasting and snorting in as much air as he'd snorted out. Water poured from his antlers as he swung toward Ian's voice.

"The car!" I yelled.

"First you yell at me to get out of the car. Now you yell at me to get back in," groused Ian.

I was already running. "Fine. Find out if he wants to spear you or mount you."

We slammed doors. Pock rushed the window, barking. The bull charged. "Duck!" I yelled. I leaned on the center console away from my window as the car rocked with the impact and then lifted slightly off the ground. I heard hooves pawing dirt and antlers on the roof.

Ian bent toward the floor mats. "What's going on?"

"I try not to look at bad stuff," I said. Pock pawed the windows, yelping and growling. I turned and reached behind my seat to grab his collar, risking a glance out the side window. The moose and I were eyeball to eyeball. I imaged we both looked alike—eyes wide and white with fear. When his head came up, the car came up. I pulled Pock's sleeping bag over his heaving body and pushed him to the floor. "Antlers are caught on the roof rack," I said.

"How does this usually end?"

"Two bulls locked together die if they can't sort out their antlers."

"How does it end if one bull is locked onto a car?"

"Not well, I'd guess. Hand me the knife in the glove compartment."

Ian rummaged until he found my folding knife. "You're not going to stab him, are you?"

"I'll try prying off the roof rack if I can get the knife into the gutter and pop out the clamps." It sounded brave, but nothing could possibly make up for the stupidity of interrupting a moose pursuing lust.

"Turn the key until the battery comes on, but don't start the car. I need to lower the window." I heard him reach for the key. "Now turn in your seat and hold the dog."

Mumbling complaints, Ian twisted around to hang over the top of his seat and push Pock to the floor. I crawled over Ian's arms into the backseat. The bull blinked several times and snorted as I partially lowered the window. When my hand and knife started a slow move toward the roof, he grunted and pushed against the car. I jerked my hand back inside.

Perhaps I'd over-romanticized moose. They kill people, more often in Alaska, but last year a Maine hunter was gored. When testosterone stops moose from eating and colors their necks black with desire, they'll charge anything fertile or, in a pinch, anything annoying. I knew that. I just didn't listen to myself. We needed a distraction.

"Ian," I whispered. "If you recorded wolf howls on your phone, play them."

Hairs on my back and neck were already erect from fear, but more strands tingled and lifted as Ian used his free hand to wave his phone at the open window. Like an air-raid siren, a long, mournful howl rose into a wail and rolled slowly between two shivering notes. The moose froze against the window. I circled a finger, asking Ian to replay the calls. Pock thrashed against Ian just before the moose exploded and the car door dented toward me.

Through the open window, one trapped moose eye closed on me with murderous intent. *Killing you.*

Not necessary. I can fix this.

Need to stomp you into a gut pile.

"Stop, Ian. Stop!" I hissed. The bull dropped to his knees and lowered his antlers. Silence settled in and around the car as I looked down at the largest rack I'd ever seen. Along the length of my dented car, cupped antlers spiked into lethal points. I assumed all twenty-five points had autographed my car.

CHAPTER 14

I drove slowly up the road—just in case the bull took an easy route—while Ian swiped through pictures on his phone. "I shot proof we're on the right track of the wrong animal, but Peter will eat 'em up anyway. He told me if I joined up with you I'd see parts of the woods others didn't know about." He turned toward the dented door. "Wonder if moose spit on a window will show up."

Pock licked the window. I drove and chewed. Ian propped his laptop on a lumpy pile of clothes he'd shed.

I wondered if this particular moose belonged on my life list. Bird watchers create life lists of species they've seen, but Kate and I have a list of animals that have threatened us: a river otter, partridges, a female moose guarding her calf, feral cats, a loon guarding its nest, a fox—probably rabid—and a female bear that chuffed a warning from raspberries we'd invaded. Our list excluded stupidity, so I probably couldn't count the angry bull.

I readjusted my tilted rearview mirror and aimed it like a curious security camera. Same blond streaks fading to gray. Same grooved worry line between eyes too close together. Same tiny upper lip that refused lipstick. But the eyes were different—more like the deep blue I knew even Kate envied. Where had I been for a year, and was I back? And what was I doing dragging a complete novice into a freezing forest where explosive attitudes were stockpiled like weapons guarded by chain smokers? Any old spark would light a fire.

"I apologize for setting us up for the attack," I said. "For the record, I think moose kill or maim more people than wolves ever have, but there's no excuse for ignoring the safety zone each animal requires. I might have been showing off a bit."

Ian shot me a dark look. "We've got an agenda. Moose aren't on it, so leave off the sightseeing tour."

"Listen, Ian. Did you think this trip was going to take you to the Bronx Zoo? Caged animals on one side of the fence and you and the coffee machine on the other side? Newsflash: *we're* looking for real live wolves."

Ian bent his head. He must have sensed I was cranking up my lecture engine.

I reached over and closed the laptop on his fingers. "Ian, are you hearing me? You've been acting like anything animal is getting in the way of *your* story, but feces, plant parts, and skeletons are clues. If someone you interviewed left the room, I know you'd sniff clues from her desk and garbage can—probably rifle through her underwear drawer. Reading animal signs is legitimate investigation." I pressed harder on his fingers but couldn't get him to grimace. "What's more, that bull's genes—ten generations away from a face-to-face wolf encounter—are hardwired to stomp my car like it was an enemy pack. That's good information. Unseen and only a sound from a phone, wolves have power."

Ian slid his fingers from his laptop and offered me a lopsided, smug smile. "If Shannon found a wolf-tracking collar, someone at the other end of the signal might know more than any animal message scratched in dirt or shit."

The sun slanted shafts of fading light through gathering clouds—a dark sky for the middle of the day, or maybe it was my mood. In the past twenty-four hours, I'd acquired a badly dented car and a surly kid reporter and realized sane professionals were ducking low. Shannon hid her tracking secrets, and, from the safety of his departing truck, Phil had aimed us at the Mahoneys. Maybe they were right. After ducking logs let loose in the road, it might be smart to keep on ducking.

Only one idea felt warm under my clothes near my heart. If Shannon were alive, she'd be tracking wolves. I could pick up her trail and carry her toward them. One gray tail disappearing into the trees would be fine; Shannon and I didn't need more than a tail.

Heat flamed up under my arms into the back of my neck as I imagined her lying cold and still. *I'm pretty sure I'm doing what you'd want. Out here instead of where you are. You wouldn't expect me to sit in a plastic chair in a bad smelling hallway when I'm headed toward what you cared about. Just feeling guilty is all.*

I eyed the collapsing paper mountain around Ian's feet. "Can't you sort out information that might be useful?" I asked.

Ian held up a scuffed copy of the *Recovery Plan for the Eastern Timber Wolf.* "This has stuff you'll like." He sniffed. "You know ... it's got *hab-i-tat* requirements." He tilted the report to read his scrawled margin notes. "Maine's got twenty-seven thousand square miles of livable territory—room for five hundred wolves."

I slowed to a crawl. "Is there a map?"

He unfolded a page over the steering wheel. Everything from Baxter State Park west and north to the Canadian border, the beaver-plagued streams, all of Monson's lands, chunks of Great Nations lands, and even the moss still pressed into Shannon's shape—all were behind wolf habitat boundary lines.

"A pack needs about one to two hundred square miles to set up its own territory," he said, squinting at his notes. "Maine could host multiple packs, and wilderness isn't required. They've found dens in logging operations. If roads are rare more wolves survive, and the fewer humans around, the better." He looked out the window and frowned. "I haven't seen a human for miles."

"What did Peter mean when he said there wasn't much time?" I asked.

"His board of directors wants to close the print side and go digital. He's hoping a juicy story buys him time so he can find an audience that avoids computers. He says the *real* Maine's not showing up online."

I wondered if Ian had picked up on Peter's hollow face. I didn't want to lose Peter. "Is there more? Something else?"

"He could mean we don't have much searching time if someone else finds wolves first." Ian interlocked his fingers and reached his arms into in a lazy stretch. My scavenged shirt popped stitches up his back. "The gun crowd might have some legitimate anxiety. This report says limiting some hunting seasons makes it less likely hunters will kill wolves."

I unwrapped more gum. "Right. Separate the affected parties. The fewer people toting guns on back roads, the more animals might survive. When the Maine Association of Sportsmen and Trappers made it illegal to import wolves, they were sure wolves would colonize Miami before they'd arrive in Maine. I think I understand them, even if the membership is a small slice of Maine's outdoor folks. Their members already hate coyotes, and wolves would be a direct attack on their right to claim each hoofed target. And closing roads. That would be a declaration of war. These people want to drive everywhere to do what they do."

I added more gum to the wad in my mouth. At least rain would end the dust. "What does it say about the prey base?" I asked.

Ian snorted. "Wolves and religion?"

"P-r-e-y. Food they catch and eat?"

More pages shuffled. "One wolf might eat fifteen to twenty deer a year or about fifteen moose with assorted beavers, rodents, even a bear cub or two on the menu. They like to eat five to twelve pounds of meat a day but can go hungry for a long time. When they do kill, they can gorge on twenty pounds … or more." He looked up and whistled. "My record's six Big Macs. I could go for a Big Mac."

"Have a granola bar. Same protein as a burger."

"When I'm desperate, I'll eat sawdust," he said.

Ian bent over his knees and clicked keys. Graphs whizzed across his screen. "Catch this. With all that eating, wolves don't do much to deer populations in Minnesota. Deer numbers and wolf numbers are both on an upward curve."

"I'm not sure we have enough deer to go around up here," I said.

He angled the screen toward me. "Wolves. Hanging out."

I pulled over to study the screen. A moose stood stiff-legged and defiant in deep snow, one wolf hanging from its nose, another hanging from its rear flank—trampled drifts around the frozen struggle stained a shocking red. I flinched. Sometimes I don't want to know how animals eat each other.

"Moose could work," I said, pulling back onto the road. "No shortage of moose up here."

Ian reached for a chart he'd wedged under his leg. "And beavers!" he said. "After large ungluelates, beaver's a favorite food."

"That's *un-GU-lates*. No glue involved," I said.

"Oh, pleeeease. Don't get all teacherish on me," he snapped. "Beavers. Maybe they're not a mystery if someone's importing them to stock the fridge—make sure wolves won't run out of food." Ian reached back into the cooler and pulled out a block of cheese. "I'm starving."

He ate it all in noisy, methodical bites. At the rate, he mowed through supplies, I'd need to beg or buy food from the inn or we'd be down to our last granola bar before we launched the canoe.

I looked over my shoulder to be sure of the grease bucket's upright position. "Beavers are bait, easy food to bring the animal where you want it. What bear bait is also supposed to do." A light flashed in my mirror and disappeared behind a sharp corner. "At Grants tonight, let's see if any guides are running dogs on bear. I like to know what's in the woods with me. Some guides sit hunters near bait, but some use radio-collared hounds to run down a bear."

In the distance a red light winked through our trailing dust.

Ian stuffed papers into his bag. "What isn't wearing a tracking collar up here? I feel naked." He pointed down the road. "When do we get to the Great Nations gate?"

"Not as soon as the ambulance coming up behind us." As I pulled over to let it rocket by, its pulsating lights lit up a haze of red dust.

CHAPTER 15

At the gate, Sketchy Sam stomped back and forth in front of Great Nations gatehouse, palms pushing the air in urgent stop messages. I'd always focused on his red, splotched face and watery eyes as we transacted business. This time his bent body crackled with energy. Taut neck sinews plunged into a patched red shirt worn over loose, flapping jeans and scuffed cowboy boots. Crablike, he scuttled sideways toward us, thin limbs twisting back and forth to wind up his momentum.

He pointed to the side of the road and bellowed, "Park there. Don't get out!" He limped to Ian's window and jabbed a gnarled finger on the glass. Ian looked at me, but Sam yelled, "It's me you have to worry about. Now open the goddamn window."

I saw Ian's eyes widen and then, as if he'd wiped a hand over his face from forehead to chin, all expression vanished. He turned pleasant cheeks toward Sam and lowered the window.

"I know who *she* is," sneered Sam. "Who the hell are you?"

"I work for the *Bangor Weekly*."

"Name," barked Sam.

"Ian Glenburn."

"Reporter?"

"Yes."

"Well, that's just damn dandy. A reporter." Sam turned his head to launch his wad of chew toward my car's back tires. I heard soggy spit splash his target.

He leaned in toward Ian, tobacco fragments clinging to his stained teeth and tongue. Grateful for the grease atmosphere that permeated my side of the car, I imagined the fetid cave smell from his mouth must be fearsome. Ian's innocent gaze never dropped from Sam's face despite the wailing ambulance and a growing chorus of yells from the gatehouse. Pock's low growl echoed my Sam sentiments. I reached back and rubbed fur under his collar.

When I leaned toward my window hoping for a better view of the scene, Sam pounced. "Don't even think of stepping out, Conover. You're in trouble for lying to me last time you came through. I'll deal with *you* when we get rid of the ambulance."

"What's going on?" asked Ian.

"Medical emergency with one of the crew." Sam's eyes narrowed. Suspicion spread from his eyes to his quivering lips. "I don't want you nosing around."

"Come on," said Ian. "The *Bangor Weekly* does a good job of reporting up here. Last year your bosses gave us an award."

"I got orders. Whatever this is, it's not for publication."

My vest-ripping deputy, now working as an EMT, lowered an ambulance window. "Sam. Need to know what you know." Anderson Barter jumped from the ambulance in a heroic leap that ended badly on loose gravel. Rising on one knee he tried to collect devices raining from his belt.

"Move it, Steve!" he yelled at the ambulance driver. "Turn that thing around. Get the doors open. Locate the large airways. Prep the AED. Don't waste time on activated charcoal. It won't work." He hobbled toward the gatehouse, pointing at Sam who was scurrying toward him. "We're going to need all the whiskey you've got. Your whole stash. Don't hold out on me."

Anderson stuffed phones, pagers, radios, and at least one knife back into his pockets while barking commands at the driver, who gunned the ambulance into a tight circle that raised more dust between us and the gatehouse. After parking near my car, the driver disappeared into the medical end of the ambulance.

"Did the paper really get an award?" I asked, popping a larger wad of gum into my mouth.

"No, but how's he going to know that?" Ian chuckled and worked his phone. "This place has the strongest signal I've found north of Boston. In the middle of nowhere."

"Wonder why Anderson wants an AED?" I asked.

"Automated external defibrillator." Ian wiped dust from his phone's screen as he swiped. "Automatically delivers electric shock therapy during a heart attack."

"I know that. I have to practice on one before they'll let me work ski patrol. Do you have first aid training?"

"No, but I can read," Ian said. "Medical website. I'm on activated charcoal now. Is that what Anderson called it? It's a binder. Prevents toxins from being digested. Absorbs poison and passes it from the system in bowel movements."

"Yes, and when that happens, plan to be elsewhere," I said. "Last year I rushed my neighbor's dog to the vet after it ate rat poison. I wished they'd warned me about charcoal and lava-like feces. The dog lived, but everything in my backseat died."

Ian shifted in his seat, grunting with the effort to extract a small black case from his duffel bag. "Something big is going down. I'm going in." He pushed Phil's yellow hard hat firmly on his head, positioned the Six Rivers insignia over his eyes, and rolled low out of the car. In a mock cowboy accent, he drawled, "Cover me, pardner."

In my rearview mirror, I saw him crouch behind the car. I opened my door, scooped up two handfuls of dirt, and tossed them on the passenger windshield, hoping Sam wouldn't see the empty seat. As Ian hopped into the ambulance, I drove toward the gatehouse and called, "Sam! The kid has to use the outhouse. Where do you want me to park?"

Sam scowled. "Make him use the woods." He waved me back and disappeared into the gatehouse.

I inched away as slowly as a car could crawl, using wipers to clean the front window. Inside the small gatehouse office no one paid any attention to me. Anderson gestured toward a white-haired man I didn't recognize. The man's unstained parka and pleated corduroy pants marked him as an outsider, but his crossed arms and curt nods signaled rank. All three stared at wild blinking lights on Sam's machines. Anderson reached to tap an insistent button and wall speakers wailed to life. Leaning out my window, I eased my foot off the gas.

We all heard the same panicked voice. "We're minutes out. He's tearing up the back of the truck. Thrashing all over. Seizures, vomiting. Christ! We need help! Now! Where's the ambulance?"

Waves of agonized screams drowned the speaker's pleas and spilled out the open door. Anderson punched his fist on a row of keys to silence the agony. He reached for the handheld microphone. "Ridge. Ridge. Anderson here. Pad the sides of the truck with clothing to protect him. Stand back. Give him room. Turn him on his side when he vomits. Step on it. We're at the gate."

I rolled to my assigned spot. Ridge was clearly in the middle of a medical emergency that made me invisible. I wiped a finger over Shannon's picture. Without dust, her smile glowed. I thought about the question I didn't want to ask. *Who's got the tracking collar, sweetie?*

A fast-moving dust cloud on the far side of the gate announced speeding traffic. All three men charged from the gatehouse and formed a stiff line, their backs to me and the ambulance. Anderson jerked first aid gloves from an orange jump kit slung over his shoulder and snapped them on his hands in loud official snaps.

Behind me air brakes exploded and exhaled. Pock dove for the floor. Sam limped past me, waving two empty log trucks toward my car. As soon as bearded men in plaid shirts and lug-soled boots jumped to the ground, Sam pushed them toward the gate. Ian was missing in action, my gum wad was no match for diesel fumes, and my contact lenses felt like rubbery fried eggs. Leashing Pock, I slipped behind a wall of pines and tiptoed toward the gatehouse. The trees were a clear invitation to snoop on the white-haired man yelling at Anderson.

"Who gave you permission to use 1080? In all my years of working jobs all over the country I've never heard of such lame-ass stupidity," he barked into Anderson's face.

Anderson focused his stare toward the expected direction of trouble and muttered a few words that fueled the already fired-up visitor.

"Don't give me that real estate division crap," the white-haired man said. Both truck drivers leaned away from his flying spit. "This is one company. One. O-N-E. One. If *you* have a problem with anything out *here* I want to know about it. Boise wants to know about it. We could have told you poisoning these animals was dumber than dumb. We're Idaho. We've already been through this shit."

Anderson turned and stared at the huddled, silent drivers standing behind him. He turned a darker look on his attacker.

The visitor cleared his throat and executed a dismissive wave that sliced across his chest and ended in the air by Anderson's nose. His voice dropped into a soothing western cadence. "I am Calvin Harworth, vice president of North American operations." The drivers wiped their faces clean of emotion faster than Ian had. "Now, you boys are going to forget you ever heard this conversation and that you were even here with us when what is going to go down, goes down. Sam here will get your contact information to my office in Boise, and I will personally see that you are compensated for any inconvenience."

Both men nodded, calloused hands seeking the safety of their pockets, feet shuffling pebbles under their boots. One of them looked at Sam with raised eyebrows. Sam shook his head and turned away.

Calvin Harworth glared at Anderson. "Will that do?"

Anderson's head jerked up as a white pickup truck roared around the far curve. On the edge of control, it fishtailed between rock mounds dumped to define the road's edge. For a tense moment, it teetered on two tires as a rut sent it airborne. The screams reached us before the truck did. They climbed as overlapping waves of fevered howling, electrifying each hair on my body. Pock lunged for deeper woods, but I pressed him down and crouched beside him.

Harworth yelled, "How many men did you say are down? Are there more than one?"

"Just one," said Anderson. He snapped the cuffs of his gloves.

"Oh, my lord," breathed Harworth. He looked over his shoulder as the ambulance doors behind us banged open.

The driver hauled out a gurney and snapped its legs into position. "You gonna help me with this?" he asked. Hard hat tilted over one eye, Ian grabbed one side of the gurney as the white truck skidded toward the ambulance. The crowd from the gate sprinted toward the truck. I ran behind the men, dragging a dog that lunged the other way. The two truck drivers reached under Anderson's butt and catapulted him into the back of the white truck while it fishtailed for control.

Wearing only an undershirt and boxer shorts, Ridge gripped the sides of the truck's cargo bed. Gray clumps of vomit streaked his arms and legs, and he vibrated with cold or panic or both. He pounded the cab's roof and swore at a wild-eyed woman behind the wheel. "Stop, dammit!"

One of the log truck drivers gasped, "Oh, my Jesus God. It's John Tario. What happened to him? He's all froze up!"

Each time Anderson tried to kneel next to the thrashing man, a rigid arm or leg lifted him in the air and smacked him against the truck's walls. John's terrified eyes locked on mine, begging for something I couldn't give. Anderson was in charge, dancing around the back of the truck, ordering Ridge out of the way, trying to sooth John with hoarse cries of, "We're here, John. We're here. Just let me in."

When the screaming stopped, the silence was broken only by stomping boots—John's heels feverishly drumming the truck's floor. Anderson's boots thumping around the thrashing body.

Anderson yelled, "Steve, airway!" just as the gurney rolled into place under the tailgate.

Steve jumped into the cab. On their knees both medics struggled with John while Ridge balanced on the cab railing, panting and crossing himself.

"What shit *is* this?" Steve mumbled. "He's stiff as a board."

"Some kind of seizure. It's like his throat's locked shut. Airway won't go."

Sam lifted two bottles of whiskey over the tailgate. "Anderson. Need the hooch?"

"Too late," Anderson said. He rummaged through his kit and whipped out a smaller airway device. He bent his finger, wiped foam from John's cheeks, and, with a twisting motion, slipped the arched plastic down the man's throat. Even if John's gag reflex wasn't working, mine was. A wave of nausea swayed me backward. When people skied their speeding bodies into trees, I'd executed that same maneuver but never on someone with open, frenzied eyes. I looked for Ian. Over us all, perched on the truck's hood and elbows braced on its cab roof, his fingers twitched images into his phone.

"Bag him, Steve," barked Anderson. "He's stopped breathing."

Steve eased a face mask over John's nose and mouth and settled into rhythmic pulses, squeezing and releasing the bag between his hands. Anderson tossed loose gear into his kit, jumped off the truck, and, with surprising speed, organized the group into a chain of hands that transferred John to the gurney. John's stiff arms and legs looked like laundry frozen hard on a clothesline.

As the gurney slid into the ambulance, Steve pumping air and fumbling for balance, John's arms sagged. "Oh, shit," said Anderson. "Drive. I'll get with the AED. He's coding."

They slammed doors and disappeared into a new cloud of dust.

CHAPTER 16

Under cover of settling dust and parked log trucks, Pock and I reached the Subaru and rearranged ourselves in obedient sitting positions. Ian appeared, a truck driver on each elbow. Only his toes touched the ground, making slight squiggly trails in the dirt. I reached over and opened his door. The men dropped him heavily in the seat, tossed the hard hat on his lap, and parted to show us an angry Calvin Harworth and an even angrier Sam. I didn't think Sam's face could get redder.

"Let me, Sam," Harworth ordered as he stalked to my window and squatted, his face inches from mine. His breath smelled lightly minted, but it turned my stomach more than Sam's nasty tobacco mouth. "I know that you are Cassandra Conover. Consider me to be Great Nations Forest," he said. He looked up at the scarred hills as if surveying his kingdom and leaned in to add, "Incorporated."

He was impressively manicured, each trimmed hair in place, buffed nails, a too-even tan and teeth too white. His eyebrows looked tweezed. This man was used to controlling everything from rogue nose hairs to thousands of employees and billions of trees. If arrogance could eat oxygen, like John Tario I'd be on life support.

Calvin Harworth sucked the air around him so others might suffocate.

I'm used to men who attempt this level of mastery. As attorneys, they try to overwhelm you in paneled conference rooms with million-dollar views of the Maine coast. I could live handsomely in one of their paneled restrooms. They strut through statehouse corridors. They promise jobs they know won't last. As governors, they religiously evoke the names of their states while they close deals that make Maine less Maine or Montana less Montana. In the conservation trenches we waste way too much energy, time, and talent trying to outflank these egos. I'm no man basher, just an experienced observer of the battlefield who decided to go missing in action. I sensed Harworth could probably do what other men only aspired to do.

His voice was cool and toneless, like a disembodied announcer in an airport shuttle train. "I am sure you know that in my Boise office you are considered a troublemaker. I can't think why the deer on *our* land are any of *your* business, but apparently they are—along with everything else that we do." He held my last registration form, the one where I'd lied about my Bluffer Brook destination.

"Sam is upset that you lied. Makes him look bad. Makes it impossible for us to come find you if you get in trouble. And you did get into trouble, didn't you? Trespassing?" His eyes traveled to Shannon's picture. He snatched it before I could raise an arm to stop him. "Your dead friend, I assume," he said.

I stared into his steel-brown eyes and took a long breath, exhaling it slowly and audibly through my nose, preparing myself for the threat. I slid my hand over Ian's arm and squeezed him a play-it-cool warning.

Harworth held up the photo. I imagined what Shannon would do if he tried to touch her. "Ms. Angeles. Your friend—but our employee. We didn't know you were friends. Not that we have any legal right to limit friendships. We can only make recommendations. Attractive woman. I hear she was smart, too. I wonder if she was smart enough to know where her loyalties should have been placed." He lifted her photo toward me. I looked away and reached for a stick of gum. He sighed theatrically and replaced the picture over my speedometer.

"Here's how it's going to go. Victoria Brinkman wants you inside our gate today and is prepared to vouch for your visit to meet with her land manager." He stood effortlessly. Not one dirt particle clung to his crisp corduroys. I felt like a dirty vacuum bag turned inside out and wondered if, like a nonstick pan, he'd been coated with something that repelled the natural world.

"We like Vicki and hope to do more business with her." He nodded at Ian. "I will be calling Peter Markes personally to check on your reporter friend and the story you *appear* to be researching."

I started the car, hoping our little chat was concluded. He placed both hands over my door, fingers denting the vinyl panel below the window. "I want Sam to hear this so we're all clear about the future," he said. Sam straightened as if a drill sergeant barked him to attention.

"Sam, this boy's paper will file a list of people and destinations connected with his reporting. Your job. See they stick to the list." He pointed at Ian through the open window. "There will be no interviews on the unfortunate accident you witnessed here today. We will operate under a complete press blackout as we research the sequence of events that caused this incident."

I gunned the motor, not sure I could limit my mouth to gum.

Harworth's fingers on my door didn't twitch. "We are in the process of revising our harvesting schedule, and that involves closing and gating numerous roads in this area. Closed means *closed*, Ms. Conover. We have the full force of the law on our side, and the sheriff's office has been notified."

If the full force of the law meant Anderson Barter, I felt better.

"All done?" I asked. No one spoke. I offered my cheeriest cheerleader voice. "You sure?"

Harworth snapped new snaps on his parka.

I eased the car forward. "Alrighty then. We'll be going. Sam, meet you up where we do the paperwork."

The last thing I wanted to do was step out of the car into a gauntlet of hostile men, but Ian begged me to stall the clipboard process. Counting satellite dishes and antennas, he'd already fired up his computer. "I need to reach Peter before Mr. Incorporated does."

"OK. I'll stall, but find out what 1080 is. Harworth chewed out Anderson for using it."

I stood outside my car assessing the scene. Ridge was crouched in the back of his truck, stuffing clothes into a garbage bag, but he stopped to fling me a middle finger. I reached into the car for a spare can of baby wipes. "Until you get a shower," I said, tossing him the can. "I'm sorry about John."

"Somehow you *have* to be mixed up in all this shit," he snarled, grabbing fistfuls of wipes. He kicked a pile of vomit-covered ropes, come-alongs, pulleys, and shovels into the road.

"It looked like John met up with poison. I haven't poisoned anyone."

"No?" He scraped at clumps of dried vomit on his legs. "No? You and your kind don't spread poison? Screaming about how we murder the forest? On account of laws your prints are all over, I'm tap-dancing around useless toads and bugs. You want to talk poison? Let's talk endangered species bullshit. That'll kill us faster than a spruce budworm epidemic."

I pressed on. "It was poison, wasn't it? What were you trying to kill?"

He tossed the empty can at my feet and stalked off toward the outhouse. "I can't be seen talking to you."

That went well, I thought.

The truck drivers and Ridge were huddled with Sam inside the gatehouse where I assumed he was arranging payment for their silence. Seeing me in the road, he hobbled out and shoved a clipboard in my face. To cut it short, I said we'd be at Grants Farm Inn for two nights and call him if we changed our plans. We always lie to Sam.

He grinned. "Don't bother. Every one of us will know where you are, every hour, every day."

Harworth sauntered toward my car, phone tucked under his chin and fluttering left hand ordering Sam back to the gatehouse. He aimed one lone finger as if I were a truant child. *Time to go.* I trotted to the car and pulled away from the gatehouse, hoping Mr. Incorporated coughed my dust.

Out of sight, I accelerated up a hill, praying my tires had enough tread to handle speed on dirt. "Are you still online? Did I give you enough time?" I asked.

Ian shook his head and clung to his computer, typing with one hand.

"Computers," I sniffed. "Be prepared to leave yours at Grants when we change the car for a canoe tomorrow. Tell me about 1080."

"Disrupts something called the Krebs cycle. Starves organs of energy. Affects the brain, heart, lungs, and—" He whistled. "Jesus—the gonads."

"I don't care if it makes you infertile. What's it really do to you?"

"What's ventricular arrhythmia?" he asked.

"Heart palpitations that can lead to a heart attack."

Ian bent low over his screen. “Not before it turns you into a drooling zombie.”

I swerved to avoid the same ruts that had launched Ridge’s speeding truck and his howling passenger. John Tario was headed south toward a trauma center and I was headed north, imagining another victim. In the woods a wolf might be howling with fear and pain, foam bubbling from its mouth, stiff legs pushing feebly against dead leaves as it flopped from side to side. Red-rimmed eyes bulged in a frantic search for pack mates. Near the end, only patient ravens in the trees heard the strangled whimpers.

Too late, Shannon. We might be too late.

The Subaru strained to gain elevation, sputtering up a steep hill into views of water spilled across the horizon. Narrow corridors of shaggy spruce and fir outlined shores and pressed in on clear rivers falling into Canada Falls Lake. The trees marked a narrow buffer between land Great Nations had stripped of trees and public land that hosted lots of trees. Technically, Maine’s Bureau of Public Lands cared for the lake and its shores, but I’m part of the public so it’s all mine. Luckily, I shared the place with a million other Mainers who don’t know what they own, so they don’t visit.

“Awesome,” said Ian.

I shook my head to clear away the dying wolf. “I know. This view hits me the same way.”

He didn’t look up. “Oh, yeah. We there?”

I turned onto a narrow road and eased the Subaru through puddles oozing from a flooded swamp. “Beavers,” I said.

Ian’s face was lit up by his flashing screen. Maybe I’d overreacted, coming down on him for his boredom with my world. Plugged in, he didn’t need supervision. “What’s awesome?” I asked, letting mud slow me.

“Idaho.” Ian turned his computer so I could read. Men wearing orange hats and vests filled the screen under a bold headline: “Feds Investigate Poisoning as Hunters Protest Wolves.” I braked and studied the crowd’s signs. “Elk. The Real Endangered Species.” “My Wolf Plan: Shoot. Shovel. And Shut Up.” The “Smoke a Pack a Day” sign was carried by a man with a shotgun slung over one shoulder and a rifle over the other.

When I let Pock out, he raced to the top of the beaver dam and tugged at sticks artfully mudded into place.

“You don’t mind if he harasses *wildlife*?” Ian asked.

“He couldn’t actually catch one. They’re hunkered down in tunnels.” I forded the stream, gripping the wheel to feel for soft spots. “Go on with Idaho. He’ll catch up.”

“Last year someone poisoned some Idaho wolves. Local biologists tried to hush it up, but one had a crusading daughter who blew the whistle on her dad and emailed pictures of dead wolves to something called The Predator Project. Those guys filed a Freedom of Information Act request to get the lab results and they—’

“They found 1080,” I said.

"Yup. Enough in a few wolves to poison packs in Idaho, Wyoming, and Montana. The nuts could have killed several hundred thousand people they didn't like just by dropping a quart or two into drinking water. The feds are on it now."

"Feds?" I asked.

"Homeland Security's hoping terrorists don't find out about 1080."

The road narrowed. Crooked alders tapped the car with bent twig fingers that made Ian twitch away from his window.

"How toxic is it?" I asked.

"One teaspoon could do a hundred or so adults. Odorless, colorless, tasteless. Dissolves and disappears. No known antidote, but liquor might dilute it if someone drinks a lot of it. Quickly."

Ian was a champion scanner. Documents swam across his screen. "Not good for Mr. Tario. Not much that's alive stays living after meeting up with 1080, but I think there's a volunteer medic who knows more than we know."

I'd forgotten Ian's ambulance investigation at the gatehouse. As I parked at a grassy campsite, Pock leaped against the car and pressed a muddy nose on Ian's window. Ian swore, pushed against his door, and toppled Pock into the road.

CHAPTER 17

Labrador retrievers think any physical contact is a human gift, so I knew Pock would recover his sense of humor, but I might not. Ian climbed on top of a picnic table. I grabbed his coat, my coat, my cheese slicer, the last package of cheese, bread, pickles, and salami, and arranged them on the table. I zipped every zipper and turned up my collar.

"I'll make sandwiches if you put on your coat and give me some credit. I know dogs aren't everyone's pal." I grabbed a stick and heaved it into dense vines. Birds screeched as Pock fired himself like a missile into their deepest sanctuaries. "There. Now he's gone for at least ten minutes."

Ian reached for a slice of cheese and held it up to the light. "I'll need a lot more of these to actually taste the cheese." He squeezed the slice into a ball and popped it into his mouth. "Back at the gate I sent Peter pictures of Tario in the truck, a video of the medic working the air bag, and close-ups of Mr. Incorporated watching the whole show." He bit into a sandwich that oozed fillings.

"What can Peter do?" I asked.

Ian pushed an escaped pickle back into his mouth. “He plans to email the ambulance scene to Harworth and offer to hold off publication if Mr. Incorporated lets us work where we want to.”

I sagged against the table. “Ridge and crew will still follow us around, and Peter can’t stop me from getting fired. On Great Nations enemies’ list, I’ll be useless to Ken.” I sucked on a dry scrap of salami. “What else from Peter?”

Ian removed a small recorder from its case and placed it on the table. “He said to use the paper’s name like a shield and come home if anything smelled ugly.”

Oh, right, Peter, I thought. *As if that’s going to happen.*

“Inside the ambulance. Listen to this,” he said.

At first all I could hear was rustling clothing and thumping noise; then Ian called, “Need help?” There was a muffled answer from Steve and the crackle of the ambulance radio.

“Come in, Anderson. Anderson, are you there? Doctor Mukarjee here. Anderson? Steve? Do you read me?”

More thumping as Steve probably lurched into the front compartment to grab the radio. “We’re at the gate, doc.”

“Status,” barked the doctor.

“Patient en route to us. ETA, minutes. From the sounds of it, he’s conscious but deteriorating.”

“The dosage for activated charcoal is one gram per kilogram of body weight.”

"Anderson says not to bother with charcoal. Says it won't work on what we've got."

A long pause. "What *have* you got, Steve?"

"Darned if I know. Anderson told me to ready airways and the AED."

"He's expecting a cardiac event?"

"Doc, this is one of his own guys. I think he's got more information than I do."

"He radioed it was a poison event. Did he name the agent?"

"Just said it was something John Tario stumbled into in the woods."

"If you have time, assign someone to collect—carefully—all materials Tario's crew handled, especially food and drink containers." The doctor's beeper dinged and he cleared his throat. "If you can't find someone to do that, we'll send the game wardens."

"Will do," answered Steve.

"Radio vitals as usual. Give us an ETA when you are close. Mukarjee, out."

For a few seconds Ian and Steve wrestled with something that snapped into place. "Let me help you get that corner," said Ian. "Why won't this fella Anderson tell you more about the poison? What's up?"

"Whatever it is, it's not like him to hold back anything," Steve said. "He tells us to cough up everything we see and hear."

"Well," said Ian, "we've never used poison at a site. Maybe this guy bumped into something nasty put out by someone else."

I had a clear image of Ian, Six Rivers yellow hat askew, face wiped clean of intention, nodding attentively while his inner voice coached Steve to spill something important.

And Steve did. "No, it was a Great Nations operation. Something quiet for sure. On the drive out here, Anderson hung over his phone in the back of the unit, swearing between signals."

Ian switched off the recorder. "Then the truck arrived. You know the rest." We sat on opposite sides of the picnic table. Near my toes, a chipmunk stuffed crumbs into his cheek pouches until his face looked prize-fight swollen, saving his food for underground tunnels he'd raid all winter. I thought Ian might find cheek pouches useful.

I crossed my arms, trying to trap heat near my chest. "If Anderson knew that activated charcoal wasn't going to work, he knew what the poison was." Pock circled our table, drool oozing off his stick.

With a pained expression, Ian pulled black, hairy mittens from his pocket, shoved them onto his hands, and held his hands over his ears. They created an Elvis sideburns effect that would have been funny if his voice hadn't been so low and serious. "Anderson called for Sam's whiskey, but Tario was too far gone. He knew liquor was the only possible antidote and he didn't tell his partner and he didn't tell the doctor. Big. This is very big."

I felt for the hood on my jacket and pulled it over my head. Sunflower seed husks rained down on my lap. My hood must have hosted untidy mice. "Yes, big," I said, "and it gets bigger. We might be too late."

Ian raised his head, gray eyes lit more intensely with the press of gray air around us. "Late?"

"Ian, John Tario could have been poisoning a wolf. Or wolves. At the gate Harworth chewed out Anderson for using 1080 on what he called 'those animals.' I didn't need to hear the 'wolf' word to know what he meant."

Ian jumped from the table and punched the air with mittened hands that looked like circling crows. He kicked great clots of grass at me but they fell short. "Good Christ, Patton. When were you going to tell me the first news I can use? After my moose mating lesson? This is a breakout story, whether the wolves are dead or alive. Don't you know how this works? I have to break this story before someone else does."

I strolled to the middle of our clearing, bent to look under the car, and stepped into the road, leaning first in one direction and then the other. "Come out, come out, wherever you are, cagey reporters of the world." I bent a hand behind my ear to hear reporters as they stampeded for the story, and then I heaved Pock's stick back into the bushes.

"OK. OK. So we're alone in this freaking place," Ian said. Pock raised a new chorus of bird protests. "Except for your *friends*. It doesn't change my problem. You have no urgency to get this story nailed down. Why did you agree to come out here?"

I stalled. "As I recall, I didn't *agree* to much. Vicki showed up to brief us for an interview I didn't arrange. You turned my columns into a blog without asking me. Peter negotiated my future schedule with my boss, and my house became a hostel for penniless reporters."

Stalking back over the grass he'd disturbed, Ian thumped each clump back into place. "Cut the crap. Why are you here?"

I hadn't worked that out. I opened the cooler, dropped food into it, and leaned against the side of the Subaru, feeling the fading warmth of the car's engine. Last week my therapist Gretchen had challenged me to get back into the game, any game. "You've proved you can survive the divorce. Now it's time to move on and thrive. What's next for you?"

I had no answer and I liked answers—well researched and tucked in my back pocket. It didn't even hurt much when rooms of attorneys and CEOs jumped to microphones to attack my testimony. I had answers. I knew where their statistics were cooked. I knew the evasions their public relations team turned into "talking points." I had a lock on what they'd said and done that contradicted whatever current image they'd fabricated. Even if our side had a stomped-on day, legislators came to shake my hand and whisper congratulations.

I took strange comfort in knowing and seeing what others either didn't see or refused to see. Forests were cut faster than they could regrow. The Penobscot River, healthy, provided more jobs than mills polluting the river. Without shelter, the deer herd was crashing.

I just didn't know Evan planned to leave me.

Pacing our living room like a dog that wears a trench at the edge of its fence, my husband tried to look pained, but he just looked annoyed. "I hinted at my feelings," he said.

"Hints?" I asked.

"I encouraged you to see a trainer. I ordered you self-help books."

"You mean the belly fat book? That was from you? I sent it back thinking it was a mistake. Hints. Hints. Let's see. Last year—was the new wedding ring you bought to replace my lost diamond a hint? Was making love on the couch last week a hint?"

Sleepless, at four in the morning I prowled the house searching his files and papers, something I'd never done. Deep in his briefcase, tucked under the last page of a legal pad, was the picture I didn't expect. A young woman lay laughing on the hood of his car while he lifted his kayak and beamed at her.

Beyond getting to Antler Camp with clothes and food, I had no grand plan, just a daily agenda. Breathe. Drink tea. Breathe. Walk the dog. Breathe. Drink tea.

"Well?" Ian picked up Pock's retrieved stick and heaved it into the farthest campsite. "What *are* you doing here?"

I studied my scuffed hiking boots. Blobs of glue advertised my attempts to patch separating leather, so my feet looked attacked by miniature jellyfish. I wore one pair of boots and two outfits, ate one brand of cereal, and washed out one mug—a faded Dunkin' Donuts travel cup whose remaining letters spelled "unkinD." No career, no husband, cereal and toast meals, and nights Pock warmed my feet. Kate's visits made me feel like the wealthiest woman in the world, and so far, that was enough.

"I don't know," I said.

"What?"

"I don't *know* why I agreed to come." That was true but changing. Ian wouldn't be happy to hear I cared more about picking up Shannon's search than making him famous. I heaved the cooler into the back of the car, thinking Ian's muscles hadn't changed my life. Pock carried his dripping stick to his sleeping bag and collapsed on it.

Ian threw himself in the car and slammed his door. "You don't know? Thaaat's great. That dog's not on *my* sleeping bag, is it? Could we get some heat and move on my story?"

I sat and cranked the fan so it parted his hair in unruly puffs. "Your story? I thought it was the wolves' story. Would *your* story get play if they were tame?"

He slipped off a sneaker and lifted one foot to the heater vent.

"Of course not," I said. "Wild wolves make the story. Wild wolves returned to the wilds of Maine. And—*you* should like this—wild animal health depends on our setting up the outdoors as a zoo—a zoo without bars. I know it's a contradiction, but today no animal can be free until we accept responsibility for its freedom. I don't care if you crate it up and ship it to Yellowstone, dismantle dams so fish can swim upriver, or pass laws that stop people hunting species into extinction.

"Human hands are all over wild, but then we have to step back and let wild ones be what they are: free to attack my car or march their children up the middle of the road. Wolves won't survive unless we make space for them to live wild. A wolf without its wild world might as well be a stuffed animal on the shelf. So you see, it's really not Ian's story. It's the wild wolf's story."

Bright yellow birds and their brown female mates hopped from the trees to the ground where I'd brushed crumbs. I pulled off my hood and rearranged my hair into a tighter ponytail. Pock whined hopefully against his window. Ian scratched something in his notebook.

"You still haven't told me why you're here," Ian said.

I aimed the Subaru at a faint ribbon of smoke rising over the trees ahead of us. "Maybe I have and you haven't figured it out yet."

CHAPTER 18

It was too late to hit the brakes when I saw the airborne bike, so I jerked the wheel, aimed for a dirt mound, and hoped for a soft landing. The bike and crouched rider arched across the road and plunged into trees as I ploughed into the pile and watched a gritty avalanche bury my front tires.

"Back up!" yelled Ian. "Gun it."

"No, we'll just dig a deeper hole," I said. Repairs were adding up. I hoped Peter was prepared to pay.

The bike's owner, clenched fists on hips, stood with his back to us yelling "Damn! Shit! Crap!" while his tight racing suit vibrated onto every muscle. My brother's football games taught me that clothing sucked onto flesh was more nude than nude. When the man turned and green Lycra caressed every curve of his crotch, I so wished for Kate. Lycra stretched over body parts made her laugh.

"Ian, got your phone? Quick. Take a picture. It's for my daughter," I said.

"Are you nuts?"

The biker bent and dropped his arms toward the ground, twisting them rhythmically so they swung over his toes into a yoga stretch that brought him upright. At his full height, well over six feet, his face smiled itself into canyons of leathery skin. A tight collar corralled a few chest hairs that were as gray as his sweat-slicked hair. Old only from the neck up, he was physically schizophrenic. His outstretched palms made lowering motions, so I dropped my window a crack and locked the doors.

He leaned down to my window. "Please forgive my going insane out there. Training for a mountain bike race and the intensity got away from me. I'm Engunn Stein. I'm gonna grab some gear and pull you out."

I stepped from the car and offered my hand, but Engunn was already sprinting toward a dollhouse-sized cabin, yelling, "You're Vicki's interview team, right?"

Ian, who'd escaped by crawling out my side of the car, trotted toward the lake and climbed to a small cliff where waves and spray smacked the dam below the rocks. Arms pumping the air, he seemed poised for takeoff. "Crazy!" he yelled. "Seriously, crazy!"

I crawled up to join him, thinking he might need a chaperone.

"There's nothing out there for miles, friggin' miles," he said.

"Nothing. Right," I said, leaning into the wind. *Nothing* was my idea of a good time. As if fierce gray-blue water was nothing. Thirty miles of rock shores guarded by pines—nothing. As if a wedge of ducks swimming into the wind to dry feathers was nothing. City folk often lacked vocabulary for vast landscapes lacking concrete.

My lobbying life had been filled with people who wanted to build something on top of what they thought was nothing. They had no idea how much life was in *nothing*, and they certainly had no idea how much money was in *nothing*. Below us a wave charged the cliff. I pivoted and caught the spray on my back. Pock snapped at it. Ian's face caught most of it.

"Whoo-wee," he yelped, windmilling both arms to wipe his face. "Awesome!"

Engunn, dressed in hiking shorts and a black military sweater crowded with zippers and pockets, stalked toward the Subaru. Around his shoulders he'd draped a thick tow rope that looked like a python coiled on moving prey. Pock bounded toward him and jumped for the swinging end of the rope. Engunn slowed his steps and leaned into a tug of war with my friend before he connected the rope to my car and disappeared into the woods.

"Why call it Canada Falls Lake? No falls. Just lake," Ian asked.

"The dam made the lake and the new lake drowned the falls," I said. "I think the dam builders had no feel for the waterfalls they drowned—couldn't understand the loss—so they kept the original name."

Killed rivers give me pain. When I stand on dams my chest feels heavy, and the ache migrates down to where I can almost feel concrete shave skin off my toes. I faced the lake, closed my eyes, and felt for buried current where a restless river pressed its dark weight against thick walls. I sent the river some hope. *One day, probably after we're long gone, you'll find the right cracks.*

Engunn's deep laughter spilled from the trees. "Piece of cake." My car creaked as the rope tightened and unseen forces dragged it from the dirt pile into the road. Ian and I waded into a complicated web of zigzagging lines and found Pock contentedly shredding a stick in the middle of the maze.

"How'd you do that?" Ian asked.

Engunn bent and rubbed Pock's ears. "I like your dog. Seems like he's always up for action. Hope he doesn't run deer, though. We're in some strange deer hotspot here. They're all over." He pointed at the roped trees. "This is a Z-drag. It's set up to deliver a mechanical advantage of six or seven strong men. Help me dismantle it and all will be revealed."

"Wouldn't it be simpler to use your Jeep or a come-along?" I asked.

He turned dazzling white teeth on me. "The Jeep's tow bar is really for looks, and I like putting my hands on climbing gear."

We unclipped anything metal we found, working the rope in and out of trees, collecting pulleys and clips into a cloth bag. Engunn made energetic pulling motions to demonstrate what had now become obvious. "Each time the rope zigs through a pulley hanging off a tree the setup creates more leverage, so less force is needed at the end of the rope," he said.

He handed the rope to Ian, who looked eager to try wearing the coil and walking at the same time. "Vicki says you two are here to talk money and easements. Let's do it," he said.

"Talk in a warm place," said Ian, heading toward the cabin. "Got coffee?"

Engunn shot him a thumbs-up while I started the Subaru, listened for loose parts, and parked next to the Jeep. Legs wide, hands on hips, Engunn clearly expected some private conversation with me. "What happened to your car?" he asked. "Looks like someone cut hieroglyphics with a pen knife."

"Moose."

"On its knees?"

"Sort of."

"I heard you found Shannon Angeles. Got some background for me?" he asked.

"On her death?"

"I already know about that." He picked at pitch on his hand and flicked it into the road. "And I already know more than I need to about her life. Yale. Forestry graduate school. Free-ride internships with the rising stars of the tree world. The rest of us got sawdust."

Ouch. Maybe Shannon and Engunn had a history I didn't want to hear. I smiled, shrugged, and started for the cabin. I was almost trotting while Engunn simply walked at my side.

"What was she doing off the reservation—off company lands and trespassing?" he asked.

I stopped to watch Pock roll deliriously from one pile of goose droppings to the next and dug down deep for a chirpy voice. "That I really don't know." As I moved away downwind toward the cabin, I smelled pitch mingled with a familiar citrus scent. Engunn used my brand of baby wipes to scrub off sweat. “Here’s what I do know,” I said. “You saved the rest of my day by retrieving my car and I owe you large thanks.”

Ignoring my effort to move on, he reached for the rusted latch on the cabin door. “I figured there’d be opportunity. Turns out no one retires up here until they’re decrepit. Ms. Angeles, girl wonder, got the only forestry job that’s been advertised in decades.”

We stooped low under the sill and straightened up into a wall of heat.

CHAPTER 19

Engunn lunged toward a window. “Christ, it’s hot in here.” He jerked off his sweater, treating us to a sleeveless undershirt and a blast of cold air.

The dollhouse decorating theme permeated the interior. I couldn’t wait to see Ian and Engunn sit on tiny chairs with matchstick-thin legs. Ian’s notebook, a recorder, and the article on easements from my storage cooler were neatly arranged on a tiny coffee table wedged under the one window overlooking the lake. We took up positions leaning against the walls.

“I know,” Engunn said. “Bizarre. It was a playhouse for an estate up the lake. When the state bought this land, it sold off the buildings and barged them away. No one wanted this cottage so they brought it here. I’m just here to use the stove when it’s cold and map out a few easement details on the ground.”

The narrow bed sagged with electronic equipment, cables, switch boxes, a video camera, and something that looked like a small round solar panel. Piles of boots and shoes looked like they’d been swept under the bed, the broom thrown in after. I wondered where Engunn slept. Maybe he didn’t need sleep.

Ian, hands wrapped around a slender mug, his back inches from the woodstove, asked, "Why did the state buy the land?"

Engunn reached for the last mug and slurped the last drops of coffee. "'Cause Maine doesn't own much public land. That's where our land trust comes in. We're better at protecting larger chunks for less money."

Wind whined down the stovepipe, and swells on the lake pounded the dam, spitting spray into gray sheets that evaporated into mist. The ducks bobbed in a more sheltered cove. I was quiet, appreciating my tax dollars at work, savoring the green tree fortress that separated Canada Falls from Great Nations' advancing stump army. Engunn leaned his shoulders against the wall and arched his back into a slow, catlike stretch. Ian raised his eyebrows at me.

"Ian," I said, "the trust's specialty is saving what they call the 'working forest'—lands still being commercially cut—with easement deals. Easements aren't as expensive as buying up the actual land."

Engunn pushed off the wall. "Working forest. We're *conserving* traditional forest uses. People get riled up about cutting trees. But then again, they don't know much."

Ian tried to catch my eye, but I turned to watch the forest hug the lake.

Engunn reached for a rolled-up map, dropped to his knees, and spread it out on the floor, thumping bulky dumbbells on its curling edges. "We're working with Great Nations on a plan that mixes up a couple of types of management."

I knelt at the map, knees protesting each loosely nailed tiny floorboard. Ian looked over our shoulders, juggling his notebook, phone, and coffee. Across the map, hand-drawn black easement boundary lines included a familiar chunk of forest: Great Nations' easement included our canoe route to the Howlers, closed roads, official lynx habitat, and a large chunk of proposed wolf recovery lands. What I saw was disputed territory—land mapped for too many different futures.

Engunn's voice dropped into the grooves of a prepared speech. "A working forest produces wood products. Trees as a managed crop. Our GNF partnership keeps the cash crop going, but we'll buy up the development rights to eliminate real estate speculation." He turned toward Ian. "Development rights. We'll buy up the company's right to sell real estate on most parcels. No houses. No big-box stores. But the company still owns the land and harvests trees as it always has."

More good news, I thought.

He rocked back on his heels, fingers flexed on the map. "We're not the first group to try this, but we're the best. Vicki will make us the largest easement holder anywhere."

Ian dripped coffee on the floor as he shoved a tiny chair next to Engunn and placed his recorder on it. "OK if I put this on tape?"

"No prob," said Engunn.

Ian assumed his innocent face. "Let's go to the economics. What's in it for landowners? What's in it for the trust? Who gets what?"

Ian wasn't asking innocent questions about money because he cared about our cover story, but I couldn't figure out his strategy when my knees felt crucified on loose nails.

Engunn reached for the broom under his bed, yanked out a fistful of straw, and passed me a few pieces. "Easements. Landowners have a bundle of rights attached to their property. They can transfer or sell some of those rights to another entity, and," he crushed the rest of the broom to his chest, "they can hold onto their remaining rights and land ownership. The easement spells out what rights the landowner keeps and what rights he sells."

Ian leaned over the chair to check the lights on his recorder. "But money's got to be involved. Why would Great Nations give away its rights to anything?"

Engunn reached for a jar of markers and scrawled "Good Deal for GNF" on the pink wall, scrawling a vertical line of dollar signs below it. "I gotta paint the cabin before I shut it down. This works."

His red marker hovered over each dollar sign as he worked his way down the wall: Great Nations got thirty-six million selling wetlands to the Ecology Fund for a bog the company couldn't harvest anyway, more millions selling real estate development rights to the Maine Forest Trust, and even more millions for trees cut off easement lands they'd continue to own. Engunn wrote "Wind Farms," and that did it for me.

"How many wind power sites in the easement?" I asked.

"At least four. Don't know what Great Nations makes off wind farms."

I knew that dollar sign. The wind power and wildlife debate had gathered heat just as I'd abandoned the legislature. Mentally I added another thirty to fifty million—per site. Whether GNF leased land to energy companies or built the sites and sold power contracts, the results were the same—bulldozing mountains where no one in his right mind would ever locate a factory. Maybe calling it a wind farm made people think chickens and pigs instead of blades bigger than jets, transmission lines carving up wild backcountry, and freeway-sized roads blasted uphill. *Oink*, I thought. *Oink, oink.*

Engunn aimed his marker at more dollar signs. "Not done yet. Haven't factored in costs or…"

Ian laughed. "What's a million or two in overhead when you're going to more than double or triple what you paid for the dirt anyway?"

My moment arrived. Sticking pitch from my hands onto the back of Ian's map, I stood and pressed it on a blank wall, pointing to where I'd seen Shannon light up the far side of a river, where the wind whipped pink flagging tape against a gathering storm.

"What's the cross-hatched area over here? The slanted lines around these rivers and ponds?"

Engunn frowned. "Looks like you already know it's Wild Pines Resort," he said.

"A resort?" asked Ian. "Vicki said this was a conservation deal."

Engunn swung toward us, his cheeks dark with defense. "Look—getting protection out of this arrangement can't happen unless Great Nations' real estate division gets a chunk of the action."

I reached into the jar for a black marker and scrawled "Real Estate Development" next to the last dollar sign. Ian crouched to take pictures of the wall's math and map.

"How much will Wild Pines bring in?" I asked.

Engunn paced back and forth tapping dollar signs. "Motivating the landowner is essential here. That and focusing on what we get to protect—fifty-eight lakes and ponds, two hundred miles of shoreline, seven hundred miles of rivers and streams, three hundred and forty thousand acres that won't ever be big-box stores. Unless there's a large payoff, no business is going to part with any of that."

I was beginning to wonder who wrote Engunn's paycheck. I slid my hand north to south down the map. "This land already double pays landowners. The tree growth law gives owners big tax breaks if they keep land in forestry operations and then, weirdly, they also get paid when they cut it to the ground."

"Look," said Engunn, his voice rising over the wind and whining stovepipe. "These companies are *all* setting up real estate divisions. Our way is the *only* way to get ahead of that wave and lock up some forest for—"

"Thirty years," said Ian. "Vicki sent a newsletter that says it's thirty years. So how much is Great Nations paying you to manage the easement? You get money for the deal, right?"

We jumped as the door banged open and slammed the wall. Flying bits of broken latch cartwheeled across the floor.

"Of course it's a deal and it's a great deal. Nothing's free." Under her fur-trimmed hood and purple parka, Victoria Brinkman filled the tiny doorway. On one finger, she passed her coat to Engunn and tiptoed to the tiny chair. Sitting primly, knees almost level with her black-sweatered chest, Vicki collected Ian's recorder from the other chair and snapped a few buttons. Her bracelets chimed merrily as she folded her hands in her lap.

CHAPTER 20

She frowned at the wall. "My goodness. *What* is going on here? I can't see how an examination of Great Nations is on topic if we're supposed to be discussing economics and the Maine Forest Trust." She lowered mascara-rimmed eyes at Engunn and smoothed imaginary winkles on her jeans.

"Our easement negotiations are private and sensitive," she said, dropping a finger onto Ian's recorder. "I cannot authorize information to go out at this time, so I have erased your interview and Engunn will soon paint over this wall. We do hope to see you at our press conference in the new year."

She pulled her feet close to the chair and looked around for a graceful way to rise off a seat only inches from the ground.

Ian knelt and offered his hand. "Before we go—"

"I have nothing further to say," she interrupted, dropping his hand as she gained her balance. "But I will email you a recent analysis. You'll find that conserved lands we acquire return eight dollars in statewide benefits for each dollar spent on the purchase. Land trusts are a better investment for Maine's economy than bond funds, but Engunn should have explained *that* by now."

I was comfortable against the wall by the woodstove, watching a new show outside the window. Their bright yellow and blue boats decorating the lawn, a group of kayakers played with Pock. I fumbled in my pocket for the leash, knowing he'd be happy to swim downriver after them.

"Patton," Vicki called as I opened the cabin door. "Let me walk with you."

I looked at her high-heeled boots. "You sure? I'm going out where there's geese."

She held out her hand for her coat, and Engunn dropped it over her shoulders and looked away. "Now, Ian," she said, "no more bothering Engunn. He's got a job to do."

I had to admit her takedown of Engunn was impressive. I thought of men I might send her way—Harworth, for one. We walked toward the kayakers, who were stepping into spray skirts that looked like neoprene petticoats. Vacuuming up peanut and raisin crumbs scattered on the ground, Pock ran from boat to boat until I leashed him and dragged him away.

"They're going to jump into the river?" asked Vicki.

"Not until they get into their boats," I said. Crammed into tiny cockpits, the paddlers secured their spray skirts and, leaning forward, slid their kayaks from slippery lawn to deep water below the dam. Pock leaned toward the pool and twitched with anticipation.

"I tried one of those sliding seal entry moves once," I told Vicki. "Missed the pool and broke toes."

"Toes gone wrong are large hurt," Vicki said, letting herself be blown toward the parking lot. "In college I dropped an ax on mine. Chopping them off would have been less painful."

I pulled my hat low to stop the wind whipping my ponytail. Vicki's hair didn't quiver. Lacking a devious way to approach the topic of Wild Pines, I tried the direct ask. "Vicki, how much more income will the resort add to GNF's bottom line? There's room for several thousand houses or condos or whatever."

"Still on that? It's a slippery figure at this point. First we have to go through a process to get the land zoned out of forestry uses and into a friendlier category for what we propose."

She frowned at my car.

"The scratches are moose. The smell is bear bait," I said.

We watched Engunn climb a ladder and crawl up the cabin's roof toward a coil of wires. "OK," he yelled. "Pull 'er in." He swung cable and rope in a smooth arc that ended in Ian's outstretched hands.

"Cheap, easy rope tricks," said Vicki. "He's all about mechanical advantage when he's really just working the man advantage."

I leaned against the side of the car, trying to sort out her motives for detouring to Canada Falls when it was so far out of her way and appreciating her slick ability to ease the subject away from something edgy. After all, didn't I do that on the flip side? Ease people away from the thorns of an issue if I needed to?

I probably needed to face up to envy. When was the last time my lobbying efforts got near to protecting fifty-eight ponds, seven hundred miles of rivers and streams, or three hundred and forty thousand acres? On the other hand, what good were ponds, rivers, and patches of trees if they were like park attractions in the middle of a landscape sliced up with clear cuts, roads, golf courses, condos, sludge fields, and wind turbines?

A forest isn't a menu of destinations. It's a broad, sticky web of relationships that matter. Silt the pond with road gravel and far away the river runs too murky for spawning fish. Scissor up terrain with roads and condos and any animal that's not a squirrel or raccoon has difficulty leading an authentic life. It looked like the trust was about to tear the forest web into separate strands too weak to stand against a greedy corporate wind. No, I wasn't envious. Just mad.

"I'll need a ride to Grants or the gate," she said. "Either you or Engunn. No float planes flew out of Munsungun Lake today. Too much wind. I bummed a ride from the local warden. A silent type. Took forever. We must have stopped at every woods operation this side of the Penobscot River collecting thermoses and—of all things—food. I thought wardens were supposed to be catching poachers."

Without noticing my frozen face, Vicki considered joining me against the car. She ran a finger over its dust-blasted surface, sighed, and looked for a convenient place to lose the dirt.

Squatting to pick up loose leaves and wipe her finger, she chatted on. "Apparently, they conduct investigations of suspicious deaths in the woods. This time, a dead logger. My ride was tight-lipped about it, but I'll find out what I need to know at the gate."

It made sense that John Tario hadn't survived 1080, but having his demise featured in Vicki's breezy travelogue felt cruel. A memory of his screams chilled me more than wind off the lake. And Moz. If he was the warden who'd dropped her at Canada Falls, I'd missed a chance to tell him about the tracking collar.

I settled Pock on his sleeping bag. "Vicki, I need to get Ian and hit the road."

Vicki crossed her arms. "You're not popular on this side of the gate, Patton. I get to hear landowners complain about you the way they bitch about black flies they can't outrun. Great Nations seems unusually miffed at you, but I made sure you'd get beyond the gates today so we could chat."

Her idea of chat didn't sound reciprocal.

She rocked on her feet as sharp gusts of wind rolled up the lawn into her back. "Engunn seems to have jumped the gun about GNF's plans, but I did warn you about his focus. We expect elements of this easement to be controversial with...with.... well, you know. You're not working with your *usual* environmental friends right now, but I'm guessing they will fight Wild Pines and someone will try to hire you. I can save you some energy on that."

She zipped her parka with one smooth gesture, never taking her eyes off me. "We'll win, you know. Politicians and regulators drool over this kind of deal, and eventually every landowner with a troubled balance sheet will seek us out for easement deals that bring them extra cash." She spread her arms wide to embrace lots of woods, but she covered only a few feet of parking lot. "There's something for everyone. Protected ponds and lands, timber harvesting, construction jobs, resort for upscale tourists, wind power—all mapped out on the landscape. Our arrangement assures a predictable future and eliminates risk. We'll lose uncertainty."

I concentrated on breathing in and breathing out and the dry rustle of lingering leaves. I could agree on the *certain* thing. Losing the forest was a certain, predictable thing, and I also knew Wild Pines Resort was headed toward Augusta trench warfare and endless hours in attorneys' offices.

"I'm happy doing what I'm doing, Vicki. I'm not looking for that kind of work," I said.

"What *are* you doing, Patton?"

I shrugged. "Just some deep breathing," I said. "Do we need to go fetch those boys?"

"Engunn has gear to pack. The Ecology Fund had a loon camera in the cove sending out live feeds on loons, and we're returning its equipment. He'll be along."

Checking canoe ropes that didn't need tightening, I hoped my voice was light and steady—let Vicki think I was only interested in lynx. "You sound confident about beating back an environmental challenge. I thought you'd want people to think the trust was an environmental organization. Have you asked the lynx how they feel about Wild Pines? I don't think they'll be checking into condos to raise their families."

She laughed. "I like your edge, Patton. And I do respect how you've added money to the environmental equation. Your work helps us attract donors." She came to stand next to me, placing her hand on the canoe. "Are you canoeing somewhere or just driving around with it on your roof to be visible in parking lots?"

I moved toward the front of the car, feeling too close to her force field. "I like to fish, so it comes with me."

She wrinkled her nose. "A messy sport."

"I don't keep them."

"No prize for your efforts? What a waste."

That comment I could have predicted. I faced her across the hood of the car. "Lynx?"

"Just a small speed bump. The governor's pushing the Department of the Interior for an incidental take permit to protect Great Nations from violating the Endangered Species Act. During resort construction, the company will be allowed to kill or injure some without violating the law."

I yanked a rope tighter on my already creaking thwarts. "My favorite part of that law. The part where we give people permission to kill animals we've protected."

Vicki sniffed and pointed her finger at me, bracelets jingling inside her coat. "Don't get worked up. Relaxing the law to allow for real events that might harm a few individual animals has been good for the process. It was too rigid before. Incidental take permits are like a pressure valve on a steam engine. Now rather than attack the law itself, those burdened by it have some recourse."

"My lynx," I said.

"Pardon me?" She massaged the fur around her collar. I didn't recognize its lavender color and hoped it had factory origins.

"They're *my* lynx. I'm part owner of Maine's lynx. What if I don't want bulldozers and cranes and speeding condo owners injuring *my* lynx?"

Vicki flicked a birch leaf off her shoulder. "You own lynx? Really?"

"Really," said Engunn.

Engunn and Ian must have used the lawn for a quiet approach. Only their heads showed over armloads of cables and electronics.

Vicki stalked toward him. "What was that, Engunn?"

He smiled grimly at me. "She's right. She's part owner of any wildlife in the state. We all are." Balancing an antenna and a solar panel on his knee, he opened the Jeep's rear door and stowed the gear.

"I didn't ask for your opinion," Vicki said.

He wheeled on her, face distorted with anger. "You never do," he shouted. "Never. If you'd paid attention to me the trust would have saved millions. I told you we didn't need to outbid Carla Monson for this deal, no matter how much she offered. Great Nations would never sign a deal with her! She'd ban everything but breathing. Our low bid would have nailed it. Now we'll have to find millions more to close it."

Vicki raised her hand. "Engunn. Enough."

He charged the dirt pile and lifted two large rocks, one in each hand. I stepped in front of Vicki and Ian tiptoed to the far side of the Jeep. Bashing the rocks together in front of his chest, Engunn sprayed the parking lot with splintered chips. "You're a head basher, Vicki," he said. "You just put your head down and charge."

Vicki's regular, easy breathing cooled my neck.

Engunn stretched his rock-filled fists toward Vicki. "I hate sneaking around. If we're partners with companies that own woods, then goddammit, stand up and say so." He dropped his arms but not the rocks. Blood seeped between his fingers. "Patton," he snarled, "Great Nations gives the Maine Forest Trust millions to manage the easement, and Wild Pines brings Great Nations at least another two or three hundred million. Vicki and her board of directors don't want that to get out, but it's got to come out. Everyone has to sign on. No resort, no easement."

Engunn dropped the rocks and flicked bloody bits toward Vicki. "I'd rather work for Great Nations any day than *you*." He backed to the edge of the parking lot, his slow, satisfied grin growing white with teeth.

I tried to clear my throat, but wind shoved the sound back down my throat.

Vicki sighed and pointed at Ian. "You. Put that stuff in his Jeep."

Ian tossed cables toward the rest of Engunn's gear, then opened the Subaru's door and stepped up on the frame so his head cleared my canoe. I recognized his reporter voice. "Vicki, last time you were in D.C., why did you lobby the Interior Department to move wolves off the endangered species list?"

Vicki's eyes widened in surprise, flicking her lashes up against green eye shadow. When she lifted her hood, fur screened her face from the first stinging drops that pelted the rest of us.

CHAPTER 21

As sideways rain beat on the car, I pulled into a campsite to wait out the worst of the storm. My windows steamed from soaked clothes and Pock's restless breath. Feeling imprisoned in a manic carwash, I lowered my head to the steering wheel and barely tolerated Ian's complaints.

He slumped against his window, head muffled in coats. "Let the dog out. He stinks."

"Have some gum," I said. I unwrapped a piece and tossed it toward him. "The flavor will work up your nose. Wet dog is ever so much worse than canine breath." His fingers crawled out and snatched the gum.

"Don't look," I said, stripping off my wet fleece to get at my dry T-shirt. The Subaru defrost system was on strike—again. I wiped down the interior windows with my shirt, swearing at one of Engunn's rock fragments growing a hairline crack in the windshield.

I adjusted my shirt. "It's OK to come out now. I'm back together. The good news is that rain will suppress both dust and wildlife."

Ian raised his head slightly. "The bad news?"

I put my head back down on the steering wheel, wondering how a few tracks scratched in the dirt had become a weight that felt too heavy to lift. "The logger in the back of Ridge's truck. John Tario? He's dead. Vicki told me she heard it from the game warden that dropped her off at Canada Falls. And I think it's more bad news that Moz was out collecting food and drink evidence from GNF work sites."

"No one should go out that way," Ian said quietly. "Where's the rest of the 1080? There's gotta be more."

"I plan on keeping a close eye on Pock's wanderings and limiting our food to what we have in the car and what we buy at Grants. So. Ian. When were you going to tell me Vicki was in our nation's capital on a mission that included wolves? And I'd like to hear your reason for blowing up our cover story back there."

"As if I care anymore about the phony story." He raised his phone, zoomed in on Engunn's map, and stuffed all the remaining gum into his mouth. "The Maine Forest Trust and Great Nations are in bed together. Phil was on target with that one. Vicki was part of a Great Nations anti-lynx, anti-wolf lobbying trip to D.C. Probably easier to roll all the problem animals into one business deduction." He pulled out his gum wad and examined it. "She came here today for a reason. She's a woman who doesn't move without one. It could be she didn't trust Engunn to manage us. I'm still working on that."

I turned the defrost off and on, hoping for success. "You pushed Engunn hard on the money."

"You pushed him, too, but you were just pissed about the resort thing. I pushed him for a good reason and here it is. You ready? What if there's so much money involved in this deal that anything that gets in the way needs to get *out* of the way?"

Of course, money trumped wolves. Peter was right. The kid was good—getting Engunn to reveal Great Nations' potential revenue from working over a large chunk of forest. "OK," I said. "That's good. How does all this affect your story?" I asked.

Ian reached over and poked me. "You mean the *wolves'* story? I think a billion dollars of incentive is not good news for any living wolf. If they're here, I'd like to get to them before someone who's after some sweet income gets to them." He kicked off his shoes and swiped his feet back and forth across his front window to clear the glass.

As I eased the Subaru over clumps of wet leaves and headed toward Grants Farm Inn, my wipers struggled to offload rivers of rain, but my defroster was back in action. In my rearview mirror a dead limb crashed onto a picnic table. On the instrument panel before me, Shannon's picture was angled so she could see the limb's twitching branches. I cupped her photo and slid it to safety under my shirt.

The sand-under-eyelids feeling was back. I glanced at my watch. We'd be on time for the all-you-can-eat buffet. I wasn't worried about where to sleep. Any floor—car floor, bathroom floor, dirty floor, cold floor—would do. Sleet and rain waved in front of me like beckoning ghosts in the road. While everyone in my car snored, I drove with my left hand and scrawled Ian a to-do list with my right: research the easement map he'd captured on his phone and update our topo map with Wild Pines' boundaries. Locate Anita Stockdale and set up a meeting. Pursue a cyber-search on Phil's Lottflex GPS 7000 tracking collar because Shannon's cheek had been lying on one just like it.

My own list wasn't long. Fish before dark, decide if Engunn's bitter attitude toward Shannon mattered, and find Moz to tell him I'd identified the missing collar as a tracking device. Outside of wishing he'd just appear, I wasn't sure how to summon him without the warden grapevine listening in, but I thought we'd ask the same question. If the thief knew the collar could locate wolves, did we have a secret friend or a secret foe?

I felt the rumbling floorboards of the one-lane wooden bridge over the South Branch River and stopped the car. Curtains of rain cloaked the visible world. I opened my window to hear it hiss into the river while I inhaled the crisp scent of scrubbed rocks. Under the bridge a voice counted, "Six, seven, eight. That's everyone. Let's hit it." Bent over, heads tucked and paddles low in the water to avoid wind, the kayakers looked like the wedge of ducks I'd seen at the dam. I wondered if there'd be any chocolate cream pie if they got to Grants before I did.

Behind me an engine downshifted as it approached my car. I left the bridge, turned off the logging road, and turned into the inn driveway, braking for a group of deer bounding for cover—eleven deer more than I'd seen north of GNF's gate all fall. The stark outlines of pasture fences, barns, and rusting machinery loomed eerily into view and vanished in moisture as I inched up the hill toward the inn.

I'm not much for museums, but the farm in fog was a stark black-and-white exhibition of a vanished world where hundreds of farms once fed thousands of loggers. Back when men were the most efficient machines, the inn stoked their fires with calories and coffee. Pock stirred and pushed his nose against his window. Grants was his favorite stop.

"Shhhhhh," I whispered. "Don't wake the boy. He's not big on animals."

My outside mirror scraped a post as I pulled close to the barn and opened Pock's window. Munching forms floated from the rain and tiptoed toward us. Like big-headed flowers on slender stalks, llamas bobbed gracefully down to sniff Pock. He nosed each offered face until sheep bleated in the back pasture, calling the llamas back into the mist. When they'd arrived at Grants, llamas came as motivated infantry dedicated to sheep safety. Heads stretched high, nostrils flared above sharp toes and quick legs, llamas were both an early warning system and deadly ammunition. Grants had smart predator control.

Ian was so asleep that I'd fed Pock, dragged Francoise's grease pail to the inn's back porch, paid for the last two rooms, and reserved pie before he appeared in the kitchen, shivering and coatless. If we ran into weather searching for the Howlers' camp, I'd have to take a command position and order him into foul-weather gear.

I was sharing a pot of tea with Mike Leavitt and from behind the staff table where we were squeezed against the kitchen wall, we watched the inn get ready to feed us dinner. We had a clear view of early diners pulling into the parking lot, and next to us, cooks ran dishes through an arched doorway into the dining room.

Mike lived for mint tea heavy with honey and didn't care if it was served on plastic picnic tablecloths or law firm mahogany. Governors made appointments, but the executive director of the Maine Association of Sportsmen and Trappers got into the senate president's office—or any office, camp, or truck—without an appointment because Mike Leavitt was the most powerful man in Maine.

His new L.L.Bean boots were propped on a cluttered counter that displayed everything from bug spray to turkey calls. An impatient waiter balancing racks of glasses nudged a staring Ian out of his way. Even without a red costume and bag of toys, Mike was used to stopping traffic.

I waved Ian toward us. "Ian Glenburn of the *Bangor Weekly*, meet Mike Leavitt, better known as the Sportsman's Santa."

Ian ran a quick hand through sleep-smashed, dripping hair and reached for Mike.

Mike reached up but didn't move. "I'd get up but when I've just rearranged my butt in the chair, it's best to let the rest of me settle." There was a lot to settle. Dimpled cheeks rolled into a beard more ivory than the soap bars stacked over his head. Full lips parted for his famous "always-glad-to-see-ya-deah" smile, and smudged, wireless glasses magnified black eyes that glittered in genuine glee.

Spreading his hands over his mounds of belly in what might have been an obscene caress if directed elsewhere, he bellowed, "A testament to thirty-five years of knowing every sporting camp cook in the entire state." He gestured to an overturned milk crate. "Sit. The Kenneths aren't here if you're looking for the owners. They're in Bangor. I haven't had time to ask Patton what she's up to yet. Too busy making her serve me." He chuckled and raised a giant brownie that shed coconut down the front of his green flannel shirt. "My guide's been looking for you and my bait all afternoon. He's picked out my next bear rug, and all I have to do is waddle out there and try not to smell human or pick my nose and spook it, and the beast is mine."

I lowered Ian to the crate, squeezing his arm in what I hoped was a warning. *Mike knows everything that Sam at the gate knows. If there's a wolf hunt, he's part of it.* "Ian," I said, "Mike's got lots of obvious Santa parts, and then there's the less obvious Santa parts that bring gifts to his members. He defeats gun control legislation.

He fends off most spending bills dedicated to animals that can't be mounted on the wall or fried in a pan. He's famous for coming up with creative ways for hunters to get more hunting time and fishermen to get more fishing time."

Mike beamed at me. "That's right and I am proud of it all." He turned to Ian. "We can't explain it, but somehow Patton and I seem to be friends who don't agree on anything but trout. What are you two doing out here?"

I leaned back and added my boots to the shelf. "You tell me, Mike. I'm curious to know what's beamed into your universe." Ian rose and drifted toward the dregs of coffee that looked and smelled singed as he poured it into a paper cup. He sighed through the first few sips and eyed us over the rim.

Mike laughed. "I haven't seen you since you were hot on regulating logging roads. Another numb-assed plot to drive business out of state." He moved a faded curtain and considered the parking lot filling with dinner traffic. "We like roads. Cuts down on the distance we have to drag game out of the woods. Francoise at Road Kill says you're looking for money. I'm not sure what that means. Sam at the gate says you're in here working for the *Bangor Weekly*. The rest of what he said would ruin dessert if I had to repeat it." He licked melted chocolate from his whiskered lips.

Wafted toward me by a grease-crusted fan, chocolate's siren song called, and I reached down and grabbed the sides of my seat to halt a swoon of desire. My mother had lived on dark syrup-choked shakes as she breast-fed her children, so my cells are conditioned to lean hungrily toward chocolate.

Mike blew coconut flakes off his shirt. “Christ. Looks like I’ve got the worst case of dandruff.” He slapped his shirt with a red bandanna and then drove it vigorously over his mouth. “Great Nations says you’re working up columns on outdoor economics, but I got the serious impression they’d rather have you gone.”

As I leaned into my mug, Mike’s delighted shout embraced the entire kitchen. “Oh ho! So they’re still pissed off about your flap over cut deer yards! Publishing private corporate correspondence won’t win you friends, my dear.”

I slapped at his knee. “I wouldn’t be such a target if you and your membership showed up to save a few more trees.”

Mike opened both arms wide. “I do love you, Patton,” he bellowed.

“At least you’re consistent,” I said.

Mike dropped a satisfied nod down onto his bulk.

Ian crushed his cup and crouched on the milk crate, notebook open. “Consistent?”

Mike grunted. “You tell it, Patton. You always get it right.”

I rattled off my standard MAST explanation. “Mike and his mostly men members side with corporate forest land owners because owners have the keys to the gates. Behind the gates, nine million acres of hunting, fishing, and trapping are the Promised Land. MAST members will work on protections for fish or bear or turkeys and other game species when those protections won't upset their more important relationships. In short, MAST votes for whatever the owners say they need."

Mike raised his voice, throwing his politics toward boots clumping into the dining room on the other side of the wall. "Well done, my dear. Some folks think the enviro-movement was started by Rachael Kenneth whining over dead birds, or wilderness nuts like John Muir." Thumping his chest with both hands, he pounded out a kettledrum echo. "We started it. Hunters. We taxed ourselves to return wild turkeys, ducks, elk, bobcat, deer, bear—and there must be more I forgot."

I knew he wouldn't mention the slaughter that originally decimated wild turkeys, ducks, elk, bobcat, deer, and bear. Curious diners lined up three deep in the doorway of the kitchen, enjoying the show.

"Here's some money for you." Mike pulled shotgun shells from the shelf by his ear and tossed them to Ian. "We pay taxes on ammo, guns, fish line, rods. Everything we need. Five million dollars a day. Off us. And then add in the hunting and fishing licenses. We've paid for and protected fifty million acres of land and water—bullet by bullet."

One of Grants' cooks leaned over us on his way to the steam table, sweat pouring down his arms toward the mashed potato tub. "You tell her, Mike," he said.

I made a mental note to avoid potatoes and cleared my throat theatrically.

"You're OK, Patton," Mike said. "You fish. Your money's in our pot."

A man wearing a white fur vest with small pink noses lined up as a row of buttons leaned in the doorway. "Is she a predator lover, Mike?"

Ian lowered his pencil. Mike crossed both arms on top of his chest, gripping his forearms to keep them stacked on top of his bulk. "Well, I don't know about that. Yet." His voice dropped into that judgmental low register I always dread in December when people ask if I've been *good*. He removed his glasses so his eyes could find mine. "We haven't had much talk on that."

Banging inches from my head, the dinner gong lifted me off my seat and vibrated my mug off the table. Ian clamped his notebook over one ear. Mike calmly placed his hands on his knees and tipped forward to loom over us. "The predator lovers don't pay, so they don't get to play." He hitched up his pants and snapped his suspenders. "When your enviro-friends raise money to pay for their own species projects, I might consider them less of a threat. Right now, they just siphon off funds we need for the animals we care about."

He groaned and wheezed over my legs, turning in the dining room doorway. "Let me revise that just a bit—for Peter and the *Bangor Weekly*, of course. And my apologies, as I understand you're having a rough week." He raised his arm, rifle-like, and aimed it back into the kitchen, squinting one eye down the length of it and finding me as a likely target. "Some animals are unacceptable. Ones big enough to take down a deer or moose—well, we'll adjust our sights to deal with them."

Rubbing his girth, he peeled away to the dining room yelling, "Who's got a gripe or good story for my next newsletter?"

CHAPTER 22

Ian slid into Mike's vacant chair. "Add him to the 'people who suspect' list," he whispered. I scraped up mug fragments and reached for a napkin to wipe up my tea.

"I knew that the minute I saw him holding court in the kitchen," I snapped. "Hunt bear, my ass. He's not up here for bear. He's here for wolves. Mike wrote the law making it illegal to bring wolves into Maine. He here because he thinks someone messed with it." I pulled my hair loose and fluffed it up a bit to see if it could stay down for dinner. It reorganized into a tight, dirty clump that I stuffed back into a rubber band. If I timed it right, there'd be hot water for a shower after the dishes were done. I settled for licking my fingers and neatening my eyebrows as a token tidy-up gesture.

Ian lifted my list from his shirt pocket. "I believe you left this in my shoes. Grants has wireless. I'll upload pictures of Engunn's money wall and map to the *Bangor Weekly*, and I'll add Great Nations' resort project to our map. I already checked out the tracking collar. It's first rate. If the one Shannon found was on a wolf, I hope your dark forces don't have it now cause their tech guys will know where wolves hang out minutes after they download what the collar knows."

He flicked the empty cup over my head into a garbage can and sniffed under his arms. "I don't think I smell like a bear, but let's eat like one. I'm starved."

In the next room, feet thundered toward the buffet table. We leaned in to assess the line snaking around chipped Formica-topped tables loaded with ketchup, hot sauce, and syrup. People squeezed past us with trays of turkey, meatballs, roast beef, baked beans, mashed potatoes, and dinner rolls that teetered like miniature chef's hats on top of food mountains.

"Not a veggie and fruit crowd," said Ian. Slowly we shuffled forward. "Weird collection of people. Like refugees from different countries."

In a way, he was right. Escaping cities and suburbs, people from different cultures ended up at Grants. Tourists passed around phones comparing leaf pictures. Kayakers with water-wrinkled fingers lowered their heads as a troop of revivalists on retreat sang grace. Hunters in head-to-toe camouflage rotated back into line for second helpings. Truck drivers speaking rapid Quebecois French drowned their plates in gravy and maple syrup. Young field trip students wearing "Beware Biology" T-shirts begged chaperones for extra brownies, and a woman so angular her windbreaker hung off shoulders shaped like coat hangers stood between mounted bobcats and poked at her string beans.

I only noticed the two men in dark glasses and string ties in the far corner when one pointed at Ian and both raised their cell phones. They didn't fit because no one else was interested in Ian, or wearing dark glasses, or more thinking phones were more appetizing than roast beef. I wasn't surprised by Harworth's GNF posse, just sad it had invaded a refuge where I'd always felt welcome and safe.

Mike Leavitt's voice boomed from the serving line. "Add more. My doctors are idiots."

Ian stepped out of line and tapped a map pinned to the dining room wall. He waved chattering children past us. "I want that map. Who could make us a map like this?"

I squinted at the map key. "It's GIS—geographic information system. It mixes layers of computerized data with new information you can add manually from a drawing program. Over here around the lake someone's added bird symbols to mark loon camera locations."

Ian dropped his voice as we huddled next to the wall. "So on top of the already mapped lynx and wolf lands we can draw closed roads, dismantled beaver dams ... any extra stuff we find?"

"If we get access to a high-tech mapping program, we can layer in any new information we find. I just don't know if we have time." Moving to the steam table I spooned macaroni and cheese into my divided tray and pitied the wilted salad.

"Vegetarian?" asked the cook behind the table.

"No, not me. My daughter. Just getting ready for Thanksgiving. If I cut back on meat now, I won't mind zucchini lasagna over the holidays."

"I won't tell. Eat up. It's Tall Tales Night." He slipped a slice of roast beef into one empty compartment.

A roar from outside whipped cooks' heads toward the parking lot. "He's back," wailed a dishwasher. They crowded the smudged window over the serving line. Whatever drama was headed toward the buffet, I was more interested in food.

Except for a small "reserved" table wedged behind the wood stove next to the tourists, all the tables were taken. I led Ian toward the tourists' table, where smiling diners stacked their guidebooks to make room for us. I was about to suggest an interview about their spending habits, when all eight kayakers sitting nearby scraped back their chairs and bowed raggedly in my direction. Dining room conversation dimmed as the nearest kayaker passed her dripping helmet across the aisle to me.

"We passed the helmet to buy you dinner," she said. She nodded to her group. Milk slopped on their table as they stood and raised glasses. "Sorry the money's wet, but it's good. You don't know us but we know you. Hoo-rah, Patton Conover. Hoo-rah for cleaning up the Penobscot River's stinking green slime."

"Hoo-rah! Hoo-rah! Fight on," they shouted, stomping their feet like stampeding buffalo. Jostling each other, they sat and pulled slabs of lemon meringue pie onto their plates.

Ian pinched my elbow. "Return the helmet. I got the money."

The rest of dinner felt like a festive community supper to benefit someone needy—or lonely. I didn't want to admit Pock wasn't enough company, but lately I'd considered Kiwanis bingo as a social option. Kayakers thumped me on the back. Tourists peppered me with green slime questions. After Ian stuffed a five-dollar bill in a glass and perched it on the end of the table, hunters tipped me on the way to the coffeepot. I wouldn't have heard the gravel voice in my ear if his cold breath hadn't already caught my attention.

"There's more than enough slime to go around," cold breath said. "Their boys are giving you the evil eye, so I assume you're on the right side of Great Nations Forest—their bad side." The men in dark glasses hadn't dropped by to put money in my glass, and their mounds of uneaten potatoes looked calcified. Cold breath leaned so close I was worried about his lips reaching my neck. "I hope you're still around when their trucks dump sludge where my forest friends dine. For sure, corporate diarrhea's just a by-product of their greed."

One hand grabbed the side of my chair and spun it toward the small reserved table behind us. Ian was left wedged into the tourists' table while I was knee to knee with an old man. He reached under dry, white blond hair, pressed his hand against his ear, and nodded once at the dark glasses men.

"I can hear them talking about you. Wanna listen?" He slid a narrow black earpiece down his neck. In slow motion, I shook my head, and he eased the device back into place and rocked his chair against the wall. Knees freed, I scraped my chair over the floor and joined him at the wall, both of us facing the room.

I nodded at Ian and he dropped back into his chair. "Who the hell are you?" I whispered.

Alert, feral blue eyes tracked mine. They glowed inside a rustling mane of matted hair and beard. I guessed his age as sixty-something, but it was a hunch. He could have been a fit ninety. His elbows explored holes in a barely-there denim work shirt. Raised gray sinews roped across his forearms as he leaned on tensed thighs. Rocking the chair back and forth on its back legs, he seemed a strange blend of lion and cobra—regally coiled.

He sighed. "Look—there's not much time. You done with the inspection? I'll give it to you straight." He slid forward and tapped a boot tip on Ian's chair and smiled when Ian's head jerked. "Sidekick—you listening? Good. I thought sludge would get your attention."

"Those guys who don't fit." He pointed openly at the dark glasses men. Their sunglasses rotated in our direction. "Great Nations Forest's corporate office is following you. They just closed a secret deal with the Ecology Fund and the Maine Forest Trust to piss all over three hundred and forty thousand Maine acres—and get paid for it. Now they can tree rape it, gouge gravel pits, explode mountains into wind farm factories, and slime woods with shit spewed from ritzy condo plumbing." He sighed again. "I actually like sludge. It's such a tight metaphor for their crapping all over us and selling it as sweet-smelling conservation."

His laugh rolled like a snarl. “Are you going to stop it, Cassandra Patton Conover? Are you, young muckraking reporter? I think not. They’re on a roll, and the only thing that stands between them and what’s left of Maine’s forest is—.” He stopped. “Well, there’s me, but I also have some helpers.” Again, he boot-tapped Ian’s chair. I held my breath as Ian’s neck flushed red.

“Soon I’ll need your help.” My gravel-voiced neighbor rocked forward, heaved a green duffle bag to his shoulders, and snapped the rubber band from my hair. “Let your hair down, Conover. Don’t miss tonight’s show.”

He bowed. “Gordon Samuels, wolf in wolf’s clothing. Soon to be at your service.” He ducked behind the retreat choir singing at the piano and vanished.

CHAPTER 23

The hymn faded as Ian and I reached my car. I brushed sleet off the door and bent in, looking for my warmest gloves. "What the hell was that?" Ian asked as I leashed Pock and checked my pocket for room keys.

"Whoever owns that," I said. Wheels half on the porch steps and half in crushed flowers, a dented all-terrain vehicle blocked kitchen traffic. A padlock as round as a hubcap swung from a locked box bolted over the rear fenders.

"You know him?"

"Grants' staff sure knows him; they save a table to quarantine him from sane guests. That's got to be Gordon Samuels' transportation. He's Carla Monson's land manager, and no, I don't know him."

"He's expensively wired for someone who looks like a hermit," said Ian. "I've always wanted a directional mike, and he's computer savvy. My sludge story's only online." He slapped me on the back. "On the other hand, *everyone* seems to know you."

As we walked to the llama barn, Pock leaned toward the smell of manure. "Sludge," I said. "You're the expert. What more should I know?"

"He's probably right about the corporate diarrhea thing. Wild Pines' toilets have to go somewhere, some kind of waste system. Up here that's probably spreading processed poop—sludge—on land. Back in civilization, people take issue with shared heavy metals and excreted medicines that might wreak havoc with their health." He waved his hand into darkness. "I'm guessing *your* animals will be walking through some of it. Of course, it's not really a problem if there's *nothing* out there." He punctuated *nothing* with a few dance steps.

I felt slightly cheered and handed Ian his room key. "We'll have to attend Tall Tales Night to learn about the wolf in wolf's clothing."

Carrying only his toothbrush, phone, and computer, Ian trotted across the parking lot. I fluffed up Pock's sleeping bag and hugged him. "Not going to sneak you in tonight, boy. You'll have to bunk here."

Grants' dining room was packed sardine-can full. Rickety chairs creaked under the weight of extra people and watchers were stacked three deep against the walls. Waiters dragged wooden pallets to build a stage by the kitchen door. When a crew of mud-crusted loggers joined the wall leaners, pitch overwhelmed the lemon meringue atmosphere. I retreated to the kitchen, hoping the dishwasher had leftover chocolate cream pie and coyote clues.

Hunters liked Grants because remote snowmobile trails gave them easy access to coyotes that also used the trails. Last February, to escape an inn parking lot fogged with snowmobile exhaust, I'd skied across the frozen South Branch River into a forest of white, iced-over trees. While Pock snorkeled into buried mouse trails, a hooded man with a rifle slung over his back floated toward me, his snowmobile appearing under him as he topped a rise in the trail. Alone, I've often met well-armed men in the backcountry. I waved.

He smiled through frosted facial hair and slowed. "I'm after coyotes, but you don't look like competition. Not sure what's up—they used to be everywhere, but not anymore. Watch the ice. Don't want to look for the hole where you went in after dark." He pointed to the headlamp under his hood and disappeared down the trail, his black shape broken by falling snow.

The dishwasher stacked wet pans into a pile to dry. "Sorry—pie's all gone and most coyote hunters, too. Gone east to Washington County, where there's a chance of bagging one," he said. He tossed his apron over defrosting slabs of bacon. "Don't get that, but there's a shitload of deer moving around, mostly over to that woman Monson's land. That pisses off people 'cause she chases 'em out. People, I mean. I don't hunt, so what do I care."

"Anyone running dogs on bear right now?" I asked.

He waved through steam at the window. I leaned over his shoulder. Parked next to Mike Leavitt's MAST van was a beat-up truck where a two-story platform of divided doorways filled the back cab. Out tiny windows in the tiny doors, dogs' drooling heads stretched toward the kitchen fan. Mike's bear guide used dogs.

Hoots, hollering, and applause followed the end of each tall tale. I hauled the staff table into a corner under shelves that sagged with canned tomatoes, assembled my fly rod, and studied my almost empty fly boxes. Most of my flies were snagged in trees, tangled in debris, or stuck in my hat, but I planned a headlamp visit to trout living behind the inn and hoped Gordon Samuels wouldn't show.

When black paws ripped the screen, and fumbled at the kitchen door, my arms flew up and flies flew everywhere. A wolf's head peered around the corner, lowered its muzzle, and growled softly at me. I swallowed and pressed one hand on my leaping heart. Not a live wolf. A bent-over man wearing a skinned-out wolf cape, animal muzzle balanced on his head, tawny ruff of hair framing his forehead. Gray-brown wolf shoulders draped his upper body, and leg skins swished down his thighs. With a throaty gurgle, Gordon lifted his head and I gasped. His eyes were waxy, yellow pupils cut by black slits. Contact lenses. A wolf man in wolf's clothing.

Dragging his green duffle, he padded toward the dining room, snarled, and leaped to the stage. A woman in the front row screamed. Like linebackers set to charge, loggers hunched low and aimed for the stage. After Gordon raised his paws and waved them back against the wall, people settled and hushed each other. I squatted on the kitchen sill inches from the duffle bag and stage and saw Ian balanced on a service cart at the back of the room, adjusting lenses on his camera.

Gordon whirled over the stage, gray tail streaming behind him like a furry windsock. "I see you know me. Fearful eyes. Fear I will eat your children. Fear I will attack your husbands in the woods. Be calm. Be calm. Fear rattlesnakes, bears, moose, and your pet dogs. They kill thousands of your kind. I do not." Paws pressing the air before him, he stalked the rapt student audience and snatched a stuffed sheep from a pink backpack. "Perhaps you fear for your livestock. On hooves, your property walks toward us. Soooo easy and soooo stuuupid."

He bent low to brush wolf teeth across the toy. A girl giggled and stretched her hands toward Gordon. He patted her head and returned her sheep.

"Perhaps you fear for your game?" Gordon's paw swiped a mounted deer head. Dust and hair floated down on the audience. "You hunt the magnificent bucks. The fertile does. Animals poised to breed their superior genes. *We* are not so stupid. *We* seek the old, the sick, and yes, the young who can't escape us."

Like automated fireflies, cameras and phones flashed.

I dropped to the floor near students pressed up against the stage. Gordon and his wolf head prowled the room—two pairs of eyes seeking prey.

"Ah yes," he snarled, pouncing on a patch of floor before the Great Nations' men. They hadn't moved all night, dark glasses and mashed potatoes frozen in place. "The forest. You own the dirt and trees, but you don't *own* me or the deer whose homes you destroy."

Dragging a small table into the aisle, he crawled on it, until, four legged and panting, he was eye to eye with the men. He thrust claws inches from their chins, but neither man flinched. He raised his muzzle, sniffed, and spat on the floor. "I smell the stink of your fear—fear my return dooms your lust to cut and cut and build and build."

In the back of the room, a deep voice yelled, "Time's up, crazy old fart!"

As one body, the audience of students, tourists, and revivalists turned and exhaled a deafening "Shush!"

Gordon swung his muzzle low over the men's table until wolf teeth glinted in their dark glasses. He flung his arms and paws wide. "I am not your property to kill. I am a Maine wolf. I belong to ev-er-y-one."

I slid sideways for a better view and bumped into Gordon's duffle. Like a small water bed, it floated and nudged me at the same time, sighing out a musty kennel odor. Gordon sprang from the table and padded through the dining room.

"I am returned to heal a wounded landscape," he yelped. The howl he rolled through the room might have come from Ian's wolf recordings.

"Oh my," said a field trip teacher sitting beside me. "He's very realistic, isn't he?"

Howling and weaving among the tables, Gordon batted his paws like furry conductors' batons until students, tourists, church group, and kayakers overlapped him in a mournful group howl—a vibrating hymn to a creature we didn't know. Gordon lowered his arms to quiet the room. Faintly, Pock howled from my car.

"Awesome," breathed two boys in the front row.

Wonderful, I thought. *Shannon, you should see this.*

Gordon lifted a chair to the stage, sat, and crossed his legs. I couldn't separate his multicolored hide from his matted blond hair. His voice was a confessional lilt. "*They* will soon try to kill me. Again. *They* are looking for my hiding places, my pups, my family." He aimed a hoarse stage whisper into the captured room. "Help me. How will they come at me?"

Gordon raised his paws and put them on his chest. "Come on, people. How do you kill a wolf?"

A woman with bright red hair, dark roots, and chains of crosses started to lift her hand but changed her mind and rocked her body to sit firmly on her fingers.

"Yes," said Gordon, nodding at her. "Begin."

She cleared her throat. "I raise Irish wolfhounds. Wolf-killing machines. Well, three hundred years ago that's what the Celts bred them to do. Dogs. They might use dogs on you." Crossing her arms, she settled back in her chair. "Lovely, gentle pets, though."

The air was full of hands, some tentative, others pumping energetically. How could a random group of people know so much about killing wolves? The children knew about wolf pits—holes filled with slick rocks and drowning water or sharp pikes to impale curious predators.

My neighbor whispered, "Our unit on Lewis and Clark's journals had vivid pit diagrams."

The list was long. Traps that crushed or choked. Drag lines that snagged exhausted captives in dense brush. The Indians used deadfalls—rocks balanced to crush skulls as wolves tugged on sticks set over bait. White settlers armed with torches and drums drove animals to the center of a narrowing human ring. In the center, they killed wolves, bear, deer, foxes, mink, rabbits—even moles.

Two brothers volunteered they'd run down a tired pack on a Canadian snowmobile vacation, and a few hunters boasted they'd shot wolves from planes in Alaska. On stage Gordon ducked a phantom airplane and bit imaginary bullets out of his hide.

"Excellent," he yelled. He pounded the pallet's boards, panting and shouting. "Chased and torn apart by dogs. Body parts strung up on fences to warn my family away. The vendetta. Still going on. Who's next?"

The thin woman who'd eaten her dinner standing against the wall slipped a faded bandanna from her neck and stepped to the stage. Knotting it into a hanging loop, she dropped it over Gordon's two heads. "Snares are the worst," she said.

Gordon gagged and dropped his tongue on one cheek.

She tightened the noose. "Wolves have muscular throats and reinforced trachea so snares take time to kill—days—while the animal thrashes and whimpers from thirst." She loosened and removed the loop, calmly facing the audience while Gordon's paw stroked her arm. "Snares catch foxes, deer, eagles, moose. I've found animals who've chewed off legs to escape."

"Come on, Stockdale," a man yelled from the back of the room. "You know the trapping laws got changed. We can only snare beavers now. Give us a break, for Christ's sake!"

"Yes, Walt. So sorry." She smoothed the hide on Gordon's shoulders and aimed a fearless, toothy smile at Walt's corner. "Fifty miles from here, over the border in Quebec, they're snaring wolves."

Ian popped me a thumbs-up signal as the woman slipped back into the crowd. We'd found Anita Stockdale. Peter would be pleased we'd found the biologist on his list. Gordon reached for his duffle bag and dragged it to the stage. More like dense smoke than air, its smell crawled down my throat and started my mac and cheese on a return journey. I swallowed convulsively and sucked at pitch on my palm to stop the rising gag.

My neighbor clamped her sweater over her nose and coughed. "Good lord. What next?"

Gordon's rasp stilled the crowd's mutters. "Now! Let's have it all out. NO. MORE. MURDER."

Without standing, the kayakers lifted drying clothes from their chairs and began dressing. People leaned away from the stage, arms crossed protectively over chests. Loggers at the wall scowled rebelliously. I stood and put one foot in the kitchen, thinking that the ugly moment Peter warned us about had arrived.

Gordon swung his duffle in an arc over the heads and dark glasses of the Great Nations' men. "You missed me!" he hissed. Although their noses flared at the foul cloud, neither man moved. Gordon thrust his head and wolf muzzle toward the ceiling, rolling a long howl into a tortured moan.

"Poison, people! You forgot poison!" He straightened his arms and shook the duffle. Not one child leaning on the stage flinched from the wave of fearsome smell. "See my poisoned brother!"

The bag's contents flopped onto the stage like wet, ripe fish dumped on a pier. I grabbed two screaming girls and rushed out the back door. I returned for the sheep, trampled in the field trip's retreat. Teachers scuffled with more children, dragging them by collars and cuffs, dumping them in the garden. I pushed my way back into the dining room, where mugs rolled on the floor under tipped chairs and Gordon had vanished.

Medical gloves on her hands and calm fingers probing the animal, Anita Stockdale examined the carcass. The sleeves of her red plaid shirt were rolled above her elbows as she cradled the lolling head on her legs, and I could smell the menthol ointment she'd smeared up her nose. A wet stain from the animal's swollen, gray tongue deepened the dark front of her jeans.

Mike Leavitt and most of the working men ringed the stage while Ian stood on a table, dish towel tied over his nose, telephoto lens lapping up the scene. With the windows open and the room cleared, I found that shallow breaths held my mac and cheese where it belonged.

"Give her room to work. Give me some goddamn air," barked Mike.

I thought Anita was almost as interesting as the dead animal. She used her wrist to brush wispy blond strands from her forehead. Cobalt blue eyes lit up a wind-chiseled face the way a lighthouse animates solid rock, and her angular elbows radiated energy as she positioned the animal and tended to it.

"I'll get the Tufts lab to work her up after she's good and frozen," she said. "I'm more interested in how she died than what she is." I thought the short muzzle and neck ruff looked like Gordon's hide.

"Shit—it's a wolf," said Mike. "That's the second one killed up here in two years. I thought we'd made the vermin illegal. Good Christ. I got enough problems keeping coyotes down." He kicked the carcass. "Shot?"

Anita raised the animal's head so together, they met Mike's eyes. "Animals are illiterate, Mike. They don't read laws you write for your legislator friends to pass. I think the crazy man's right, though. Poison. Her orifices and internal organs feel like jelly. No bullet holes." She smiled and bent toward one limp ear. "There it is."

She smoothed the body's tattered fur from neck to tail and rose to her feet. She towered over Mike. "Sorry to disappoint you, Mike, but this is one of Taylor Arbuckle's wolf hybrids. A wolf dog. Or dog wolf, if you prefer."

"You can't know that," he snapped.

"Oh, yes, I can and do. In the Fish and Wildlife Service we had several go-rounds with Arbuckle over letting his hybrids run loose. They created too many crazed wolf sightings we didn't want to waste time on. Three years ago, we worked with game wardens to serve him with a court order, and I searched his kennel. I notched ears until he ran us off. Notches remove any doubt. I can feel her carved ear."

Anita stripped off her gloves and reached into her pack for a can of disinfectant wipes. No one spoke as she scrubbed her hands, picked up a mug and squashed the gloves and wipes into it, and dropped the mess into an orange biohazard bag. She pulled duct tape and more gloves from her pack and turned to the waiting men. "Walt, would you get some help and wrap her in garbage bags? Wrap the outside with tape and lay her in the cab of my truck. Would be much appreciated."

Walt nodded.

"Use these gloves and scrub up in the fish cleaning station. No telling what we've got here. Give the cooks a heads-up to wear gloves and haul this pallet out and burn it. Tonight." Walt nodded a second time and walked toward the kitchen.

I felt a pang of jealousy. Even people who didn't like this woman listened to her.

CHAPTER 24

Outside, Ian and I found the rain stopped and Gordon's ATV tracks mashed into Rachael Kenneth's garden. Anita crouched behind her truck, using a stick to push her pants into another biohazard bag. "I can't seem to keep a pair of jeans long enough for them to fade," she said. She tossed the bag into her backseat and vigorously tucked her oversize shirt into new jeans, twisting to rip store tags off her rear end. Her hand slapped firmly into mine.

"Anita Stockdale, Patton. Good to meet you. I'm with the kayakers. Thank you for returning the river." I ducked my head, looking for darkness to hide quick tears. In one night, more thanks than decades of trudging in and out of the state capitol. "Ken says you make a first-rate assistant, and he's picky," she said. "If you need more work, look me up when I'm banding birds in the spring or collecting dead bats at wind power sites next fall. Bats bother you?" She fumbled in the front seat of her truck and then extended her hand to Ian. "You must be Ian Glenburn. My card. When you're ready to put information on a map, call me."

"Map?" he croaked.

"Didn't Peter email you? Today? You have a chance to get online yet?" Grants' roof was decorated with electronics and last year's damaged Christmas lights. Ian's surprised face winked on and off in the glow of partially illuminated reindeer. "He's hired me to make you a GIS map. Any ready-to-go data layers I can whip on it before we sit down in person and add stuff only you know about?"

"Can you lift a map from a picture I have on my phone?" asked Ian.

"Send it off to me tonight. Email's on the card."

I imagined three hundred and forty thousand acres of Maine Forest Trust map floating through the air from Canada Falls to Anita's desk, flying high over Vicki's purple parka and scowl. I liked thinking of her waving helpless arms at the sky. It seemed a good omen that migrating geese honked hoarsely overhead.

"Now their wings," Anita whispered. "Wait for it." Streaming black ghosts thumped rhythmically above us, visible only as they winked out stars with feathered silhouettes. She sighed and stepped to the back of her truck, dropping the tailgate. "Fall's too short. I can't suck it up fast enough."

We watched two shapes move across the lawn toward us, holding a dark package away from their legs. Anita dropped her voice. "On the map—Peter said you'd want several hundred square miles around Canada Falls and Carla Monson's holdings, all other land ownerships and boundaries, mapped lynx habitat, and lands identified in the *Recovery Plan for the Eastern Timber Wolf*."

I bent low over her tailgate. "Can you also access maps of Great Nations' latest road closures in this area?"

She rubbed her hands together the way I do for chocolate. "Sounds like fun." She motioned Walt to place the wrapped animal in the back of her truck and thanked him. Both men backed away from the truck and trotted toward the inn, hands held in the air.

Ian patted his pocket, feeling for his notebook. "We've got questions."

She bent, poured a bottle of water over her head, and from her truck pulled a bulging bag of lemon slices. After rubbing lemons on her hands, she combed her fingers through her hair. "No excuse for smelling that rank," she said. "What do you want to know?"

Ian leaned into my headlamp to read from an open page. "One wolf by itself—would it trigger the Endangered Species Act?"

"I don't work for the Fish and Wildlife Service anymore, but technically it could," she said. "The Maine biologists might want more, maybe a breeding population, but there's plenty of statutory language to anticipate the needs and protection requirements of singular dispersing wolves. You know, Canadian individuals that wander in looking to hook up and mate, although that's not likely given the terrain between here and there."

She gathered her wet hair under a bandanna, climbed into her truck, and leaned out her window. "Even if it takes wolves another century to figure out how to cross the Saint Lawrence River, the debate about how to manage them will be vicious. The only thing not vicious is the wolf itself. *Vicious* is us moralizing about animal hunger. A wolf just does what a wolf is supposed to do. Yes, it crosses the line into domestic animals we care about, but not as often as locally manufactured horror stories suggest. Opponents love to orchestrate a few episodes into revenge on the entire species. They post pictures of calves ripped out of cows' bellies and horses' legs that look like spaghetti dripping red sauce.

"Out West I had to investigate those claims, and take it from me, in eight years I only had to shoot a few wolves addicted to domestic dinners. But if I'd been asked to shoot the real culprits, I would have been gunning down coyotes, bears, eagles, and, most certainly, pet dogs. And, hell, I couldn't shoot the weather. Each season Mother Nature slaughtered scores of sheep and cattle, but wolves get all the sexy press." She leaned out the window as she shifted into gear and rolled slowly away. "At least as a species wolves haven't burned the faithful at the stake, dropped nuclear bombs on innocents, or sent millions to the gas chamber."

Ian used his phone's glow to find his way across the parking lot, mumbling loud enough for me to hear, "If the closest we get to wolves is Samuels' skin theater there's no story." Anita's truck lights hadn't cleared the far hill when I saw him open his computer on a deserted porch table and wrap his hands around a coffee mug.

I walked Pock to the river for a drink. Rain-soaked grass crackled with frost. I liked Grants the way it used to be: one cranky phone line easily toppled in storms, mail delivered weekly with limp vegetables, and no Internet, but I also understood Rachael's need to provide technology for guests who insisted on having it all.

"I got to compete to pay the mortgage. I've quarantined them on the back porch no matter how freezed up they get out there," she sighed last August, wiping bread dough on her apron. "The rest of the place is still board games in the dining room and river noise through the window."

Pock leaned hard against his leash as something whooshed from rushes near shore. Fish rose to sip insects from my favorite pool and I felt deprived of the fall hatch. I heard small licking sounds—fish lips slurping like someone sneaking a drink from another's cup. River muck sucked at my boots. I tried to inhale river perfume and exhale the scent of senseless death. The wolf dog's. John Tario's. Shannon's.

Shannon cherished both perfume and river muck. I pulled her picture from my shirt and held her up into the night. There was no lonely when she filled the empty chair by my woodstove. We were the laughter in each other's lives. I didn't expect much more of that. How could laughter make its way past an ache that filled the throat?

Pock jerked his nose from the river, hair up, growls spurting water from his mouth. Gordon Samuels crouched on the riverbank, his teeth in my headlamp's beam. Wolf eyes glowed like tiny candles resisting night. Spread next to him like a fellow watcher was the folded wolf skin, legs fanned out in four directions, muzzle tilted downhill. Pock whined softly and trembled against my back.

"Quite enough for one day, Gordon." I pointed to the skin and pushed Pock into a sitting position. "Put it away. I'm only interested if you've moved on to something sane." My fingers closed over Shannon's picture.

Like a pagan priest he raised both hands and tilted them toward the sky and then the river. "You and your friend Shannon. You feel it. Feel its loss. She *did.* You *do.* My guess? You're humping odd jobs to avoid the futility of what you used to do for work. Nothing worked, did it? Press conferences, reports, editorials, begging legislators?"

No. Not much worked. I agreed with Ian. For someone who looked like a hermit and behaved like a crazy man, Gordon knew way too much. "Go on," I said flatly.

"Let's talk *sane.* Who's in charge of the woods? Some bogus government agency with a comatose mission? Is it sane to say yes to every greedy wingnut who wants to mow down forest and replace it with concrete? Only so much forest, but assholes can mix up concrete forever. *You* can be here to see how it all turns out."

"Going somewhere, Gordon?"

"I'm done. Your turn. I assume all your lost causes made you steel tough. Ready to do battle."

"I already have a therapist."

"Oh, good Christ, I know that. It's Gretchen *this* drama and Gretchen *that* drama."

"You son of a bitch," I said. "Are you stalking me?" Another scary thought slammed in behind that one. "Were you stalking Shannon?"

"No." He calmly rested his chin in his hands. "I found Shannon's graduate thesis online years ago. It's been my bible for fixing up Monson's forest so there's food and cover for all us wild ones. You. You're splattered all over the web, but I've been sniffing out your subtext. You see the soft underbelly of the corporate beast, the hypocrisy contaminating their slimy marketing departments. You don't get heard because you've been tamed and watered down to a pathetic squeak instead of righteous thunder that should fry their asses. You're always handcuffed to some lame-ass committee that's jerking off on consensus bullshit."

Saliva pooled and matted his beard. I retreated a few more steps as he pulled the wolf's head into his lap and rotated the skin inside out, feeling his way up its legs. "The natives carried magic herbs sewn into its coat. Helped them kill more buffalo." Something glinted in his hand. "I have modern magic for you."

"What are you babbling about?"

"The end of compromise. Where we're alike, Ms. Conover. You know. Con? Over? Kindred spirits. We're both done with compromise—only you don't know it yet."

My legs ached and part of my brain was trying to calculate how much sleep I'd need if I got up before dawn to fish. "Get to it, Gordon."

Metal flashed up my headlight beam. "Catch."

I dropped the leash and fumbled in the air. Pock raced for my car.

"A flash drive?" I asked. "Something I have to plug into a computer is your big handoff to save the woods?"

He stood, grinned wickedly, and arranged the cape around him. The wolf's head, mouth open in mock laughter, fell down his back. He scraped his eyes and blew contact lenses into the breeze. "They're your wolves now. You're always whining about how you *own* wildlife. Tag. You're it. I'm gone, so if you have one question—just one—ask it. Don't waste it on the wolves. Hook reporter boy up to my gift."

"Two. I have two questions."

He crossed his wolf arms and wolf legs over his chest. Old black-and-white prints of Geronimo and other last-stand warriors offered up that same grim, determined jawline drawn tight over rigid shoulders and feet anchored to the ground. Gordon was part of some last stand.

I grabbed for a small birch, suddenly dizzy and unsure of my footing on slippery grass. "I want to know about deer. Why are they on the move to Monson's land?

"Last winter shelter in the watershed. Deer know where they need to be." He cackled. "I made Carla Monson's land a sanctuary—seduced deer with uncut hidey-holes, salt licks, and tasty tree limbs piled here and there. And there was coyote target practice to keep my aim sharp and clear the terrain of inferior canines that might mess with my mission."

"Why?"

"You've used up your questions."

"Why, Gordon?"

He bunched the wolf skin under one arm and padded down the bank. I swung my head trying to find him with my headlamp, but his gravel voice rose from the river beyond the dimming light. "The wolf and the deer need each other."

"Shannon Angeles," I called. "Are you involved in her death?"

He waded upriver. Water covered his tracks. The splashing paused, replaced by an echoing answer. "Yes. Hers and more. Many more."

Maybe I imagined what he said next, or maybe like invisible fish and ghost geese he sounded more substantial without form. His voice faded into a congealing mist—warmer river water colliding with cold air.

"Shannon. Without wolves, she would be alive. I made the wolves happen. I am in the wider chain of her death."

Morning darkness isn't as scary as night darkness. A thin, gray film coats the air, suggesting light before it arrives. Maybe there's less harm lurking before dawn. I like to think predators of all species have done their worst and returned to bed. An hour before dawn is also the best time to sneak up on trout, conduct a survey of insect availability, and choose a fly that looks tasty.

An hour before dawn, bleary from the rapid pace of life, I slipped through the Grants' kitchen and thanked the breakfast cook for wrapping steaming blueberry muffins in a paper towel. I was too proud to beg bacon, but I could have downed most of the slippery mountain stacked on the grill.

I checked the kitchen calendar and took a brief inventory of recent events. Wednesday. Day two of my road trip with Ian. Five days since Shannon's death. Four days since Moz intercepted Anderson with a searchlight and warned me about the dangerous endangered species. One day since John Tario's unspeakable end. Four blogs on outdoor economics sent to the *Bangor Weekly*. Attacks by log truck, partridge, and moose. Multiple attempts to dress Ian appropriately for bad weather. Engunn's wall painting depicting wholesale forest plunder on behalf of GNF stockholders. Vicki telling me what I could and could not do. A messy map accumulating pieces of information that might or might not help us find wolves. One tall tale evening I'd never forget.

Wednesday. Ten hours since Gordon vanished upriver.

Eight hours since I'd looked for Ian and his computer on the back porch, flash drive shifting restlessly in my pocket. I'd resisted the urge to wake him, sure we wouldn't sleep after seeing how Gordon "made wolves happen." Sure I wouldn't sleep after he'd admitted he and *his* wolves had somehow killed Shannon. Maybe indirectly, but they'd done it. I was already on to that.

Wednesday. One hour since I'd tiptoed to Ian's room and slipped the flash drive and a note under his door. If I didn't have to look directly at anything "Gordon" for a few more hours, that was fine with me. Something metal plugged into something else metal wouldn't resurrect Shannon.

Minutes after leaving the kitchen, I parked my Subaru near the boat launching ramp and rubbed my berry-stained fingers on fading viburnum leaves. I treated Pock to a brief bathroom break, shoved his disappointed body into the car, and poured him a bowl of food. "Swimming behind the canoe today, buddy," I said. "And I'd mind if you scared the fish. Rest up."

I'd already arranged for one of the cooks to drive us and our canoe to an upriver launch site, and I'd ordered five days of boxed meals to hold us—Ian, hold Ian—for two days. After a night with the Howlers, Ian and I would have an easy paddle downriver toward my waiting car.

Popping a handful of pills and massaging pain from my fingers, I slipped on fingerless mittens and gripped the cork handle of my fly rod. All my cells screamed for a place of water, birds, balsam, and peace. Last night's mist hugged the river, and rafts of geese swam in and out of its filmy edges, honking their way into wake-up calls. Llamas on coyote patrol elegantly tiptoed the pasture edges, sniffing clumps of sheep. Wood smoke wreathed the inn in a dark, warm halo. I crushed a path through blood-red leaves spilled carelessly on impossibly green grass.

Here was everything a north woods traveler might need. Bright welcomes into a steamy kitchen. Quilt-covered sagging beds. Enough hot water to shower every few days in shared bathrooms. Racks of crumpled paperback novels and board games missing parts. Gas and ice, packed lunches, and intelligent conversation—or no conversation at all if someone wanted to sit with a beer and watch the river find Seboomook Lake.

I suspected Wild Pines Resort would destroy Grants Farm Inn as well as this part of the world. A relic of log driving days, if the inn had to compete with paved golf cart trails and the Bogside Bar, I feared for its future.

My destination was a narrow gorge guarded by smooth ledges and a stream still wearing away the rock. I stretched my headlamp band over a thick wool hat with purple earflaps, and, as always, I heard Kate's sneering censure. *Don't ever wear that in public with me or without me.* I liked to mail her snapshots of it on my head in stores and libraries.

I turned to watch the first gray fingers of light touch the barns, pastures, and slouching inn buildings. Turning a circle to make sure I was alone, I stepped between the nearest dark pines.

CHAPTER 25

In the gorge caddis flies poured over the falls' edge before they could hatch off the water. Insects swirled around my feet, tissue-paper wings battered and useless. I tied on a mangled fly that resembled a crippled caddis. If I had to explain fly-fishing to people who'd never waded a stream, I'd say it was three-dimensional, wet chess: moves and countermoves under the water, over the water, and on the water itself—on that thin membrane that divides fish from folks.

I cast upriver into the current. My fake fly floated loosely among the bodies of its real relatives. I jerked the rod tip to twitch my deception into life. The brook trout that swallowed my fly was as cold as a fish can get without being wrapped in the freezer.

Extracting the hook, I faced the brookie upriver and waved it slowly in the current, reviving it to sample other flies on other days. *You tricked me.*

That's what we fishing folks hope to do.

Embarrassing.

You went after the only twitching bug. A good choice.

You won't tell?

No one to tell and no one to listen. And soon, I'll set you free.

Like a competitive swimmer kicking off the pool wall, the trout bucked against my hands and shot into the current, iridescent red spots shimmering over tan boulders as it flashed into shadow. I scrubbed fish slime from my hands, adjusted my armband over an aching arm, and looked for my water bottle. I might have missed the faint outlines of Moz's green uniform camouflaged in cedars if his moccasins hadn't overlapped the ledge above me.

He landed in a soft crouch and touched the black band on my right arm. "Would you like to cast without pain?" he asked.

I passed him my rod.

He pressed it back into my hand. "I will lift your arm."

Moz moved behind me, left hand light at my waist, right hand firm on my right elbow. I knew he'd have to hug me from behind for our arms to cast together. I thought male contact— if it came at all someday—might be scary, but then I hadn't thought about Moz.

"You must be relaxed," he said, "but the lower arm must be straight like the rod." His hand traveled up my arm, smoothing lumpy layers of jacket. "Pretend you have a broken forearm that is now in a splint." His breath blew wisps of hair over my ear. His neck smelled more like the river than the river—scrubbed, earthy, and alive. The pressure of his fingers molding his arm to mine traveled up my bloodstream against my heart, pressing extra beats out of it.

"Where do you want to land the fly?" he asked.

"Behind the egg-shaped rock on the bubble line."

"Feel the stops I will make," he said. He pointed our joined arms and my fly rod toward the river and lifted them abruptly to the sky. Stop. I felt the line load behind me. Pushing my arm forward, he pointed the rod at the corner of my chosen rock. Stop. The line zinged by my ear.

"Wait for it," he whispered, slowly lowering the rod tip. "Follow your line down to the water. Do not lead the line."

Without pain my line uncoiled to its full length. My fly popped the largest bubble like a dart might explode a balloon nailed to a target.

I jumped and spun to face him. "How did we *do* that?"

His night-black hair swung forward, but he couldn't hide a piece of smile. "We gave power to the rod and line."

He made room for me on a bleached tree trunk, and we watched the last caddis emerge as transparent wings that shivered off the stream. My news tumbled out in unfinished sentences: John Tario writhing in Ridge's truck, Calvin Harworth's paying Great Nations' crew for silence and chewing out Anderson for using poison. Anderson withholding 1080 information, leaving the emergency room doctor in the dark. Gordon taunting GNF's men at Grants. Anita Stockdale carting off a poisoned wolf hybrid. Gordon's flash drive. "Oh, and Mike Leavitt's here, but he's hunting wolves, not bear," I said.

Moz pulled a knife from his belt, snapped a branch, and dug the blade into it. His wrist flashed in the growing light as he slashed heartwood into thick shavings that fell over his moccasins. "Please keep what you know about 1080 quiet for now." The branch was chips in less than a minute.

I reached for another branch and propped it by his side. "I can't promise Ian and Peter won't be working up a story, but nothing's clear enough to publish at this point."

"Harworth is from Great Nations' home office?" he asked, running a dusty finger up the blade to clear it.

"Yes, and he was furious about 1080. Is he here for wolves?"

"I assume he is here to manage a situation. My lieutenant said Harworth issued orders to have roads closed." He nudged his pile of shavings toward the stream.

The sun cleared the edge of the gorge, crawled up the rocks, and turned my clothes to sweat. Struggling to exit my parka, my flailing arms slapped Moz. I was trapped in a turtle-in-shell moment, head halfway down my coat, arms dangling. When Moz grabbed my collar and freed me, I reached up and felt my ponytail spurting hair in all directions.

He examined the zipper. "Your coat is sewn shut."

"I sewed up the broken zipper and made a pullover."

He reached for my hands. That his hands smelled like an entire forest was not a surprise. Sent to Moz's home to retrieve skunk traps Ken needed, I'd been nosy, but then I'd been given permission to be nosy.

"Find out how someone who lives rough can show up wearing a uniform that's ready for royalty," Ken said.

There were no clues in Moz's canvass tent, pitched on a wide platform that angled toward a stream—a tent that housed only a hammock hung near a small woodstove and cast iron pans hung on the center pole. His barn was the surprise.

Pencil sketches of leaping, dancing animals crowded the unfinished trim around his windows. I ran my hands over cedar closet doors and willow bookshelves. A birch bark canoe hung from the loft, and stacked in every corner were paddles and trim from ash, cedar, spruce, and wood I couldn't recognize. I found his ironing board and spray starch under a window crammed with shelves of tangled herbs. I closed my eyes and breathed oak's vanilla scent, rubbed shavings into my hands, and then, like it was perfume, dabbed wood dust behind each ear. I knew exactly why Moz smelled more like wood than wood.

Laying the knife on his knee, he squeezed my hands and I felt the ridges of his callouses. "If you find fear—or fear finds you—know that you may come to me," he said. The closest I'd ever come to his hands was handing over my splintered paddle and then getting it back again, red and blue coyotes dancing on its repaired, varnished blade.

I pulled my hands back to my lap. "Ken was sent to find suspicious tracks. Did he?"

"He has produced a map of what he calls wolf-sized tracks—large prints he found north and east of Canada Falls." Moz started carving the stick I'd given him, so I knew we were done with Ken. "Last night I retraced Shannon's route behind Monson's gate."

He unsnapped a pocket and placed a bag of Tootsie Roll–looking chunks in my lap. "Please take this sample to the Mahoneys. They will know what to do."

I dropped it next to my pack. "Looks like dog. You think it's wolf? Where did you find it?"

"Near Shannon's tree." Moz's black brows drew together in a warning as shavings flew into ferns hanging from wet rocks above us. "I have more."

We sat with our thoughts covered by the running stream and the *strip, strip* of his knife biting wood. His brows weren't good news.

"The state police have ruled Shannon's case an accidental death," he said.

That should have been good news, but somehow I knew it wasn't.

"The autopsy?" I asked.

"They found airway obstruction, internal hemorrhaging, and broken bones. Some bruising at the base of the neck." As Moz studied my face, I could almost feel each line and crease present itself for inspection. "I did not expect to disagree," he said.

There it was. Whatever you called it. The elephant in the room. What lies just beneath the surface. Things you don't want to touch with a ten-foot pole. The don't-go-there moment. All that. I shifted further away from him on the log.

"You what? You disagree?"

His knife hung in the air like serious punctuation. "I disagree with the findings. I believe her death was not an accident. I have always believed her death was not an accident."

I rocked to my feet and leaned away from him into the wall of ferns. 'Why would anyone kill Shannon?" Leather creaked as Moz reattached the knife to his belt; then I felt him behind me. "Why would anyone kill Shannon?" I whispered.

"For what she found and for what she knew. The tracks. The wolf," he said.

I wheeled away from the wall. Moz fell back a few steps. "But a tree *fell* on her! You can't just drop a *tree* on someone!" I said.

He pulled a crinkled piece of paper from his pocket. "Did you ever create grave rubbings for a school project? Run charcoal over a headstone so the raised words transferred to the paper?"

Confused, I stared.

"This is a tree rubbing. I used charcoal from an old fire on the trail and ran it back and forth on paper I held over a tree trunk at the scene. What is missing?"

I snatched the paper and squinted.

"Tell me what you see," he said.

"Rippling black marks. Maybe that's bark."

"What else?"

What was I missing?

He pushed. “What else?”

“In the middle there’s a wide, smooth line—like there’s no tree shape behind the paper. A kind of empty spot.”

Moz calmly folded the paper back into his pocket. “I thought you might need proof.”

“Proof?”

“The tree across the clearing had fresh scars, slashes that appear as a smooth, empty strip between the bark impressions. That line tells me the tree was rubbed raw to its heartwood.”

“I don’t get it,” I said.

“Bears scratch trees. Deer and moose leave antler rubs. Beavers chew a slanted groove. Only one animal could leave this sign—an animal that used a rope.”

“I still don’t get it,” I said.

“I believe someone pulled the tree down on Shannon—attached a rope and forced the pine down upon her.”

“How could anyone do that if she was alive? She was alive!” I grabbed more ferns, closed my eyes, and rubbed cold dew across my face. “She was alive under the tree. Her hands clawed the ground. None of this makes any sense!”

For the second time Moz gripped me from behind. His voice was law enforcement low. “If the bruises on the back of her neck came from a blow. If she’d been stunned before the tree fell on her—it makes sense.”

I opened my eyes and walked toward the stream, crushing caddis carcasses under my boots. "You know more than the coroner?" Of course Moz knew more than the coroner. I shivered and—just for practice—thought it. *Shannon. Murdered.*

Moz dropped his voice so low I had to turn at least one ear toward him.

"I did call to ask him about Shannon's neck. He said the bruises were consistent with a fall on rocks. That did not fit what I found. I examined the ground where her body fell, feeling for what my team may have missed. No rocks. Only moss. Soft moss."

"This is insane," I cried. "It's not enough to go on."

He sat on the log and patted a place for me. "Not enough to reopen the investigation, but when added to John Tario's poisoning and Gordon Samuels' taunting Great Nations crew into a wolf hunt, it is sufficient to send you home when you return from the Mahoneys."

I hadn't expected that. Not from Moz. Time for the women to pack up and head back to the fort or compound or wherever it was we gathered with the children, pigs, and goats behind stockade walls. I felt the air snap, as if I'd stepped out of my skin to whack myself on the head. Any shock I felt over the idea of a murdered Shannon evaporated into something hot.

I backed away. "I'm not afraid, Moz."

"I did not say you were afraid."

"You said I could come to you if I found fear or fear found me. I'm not afraid."

"No. Here, now, you are not afraid."

I reached for my pack and wrapped the poop in more plastic. I had people to see and places to go. "Good. We're agreed, so you don't need to rescue me. And apparently, I'm needed to get this to people who might prove this is wolf scat."

Shoving the bag in a pack pocket, I found the crumpled instructions for the tracking collar. "I can't believe I forgot this. It's from Phil Bryan's office." I handed it to Moz. "The strap I saw under Shannon's head looked like this."

He scowled and tucked the flyer into his pocket. "Do you know what this device does?" he asked.

"Shannon found a wolf tracking collar, Moz. Not just tracks. She found a tracking collar!"

He folded his arms across his chest. "Phil Bryan's lynx research uses such devices."

"Phil's not missing any collars," I said. "I checked. Someone must be tracking wolf movements. Maybe right now someone knows where they are. Right? So I can jump you ahead to Great Nations golf resort, OK? I assume *you* know all about Wild Pines. Warden grapevine," I said.

Moz shaded his eyes against the sun. And me.

"What happens if wolves are on or near the project area?" I stepped in front of him. "Don't get all inscrutable on me. I'll tell you. Game over."

Moz stared over my head like a compass locked on a tight bearing. He stalked to the edge of the stream and rinsed his face. I must have missed it jelling into granite until it was too late.

I swayed past him and paced the ledge. "Wild Pines is probably done for if it's official wolf habitat. Condos, golf courses, toilets, sludge, landing strips, mowing down deer yards—all that has to go. What if wolves stop the madness? Don't you see? If we don't find the wolves before Great Nations finds the wolves, they'll kill them. We've got to—"

"Stop." A hard hand grabbed my shirt and forced me down on the ledge. I tried to rise, but Moz planted his moccasins on my hiking boots. "Stop, Patton. Stop." He crouched inches from my face, his mouth rock hard, his cheeks tight with anger.

"Whoever killed Shannon might kill you or anyone who tries to interfere. You must understand. I think you are correct. Wolves may be opportunity but also great danger. Much is at stake. Today you told me Gordon Samuels spent years arranging Monson's woods to feed and shelter deer and beaver so he might feed wolves. Like refugees in a hostile land, wolves need allies. Whoever attached the collar to the wolf may also have much to lose."

I placed my hand over his, giving it a slight push that yielded no territory on my shirt.

Moz's face leaned closer to mine. His breath smelled like he'd eaten wood chips. "Someone is responsible for John Tario's death as well. It may have been carelessness—maybe a deliberate act, but it was connected to wolves, or a wolf. The state lab found traces of

1080 in a thermos no one claims. What would someone do to avoid responsibility for John's death? So much we do not know."

I reached up and used both hands to move one of his fingers. "Moz, let me up. My butt hurts and I feel pinned." He shifted his grip and lifted me from the rock.

I tugged my sleeves into place. "I get it, Moz. Really I do. The wolf is officially now more than the most dangerous endangered species. It was serious enough when it was just an animal people loved or hated. Now wolves are either a multimillion-dollar disaster for Great Nations' resort plans or a serious conservation tool *if* someone figures out how to use them to stop construction. And ... and ... most of all I get that Shannon didn't get it. Not really. Not enough to protect herself from someone who saw her as a threat."

Moz's pocket chirped. He pulled out a phone and frowned. "A disturbance at the inn."

I snatched up my clothes and gear. "We're running out of time. I'm going to Grants. See what's on the flash drive. Then I'm going to paddle your baggie to the Mahoneys." I grabbed my pack. "You coming?"

He'd moved to block the path. "Will you promise to return to Greenwood after that visit?"

I stuffed my pack and considered options. Would Gordon's flash drive help us find wolves? What did the howling Mahoneys know?

Our best wolf finding tool might be Stockdale's map, but how to get back inside Great Nations' gates to use it?

Ian and I needed a gate-crashing strategy. Ken had a float plane and could land us on water, and I knew at least two people who'd loan me a truck once we landed behind the gates. Would we have time to work this strategy? Gordon's poisoning performance was a smart, defensive move if it made Great Nations so cautious it slowed its search. If Ian and I left the woods and went peacefully to town, would GNF feel the heat was off?

It couldn't hurt to say yes. "Yes," I said, shouldering my pack. "I *will* go back to town.

Legs wide, Moz filled the trail. Not an eyebrow or cheek muscle twitched.

I threw up my hands. "Once I leave they're not going to let me in here again. Guaranteed. So what are *you* going to do? You *are* going to do something, aren't you?"

Moz pointed at my rod, leaning against the log we'd used. "I will see you keep your word."

I turned and reached for my rod. "And then?" I asked.

And then Moz was gone.

CHAPTER 26

I almost ran into him crouched on the trail near Grants. "Someone running," he said. Dull thuds echoed up the trail. Fending off branches with his left arm, his laptop gripped under his right arm, Ian looked like a gangly quarterback advancing against impossible odds. He went down over a slippery log, but I saw him lift his laptop as he hit dirt. Moz yanked him to his feet.

"Quick!" Ian shouted. "Almost out of time. You have to see this! Sit! Sit!" He dropped on the log, opened his computer, and fumbled with commands. Keys clicked. "Only minutes. Come on, come on signal!"

Moz and I eased onto the tree, testing its weight. Soggy bark soaked through to my underwear as I reached over to tap Ian's arm. "Why don't we—"

"'No ask' time," he panted.

On the screen a flailing cow moose attacked a clearing, snorting and ripping roots from the ground, stomping small trees into splinters. Then she head-butted the camera. I jerked back and almost lost my balance. She whacked the camera a second time before the scene faded to darkness and laughter. Gordon Samuels' laughter. "Good thing I hung my camera in a wire cage," he said.

"Witness the power of the wolf. It's not even here. Just left its urine, a few bones, and the scent of death. She wants to kill the air it left behind."

"What's going on?" I asked.

"Quiet," barked Ian. "Samuels is taking down the website."

The camera found Gordon's hand, suggestively wiggling a copy of the *Recovery Plan for the Eastern Timber Wolf.* He coughed up a hoarse voice. "Nice of the feds to provide a how-to manual. I have been ordered to document our reintroduction process. I suck at editing this shit, but here goes." The report reappeared, flipped to a page headlined "Wolf Reintroduction Guidelines."

Gordon dropped into a sonorous judicial voice. "Number one. Obtain permits from appropriate agency."

The insolent Gordon returned. "Well, shit, I got permission from my boss and that's good enough. I hate numbered lists so no more of that crap. As if lists mattered to a bunch of kidnapped animals." Clearly we'd get his judge voice for instructions and his Gordon voice for editorial comment.

The judge droned on. "Obtain disease-free wolves from nearest population."

He bellowed with glee. "Well, that's another dumb-ass one. The nearest Quebec wolves are watered down and screwed up with coyote genes. We made an outfitter in Alaska rich for getting us real-deal wolves."

New images tilted violently across the screen. Endless snowfields bobbed outside a cockpit window. Rifles pressed against the shoulders of harnessed men who leaned out open helicopter doors, shouting commands over the relentless *whomp-whomping* of rotor blades.

"Nail that one slipping away."

"Left, Bob! Shoot left!"

"Take her up the hill. Hold it steady." Their guns popped single shots between frantic reloading, and then the pilot hovered over sprawled forms—limp gray shadows dusted with rotor-driven snow.

"Put it down. Put it down. I think we got the male and female you wanted, Maurice. And a few more."

Again, Gordon's hand twisted the federal guidelines into view, but all I really saw was a blinking notice in the corner of the laptop screen. "Site Deactivation Imminent."

"Prescribe manner and season of live trapping," judge Gordon said. I could hear the smile in his voice.

"Not as difficult as we thought it might be. Hire a hunter who's shot wolves from the air. Pay him hundreds of thousands of dollars for a breeding pack. Yearly payments for life to buy his silence. Lure the targets onto snowfields with dead elk. Dart them. Rough, but they made it."

The screen filled with a black nose pressed on a thick metal fence. "Don't hand-feed him. I don't get paid if they aren't delivered wild and crazy," came the drawled voice.

The camera pulled back to reveal a large corral ringed with double fencing and rows of shaggy pines that grew nowhere east of the Rockies. Two gray-brown wolves crouched over a bloody carcass, growling at others who slunk around them at a safe perimeter.

The judge voice droned on. "Provide holding pens in captive area. Examine, ear tag, radio collar, vaccinate."

Ian and I jumped with surprise as Gordon walked into the scene carrying a rifle and a cardboard box. He turned toward the camera, grinned wickedly, and held up a radio collar in one hand, a syringe dart in the other.

"Medic by day. Sniper by night. A good time was had by all." He raised the gun and fired at the nearest wolf. The dart's landing *thwack* was as sharp as a genuine bullet.

"Holy shit," breathed Ian.

The wolf snarling guard over the carcass staggered sideways, dropped his front legs, and tap-danced on rear paws, struggling for balance. Finally, muscles melting to quivering putty, he collapsed and rolled away from the camera.

Ian and I leaned close to squint at the next confused scene. Men wearing headlamps grunted and shoved shapes into the dark. I recognized a mobile dog kennel, two tiers of small doors in the truck bed, a dogsled strapped to the roof. Spotty paint on the truck door advertised Maynard's Dog Sled Mushing Champions.

Waving, uneven light caught two massive aluminum canoes lashed together to create one metal raft. Shrouded figures in black wool hats and dark face paint wheeled a canvas-covered dolly over rocky ground. Swearing, whispering, and lapping water were the only sounds until Gordon resumed his official narration.

"Deliver to release point. Arrange shortest, direct flight," said the judge.

One fading beam caught the backs of bent-over paddlers stroking furiously toward dark water that swallowed the boat's disappearing wake.

"A no-go on the direct flight." Gordon chuckled. "Six days' special delivery to Quebec, our wolf guests motoring in sneaky sled-dog luxury—then paddled to Maine on ancient water routes navigated by people with ancient grievances."

His voice dropped again. "Select appropriate release site."

He sniffed in disdain. "Well, duh. Only Maine has enough territory for an undercover operation. Lots of food. Look at the time. Chop-chop. Final instructions. Build appropriate pens at release site. Hold wolves on site for six months. Feed local wild prey. Allow wolves to leave pens at will."

The next scene was a thick chain-link fence enclosing a clearing where one wolf lapped a stream that came and went through the enclosure. Next to a trailer heaped with dead beavers, two people wearing wolf capes reclined in lawn chairs, raising flutes of champagne toward the pen door as the wary face of one wolf peered through the open pen door.

Inside my chest something leaped and mentally opened the door wider—urged the wolf into the woods. Cheered him on. *Go. Get away. Disappear. We don't have to see you to know you're home.* Home. Shannon would have used that word, too. *Welcome home.*

Gordon returned to the screen wearing his wolf cape and dragging a deer carcass by a rope wound through its antlers. "Consider providing carcasses of wild prey near release site."

He slipped the line through the antlers and stood, stretching and groaning. "Must not touch the offering with too much human scent, must we? Attention! The next image contains graphic material unsuitable for small children and assholes who should know better. I include it because you need good intelligence on the enemy."

Three men wearing bandanas tied over most of their faces and medical gloves on their hands bent over a dead moose calf. I recognized John Tario's voice.

"Christ—hurry up. I don't want to be near this shit," he said. Deep sweat lines pooled around his upper arms.

Using tree limbs, he and his partner widened the slit-open moose stomach. The third man held a small can, dipping a paint brush in and out, spreading glistening, exposed organs with a grainy paste. The screen hiccupped to a later scene—Gordon and the dead moose alone in the clearing. Gordon stacked a mound of brush on the carcass, picked up a red gas can, and sloshed liquid on the pile. He stepped back, tossed a pack of lit matches on the brush, and a whoosh filled the clearing as fire ate the pile and licked the moose.

He tiptoed to the camera and leaned into what must have been the microphone. "Just who the hell do they think they're dealing with?"

Moz shifted on the log. While Ian and I bent over the computer, he'd remained upright. Sitting close enough to feel his rigid arm, I couldn't feel him breathe.

Gordon's voice rasped into what I hoped was his wrap-up moment. "Well, that should do it, my dears. Recent history, now ancient history. I think I slowed the boys a bit this week, but they're a determined lot. Inept, but mission focused. I've left enough food on the ground for a week. Winter is roaming-the-land time. This year's pups are ready to travel. Everyone's restless. Especially Katu. He may strike out on his own any day. Adolescents do that."

He stalked to the camera, cocked his head, and peered at it like a mirror whose reflection was disappointing. "You may ask why I dismantle my cameras. Drop the collars from our furry guests' necks. Remove our website. My employer and I will never breathe uncaged air again if we're sent up for half of the laws we've screwed with, so we'll cover our trail. Our vanishing act is necessary to give our wolves a fresh start. The arrival must be magic. Impossible to trace. Would you have the law capture and return them to—where?"

He clapped his hands, applauding himself. "That's the beauty. They're here. Step up now, Patton and reporter boy. You be trusted with the magic."

He ducked below the camera but popped up again, face so close I could count red rings orbiting through the whites of his eyes. "I sent you some snaps. Now that you are wolf foster parents, you should know them as we have known them."

Gordon clutched the wolf cape around his shoulders and hauled the head and muzzle over his own wild hair. His face melted into gray strands, but his voice grew louder as the screen grew black. "The wolf has no shame as he stalks his prey. I take that lesson with me."

"Crap," cried Ian. "Crap, crap, and double crap!" He slammed his computer shut and bounded off the log.

I couldn't read Moz's expression. It was as dark as the mound of dirt he'd been grinding under his heels.

"Why the gloom?" I asked. "We just had wolves dropped in our laps. A breeding pack. It's just what we need and—"

"And we can't prove it," scowled Ian. "I can't run a story on wolf pictures I could have copied from 'Little Red Riding Hood.' There's no way to prove it! More crazy man stuff."

Moz bent and fingered one of the beads on his moccasins, hair falling over his face. I'd never noticed the animals that ran races in a circle from his toes to his heel. When he straightened and turned to me, his eyes were deep, black pools of sadness. There'd been no time to consider the consequences of a game warden viewing a site

Gordon intended for Ian and for me. I couldn't imagine how many crimes he'd witnessed.

"What are you going to do?" I asked.

Ian clomped off down the path. "Find the friggin' dogs, that's what."

"You," I whispered. "I mean you."

Moz shook his head and followed Ian down the trail.

I found them ducked behind trees that screened them from the inn's driveway. Moz held up his hand and motioned me behind him. The parking lot looked like an ATV convention. Five trucks, each towing a trailer and muddy four-wheeler, surrounded the front porch steps, and a circle of men scuffed their feet as Rachael Kenneth flew at each like a crazed hawk defending her nest. I recognized Mike Leavitt's Santa outline, Ridge's truck, and Sam's lean, twitching silhouette. Only Calvin Harworth had an unbowed head.

"What do you want to chase that woman for?" Rachael yelled. "What's she ever done but call you out for good reason?" Someone must have smirked. A mistake. Rachael reached up and cuffed his head the way a coach might discipline a surly player. "Wipe that off your face. You're on my property."

When Calvin Harworth shook his head, she flew at him. "That's right. I know Grants sits on land we lease from you. I know I should suck up to you. All of us who signed leases are expected to act like we *love* what you do—so *we* can do what *we* do. Well, we don't. Love what *you* do."

Harworth raised both his palms at her. "Mrs. Kenneth. Think carefully before you go on."

If Rachael had been a porcupine, Harworth would have been pin-cushioned with quills. "This is *my* business. You just ate *my* food and you'll take whatever *I* dish out before *I* kick you off."

Moz leaned close to my ear. "Are you packed to travel?"

I pulled Ian closer. "Ian, did you drop your gear at the boat ramp?"

He nodded and aimed his telephoto lens up the driveway.

"We're good to go," I said.

Moz pointed at Ian's computer. "I will leave it in Rachael's office."

I reached for the laptop before Ian could free a hand to grab it. "You won't need it," I said. "And I don't want it."

Moz tucked the computer under his arm. "Soon I will walk up the hill and entice the gentlemen around the back of the inn. I will tell them I drove you further upriver to a canoe launch site, and they will make a fast exit trying to catch you. Go to your car and canoe. Load what is needed and paddle upstream against the current. You know where to leave the river?"

I patted my pocket and the map he'd drawn for me at Antler Camp. "Collapsed beaver dam under a split white pine." I nudged Ian. "Can I look at Rachael through that?"

Ian passed his camera to me. “That is one steaming woman,” he said.

I raised the heavy lens to watch her. She was a stocky woman who stood lower than the shirt collars of the men she taunted. Her crab-apple-sized cheeks were actually apple red. High white sneakers cut into black pants stretched to seam limits, and she camouflaged her outsized breasts under men’s shirts grateful guests gave her. I smiled to see her wearing my shirt, where tiny salamanders leaped off faded letters that said “May the Forest Be With You.”

She reached up and poked Harworth’s stomach. I figured it must have been a rock-hard stomach to poke. “Go ahead. Kick me off, Mr. Great Nations Forest. You know what my accountant told me yesterday? We can’t afford to run the place another year anyway. We’re going to lose it, and today I can put the blame where it belongs because I’ve worked my ass off for eighteen years only to see it all destroyed by you idiots here.”

She jabbed more parts of Harworth’s anatomy to punctuate her lecture. “You cut the workforce by half. The half that used to stay and eat here. Then you cut it again. Now big machines do it all. It’s the secret you don’t want governors who *love* you to figure out. You make money, not jobs. You strut all over Augusta as if you were our economic savior, and no one has the balls to speak up and say that’s ancient history.”

She pounced on another victim—Anderson Barter, who'd been keeping a low profile behind Harworth. "I see you, Barter. You told your bosses to hike the gate fees. Getting ready for rich condo folk? My business is real Mainers. Now a night out to dinner here costs a carload of people the price of another dinner just to get here. More lost customers. Maybe you can give my checkbook mouth-to-mouth resuscitation, Mr. Big-Shot Ambulance Man."

Sam leaned forward eagerly. "I won't waste time on you, Sam. You're just plain creepy. There's no limit to your spying and snooping. My kids are under orders to never tell you where they're going unless it's home."

She moved on Ridge. "For eight years, you've cut every deer yard in the valley. My hunters are off 70 percent. Hunters are *my* mortgage payment." She turned away and then wheeled back on him. "Shame on you, Ridge. Your daddy was the best hunting guide we had."

Grinning, Mike Leavitt dropped awkwardly onto one knee, hands pressed together mocking her for mercy. "Get up, Mike, you spineless excuse for a sportsman," she said. He struggled to push himself out of the dirt. "Shame on you for blaming coyotes for the crash of the deer herd ... getting your members hot and bothered to kill what's only a distraction. You damn well know it's Mr. Great Nations and his buddies cutting what deer need that's done the deed. If you told the truth all their bribes would disappear. What would you do without your cushy paid-for out-of-state hunting trips to Idaho?"

Suddenly she bent over panting, hands gripping her knees. Her red face filled the narrow circle of the lens pressed to my eye until Anderson reached for her.

"When I'm dead, Barter. That's when you can touch me," she said. Limping away, she wiped her eyes with one hand and stuck her middle finger in the air with the other.

Bravo, Rachael Kenneth, I cheered silently. *Standing ovation for you from out here in the woods.*

When the men turned in our direction, I lowered the lens and realized they were watching Moz stride toward them. I raised the camera one final time and found them staring at his moccasins. He started to run, jogging past them as if they weren't there, Ian's computer under one arm, his radio held against his ear. They trailed him like expectant puppies.

CHAPTER 27

There's nothing like paddling upriver against current to fire muscles into serious effort. I was off the seat and, kneeling low to improve the canoe's balance, my kneecaps burned as if I'd knelt on a hot stove. In the bow enduring my curt commands, Ian suffered through a crash course on paddling, so I didn't expect him to notice the scenery.

To our left, Great Nations' land stretched away in a jumble of raspberry bushes with no shade in sight, and scraggly alders at the river's edge looked like useless fringe on a mostly shaved dog. On our right was the real forest: Monson's land was a wall of dense spruce and fir lit by flashes of white birch. Between strokes I heard woodpeckers hammer insects out of dead trees.

Pock ran in and out of the river, working too hard to keep us in sight, but I needed a lighter boat to fight the current. Ducks drying their wings on rocks in the middle of the river tilted their heads in disbelief as we struggled north. When clouds dropped to tree level and spit sleet, I lied and told Ian a freak storm signaled warmer weather.

He bent over his paddle and grunted. "As if."

I balanced my fingerless mittens on my paddle and slid them forward to Ian so he could snatch them. I wasn't ready to tell him about Moz's visit to the downed tree and not ready to say *murder* out loud when it looked like wolves could take a human life without sinking their teeth into anyone. Was Shannon's death supposed to protect the pack or protect its enemies? Were wolves worth more dead or alive? Questions made my head ache more than my knees, and that was a good thing so I kept them going.

Had Gordon Samuels left the field of battle or just retreated to a high-tech control room? Where was Great Nations' posse and where was Moz? I felt smug about white trucks aimlessly wandering dirt roads, and then a real smile cracked my cold cheeks. For months, Kate had tried to make me smile into her camera, but here it was in the middle of sleet, headed the wrong way up a river—a wide smile for the arms that fished around me as if we were one person.

I hadn't felt much passion since I'd moved to Antler Camp, not for food, clothes, domestic comfort, and certainly not the promise of domestic bliss or even a one-night stand. But suddenly, feeling the memory of Moz's arms, buried parts of my chest thought there might be more to life than rough, line-dried shirts.

I saw the lightning-burnt tree and collapsed beaver dam that signaled our turn into a side stream. The sleet stopped, the sky reappeared, and Ian used his new skills to paddle us onto a beach, where Pock thumped his head against the canoe, insisting we take him in.

Ian whipped his paddle around in the air. "Beats the gym. I'm going to create something that does that, a machine that won't let you wimp out. Won't let you stop until you blow your limits."

That would be childbirth, I thought. I pulled a crumpled bag from my parka and shared the last peanut butter sandwiches, tossing one to Pock, who was dripping water over our gear bags.

Ian tried to peel bread from filling. "How old is this?"

"It's perfect and it's lunchtime. After a few days, there's complete gourmet fusion between ingredients and we're there."

The stream had little current, so I released Ian from paddling and stroked us upstream, replaying my morning with Moz. Ian bent over his notebook. "I'm with Moz," he said. "Let's go back to town—work with Stockdale on a map that gets us somewhere." Without looking up, he waved one arm in an air circle. "We're nowhere, and I'll use an animal so you can relate. This is a wild goose chase."

I stared at the back of his head and told him what I wanted—but not out loud. *I want wolves, Ian. I want them alive. Alive, they might take down Anderson Barter and Great Nations' resort. And somehow, in some way I can't imagine but can hope for, wolves may also take down Shannon's killer and if she were here, all that would make her happy. Especially the wolves.*

Ian was captive in my boat, so I let him have it. "Seriously, Mr. Cub Reporter? You can't investigate what got dropped in your lap?

Someone hired Gordon Samuels to import wolves from another country, paddle them to Maine—in canoes, for God's sake—and hide them until they produced pups. Gordon and his boss Monson are on the hook for pursuing, shooting, wounding, trapping, transporting, and harassing an endangered species. You know, all the illegal activities you read off to me yesterday? They had a truckload of beavers—that's got to be illegal—and then there's Mike Leavitt's Maine law against importing wolves without legislative approval. Lucky you. Now it's a true crime story, too."

I shoved us off a rock with a bit too much force and Ian clutched at his notebook. "Except for Gordon, Monson, and Moz, we might be the only people who actually know wolves are here, so your scoop is still in play," I said. "Gordon says he left food to hold the pack for a while, *and* I think his Grants' performance might slow GNF's search or make them change tactics, *and* I'm guessing Moz wouldn't send us toward the howling folks if they weren't essential."

The leaping animals Moz had painted on my paddle flashed in and out of the river as if pursued. He'd seen enough wildlife crimes on Ian's computer to earn him a slew of citations if he wanted to catch the perpetrators, but he also worked for an agency that could order him to hunt down wolves as if they'd violated some law. What would he do—or not do?

It was a relief to find wildlife reliably at work on fall errands. Like blue-gray sculptures in an overgrown garden, migrating herons froze on shoelace-thin legs, flapping wide wings and dipping around the next bend to land in front of the canoe. The birds and I enacted discovery and escape each time I entered a new pool.

Rafts of ducks gathering for fall flight paddled in and out of marsh grass, more interested in foraging for minnows than fleeing our approach. In a sheltered cove, a doe froze, muzzle draped over her drinking fawn, twitching ears flicked in our direction. In one bound the pair vanished, tails raised in white warning. We glided by a circle of mashed grass where Ian didn't need to know a bear had napped after a meal of berries.

In the bow, Ian scribbled intently. "What's Moz doing about all this?" he asked.

"I don't know. He might be after whoever killed Shannon. Or John Tario. Or he's searching for wolves or he's on duty somewhere."

"Perfect. You didn't ask him?"

"It wouldn't have done any good. I saw his face."

I had no idea if we'd find the Mahoneys behind the towering dam that hung over the stream ahead. Generations of undisturbed beavers had woven brush and mud into a vertical three-story wall where weeds and goldenrod sprouted from tidy dirt terraces. On either side bulrushes advertised a swamp, good information we'd be wading muck if we tried to portage around the wall.

Confident he'd seen enough of Engunn's rope work to winch our loaded canoe over the dam, Ian pointed to my coiled rope and suggested a Z-drag. It wasn't until we'd rigged the ropes, hauled our canoe to the top, and lowered it into the pond that I really believed Moz. My rope had carved smooth, deep scars into the tree we'd used.

I almost hated to wreck Ian's jovial mood when he looked better, more relaxed. A two-day beard shadowed his cheeks, and undisciplined hair and mismatched clothing masked his city origins. Swinging my rope in a circle, he even grinned at me. "Yup. That's a slick trick."

I reached for the rope and enunciated each word as if we had a bad phone connection. "Ian, Moz thinks Shannon was murdered. That someone. Pulled. A. Tree. Down. On. Her." I spread my fingers over the smooth gashes we'd carved into a sturdy birch and explained Moz's theory. "Take my word for it," I said. "These marks are just what Moz copied for me—proof someone used a rope system to move a heavy load. Proof someone could have pulled a tree down on someone who couldn't move."

"Well, now that's a bigger story," said Ian, his face growing red as he realized he was a more of a news hound than a compassionate fellow traveler. "Sorry," he mumbled. "But you gotta feel a little better there's a reason your friend didn't screw up. You know ..."

I picked up a loose sheet of birch bark and whipped it like a Frisbee out over the pond, surprised at how far my anger sent fragile white paper. "Let it go for now," I snapped, climbing into the canoe.

"Could be Engunn Stein," Ian said.

"... or any number of construction workers, guides, or loggers who know the Z-drag trick," I said. "Just get in and drop it."

On the top of the dam Pock rolled ecstatically in something beaver, but before I could whistle he was on his feet, hair rising off his shoulders in a stiff warning. "Whatever it is, I don't see it," I said. "Come, boy. Yip, yip. Zip, zip."

The howl that rolled across the pond flattened him in fear, but he was instantly up and launched into the air, scrabbling legs aimed at the canoe. "Paddle in the water!" I yelled, stabbing my blade into the pond. "Paddle in the water, Ian. Don't lean on the boat."

As Pock landed, half in and half out of the boat, Ian buried his blade in the pond, and we struggled to keep the canoe upright.

CHAPTER 28

A musical voice floated across the water. "Are you with Shannon?" Ian and I looked at each other. He shrugged. Again, we heard the lilting call. "Are you with Shannon Angeles?"

"Shannon's friends," I called. "And friends of Robert Atkins. Friends of Moz."

"Approach, please."

"There," murmured Ian. At the far end of the pond I saw two figures extend their arms wide and hold them open, waiting. The Mahoneys.

"They're good," whispered Ian over his shoulder. "Sounded like a wolf to me."

"Pock thought so," I said.

Wind on our backs, we needed only a few strokes to bump against the makeshift driftwood dock where the couple smiled peacefully at us.

"Out of the canoe," I hissed. "Some kind of welcoming ceremony."

I'd never seen two people who looked so like each other. Not twins—more like littermates bred for species purity. Both wore waist-long hair in slick brown braids that fell over their shoulders as they leaned to grab our hands, and four brown eyes twinkled behind rimless glasses. Their complexions were unearthly—indoor pale, but each had bright spots of color sweeping rounded cheekbones. Wordless twitters and clicks came from generous mouths filled with wire retainers.

Humming, they pulled us into a circle. Pock thumped his tail and watched us from his canoe refuge. Hands joined with theirs, I had a strange sensation of being examined and decided it came from their habit of nodding to each other even though we had yet to speak. Green tie-dyed lab coats completed an exotic wardrobe that ended in white mukluks. Their rounded, soft bodies seemed to sway rather than stand, and they talked as one person.

"You complete the circle," they harmonized. "We are Bart and Marta. The Mahoneys. Friends of Shannon, who are you?"

I wasn't sure what to say. While we waited in silence I took in their campsite. Perched on a rock outcrop overlooking a brook that tumbled into the pond, it had a commanding view of the beaver dam, the stream below it, and, in the distance, the North Branch of the Penobscot River—our wet highway into their world. A spotting scope capable of seeing Ian's and my upriver struggle was tilted toward the beaver dam. Two upside-down canoes with stumps for chairs made a dining room, and Coleman stoves bubbled on a rough worktable of stained planks. Metal crates were stacked under the table near the same type of solar panels and batteries I'd seen at Canada Falls.

Two large tents with dark rain tarps were clustered under mottled green and brown netting strung in overhead trees, where a pulley system yanked the nets into position. From the air, the Mahoneys were almost invisible.

On a clothesline strung between the tents, bright orange clothing dried in the sun, each printed with graphics that screamed "Don't Shoot." Shirts, bandanas, vests, ball caps, and—while I didn't want to stroll over and examine them closely—orange "Don't Shoot" underwear in men's and women's shapes flapped in the breeze.

"I hope you won't think this nosy," I began, "but your clothing is bright orange and your campsite well hidden."

Bart smiled. "We only wear Carla Monson's apparel when we are ..."

Marta finished, "... when we are paddling or hiking. It needed drying after the storm."

I made a mental note to separate them so Ian and I could converse with one complete Mahoney at a time, and another mental note to ask about Carla Monson's "apparel."

"May we sit?" I asked.

They waved us toward the stumps.

The same nodding, clicking communications passed between them. "Your dog," they said.

"I am sorry," I said. I grabbed Pock's collar and forced him down at my feet. "It's rude to appear in your solitude without an invitation but doubly rude to bring a dog. He might disturb your work."

They sat.

"Good."

"You see ..."

"... it's just that ..."

"... that wolves are attracted to domestic dogs as easy food."

"We wouldn't want ..."

"... want anything to happen to such a lovely and happy creature."

I leashed Pock to my belt.

Marta rose and drifted toward the stove. "Goodness. I've lost my manners," she cooed. "I brewed tea while enjoying your progress over the dam and your dog's antics."

Bart arranged carved wooden mugs on the nearest stump. "Your canine is a close wolf cousin, so close it would be almost impossible—almost—to tell it from *Canis lupus* DNA. Of course, his antics imitate wolf behavior. Rolling on odiferous objects is a communication tool to bring you scent information about intruders or a maybe a recent kill, but of course you would need to smell the message to understand it, and we've lost that ability."

I hoped Ian could silently suffer Bart's wildlife lecture, but I heard the boy's teeth grinding, and he impatiently rocked his stump seat against gravel under it.

Marta poured boiling water and leaves into our cups. "And wolves raise the hair on their backs to appear larger and more threatening when they are upset. Your dog's display wouldn't save him from determined wolves, but it might ..."

"... might dissuade a less determined attacker," Bart said.

More silence. I laid Shannon's worn picture on the canoe between us, my fingers lingering on the paper as if it were warm skin.

Marta finally broke long minutes of silence. "Something has happened, hasn't it?" She also traced fingers over Shannon's smile. "We were expecting her, but something has happened."

Bart looked off into the distance, eyes suddenly moist. I bent and rubbed Pock. My throat felt like sandpaper.

Ian looked around the campsite. "The sticker on your crate?" he asked.

"Oh my, yes," said Marta. "Our mission as well, 'to cherish the life of the world.' You must know that is a Margaret Mead expression as well as the epitaph on her grave."

Ian cleared his throat and nodded at me to pick up the story.

"Maybe Shannon would want that epitaph, too," I said.

The couple exhaled long sighs, sad air that sounded like leaking balloons. "Shushshannonshushshannonshushshannon." A breeze from the pond tapped hanging pots and pans into wind chimes. Marta wiped tears with the edge of her lab coat.

I explained how I'd found Shannon's body, and the Mahoneys sighed again. Ian introduced us as the *Bangor Weekly*'s team investigating the wolf's return, and, omitting any mention of a

Canadian journey, he selectively shared Gordon's website information. At news of the pups, Bart and Marta grasped each other's hands, their retainers clicking in glee. I could almost feel Mahoney cells chanting, *Yes! Yes!*

Ian shifted restlessly on his stump. "The game warden who investigated believes Shannon's death was not an accident. He believes she was murdered."

The couple nodded as if they'd been expecting bad news.

"You know Moz?" asked Ian.

Together they hummed a breathy, vibrating Zen note on his name. "Mooozzzz. Our favorite guest."

Except for the bubbling pots and the stream's splash, the camp fell silent.

Bart cleared his throat. "What do you want from us?" A hard request coming from people who, moments before, appeared to float a few inches off the ledge in transcendence. I folded my hands and examined crusty paddling blisters.

"We'd like your help proving wolves are here," said Ian.

Eyebrows quivering, Marta turned to her husband. "Shannon said not to trust anyone."

Ian sipped his drink. "Why did she trust you?"

Her smile returned. "We are research scientists. Shannon was a forest scientist."

"Then how did you get named the Howlers?" he asked. It felt like a slippery moment.

Both Mahoneys leaned their heads back into musical laughter—his deep and rolling, hers airy and musical.

Bart wiped his eyes. "One month ago, in the August full moon, we invited friends and colleagues to join us for wolf culture camping. We called it our Howl Weekend."

Marta's eyes gleamed. "Wolf legends at the fire. Howling at the moon. We were not ..."

"... were not ... are not ... ready to reveal scientific proof of the wolf in Maine, but ..."

"... but we wanted to celebrate our early efforts."

"Unfortunately ..."

"Unfortunately a reporter visiting our office read the Howl Weekend invitation on a friend's desk and turned it into a mocking story."

"At first ..."

"... at first we were outraged but then ..."

"... but then we saw the advantage."

I thought about asking one of them a direct question, maybe a strategy to get one complete answer from one person.

"Marta," I said, "Would *you* explain the advantage?"

Marta crossed her arms and looked toward the pond. "Shannon said not to trust anyone."

Bart squeezed her shoulder. "Moz asked us to cooperate if we were needed."

Ian threw his arms up in frustration and glared at me. "Your warden. Everywhere and nowhere. Like jungle drums."

"The advantage of being laughed at as the Howlers," said Bart, "is that no one takes us seriously. We can work in peace." He wrapped towels over his hands and lifted the pressure cooker from the stove. "Now that you say Mr. Samuels has destroyed his website, our evidence may be useful."

Marta hummed. "Moz often sends earth gifts. Did he give you something?"

Ian and I trotted to the canoe, where he retrieved Phil's bone, his pack, and his pungent T-shirt and climbed back into the camp. I tottered back up the incline with my gear bags, tent, both sleeping bags, and the Tootsie Roll-looking feces. I wasn't sure what I had to contribute to dinner, but I'd work that out when the time came. Miserably leashed to my belt, Pock tried to tug me back to the pond.

"Show and tell," muttered Ian.

The Mahoneys had arranged, bones, plaster casts of tracks, and laptop computers wired to impressive batteries on planks spread across their canoes. Courteous hosts, they waved hands at our stump seats and placed mugs of raisins and walnuts within reach. Ian rolled his stump next to mine and placed Phil's bone on the edge of the canoe table. Bart dumped the bag of scat into a large glass jar, moistened it with boiling water, and snapped on medical gloves.

"They're cooking shit!" Ian whispered.

Bart held up the jar and swirled its separating contents. "Looks promising. Bone chips, splinters, self-groomed hair."

"Oh, and—Bart, look. There's partially digested hooves in the hair," added Marta cheerfully. "That slick bit of hair speeds it all down the colon."

"The location of the sample?" they asked.

"On Carla Monson's land. Near Shannon's body," I replied.

Instantly sober, they felt for each other's hands and bowed their heads. We waited through more reverent silence.

"Each of us will speak to different areas of discovery if that's all right with you," Marta said.

We nodded hopefully and chewed our raisins.

"And we will move quickly, as we want to be ready to howl." She chuckled when we stopped chewing and a few raisins fell out of Ian's mouth. "Oh, yes. We've been speaking with them. After the searching, they came to us."

CHAPTER 29

Marta lifted Phil's bone, set it aside, and smiled at Ian. "I imagine Phil Bryan sent that? Sometimes the forest has more magic than the phone in your pocket, Ian." She held up two halves of another bone. "Two leg bones. Two different carnivores. Ours is also a moose femur but snapped in two. It was our first clue."

Waving both halves in the air, she explained they'd found the bones scattered on a beach north of Grants. Fresh from a sales trip to demonstrate mobile equipment vets could use to x-ray large animals in the field or barn, Bart and Marta recognized opportunity. They set up their machines in Grants dining room, x-rayed the bones, and rotated the two scanned images into place as one bone.

Marta angled her computer toward us. Scanned pictures of bone halves floated across the screen to fit into each other. No stress fractures or cracks radiated from the break line. With a click she reversed the process, severing the bone in a quick explosive move. Bent toward the screen, I had to remember to breathe. On ski patrol, I'd loaded dozens of skiers into ambulances, vaguely aware of brute forces that snapped their legs. Strange that a computer perched on a canoe should teach me more about brute force than a season of sobbing skiers.

"Of course there was only one question." Marta's grin was wide and proud. "What could snap a moose femur like a cheap chopstick? That night we logged on to locate an animal capable of such strength. How amazing when life hands you a desire. We've been devotees of restoring wolves since our Madison college days when we studied their migrations into Wisconsin." She lifted the severed femur and gaily clicked its two halves together. "We found that the wolf's bite exerts fifteen hundred pounds of pressure per square inch, and that's with forty-two teeth. The canines or fangs impale the prey and bring it down. The incisors are knives tearing hide from the carcass. Molars snapped this bone."

When she jerked the bones apart, tiny white chips rained into our walnuts. "Coyotes gnaw into bones." She held up Phil's intact femur. "See the splintering and damage along its edge? If we scanned this, we'd find their teeth marks gnawing toward marrow, but the bone would be whole. With its miraculous molars, only the wolf can snap a moose leg in two."

Bart lifted four ghost-white plaster disks. "Our next experience brought us closer to proof." The setting sun shadowed small pad marks in each casted print. Light and shadow animated the footprints' depressions—like wolves walking on air. Bart padded the casts across the table as he talked.

In June, the couple returned, seeking more proof than one bone. They hiked riverbanks, drove rutted roads, and bushwhacked through swamps, but found only poison ivy. As they packed their truck to return to their jobs, a “wild-looking man” sitting on Grants’ porch suggested they visit two North Branch beaver dams.

I was so sure Gordon Samuels was their “wild man” I didn’t need to look at Ian for confirmation. Of course the wild man made sure they found fresh tracks in soft mud—inches larger than coyote tracks, and by that time they’d seen hundreds of coyote tracks. “We took pictures, we made plaster casts, and we measured intergroup spacing between front and rear feet.” Pulling a cloth measuring tape from his pocket, Bart arranged the tracks, two large in front, two smaller behind. “This is the usual separation zone between coyotes’ front and hind feet. About sixteen inches.”

He moved the rear prints back another ten inches and whistled. “I still can’t absorb it. The spread between front and rear paws is almost twenty-seven inches. Between these sets of paws trots a much longer body than a coyote. A much larger animal. We were, however, rank amateurs so we sought out the state’s experts.”

In Augusta, state biologists dismissed their casts as large dog tracks, possibly wild and feral, but a large dog. Bart scowled. “They told us the Saint Lawrence River, inhospitable farm lands, and wolf trapping in southern Canada were barriers wolves couldn’t overcome.”

Bart and Marta bent with laughter, nudging each other like two birds on one companionable twig. “They were so wrong!”

Ian raised his head and cleared his throat. I nudged him into silence and smiled politely. *Yes, they made it. With help. Most of it illegal, but they made it.*

Bart sobered and studied the darkening sky. "I won't bore you with the science." And then he did. He punched a computer key, unleashing a parade of graphs. "Together we have made progress analyzing the protein code that allows us to identify wolf DNA as distinct from coyote DNA. Up until now this isoelectric focusing process has not helped us separate the species. IEF's been a dead end."

Ian raised a studious hand. Without calling on him Bart explained IEF. I'm always more interested in what's buzzing, chewing, mating, tunneling, or nest building. Chained to my leg, Pock was alert to an otter family grooming each other on flat rocks where a small brook met the pond. The pile of slick animals looked more like a writhing mound of brown pythons, but energetic squeaks gave them away as socializing otters.

Somehow I absorbed enough of the IEF discussion to understand that different hair molecules could be separated by different electric charges. Bart squeezed gel onto a laboratory slide, but the process reminded me of the pitfalls of contraceptive jelly. I hoped he'd get to a place I could understand.

"Previously there was no way to differentiate various kinds of wild canid hair. Now hair samples may be conclusively identified." He turned off the Coleman stove and lifted the disinfected can of scat from the pressure cooker. "I have no doubt that when I am finished with them, the samples Moz collected will prove Shannon tracked wolves not coyotes."

Ian jumped off his stump. "The isoprotein stuff is the strongest proof we've got. Someone could claim you faked the broken bone and tracks. With hair proteins nailed down, more people could find more wolf doo-doo and prove it. Really prove it!"

He reached for his phone, but I grabbed his hand. Bart pulled wires from computers and whisked them into crates while Marta wrapped casts and bones in white sheets and scurried into her tent. Ian sagged on his stump.

Bart straightened and stretched. "And finally we can offer you the opportunity to talk with wolves tonight. I am sorry that our isoelectric process is not ready for publication. Until the patent is secure, it remains our proprietary research, and this is to protect the wolves as much as our discovery. We have been told many times there are no state funds to study or manage wolves. We felt—and Shannon agreed—that without proper protections to separate wolves from intense human interest, we should not go public with our discoveries at this time."

I had a flash of crackling radios in white trucks searching logging roads and a clear image of Sam hunched in his shack relaying search coordinates as Harworth spit commands into his phone. Going public had to be better than a private death squad.

"You said 'our discoveries.' What did Shannon discover?" Ian asked.

"Perhaps it was our mistake," Bart said, "to involve Shannon. After our Augusta disappointment, we shared our evidence. Her sober reaction was unexpected. She said the closed roads were a dangerous development. Great Nations either suspected or knew. She planned what she called a 'grid search' on closed roads. We assume that's how she found the den. Empty, but she said it was recently occupied."

Sitting upright from my slouch on the stump, I knocked nuts and raisins to the ground, where Pock lapped them up in wet, happy bursts of appreciation. Den? Den? I thought Shannon and I had no unshared secrets, and here was another secret that might have killed her.

Ian slid his notebook from his pocket and scribbled furiously. "When did she find the den?"

"Seven days ago," Bart said. "She left a message on our satellite phone asking us to remain in camp for one more weekend. The connection wasn't clear. She talked about the den, a porcupine—we didn't understand that part. She was very worried about a shooting competition that would flood the region with hunters. She was adamant about it being an extremely unsafe time."

Marta must have missed our coming alive at the mention of a den because she emerged from her tent with a basketball-sized jar of peanut butter. "We've had no time to prepare dinner. Everyone must be starved."

Ian scowled at the jar, his lips so low they almost touched his chin.

"Now, young man. You haven't lived until you've had Bart's crepes," said Marta.

I thought it more likely Ian planned an after-dark downriver escape to find the den site and made a mental note to hide the paddles. Bart floated leftover pancakes in frying pans of butter and swirled berries, nuts, peanut butter, and cinnamon into each, making folded crepes with a flick of his knife. Marta, Bart, and Ian swallowed each as it left the pan, but my fingers could only grip the edge of my plate.

Ian reached over and forked my cold dinner into his mouth, but I didn't care. Shannon found the den? Had a plan and I didn't know? I felt like I didn't have a friend in the world, and that was a hunger crepes couldn't cure.

Collecting plates, Marta tapped a fork on the front of Ian's butter-soaked shirt.

"Remember to wash off grease before getting into your tent this evening," she said. "The washing station's on the way to the latrine."

Ian frowned a "now what?" glare in my direction. We hadn't discussed camp toilets. Bart, who didn't miss much, led him away for a latrine lesson. I pressed warm, soapy hands to my cheeks and reached for more in the dishwater. "How did you first meet Shannon?"

Marta strained dirty water through ancient pantyhose, tossing bits of food into the fire pit. "She arrived as a guest of a guest on our howling weekend. Shannon was a hit. There was nothing she didn't know about plants and animals. And laugh? We were sore for days. Simply hung over with fun."

I rubbed my face with wet hands, mixing warm soap and warm tears, but Marta pulled my fingers into a clean orange bandanna.

"Dear," Marta said, leaning close, "don't be hard on her. We swore her to secrecy and she swore us to secrecy. We discussed you—her best friend who knows powerful people—and decided you might feel compelled to do something. We just weren't ready for that step. I hate to think we came between you. She was in quite a funk about the closed roads and her transfer. That's when she said not to trust anyone."

I grabbed Marta's arms and sat her on a stump facing me. In the spreading pond darkness, a beaver slapped its tail angrily, letting us know we weren't welcome.

"Marta. The situation is different. We—the wolves—may not have much time."

She returned the pressure of my arms with a slight squeeze. "Yes, it's all changed. Death does that."

"Did Shannon say anything that might help us know who killed her?"

She inhaled a long, slow breath. "She did tell us she felt followed without being followed."

"That doesn't make sense."

"It seems that wherever she went, someone from her company knew her destination, even when she lied at the gate. Well, we all lie to Sam."

"Was she followed?"

Marta's braid danced from shoulder to shoulder as she shook her head. "She said no. She pulled off onto side roads. She doubled back. She even borrowed a truck. You know. In case her vehicle had a bug in it. Nothing was visible, but she still felt followed."

Ian's voice rose over my shoulder. "When did this start?"

"I'm thinking late summer," I said, surprised I knew the answer. "Probably soon after GNF started closing roads. Sometimes she was jumpy. She swept her headlamp over parking lots and locked her car. She blamed it on work and feeling like she was being eased out without anyone confronting her. Her recommendations were ignored. Road closings happened without her advice."

Head pressing on my hands and hands pressing on my knees, I scanned six months of memories and saw it. Mired in my own drama, I'd failed Shannon. She'd been busy devising strategies to get me over what she called "Divorce Falls," but I should have seen her anger. No. I should have felt it.

"Right," she'd snarled in a late-night Scrabble game, slapping two letters on my word *tray* to make her word *betray*. "Right. I'm sure the corporate clowns in Boise know what Maine looks like on the ground."

"You doing anything controversial?" I'd asked. She shrugged and ripped the edges of the game board stuffing it into its box. I revised my approach. "Anything GNF might have viewed as overstepping?"

She closed her eyes and sighed. "Recommendations. I got all excited about being asked to comment on a few things. I forgot to keep my head low."

"What did you say with your head up?" I asked.

She looked at the camp ceiling as if counting spiders and listed her transgressions. "One. I called for more mature trees to stand uncut. Two. I suggested harvesting restrictions on some easement lands. Well, damn it to hell, it was supposed to be a conservation easement. Even Vicki Brinkman warned me not to go there. She had no problems with GNF's take-all-the-trees approach. What's up with that? And three. Anderson asked me to write up a memo to prove lynx protections would devastate our operations—a memo Great Nations' lawyers could use in Washington as they attacked what they liked to call the 'endangered species train wreck.'"

She'd rolled her eyes and mumbled into her wine glass. "I also said lynx wouldn't harm forestry operations."

I giggled.

"Come on," Shannon cried. "Lynx eat snowshoe hare and snowshoe hare like regrowing trees. This was a species even Great Nations could work with."

I'd hugged her and poured more wine. "Well, I'd have fired you on the spot," I joked.

She'd forced a tight smile. "I've been trying to figure out why they haven't—yet."

I lifted my head off my knees and found I'd been talking out loud to a rapt audience. The Mahoneys were on the edge of their stumps, and Ian's jaw muscles twitched. "Of course they didn't fire her," he said. "They wanted her where they could watch her."

He rubbed his hands and looked hungrily at the cold fire pit, his breath visible in the dark shadows crawling up the stream toward our ledge. I dropped my head back into my hands. Like the mist off the river where he'd disappeared, Gordon's words rose up to haunt me. *Without wolves, she would be alive.*

Bart reached for a shaggy orange coat draped over tent ropes and helped Marta into it.

"It's time," whispered the Mahoneys, stepping off the ledge.

CHAPTER 30

Cleared of brush, the trail was as wide as Bart's shoulders, and our headlamps caught white paint winking from tree trunks to mark the route. Ahead of me three shadows scrambled up the steep slope and slipped behind a black wall of balsam fir. By the time Pock and I reached the top of the ridge, the river mirrored the last few silver shards of daylight.

Leaving Pock tied to the canoe seemed like a bad idea, and taking him to a wolf howling session wasn't a good idea either, but at least I could squeeze his mouth shut if anything happened. Bart and Marta, fingers on lips, tapped their dark heads. I killed my light. They sat on a split log balanced on piles of crumbling rock. Bart's hair glowed green over raised binoculars—night vision binoculars.

"Who goes first?" whispered Ian, bending over them.

Marta frowned and sighed, disappointed in our inability to communicate nonverbally. She made room for me to sit, motioned Pock down with a firm raised hand, and spoke into her jacket collar, barely breathing her words. "Sometimes we howl for a response, but we're getting better at joyful listening."

Bart swept his binoculars up and down the river. “Dear, we’ve only experienced three sessions.” He lowered the glasses and peered into the gloom. “You say Mr. Samuels had seven wolves?”

I whispered into the dark. “Two adults he called the breeding male and female. Two more wolves captured with them, from last year’s litter and pups born in Maine this spring.”

Marta stretched her hands toward the river. “So close—over the river.”

Bart handed the binoculars to Ian. “Please scan down the stream below the beaver dam and out over the river to the far shore.”

A wide green smile illuminated Ian’s face as he fitted the night vision binoculars to his eyes. “Black trees. A green deer drinking by the dam. Holy shit. I can see its tongue.”

Marta sniffed. “I’m not sure I want to see a green wolf.”

In the dark, I separated Mahoneys by attitude. Marta gushed. Bart was practical.

“We’ve been analyzing their vocalizations.”

“... the rousing group howl that precedes the hunt ...”

“... the short, high-pitched intermittent howls directed from one location. Perhaps the waiting young.”

“... and finally at dawn, a final, joyous symphony of wild voices.”

Ian ducked a swooping bat and lowered the binoculars. “Dawn? We’re up here at dawn?”

Pock’s ears flicked up and his body was instantly rigid. “Stop,” I breathed, hair stiffening as if unseen hands pressed a cold compress on my neck. “Stop talking.” A ghostly echo bounced around the pond below us.

“A-rah-ooooo.”

Ian swung the binoculars left and right trying to follow the sound.

“A-rah-ooooo.” Three wild notes rolled up, shivered, and retraced themselves into a low wail.

Bart grabbed the glasses. “From across the river. Have yet to see them.”

I tightened my grip on Pock’s leash, pulling his head on my thigh so I could reach his muzzle. As more wolf voices joined the chorus, three or four-note wails melted into an urgent, ragged hymn—an ancient a cappella of raw harmonies flung into the air. Deep, lingering notes twisted my chest into a pain that felt like desire. For less than a minute, overlapping howls sounded like an army of invading wolves. I forgot to breathe and then, suddenly—silence.

I wanted a world that held its breath—a world of wolf music, bat shadows, tall trees, and a river that was a dark gash in the night. I thought the wolf might knit us all together in an unwounded land, but that was too much to hope for. Pock’s teeth chattered and Ian had an opinion.

“Gordon’s wrong. That’s gotta be more than seven wolves,” he muttered.

"Wolf magic," sighed Marta. "Each selects a unique howling pitch that swells the chorus. Some think it a strategy to intimidate other packs."

"There," cried Bart. "On the beach. One wolf wading into the river." By the time the binoculars reached me, the wolf was on our side of the river—a canine head of matted green hair, alert forward ears, short blunt muzzle gliding over black water. Wide ripples surged off his chest, faint evidence of brute power gaining upriver traction against current. He could have been wearing an outboard motor strapped to his backside.

Marta clapped her hands. "Our first wolf sighting. Isn't he—or she—magnificent?" She paused. "Where is he going, I wonder."

Bart lowered the glasses. "Disappeared. Shook himself. Rolled in the sand and trotted upriver."

"Katu. The restless one," said Ian, starting to pace the small clearing. "Gordon said one was ready to head out. Maybe it's Katu."

"Again. What are Gordon's wolf names?" Marta asked.

I sat on the log and scratched Pock's quivering ears. "I'm not sure I'm saying them right, but Mekong and Hmong are the male and female. Katu and Alak are yearlings."

"What strange names for our wolves," Marta said.

Bart sat cross-legged on the ground, binoculars resting in his lap. "Mekong. A river in Laos and Vietnam. Hmong—a Laotian hill tribe that fought the communists for us. We Americans left the Hmong to die when we pulled out, although we never admitted we'd moved the Vietnam war into Laos, where we made it the most bombed country on earth. Surviving vets call it the secret war. Samuels is the right age for that."

"Why, Bart, how do you know all that?" Marta asked.

"The janitor in the lab who never speaks? The one we let sleep in the boiler room?"

"Oh my," she said.

He aimed the binoculars back toward the river. "He speaks to me."

Still pacing, Ian threw up his arms. "What do we do now?"

"Do?" asked Marta.

"What happens next?"

"We wait."

"For more howling?"

"Why of course."

"Isn't it all the same?"

Marta's voice sounded like a smile. "Not when you make space to hear nuance."

Bart was gruff. "Return to camp. I put up your tent."

Ian kicked a few rocks off the ridge toward the river. "I know I'm a pain in the ass, but while we're waiting for wolves to do their wolf thing, others are not waiting. They're tracking or plotting or arming themselves. For sure they're not having a church service."

Marta squeezed his shoulder. “Let us have tonight. Tomorrow we’ll organize. I don’t know what Shannon planned to do, but we’ll have to pick up where she left off.”

Bart grunted, “Go ahead. You’ll be safe enough.”

“And stuff your greasy clothes into the larger crate,” Marta said. “Wearing them is an invitation to nocturnal food seekers. You might rub some stream gravel on your arms and splash a rinse before you crawl in.”

Ian growled. “Forgive me if I don’t purify my body with ice water. I need sleep.”

He adjusted my spare headlamp and turned the blinding beam on me. “Tomorrow we’ll go over suspects. I need to be upfront with you even if it sounds crass. I think Shannon was killed because she knew too much about the wolves, and she intended to go public with what she knew. She’s part of the wolf story now. Part of the story I intend to tell.”

After his light faded, Bart, Marta, and I settled on the ground with our backs against the raised log. No one spoke. I split a chocolate bar into three pieces. Pock laid his head in Marta’s lap, and she stroked it absentmindedly. Occasionally Bart raised his binoculars and peered into the darkness.

I woke thinking the binoculars’ green halo was Antler Camp’s nightlight. It took me a few moments to realize I was cramped, cold, dirty, and far from home.

"Just a few yips," Marta said, nudging me. "Maybe only restless pups. No celebration tonight."

At camp, she led me to their equipment tent, where she'd spread my sleeping bag and Pock's foam pad between crates and more jars of peanut butter. "Of course you don't want to share a tent with the lad," she said. "If you're like me, you spend half the night mopping up."

How did she know I dreaded a night sweating next to Ian? She undressed and slid her folded clothes into a crate, her cream-colored buttocks shining like twin moons. Naked, she pulled a wool hat over her hair and blew out the sputtering candles. "If women could connect batteries to hot flashes, we might light the earth. Don't forget to leave clothes in with mine. It's bear time, too. Hunters running dogs make the bruins a touch crazy." She waved a few fingers at me and zipped her tent.

It wasn't a bear—the soft feet in the dirt near my head. I pushed my hat off my face and lifted one loose tent flap. A wolf sat staring at me. Through threads of mist, coal-black markings like heavy mascara outlined his eyes and the tips of his ears. The rest of the visible wolf was a mouth curved like a smile. I thought of *Alice in Wonderland*'s Cheshire Cat appearing one body part at a time, smile first. The wolf I saw was only ears, nose, eyes, and mouth—anything black that parted ground-hugging fog.

I smiled because the wolf seemed to be smiling at me, its mouth at a quizzical angle. Yellow-gold eyes calmly examined my face, holding my eyes. I'd never had an animal initiate a penetrating stare with see-everything eyes. Pock, sleeping heavily on my feet, brought me happy dog faces, not a searching interview. The wolf's fur glowed with approaching daylight, patches of tan-white hair electrifying the black bristles that fluffed his cheeks. I'd seen dead wolf hair on Gordon. On this animal, every hair breathed. Colors vibrated toward each other as he panted.

I thought his proportions made him male, but I couldn't be sure. He was twice the size of any coyote that dodged my headlights. Two bold swipes of black hair crossed under his chin and plunged toward his legs. He looked like a bandit, cartridge belts slung over his chest, swaggering attitude on display. He yawned, curling black lips to show off incisors. My chance to see—close-up—three-inch fangs that could drop a moose, nose first. With liquid ease, he slid saucer-sized front paws to the ground, leaned his head on them, and considered me from a level perspective. Stretched before my tent he was almost as long as my five-and-half-feet of tall.

I was tempted to squeeze my eyes shut—not look at the bad headed my way—but nothing felt wrong with our lying on the ground separated by a sliver of mosquito netting.

He cocked his head. *Where is the creature that leaves us meat?*

I exhaled. *He escaped before he could be caught and caged. Why did you leave the pack?*

To follow something humming in my blood.

Stray too far from this land and you will be hunted.

I am hunting now. Is the animal I smell near you available for food?

Pock whimpered in his sleep. With a silent snarl the wolf found its feet, hunched, and froze. All my pores pricked open with sweat. A scrap of nylon tent was nothing. Slowly the wolf backed toward Ian's tent. Long, stiff guard hairs rose off his back like miniature knives. His ears flicked forward. His nose lifted slightly. Eyes on me, he scratched at a lumpy pile of gear—Ian's offending garments, Phil's femur, and a squashed toothbrush.

The wolf nuzzled Ian's T-shirt and wagged his tail. Wagged his tail! Dropping one shoulder he angled into a familiar position. One shoulder made contact, and then the wolf wiggled rippling fur through the clothing pile and over the bone. Closing his eyes in ecstasy he slithered his other shoulder through the shirt. I could relate to the pleasure, but would have chosen a bubble bath over anything Ian.

Legs stiff, tail held straight behind him, the wolf patrolled the campsite as if he owned it, licking surfaces, gnawing on the edge of a stump, pushing his nose against crate latches. I felt like a prisoner behind my mesh screen, until I remembered the caged wolves on Gordon's website. This wolf must be familiar with humans behind walls. I hoped that when one of us appeared without a wall—if Ridge or Sam or Mike appeared without a wall—he'd be wild enough to run. He dropped from the canoe tables to the edge of

Ian's tent. My tent. Casually he raised one leg and splashed a stream of urine on it.

"Is it raining?" Ian's groggy voice froze the wolf. Dipping his head toward me, eyes seeking mine with a gold-flecked warning, he barked—once. Maybe a dare not to fight him for the femur he grabbed. Clearing the canoes and ledge in one blurred leap, he disappeared.

CHAPTER 31

Excited twittering spilled from the Mahoneys' tent. Of course, they'd watched the entire wolf performance. Still in his sleeping bag, Ian lowered his tent zipper, shook drops from his hand, and gawked at the disturbed dirt. He reached into the clothing pile and tore through his jeans' pockets. Holding Shannon's rumpled chart, he spread shaking fingers wide over Katu's prints. When he'd stolen her chart from my bookshelves, I hoped he'd left Shannon's notebook where I'd hidden it under *Where the Wild Things Are*. In the dark of our tent, nerved up by night noises, my friend and I often growled its famous lines. *This time, Shannon, the wild thing had no terrible roars or terrible teeth ... no terrible eyes or terrible claws—and you would have loved him.*

We assembled at the fire pit. "I think he was too magnificent to discuss," Marta said softly, her long hair sliding over an orange vest. "I don't want to ruin it by talking about it."

In silence, we ate Bart's freshly-caught brook trout fried with limp apples from my food bag. Ian sulked on a stump and tossed pebbles at Pock, who, tethered to my canoe, was far from anything that smelled like wolf. The pond's beavers and otters were silent, too. Katu must have poked his nose into every tunnel and marked his territory on every muddy stick.

Bart rummaged through a crate and lifted out a tattered brochure. "You should expect a Great Nations welcoming committee. Here's something to distract them."

"Oh, come on," Ian moaned. "Are we really going on with the dumb-ass cover story?"

"It's still a good defensive posture," I said. "To go after us, someone would have to tangle with Peter and the press. What have you got, Bart?"

"Proof you interviewed us—a Wildlife Fund newsletter with our address. He folded over a page. "This month the fund discusses fresh water fishing state by state. Here's Maine. Impressive. In excess of two hundred million dollars."

Ian asked about coffee, but Marta patted his hand and fairly bounced on her stump. "I hate to think about animals like we've put them to work, but it happens. I always had a thing for wolves and one summer I worked at the International Wolf Center way up in Minnesota. That was ages before I found you, Bart, but even back then everyone knew it was a wild creature brought that tiny town millions and put half of those people to work."

"Enough," Ian said, spreading our rumpled map over the nearest canoe. "Let's get back to what matters. Shannon found the den. Real proof. That's what I need."

"What *we* need," Bart corrected. He popped the latch on a crate and assembled his portable lab. "We'll be on our way tomorrow. If the feces Moz sent us test positive for wolf DNA, Friday night I will send the results to a colleague in the Interior Department."

Ian kicked at the dirt. "You have poop, not a pack."

"Interior's Fish and Wildlife scientists will envy the diagnostic process we've discovered. If we attract their respect, we might attract their help."

We arranged a Saturday night phone call to compare our efforts. Ian wanted to find Anita, produce a map, and get back inside GNF's gates, so he was flinging our bags into the canoe, careful to handle my soggy tent by his fingertips. He was smartly dressed in boots, wind pants, and fleece jacket, pockets bulging with *my* mittens. His sunglasses had returned to a jaunty angle on his forehead. People eager to get out of the woods like to look spiffy and accomplished on the last day of their trip. Pock lay in the sun, belly in the air, legs and paws limp with breakfast satisfaction.

On our way to the canoe, Marta slipped her folded vest under my arm and whispered, "When Gordon bequeathed you his flash drive, you were anointed, my dear. Perhaps acceptance is the next step in your journey."

I smiled. *All right, Marta, but maybe not so cosmic.* Gordon Samuels was a smart man. Crazy was cover—veneer. He'd researched Ian and Shannon, hacked into my emails to analyze my refugee life, and planned each wolf maneuver down to the last deer carcass. Disappeared, he could no longer direct his campaign, but he could bury some land mines. He'd aimed me at the wolves' future, but I had no idea what kind of ammunition he thought he'd loaded up. I found Shannon's folded picture in my pocket and ran my chilled fingers over its wrinkled edges. I assumed Gordon's first choice had been Shannon.

Despite cheerful Mahoney hugs and promises to support our search, the canoe felt heavier as we paddled the pond toward the beaver dam. It could have been Marta's vest on my back or the apples and cheese she wrapped for lunch, but that added only a few pounds. On our map, the Mahoneys' black lines marking their finds were significant but weightless. As we lowered the canoe down the beaver dam into the stream below, I decided it was Ian's blacker-than-black mood.

"What good is it if Bart cooks up the shit as wolf DNA and calls some federal agency? Bureaucrats in a D.C. office might do a few backflips. Whoopee. Just get me out of here so I can find Stockdale and get a map that gets me close. I can do the rest."

I saw I wasn't included and that sounded about right. I wanted the collar thief and knew I couldn't ask Ken to burn all his bridges and fly me behind enemy lines to find it. I almost prayed Moz's mysterious sense of timing would put him on Grants' beach so I could ask him for help, but I was probably going to be going it alone—except for Pock.

As we left the meandering stream, the river grabbed our canoe in faster water.

"You don't have to paddle much. The downstream current will catch us and I'll steer," I said. "If you want to root around in your gear, I'll pull into slow water so you can slide your rear to the floor."

"Then pull over," said Ian.

I angled the canoe into slack water behind a house-sized rock in the river. Ian straddled Pock on the canoe floor and assembled his workstation: phone, notebook, pencils propped in thwarts, and—a Marta gift—hot coffee in a battered travel mug.

Inhaling the scrubbed smell of the rock, I remembered Marta's parting advice. She'd laughed her wind-chime laugh and plunged my hands into breakfast dishwater. "I always volunteer for dishes in cold weather. Don't forget the woman behind the man. Carla Monson and her money made a wolf miracle. Find her. Ask for help."

"How did you end up on her land?" I asked.

"I'll share our Carla history while I pack the kitchen," she said. Newly hired to a veterinary biotech firm and new to Maine, Bart and Marta had looked around for wolf territory to explore. They were dismayed to find wolves hunted in Canada and hotly disputed in Maine. After they saw a letter-writing campaign blasting Carla Monson for closing her land to harvesting and hunting, the

Mahoneys figured she might own an attractive refuge—*if* Canadian wolves ventured south.

They wrote Monson asking for a campsite. A year later she sent them a map and permission to camp at the pond if they agreed to remain on the east shore of the river. Their first night Carla paddled up the pond, set up her tent, and handed them a lease to five acres. In return, she asked Bart and Marta to test her clothing in a rugged location.

"That night as we howled, she sat in the dark with tears. Of course, we later learned she'd researched us down to the moles on Bart's butt. I think she let us in because we had Wisconsin wolf training and she wanted sympathetic eyes inside her refuge."

"Is her money from a clothing business?" I asked, stacking wooden bowls that were already well oiled from years of peanut butter.

"Heavens no," said Marta. "Carla was worth millions when she was born. Her 'Don't Shoot' line is revenge and philanthropy. Ten years ago, a hunter killed Carla's aunt as she chopped wood at the edge of her yard. Cynthia Vanderlin had two children in diapers. It was November. Almost dark." Marta waved her wet hands in the air. "She was wearing white mittens and the hunter sited his rifle on those mittens. You know, a deer waves its white tail when startled. The court found him innocent of all charges. Manslaughter. Reckless discharge of firearms. Innocent. Editorials and letters blaming Cynthia for wearing white in hunting season burned Carla toward justice and, I believe ... her own brand of revenge. She instructed her attorneys to buy one hundred thousand acres and post it off-limits to everything and everyone. Except her."

"And the orange wardrobe?"

Marta dried her hands on an orange bandanna looped around her neck. "A trust fund for Cynthia's children."

Carrying an armload of wood Bart had heaped on him, Ian stalked through the camp kitchen. "If she's rich, why not give the kids cash?"

Marta shook her head. "She wants people to understand Cynthia's tragedy. Look inside my vest, Patton. My hands are soapy."

I found the label at the bottom of the zipper. *All proceeds from Don't Shoot flow to the Vanderlin White Mitten Murder Fund and a non-violent future for Cynthia's children.*

"Not subtle," I said.

Marta tucked stray hairs under her hat. "No. Our Carla is not subtle. Right away we found the clothing enraged gun rights people, hunters, and rural folks who serve hunters. Carla was thrilled. The fund makes most of its money in other countries where young people wear 'Don't Shoot' on their heads, backs, legs, and feet as they walk their beliefs into the street. It's very in-your-face and exactly what Carla hoped to do."

CHAPTER 32

The wind found us when weighty-looking clouds muscled the sun into hiding and the river's banks spread wide into bushy lakeshore. Marta's orange vest, feathered and warm, felt like Marta's departing hug. "I need help paddling now, Ian," I called. "We're in the lake and swells are coming at us."

He crammed a smeared chart into his dry bag. "Suspects," he said.

I scanned the far shore for a red dot that could be my parked car. Like angry wet fists, choppy waves pummeled the canoe. Anticipating a bumpy ride, Pock wormed his head under our dripping bags. "Ian, up on your seat," I said. "Easy. Easy. Don't lean on the side of the boat. Just paddle."

A canoe is a fairly stable craft unless someone leans on it. On summer days in Boothbay, my brother and I had played a game we called coffin. Standing on the edges of our canoe, we bounced until it capsized, and my mother shrieked as the canoe rolled and offered its bottom to the sky—a coffin lid closing over her children. In the dark we breathed the captured air bubble and laughed at her terror.

"Throw the dog out again," Ian said.

"The lake's too rough, and when we get to the car I want to move fast—toss the gear and Pock in the car and have you flip the canoe on the roof. We'll pick up your computer and then leave by a different gate where Sam won't expect us."

We were too busy bailing water and paddling to notice the welcome committee lounging in the trees behind the boat launch beach. I smelled cigarettes as soon as the canoe ground into sand. On three ATVs, riders reclined their backs against the controls, ball caps over faces, feet propped on rear luggage carriers. White pyramids of butts littered the dirt. No one moved.

I tossed Ian my keys. "Take my dog, please, and put him in the car." Pock was already whining by the Subaru door as Ian backed up the beach, eyes on our welcome party.

"Don't shoot," rolled a deep voice. Sniggering seeped from under the other hats, and boots slowly uncrossed. Ridge sat up, grinned at me like he'd never been angry, and lifted a tiny camera, pointed at my vest, and snapped pictures. "Don't shoot," he chuckled. "Proof. What we've guessed for years. You're as *anti* as they come. Anti-hunter, anti-gun, anti-cutting—anti-us."

Sam unrolled from his ATV and hacked tobacco into the driveway. I tried not to register surprise when Engunn Stein stood and thrust his hands in his pockets. As I glared at him, tendons flexed up and down his bare arms, but he didn't look away.

"So, Engunn. Is posse membership part of the easement deal?" I pulled a bag from under my seat and tossed it on the beach. "Let's unload, Ian," I called, but he slammed the car door and tried to lounge casually on it.

Sam spit more tobacco at my car tires. "Need help?"

"No, Sam. I'm good. You just wait it out over there with Ridge," I said. "We'll be on our way in no time."

Sam aimed a lean, shaking finger at me. "We'll be on you all the way to the gate. Maybe hand you over to the deputy after that."

"I'm not sure how to warn you away from Great Nations' business," Ridge drawled. "While you've been lost, we've been thinking about it."

Ian was back on point—standing just as stiff and angry as his first Ridge encounter—fists clenched, legs straight, shoulders raised and rigid. Like ground lightning, testosterone sparked sideways around the clearing.

"Didn't *our* boss get in touch with *your* boss?" I asked. "We've been doing what we said we'd do. *Bangor Weekly* articles? Interviews?"

"You were supposed to tell us where you'd be," Sam sputtered.

"Sam, I'm surprised at you." I laughed. "I thought you always knew the whereabouts of every *body* on your side of the gate."

I'd just pulled the plug on scary, electric air. All eyes dropped to the ground and lips tightened into hard lines.

"Ridge," I called, "am I being ejected because you just don't like me?"

That brought another wide grin. "It's more your politics, Conover. We don't like your politics. When you're not after my paycheck with some regulatory bullshit, I think you're kind of spunky. Personally, I like women who aren't afraid of much."

I looked at Engunn, who had turned a bright tomato red, so either his hatred of Vicki and Shannon showed up quickly around talk of fearless women, or some other memory sent blood vertical where he couldn't hide it. Balancing in the canoe, I heaved another bag onto the beach.

Ridge scraped my bag off the sand and handed it to Ian, who collected it with one surly finger. "There's been a Boise home office decision to end our policy admitting all comers inside our gates. We'll refuse unfriendly people and weed out distractions." He lifted his hat for a small second and then yanked it more firmly over his forehead. "Congrats. You made the distraction list."

Great Nations couldn't close the gates forever. The Twenty Mile Road had a long history as a public right-of-way, but lawsuits are slow solutions. By the time the law returned our access, wolves could be bleached skeletons.

Out of sight a truck downshifted on the dirt road beyond the boat launch. A truck that howled and brayed—a truck full of hounds. Pock charged back and forth in the Subaru, splashing saliva on the windows as the men on shore spun around to face a mob of dogs flying up the driveway. I'm sure no paws hit the dirt until the dogs landed on the beach, growling muzzles thrust into my canoe, frenzied eyes locked on me.

I dug my paddle into the sand and pushed back toward the lake. Outside the cove's protected shallows, wind-whipped waves crawled up the canoe's backside and crashed over my back, but I was too busy keeping the canoe afloat to bail incoming water. Capsizing was seconds away—sooner, I thought, watching faster dogs swimming over the backs of slower dogs. I slapped two attackers away from my paddling side but missed the massive hound hooking one paw over the edge behind me.

Ian's faint voice came late. "Behind you! Dog on the side."

Raising my paddle to swing it like a club, I leaned toward the dog and added my weight to his thrashing. His claws were wedged into a narrow slit in the side rail, dog eyes white with pain. When it happens, it happens quickly—the slam sideways into water followed by slow motion as the sky disappears behind the graceful arc of an overturning canoe, the coffin lid closing off sky.

Under the overturned canoe everything was black water and panic, but I wasn't panicking. I breathed the air bubble while the trapped dog panicked. Each time he thumped against me or the overturned boat, he yelped and flailed with more effort and less breath. His claws tore my pants and long underwear, and ice water and pain rushed in to cramp my leg. I had only seconds before hands and feet lost feeling.

Marta's down vest was a drowning machine. Its soggy bulk pulled me toward the bottom of the lake until I grabbed the edge of the canoe floating above me and kicked the dog away in the dark. His teeth snapped for my boots and missed. I unzipped the vest and stuffed it up under a thwart, feeling my headlamp out of a pocket in the dark. I could have ducked under the boat, popped to the surface, and left the flailing dog, but I am a hopeless lover of all dogs. Even bad dogs.

With light and my legs under his belly for support, my dog inmate turned a whimpering, hopeful face toward me. I whispered hopeful words in return. "Hungry? Biscuit? Steak? Bacon?" I planned to pull him down under the canoe, hoping he'd thank me when we surfaced away from the boat. Debris floated around his collar. I yanked it free and found the sleeve of my missing jacket, Maine Guide patches glowing green and red in the wobbly light. Someone had cut my jacket and attached my fresh and motivating scent to the dogs' collars. Someone had sent a pack to hunt me down.

Full-body shivers vibrated my limbs into uncontrollable spasms, but I was too cold for fear. I jerked the dog's head underwater, pulled him down with me, and kicked away from the canoe. Clutching my ripped jacket sleeve, I coughed and flailed toward shore. Ian and Ridge waded out to grab me. We tangled in a soggy heap on the beach.

"Are you OK?" Ian yelled. My ears felt like cold glass about to shatter. I whimpered and squirmed away from him.

Ridge struggled to his knees, pulled me upright against his chest, and rubbed my back. "For shit's sake, numbnuts, she's too cold to talk." He snatched Ian's wool hat and mashed it on my head. "Find her some dry clothes."

Ridge smelled like motor oil and cigarettes. He tasted like sand. Looking over his shoulder, my eyes focused and my breath eased into watery hiccups. The dogs were gone. Engunn was gone. Sam was gone. Ian frantically emptied my duffle bag on the car's hood as Mike Leavitt lumbered down the driveway shaking his head. Mike Leavitt? At first I couldn't place him, but up the road I heard a truck start and dogs bark a furious chorus in their cages. Ian tossed Mike a pile of my clothes and bent back into the car. Anger thawed my voice.

"Stop!" I screamed at Mike. "Get away from my car. Don't touch my stuff." I leaned on Ridge.

"Easy, Conover," Ridge whispered.

"Are you in it too?" I asked, shoving my face inches from his. I spit snot and water but he only leaned closer.

"No."

"Did you steal my coat?"

"No."

"Did you know about the dogs?"

Ridge frowned at Mike. "No."

Mike scowled at Ian. "No camera," he hissed.

Ian adjusted his long lens and aimed it at Mike. "*Bangor Weekly*, Mr. Leavitt. Smile."

Mike lumbered toward me, arms outstretched, my jeans and sweater dangling from wide, furry hands. He'd reorganized his face into a smile, a smile I recognized from legislative hearings he'd won and I'd lost. "Now, Patton, this is a sorry state of affairs that I hope has nothing to do with our friendship."

"Cut the crap, Mike. *Your* guide. *Your* dogs. I don't remember asking Santa for a pack of crazed hounds."

I staggered upright, grabbed my clothes, and threw them on the ground. "Explain this," I cried. I slapped Mike's beard with my wet, shredded sleeve. "Parts of my jacket tied on a dog. A dog set on my scent. No accident, Mike. What's the message, Mike? It's a message, right? Back off? Give up? Disappear?"

Mike pulled a toothpick from his pocket and slanted it between his teeth. "I have no idea what you're blithering about, Conover." At least he'd dropped the cozy first-name thing. "My guide let his dogs out to do their business before we headed home. Your dog must have set them off. They hate pets."

I coughed up more snot and bent double as my stomach twisted into violent cramps. I needed warm tea, warm food, warm clothes.

Mike spit the toothpick on the ground. "But since we're on the topic, I think it would be a good time for you to give up. For years I've watched you waste your time pushing up against what you can't change, so it's high time something shocked some sense into you. A cold swim should do it." He turned and leaned uphill away from the beach. "Give up. *You* won't be finding anything behind these gates."

The message was clear. Either there'd be nothing to find behind the gates—wolves gone—or I wouldn't be coming back to find them. When I tried to run, my legs knocked together and I collapsed at Mike's feet. Through torn pants, I could feel gravel shred my skin, but I was too cold for pain. Above me all I could see was the curve of Mike's round belly and his straining fly zipper. I heard Ian and Ridge start up the hill, but I waved them away.

Hands on knees, Mike bent jovially into my hacking fit. "I'm not a bad man, Patton. Under my leadership, game populations have exploded. I've secured our sporting heritage when it was headed into the toilet. And yes ..." He leaned as low as he could without toppling over and rolling downhill. "Yes, I *am* more powerful than governors. The whole spineless, dithering flock of them."

He lifted a limp strand of hair from my cheek. I thought about slapping his hand but couldn't raise one of mine to do it. I rolled on my side and squinted at the lake through tears, sure I'd never been so dirty or cold or low before.

Mike panted at me. "Know when you're licked, Patton. Nothing gets to live in the woods unless we say so."

So, Mike, does that include my friend? The lake seemed to swirl over my head in blue circles. I've never fainted before but Ian has a picture to prove that I did.

CHAPTER 33

After Ridge and Ian tied my canoe to the roof rack, I stripped next to the car behind a dog blanket Ian held in the air, shivering violently as I layered sweaters onto cold, purple flesh. Ridge dropped my dry sleeping bag on my lap and slammed the car door.

"I am sorry about John Tario," I said, "but I'd like to know who poisoned him."

"Goddamn accident it was."

"We both know that's not likely," I said. "If I tell you what I know, will you answer one question? Give me a straight answer?"

"Depends."

"No 'depends,' Ridge. Trading information." His nod was almost invisible.

"I know that 1080 probably caused John's death—very likely it was the same poison you and John brushed into a baby moose." Behind his dusty beard his cheeks drained white. He rammed his fists into his pockets and narrowed his eyes into guarded slits, but he didn't bolt.

"My turn," I said, tucking the sleeping bag around my shoulders. I had to grit my teeth against the shivering. "Who was the first person to get inside Monson's gate? The first person at Shannon's body after I called it in?"

"Why?"

I wanted to speak truthfully but give him nothing to take back to Harworth. "She was my friend. I left so quickly after I found her. I think I was in shock. Now I want to know about her rescue."

Ridge shifted weight from one steel-toed boot to another. "Monson gave Sam permission to use the gate key he holds for game wardens. He went ahead and set up lights to help them out."

Sam. Sketchy Sam. When he dragged the collar away from Shannon's cheek, did his fingers come away smeared with her blood? Did he even know what the collar could do? Had he passed it on? If the wardens investigating Shannon's death didn't have it, Sam was on the other side of the law.

Ridge slapped the car's roof, a "get going" command as he stalked toward the trees and climbed onto his ATV. He roared past us, his face a grimace framed in fumes. Ian also drove too fast, finding every hole in the road. I opened the window and lifted layers of the down bag over my head until just my nose was free. I slowly inhaled air infused with what I couldn't have. I wondered if dogs could do it better...imagine a tempting world from just a trace of scent. It was worth a try.

At first even the road smelled good. It's too bad mud has a reputation as wet dirt because it's more than dirt. It's something before birth, before consciousness, before language, and inhaling it made my heart slow against my ribs.

Then there was a rush of balsam pine so powerful it tasted like strong tea. When I was young, I cut green branches, wove them into small houses, crawled in, and pretended to survive wild weather. Freed from the car, I was pretty sure mud and balsam would cure everything that ached, but Pock leaned over my seat and licked my wet hair, reminding me I was a passenger and not in charge.

"That was gutsy," Ian said. "Going after Leavitt when you were down for the count."

I pressed a bandana to my oozing knee and dug out road grit with a nail file.

"So Sam's probably got the collar," Ian said. "Does he know what he's got?"

I leaned my head against the window and squeezed gravel into my fist until I knew I'd have to dig it out of my hand as well as my knee. *Thanks for the grit, Mike. Never again going down on my knees before you or the rest of the Forces of Darkness pack. Not on a road, in the forest, on a river, and certainly not in some stinky stale room where money's stacked the odds against me.*

Ian reached into the backseat to pop the cooler lid. "We out of food? Marta's lunch is in the lake."

I chose my words carefully. "Ian, humor me since I almost died. At least it feels that way. Shannon got too close to the wolves. It's likely her killer knew about her finds, the tracks, the den, all of it.

If we find a promising murder suspect, we might find someone who gets us to the wolves."

"I agree," he said. He lifted a dripping chart off the dash and balanced it on the edge of my sleeping bag. "Suspects and reasons. Thanks for giving me the leaky bags."

I lifted my bare feet to the heat vents and curled my toes over them. I pulled a stale chocolate bar out of a tissue box wedged into the door's side compartment, tucked half of it inside my cheek for a slow melt, and handed the rest to Ian. "Who gets most derailed if Shannon discovers wolves?" I asked.

He pushed a pencil into my fingers. "Gordon and probably Monson have the most invested. Shannon could have exposed their import operation and sent them to prison."

I shook my head. "Gordon said the wolves were ready to travel. It makes no sense for him to kill Shannon when he and Monson were about to lose control over the pack anyway."

"Gordon's got genuine killer credentials learned somewhere we're not supposed to know about, and he owns an ATV. He could have left the tracks you saw behind the gate," Ian said. "Then again, that's not important since everyone up here seems to be growing an ATV out his rear end. But I'm not ready to let Gordon go. He wired the whole frigging forest and he could have orchestrated Tario's death. Who knows what Gordon really wants."

A secret war he can win, I thought. "If you're talking investment, look at people connected with Great Nations' easement deal. If wolves disappear, the project happens, and Wild Pines gets built.

Then pretty much everyone associated with the deal gets millions."

I pulled Ian's notes inside my sleeping bag and studied his chart. "So you don't think Sam or Anderson could handle a Z-drag as well as Ridge or his crew?"

"Sam's crippled. Anderson's soft."

"That's the whole idea. A Z-drag compensates for what you lack. Sam can barely walk, but he's mean and loyal enough to do the deed. Anderson Barter's staked his future on Great Nations' success. I can't imagine him messing with pitchy ropes, but we know he was cold-blooded enough to hold back life-and-death information on John Tario. Then there's his threat."

Ian poked my sleeping bag. "What threat?" He poked it again. "What threat?"

Given four days of loose logs, poison run amok, corporate threats, and a special-delivery dog message, Anderson's threat seemed more real—not the part where I was a woman alone behind the gates. The real menace was his fevered "property is sacred" vest-ripping passion, and that's what I told Ian.

He scowled and wheeled us back and forth across the road in search of rock-free terrain. "I hope that's your last secret, pardner," he said, pouncing on the word so it sounded like *trai-tor.* I felt for Shannon's picture. Gone. Either in the packing or the swimming. I sunk lower in the bag and rubbed my eyes. I'd lost her smile again.

Ian raised the candy wrapper and shook crumbs into his mouth. "Does Engunn's being with the posse mean he's working for Great Nations?"

I pressed a water-wrinkled finger on the list. "Either way we keep him where you've got him. Aside from his physical talents and his passion for the easement deal, Engunn wanted Shannon's job and he's got an edgy grudge."

"Move on to Brinkman," Ian said.

"Victoria Brinkman," I said. "We *know* money moves her. Millions for the trust, but I see you think she couldn't drop a tree. You think bracelets disqualify her? Don't underestimate women. We're situational cross-dressers. Opera by night—clam diggers by day. She bragged that sooner or later more corporate owners would bring their money troubles to the trust so she could buy easement deals, and she's got philanthropists so confused about her forest mission they're willing to give her millions to partner with businesses that cut it down. She's got a large life plan she doesn't want to risk."

It must have been late in the afternoon, sun directly in our eyes as we skidded to a stop at GNF's gate. I was camouflaged as a stuffed green-pepper passenger, sleeping bag over my head, but I heard Ian shuffle paperwork and the voice of a cheery, unfamiliar gate attendant. What was Sam up to?

Cursing, Ian swerved to avoid log trucks straddling the middle of the road. He pounded the emergency lights and jerked us from the road. Waiting for the convoy to pass, we agreed that Mike Leavitt was too recent a wolf hunt contestant to know about Shannon's discoveries, but I was sure he'd arranged the dog attack—maybe as a favor to Harworth. Mike lived in a world of favors, and his Great Nations hunting junkets to Idaho probably weren't really free.

I was surprised to see Phil's name. Ian had him down for his ability to roam anywhere behind the gates and his decades of experience with gear in the woods. I couldn't see how Shannon was a threat to Phil. My jacket disappeared outside his office, but anyone could have driven up his driveway and stolen it. I thought his giving us the bone was a message. *I know about wolves but I don't want to officially know. I'd have to choose sides—the wolf or my work—and I can't do that.* I scribbled question marks next to his name.

Ian turned on the wipers to clear mud before he turned into the road. "I'm only interested in suspects that get me close to wolves. So far that's Gordon, and he's gone."

"I'll ask Moz to check Sam's gate records for last weekend."

"If Great Nations is involved, their gate records are doctored or gone by now," said Ian. "*You* think everyone could have done it except Gordon. Gordon gets my vote. He's into jungle justice." He snatched his chart and tossed it out the window. "Waste of time. I'm going to work with Anita to map a search area and find the den. Something I can touch that isn't noise in the air."

I pointed to a stick decorated with flagging tape and a cell phone case. "Ian, there's a signal. Maybe we have a Peter message."

He climbed from the car and waved his phone in the air while I curled deeper into my bag and thought about Gordon. Why would he execute a meticulous reintroduction plan and then leave his wolves to an uncertain fate? Leave them to hostile landowners and Mike's amped-up hunters? I wasn't military, but I understood the imperative to accomplish the mission. Gordon would be all over accomplishing the mission. What was I missing? My heels slipped through water puddled on the floor mat and found Marta's soaked vest under my seat. Marta. Marta had the answer. The woman behind the man.

Ian slammed the car door and gunned us back onto the road.

I made a small opening in my bag cocoon. "Ian, listen to this. Gordon worked for Monson. Monson must have a plan for the wolves. Phase one, hire Gordon. Prepare food, surveillance, and protection. Two. Capture and transport wolves. Three. Create ideal conditions for a female and pups in a secured area. Four. Eliminate proof the pack was illegally imported. Make Gordon disappear. Make wolves' return look like a natural event. What's next?"

Grinning, Ian waved his phone. "In two days, ask her yourself. It's two days to our Monson interview. She's asked Peter for a meeting. Saturday outside MAST headquarters, and Peter wants us in Augusta anyway. He's wrangled me a press pass to some big hunter event, but it seems you're an outcast." He danced his butt around the seat a bit. "No pass for you! It's been a busy two days out where there's coffee and toilets. The wolf issue is boiling."

"How could anyone get ahead of you on the story?" I asked.

"We're still OK. It's politics. The politics are hot. Someone on the governor's staff signed the governor's name to a proclamation naming the first week of October 'Wolf Awareness Week.' And get this. Next week really is 'Wolf Awareness Week' in nineteen states. Governor Lord's on his way home from a Japanese trade mission but caught serious flak in the air from the wolf haters, especially the Maine Association of Sportsmen and Trappers. He'll be at MAST to apologize. He'll be the first Maine governor to recall an official proclamation."

Wolf awareness. I thought we could do without Whoopie Pie Week and Tomato Week, but I liked the idea of Wolf Awareness Week. It wasn't Wolves Are Wonderful Week or Ram Wolves Down Your Throat Week. Suddenly I ached to be above the beaver pond, nose to nose with Katu, watch his fur ripple tan waves down his back and his ears twitch at sounds I'd never hear, feel his gold-flecked eyes fire questions at me. I'd already had my wolf awareness week.

CHAPTER 34

I found Gordon's pictures in my mailbox, wolf names neatly printed on the margins, and in the gathering darkness I recognized Katu's bandit stripes. Ian snatched the pictures and climbed to the roof, determined to get the wolves' faces into his phone and to Peter before we lost the light.

Francoise sent an invitation for Shannon's party, a Friday potluck at the cantina. I had one night to recover before the party and two nights and one day to deep breathe my way through the dread I felt about Saturday's Augusta trip. The thought of the capitol dome's grim shadow sent my stomach diving toward my calves—a reasonable reaction. What sane person would walk back onto a stage to try more stand-up routines when her last shows had played to audiences who stayed in their coats for a fast escape?

I whistled for Pock. Inside the cabin door he froze, neck hairs erect and vibrating. He prowled the cabin, sniffing kitchen counters, the dining table, and, strangely, the bathroom door. I walked out the front door and then back in, looking for disturbed items. I was missing a sound. The gurgle of ancient plumbing. The toilet wasn't running and the bathroom door was closed, but I'd left the door open so the woodstove would warm the pipes. I tapped the door open with my foot. The toilet bowl was a blue ice sculpture.

"Ian," I called out the window. "Did you use the toilet or the outhouse Tuesday morning?"

"Oh, *pleeeaase*," came the reply from the roof.

"I need to know."

"The outhouse. You had the bathroom. I frosted my butt. Are you done?"

I piled wood in both stoves and filled a kettle. If I could thaw the bowl slowly I wouldn't have to call a plumber. My economic bracket didn't include plumbers. It was a place of prayers where nothing broke: plumbing, car, appliances, teeth, and, of course, the dog.

Pock vanished without touching his food, so I assumed he was re-marking trees coyotes had claimed in his absence. Ian spread Gordon's wolf pictures around our bowls of chili while my phone message light winked hopefully. I even forgot the bathroom door when Ian lifted a shredded letter from Gordon's envelope. Either the "wild man" had mangled it to protect his photos, or he'd sent us an edgy message. We pieced it together.

To Only the Concerned. The wolf names are Laotian. Creeping around the Maine woods is a cream-puff picnic compared to jungles, but same rules. Win at all cost.

Mekong's the breeding female. Mekong means mother of water. I want her pups flowing across forests like toothy howling rivers. She's ferocious in defense of her young. Hmong's the breeding male. Don't call them alpha this and alpha that. Wolves are too complex for a vertical command structure. He's generous and playful when he's not hunting. In Laos, Hmong means free. Well, the Laotians aren't free so he might as well be.

Katu and Alak. Siblings from last year's litter. Ancient tribal names. The tribe, the pack, is the wolf's place in the world. Katu's a creative, curious fella. Alak's a shy and sneaky girl. This year's pups: Pakse, Salavan, Bolaven, and the dead Attapu—all named for sacred places I repaid blood debts.

Don't underestimate Monson. She has deep reserves of cash and courage. She will tell you what you want to know. Work for your story, reporter boy. Your story, not mine. Let loose, Cassandra Patton. Let loose with everything in your arsenal. Be a holy traveling woman, unconcerned about your next meal as you thunder down the road.

In tiny, upside-down print he'd added, *eat or burn communiqué.*

I spent half of the next day, Friday, sleeping. Pock came and went, nosing my arm to check for a pulse. He smelled too good to be a dog, and I wondered if Ian had sprayed him with air freshener. Ian spent the day on the roof, wearing my dad's fur hat like an unruly toupee. He climbed down to refill his coffee mug and update me on Peter's world.

Peter didn't believe a wolf had pissed on my tent. He believed Gordon's pictures were proof—not enough to publish given the source, but enough to ramp up our search—and he had a plan to sneak us inside Great Nations' gates if we mapped a helpful search area.

My *Bangor Weekly* blog was wildly popular, drawing hundreds of emails from readers sharing what they'd spent to be outdoors. Someone started a mail-in-your-proof campaign that had reporters stapling receipts to the walls in the newsroom, bathrooms, and stairwells, and somehow the unusual stapler campaign ended up on YouTube. That digital buzz only made Peter more depressed about his odds of saving the printed paper.

Ian had a press pass for the upcoming MAST event, but I was an outcast because Ridge had emailed Mike Leavitt a photo of my chest in Marta's "Don't Shoot" vest and Mike had sent it on to the paper. According to Peter, Mike was too gleeful about "Conover's true anti-gun heart," but I'd already restored the vest's matted feathers with my hair dryer and planned to wear it anyway.

Ian and I were spreading our crunched map onto Antler Camp's table when Ken's wife, Millie, burst in with a cookie jar and a thin roll of paper. She was even shorter than Ken, well-padded, and wearing an apron smeared with dough. She wore that same apron to town meetings, where she reigned as the only female selectman behind a nameplate that said "select-a-woman." Apples bumped in her wide pockets as she dropped the paper in front of Ian. "Moz called to say your message machine's full so my man should bring his tracking notes by and not wait for you to appear," she said. She slipped Pock a chocolate chip cookie under the table. "Ken sends apologies. He got called away to bust a bear poaching ring selling gall bladders to China."

Millie leaned back and stuck out her pelvis in a lurid thump. Apples in her pockets shifted like wayward testicles. "As if eating ground-up bear organs would help any man with *his* organ," she said.

We fell into each other's arms and howled. Ian ducked his red face into Ken's map.

"Let's see if I can remember it all," she said, winking at me and tucking wisps of gray hair under a hat that swirled with mismatched yarn scraps. "Ken says he's not sure if the tracks are wolf or large dog, but he couldn't find anyone running bloodhounds up there." She tapped the map. "He made little pencil stars but clumped them together when tracks repeated in the same general area."

Ian mumbled and bent over the table, head pivoting between our map, Ken's map, and the cookie jar. Crumbs rained on our chaotic margin notes, colored lines, arrows, and question marks. "Anita's going to love this," he said.

I looked over his shoulder and imagined Ken's starred tracks, the closed roads, dismantled beaver dams, chained skull, snapped femur, and plaster tracks swirling into place on top of the government's proposed wolf lands and Wild Pines Resort as Anita clicked a key and snapped them all together. I didn't need to be there to see the den appear somewhere near Bluffer Brook.

I'd be searching for the collar and who had it when our map's wolfish places collided with Great Nations' resort ambitions on Anita's computer.

Millie hugged me. "Shannon's party's tomorrow night. Don't bother cooking; I've got your apples and I'll put your name on the applesauce." Plump, chapped lips pressed together with disapproval. "What name do you want? The Cassandra name or the Patton name? I like the girl name. Wasn't she a goddess? I survived seventh-grade mythology but that was before the last ice age."

I tugged her apron down over her sturdy frame and squeezed her shoulder.

"Cassandra was human," I said, "just considered crazy because she was a seer."

"We all have eyes, honey." Millie said.

"No. She was a *see-er*, you know, a prophet, but maybe not a very successful one. Cassandra saw truth—saw the future. She rejected Apollo's advances so he put a spell on her, made it so no one believed her prophecies." I felt dry face lines crack into a smile. Across the ages, what did we have in common? "She warned the city of Troy not to bring a gigantic wooden horse inside its fortified walls," I said. "No one believed her. After dark, soldiers jumped out of the horse, opened the gates to the attacking army, and Troy was destroyed."

"There you have it," cried Millie as she reached up to tweak my cheek. "That's you. Cassandra sees what's going to happen, warns people, and they don't listen. Mayhem dismantling the world continues. Sounds like your old job. Good you ditched it," she said.

I put two cookies in my mouth and chewed so my face would be busy. No one knew how much the Cassandra curse haunted my lobbying life, but I was pretty sure there wasn't any way to talk about being ignored without sounding like a whiner.

"I've missed you, you know," Millie said. "But you're clearly on a mission and bright-eyed and bushy-tailed over it. I wrote the warden's cell number on Ken's notes, but don't bother. He never answers his phone and, no, I don't know where he is." She gathered my dog's front end in a smothering embrace. "Lordy, he smells good. Are you trying to help him find a lady friend?"

That night the Road Kill Cantina rocked with laughter, off-key guitars, and raucous toasts that wafted to where I shivered in my car. Shannon would have loved it all. Ian's silhouette, identified by ridges of spiky, moussed hair he'd sculpted in my kitchen, glided from window to window. "Fact finding," he'd said, slamming my car door. "Someone in there will know something, and anything's better than your canned chili."

I didn't see Vicki Brinkman until she tapped my window. She tapped again when I didn't move.

"It's safe to come out," she said, smiling. "All I've got is potato salad."

I lowered the window.

She placed a massive wooden bowl on my roof, unzipped her purple parka, and ran one finger lightly over her brows to smooth disobedient hairs. She wore pale blue earrings that dropped from long silver chains toward her shoulders—earrings that matched her pale blue eyes. The effect was arresting and unnatural, like looking at constellations that offer up distant light. She tugged her short black skirt down toward her boots. "It's the one Aroostook County skill that gets me in any door, no questions asked. I was peeling and boiling them before I could read, but I wouldn't eat a potato now if you force-fed me."

"I was just heading out," I said.

"Oh? I thought you and Shannon were best buddies."

I shifted in my seat.

"Listen, Patton. I am sorry about the other day," she said. "We left things hanging and tense, and—what was that nasty feeding frenzy whipped up by those young men? Come inside, have a drink, and let's patch over our differences."

I wanted to smile, but I couldn't. On Shannon's night, Vicki's invite was all about Vicki. "Thanks, Vicki," I said. "Maybe another time. I am a potato salad lover, but I'm waiting for someone."

She lifted her bowl off the car roof, raised a hand in a salute that lingered by her eyes, and walked away. At the front door, she lifted her offering and eager hands pulled her into the cantina. Waiting wasn't exactly a lie. I was waiting for my next move, hoping it would just show up. I pressed my cell phone's cracked case back together and wondered who waited in my mailbox.

Kate's scolding voice boomed at me. "Mummy. Where are you? Shame on you for not filing a flight plan. We had a deal. Maybe I won't file one next time one of those steroid frat boys tries to lure me away for a weekend." She laughed. "As if I'd be stupid enough to listen to that crap. No, really. Like usual, Dad's a no-show, and I count on you not to be. Don't do that again, or I'll have to leave college, find Sketchy Sam, and track you down. Ick. Ick. Ick. Love you! Gotta run. Call me!"

I had six messages from my mother's nursing home. I fast-forwarded through the official notifications of bruises, swallowing evaluations, and assessment meetings that came to me along with her power of attorney. I had no real power to change how the mattress inflating my mother's body away from bed sores had more vigor than she did. I had no power against the riptide of guilt that tugged me toward her when I'd been days away from her bedside, and I had no power over Giffy's refusal to call me Patton.

"Giffy here. Cassandra, where are you? Mother's status review is next week. The hospice team expects you here. Call me!"

I replayed my mother's message three times just to hear her voice, because a mother's voice is a mother's voice no matter what. "Dear, you should know the only status report of interest to me, your mother, is God's divine plan. I am quite sure he has a plan for you, too. Please call me."

A plan. I needed my own plan and didn't have one.

Inside the restaurant, two men parted a curtain and stared at me through sunglasses I recognized. Behind them Shannon smiled from a billboard-sized poster, her boots crossed on my canoe. The restaurant was papered with identical Shannon posters. I wanted another copy of that smile—a good excuse to go by her apartment and find one. Without headlights, I drove a back street to Shannon's apartment.

Her home had been searched. Not tossed into disarray, just disorder on the edges of her neatness. Drawers open an inch or two. File folders no longer alphabetized. Black underwear mixed with everyday pairs. Shannon saved her monogramed black underwear for special occasions, but mostly she wore it to the Laundromat when she was out of white ones. Did I stand in the phantom footsteps of her killer—or killers? Looking for wolf evidence, had they pawed her treasures?

I held my breath. Only Shannon's ticking alarm clock and bubbles from her fish tank filter. Exhaling a deep, cleansing breath, I resolved to rescue what had meaning to me—to us. I tiptoed over her Navaho rug, peeled away canoe trip photos she'd taped to her bathroom mirror, and slid them into the side pocket of my pack.

In her closet, I found the fleece jacket I wanted. Crushed in my hands, it smelled like lavender, wood smoke, pitch, and the pockets bulged with flagging tape—great wads of pink tape scrawled with black survey notations, "Great Nations Forest LLC" stamped every few feet. I whipped off my pack and started to stuff it full of tape, sobs shuddering down my arms. Pulling survey stakes, ripping flagging tape—people went to jail for that. Shannon was dead. It shouldn't have mattered—but it did.

When the back porch door slammed open, a flashlight beam froze my hands full of tape.

"Deputy," Calvin Harworth hissed, "arrest Ms. Conover."

Anderson Barter, in uniform, gun clearly visible, fingered his handcuffs.

"Hold on, Harworth," I snarled. "You know I didn't remove this tape."

"We reported the theft from our property last summer," Harworth said. "Your hands are full of what we reported."

Anderson reached for my arm. "I warned you about property. *Our* property."

"That wasn't a warning. That was a threat." I arched away and wheeled on Harworth. "And what are you doing searching Shannon Angeles's apartment? I have a key and permission to be here any time. What's your excuse?"

Harworth looked around the living room, crossed to Shannon's desk, and unplugged a laptop. "Our computer. I contacted Deputy

Barter and requested he allow me access to retrieve corporate property. All legal. We need her files to continue her work."

I laughed. "Oh, please. Let's not pretend Great Nations cares about what *she* cared about. Unless—"

No one spoke except the ticking clock and the bubbling tank. Everyone waited for me, except Gordon in my head: *Catch. Your wolves now. Done compromising and you don't know it.*

I laughed again. "Unless. Unless you care about the *wolves* just as much as Shannon did. Of course, she planned to make them public, and *you* want them gone." Dark color flooded Harworth's neck and washed his face into shadow. He grimaced and waved his hand dismissively—an order for Anderson to execute.

I faced Anderson. "And who are we tonight, Anderson? Are my taxes paying for this uniformed visit, or are you Great Nations' stooge in a deputy costume?"

He stomped toward me, lifting the cuffs as if I'd be willing to offer him my wrists.

Voice low, I backed off the rug and held my hands up in a crisp, football time-out gesture. "Whoa, Anderson. We can prove Great Nations' men tried to kill a wolf. We have video of them stuffing poison into a dead moose. Tape of them trespassing on Monson's land." I moved from the solid limb I was on to a more outrageous slender twig. I felt weightless. "And you had to know John Tario was dying of 1080, but you refused that information to the hospital. We have that on tape too. We can connect the dots from the dead moose to the dead man."

With a strangled oath Anderson lunged. That I expected. I bent and yanked the loose folds of Shannon's rug, upending Deputy Anderson Barter on the floor. He slithered away, popped his holster, and tossed Harworth his gun.

Harworth scowled. "Not sure how to fire it? Let me solve that for you." He dropped the gun into the fish tank. "Now get up and tackle her."

Deputy Barter hauled himself up on Shannon's kitchen counter and spread his arms into something that looked like a drunken hug. And then he hung there.

"Christ," said Harworth, and then he was on me, one hand gripping my ponytail, the other slamming me into the wall. That turned out to be a good thing because Pock's frenzied barking didn't warn me about the light, and pressed into the fake paneling I wasn't facing the window when Moz pressed his searchlight against the glass and yelled, "Maine Warden Service."

CHAPTER 35

After the barking, swearing, and yelling, Pock and I were ordered to the porch swing. I rubbed my dog's ears and my freshly skinned nose. As Moz escorted Harworth and Anderson to their truck, his head had an official slant while he listened to their complaints. Later, he sighed as he lifted Pock to the floor and sat heavily next to me.

"How long were you outside listening?" I asked.

"I thought I'd see you at the cantina, but Francoise cornered me to say you had strong grief and I should do something about it. I felt you might visit here." He shifted and stretched both arms over the back of the swing and straightened his legs until he could rock the swing with his heels. "I saw those two leave Shannon's shed and charge her back door. You appeared to be holding your own—until you taunted them. Were the insults part of a calculated plan or the strong grief I am sent here to attend to?"

"I had him," I said, trying to comb my tangled hair with shaking fingers. In the scuffle, I'd lost my careful barrette arrangement. "I had him on his scummy 1080 behavior. Even if he'd tackled me, Harworth wouldn't have let him arrest me. I saw his face. When a boss looks that disgusted, the employee's days are numbered."

"And your days are not?" he asked. "I repeat. Barter wears a gun."

"It was time to say *wolf* out loud."

Moz's fingers sorted through stray hairs at my neck. I thought the moment might go either way, not that he'd really strangle me, but he might consider it. When his hand slid down my spine, I didn't lean into it—but I wanted to.

He tapped my back gently and stood. Like hairline cracks in wood, tired lines carved his cheeks. "Does Shannon have food?"

In the apartment kitchen, I dumped spoiled food into a garbage bag, filled a cooler with items Millie and I would find useful, and chopped the remaining ingredients for Moz. He heated butter, swirled eggs with cold water, and then added mushrooms and goat cheese seconds before he folded the contents into a puffed omelet. Bending over the steam, he moaned a hungry sound in his throat that jumped to my throat so I fumbled around for forks. We shared the pan back and forth over Shannon's counter.

We'd both asked Ridge the same Sam question, so we both knew Great Nations' gatekeeper was the likely collar thief. If Moz knew about the dog attack and my rumble with Mike, he said nothing. Like most hostile encounters tracked by warden chatter, he had to know I'd crawled on the ground. Maybe he was giving the incident the quiet space it deserved.

When I explained the Mahoneys' discoveries and their plan to analyze the scat's DNA, Moz reached for his notebook and took notes. He wasn't surprised Shannon felt followed. He was surprised she'd found the den, and his black eyes snapped with light when I talked about the howling and Katu swimming the river. He lowered his pen and closed his eyes when I said I'd been nose to nose with a wolf.

Ian flipped on Shannon's overhead lights and glared at the egg scraps. "Anybody working here? Does Francoise always know where people are? Not much to report from the party. It looked like Shannon was popular with everyone except the same men who stared at us at Grants two nights ago, and they didn't crack a smile. The land trust Brinkman woman showed up. She makes a mean potato salad, but she didn't stay long. She muscled her way through the conga line and extracted those guys. I think Francoise was not happy that so many of Shannon's Great Nations' coworkers were no-shows."

Moz reached for his gun, radio, and phones piled at the end of the kitchen counter. "That is because they are occupied trying to infiltrate Monson's land, and we have been assigned to stop them."

"Stop them?" we asked.

"Three wardens, including me. Apparently, Monson has strong leverage if she's arranged extra manpower. Then there is her ranger squad."

"Ranger squad?" we asked.

"At the moment they are not clearly identified, but they appear to be a rough crew of Maine Guides and unemployed mill workers patrolling her perimeter. They ride new ATVs, wear headsets, and are forbidden to talk. Each has a pocket of business cards with her attorneys' phone numbers."

Ian glowered at Moz. "So *you* won't be helping us?"

Moz strapped on layers of leather and a fearsome law enforcement voice. Ian slid around the counter to stand behind me.

Thumbs hooked inside his belt, black brows pulled together over tight cheeks and lips, Moz fixed each of us with a stern nod. "My colonel is not aware he is paying his wardens to protect wolves. He fears a dispute between powerful landowners—Great Nations against Carla Monson. He has stationed us in the demilitarized zone. At the moment he does not know we are protecting people who have broken every law I am required to enforce."

He notched his belt tighter. "You two are to go to Augusta and meet with Monson. If you can, please discover her plans now that Gordon Samuels has disappeared. Bring me information on a shooting contest MAST is planning and produce a GIS map that might be useful. When I am not pursuing trespassers, I will search for the collar."

He pointed at me. "Ms. Conover." He ran his hand over rough stubble on his face and around to the back of his neck and briefly closed heavy-lidded eyes. "Patton. Please. Avoid Anderson Barter. Leave him—and the rest of them—to me. I do not believe the men who attempted wolf poisoning are finished, so I will ask that you eat food only you prepare." He didn't bang the door on his way out, but his boots rattled floorboards.

"Well," I said, lifting Shannon's cooler into Ian's arms. "We just had a briefing from the men in charge. He's been talking to Peter."

"It's what we'd be doing anyway. Let's get going." Ian banged out the door and across the porch, Pock at his heels. I heard him shout, "Oh, please, dog, chill," as he leaned in the driver's window to start my car.

When I reached for Shannon's coat and my pack, the pictures I'd pulled from her mirror slipped to the floor. They felt strangely thick, so I picked at their edges and found each shot taped to another picture. I spread the hidden shots on her counter and stared at soft tracks in dirt. Next to each she'd positioned a measuring tape. One red nail pointed to the five-inch line.

The last photo, thick and clumsy, was actually four pictures taped together. I peeled away tape and saw a dirt hole the size of a small doghouse door. The den. Then two more flash pictures of a dark tunnel that opened into a scooped-out saucer of earth. Shannon was inside the den. The last image was her gloved hand cradling a limp body matted with twigs. I stepped under a light. Not twigs. She held Attapu, the dead wolf cub, porcupine quills bristling in the camera's quick glare. Scrawled up the picture's side was a toll-free number.

I walked to the car and quietly handed Ian the pictures. He leaned into the headlights and studied each picture. As he dialed the number, he lifted his phone to air between us.

"Thank you for contacting the Department of the Interior's Endangered Species hotline. Our office hours are Monday through Saturday, 6 a.m. to 7 p.m. Eastern Standard Time. Select 1 to report a suspected ESA violation or harassment of a listed species. Select 2 if you have found a deceased animal from a listed population. Do not touch or remove the dead animal. Contact your nearest U.S. Fish and Wildlife Service office or your state's game warden service to report its location. Thank you for assisting our protection efforts."

I threw my pack in the car and hopped into my seat. "*That* was Shannon's plan," I said. "Report the pup and the den and deliver proof Maine had breeding wolves."

"She'd blow off her job?" asked Ian.

I squashed my hair through a rubber band and started the car. "When your real self shows up to occupy every cell in your body, the phony self's got no room to operate. Shannon showed up. She showed up. Ian, who else knew about the den? Knew enough to go after Shannon? Stop her before she went public?"

Ian stiffened next to me. "I think only the disappeared wild man and Shannon knew about the den and the dead pup. GNF's searching too hard, so I think they have nothing—yet." He pulled dark glasses out of his pocket and stared at street lamps. "Bring it back to the wolves, Patton. It's *all* about the wolves and proof. Find the den and the dead pup. Smear the news all over the *Bangor Weekly*'s front page. Research dead friends on your own time."

CHAPTER 36

On Saturday morning I'd already put in a full day before I even thought about waking Ian. I'd showered, stowed Pock in his go-to-town travel crate, tucked nail scissors and a file in my pocket in case I went unnoticed enough to pursue personal grooming, and restocked the cooler with cheese sandwiches. My black dress pants were so loose the cuffs sagged low on my hiking boots. I didn't have dressy shoes. They'd disappeared into a district court dumpster moments after the divorce, when I'd walked barefoot out the double glass doors as security guards lifted their radios just in case.

I munched a frost-bruised apple, working my way around the worm holes, thinking I might dissolve the partnership and let Ian have his shot at fame. For me, something lurked in shadow, like a savvy trout gliding under rocks: just a fin shadow or flash of white belly in a deep pool. Something or someone telegraphed more by absence. A more clever, determined intelligence was at work than the brains of people who'd made my life miserable during the past week. Someone who'd evaded Gordon's jungle skills, searched Shannon's home long before Saturday night—maybe someone who'd staged her murder to look like nature gone impersonally cruel. I started to choke up apple bits on the next thought: someone who might patiently observe my friend, aware that Shannon Angeles would find wolves long before other clumsy pursuers.

I poked fresh holes in my belt and resolved to be in and out of Augusta and after Sketchy Sam before the day was over. Either he had the collar and was keeping it secret, or he'd passed it to someone else and was lying low, and I knew how to find him. He shouldn't have tacked a scruffy copy of his family tree over his gatehouse desk.

"Researchin' my roots," he'd told me, trying to peer down Kate's shirt as she signed her form.

"Disgusting," whispered Kate as Sam clanged in his cash box. "To think of an entire line of Sketchy Sams breeding."

"Where you from, Sam?" I'd asked.

"Kingfield before it got all slicked up with ski zillionaires. Now we're in Stratton. My brothers work the sawmill."

I could be at the Stratton Diner before the last piece of chocolate cream pie was served.

Sam or no Sam in Stratton, my next stop had to be Phil Bryan's office. Either Phil could tell me who else had noticed and appreciated Shannon's tracking skills—maybe Anderson had noticed something, but I doubted it—or I'd have to reevaluate Phil as he walked a tight line toward a Six Rivers pension. Pensions were powerful. I fantasized about them the way others dreamed about tropical vacations, but I'd chosen a nonprofit career and learned too late my peers and I had to be fulfilled by badly paid work.

The Maine Association of Sportsmen and Trappers parking lot looked like a four-wheel drive dealership on military alert. Parking attendants in camouflage vests waved American flags and directed us past the front door, where a flashing billboard advertised the grand opening of MAST's new education center. Ian leaned out his window, camera lens swinging at bumper stickers that accomplished humor and venom at the same time. "Help Preserve Wolves. Take One to a Taxidermist Today." "Earn a Buck. Shoot a Wolf." "I Brake for Wolves Then I Back Up and Run 'Em Over Again."

A log truck filled with red plastic shovels sported a red, white, and blue "Shoot, Shovel and Shut Up" banner and a sign offering free shovels. The crowd was mostly men forty and older wearing flannel shirts, khaki pants over rugged shoes, and expanding waistlines. Ball caps advertised fly rods, rifles, and ammunition. Full beards and mustaches sprouted from weathered faces creased with kind wrinkles—faces that didn't fit the mayhem theme on their trucks. A few women wearing fake leopard spot, zebra stripe, or snakeskin-themed clothing were easy to pick out.

Ian's phone howled. "New ringtone and a text from Bart." He whooped and twisted in his seat. "The scat cooked up as wolf

DNA and he's offered to be interviewed for my article. I'll get him before the feds get him. Oh, yes."

The phone howled again. He listened. "Back end of the lot. Large orange truck. Peter's already here."

Large was an understatement. Monson's truck was a carnival attraction, jacked high off the ground, with tires the size of compact cars and black security windows decorated with shadows of running animals. Maybe she saw a world of leaping wildlife as she drove. Multiple antennas glittered off the roof, and thumping music boomed from inside.

Peter eased to the ground and hugged me. Thinner, he had luminous eyes radiating energy from an out-of-body source. I gripped his arm, but he waggled his finger at me. "No time to talk about me now, Patton. Focus on the big story." He waved me up into buttery-soft leather seats. "We were appreciating the last notes of 'The Mouldau.' You'd like that composition, Patton. A river filtered through an orchestra."

Reaching for Ian's pack, he pointed at a battered delivery truck. "Your new ride includes a food delivery ordered by Rachael Kenneth at the inn if you need a story to get you behind GNF gates." He hung Ian's pack on the outside mirror. "Ms. Monson is phobic about recording devices. Your phone too, please."

Ian slapped his phone into Peter's hand and slid over me to sit behind the woman in the driver's seat. Peter grunted his way up into the passenger seat. "Brace yourselves," he said.

Carla Monson swiveled her seat toward us. Annie. Orphan Annie. Carla Monson was almost a twin of every young actress who'd been on stage in *Annie*. She'd grown longer, coltish legs but she was definitely an Annie. Red curls cascaded over her ears. Dimples on each cheek asked for pinching, and red freckles danced across her nose. Her orange "Don't Shoot" T-shirt was tucked into a ruffled skirt over legs that disappeared into clunky all-terrain sandals. Pea green nail polish matched her eyes, and they laughed before she did.

"Oh, the shock," she said. "My publicist is brilliant. He releases snaps of me forty years into the future, ones that look like I survived a chain gang after I'd weathered an ocean crossing in an open boat. We like the intimidation factor. Age. Money. Mystery." She reached her hand toward Ian. "Hello, Ian. I'm year one at Columbia, but I gotta tell you I've been reading what you left behind at the school paper. Your reporting is still shellacked to the *Spectator* wall."

Ian gaped.

I gaped. I was thinking twelve, maybe thirteen. Not college.

Peter sighed. "She's seventeen."

Carla turned to me. "I hope I can call you Patton. Like Peter does. I'm Carla."

My voice squeaked. "Did you hatch the wolf scheme watching *Sesame Street*?"

She glanced at the crowd pressing on the closed MAST doors. "We don't have much time," she said. "Peter's briefed me on what you sent him this past week. You up for keeping my age and identity secret? At least for now?"

Without speaking, Ian and I looked at each other and shrugged. Peter turned in his seat to create a vehicular conference room.

"Hang with me, Patton," Carla said. "I'll explain. Peter and Ian need to get inside."

Ian shifted forward in his seat. "MAST doesn't look like your orange clothing crowd."

"I've got the biggest truck, so that's gotta count." She tugged Peter's sleeve.

He cleared his throat. "Patton, we need to come clean on what you don't know. Carla called me last summer. She liked your columns and offered me an anonymous grant to support your work. Of course I declined so we'd be independent, but I thought she might be a story—sitting on a chunk of forest she bought when she was fourteen. She's got company. There are other wealthy individualists with private reasons for buying up what we call kingdom lots, but she's the only owner who'll talk to me."

Carla shoved Peter affectionately. Ian sulked in his seat. I wondered when he'd resume his reporter shape.

Peter winked at me. "When Ian turned up at the paper with his proposal, I called Carla and asked if she'd heard wolf rumors." He frowned. "I should have been more alert—been suspicious when she said she hoped the paper wouldn't take a negative position if they showed up. Two days ago, she emailed me video of your friend Shannon Angeles measuring wolf tracks. Footage shot by her land manager."

"Well," I said, "two days ago I was upriver with the Mahoneys. *We* saw a wolf swim the river."

Carla pointed at my vest. "How are Bart and Marta?"

"Oh, fine, fine," muttered Ian, clipping his press pass to his shirt. "Maybe should be committed, but fine."

I crossed my arms and looked out the window. "If you have everything we sent Peter, you know they're fine."

Peter fumbled with his pass and I reached forward to help him. "Carla also sent me photographs that show the pups on recognizable Maine terrain," he said. "Date stamps on each shot. We can publish them if we credit an anonymous source."

Recovered, Ian learned toward Peter. "Do we even need her stuff if I have Shannon's pictures of the den and the dead wolf? I don't like being managed by the subject of my investigation," he said, glaring at Carla. "You can bet she's used to buying her way everywhere."

Carla raised her hand. "It's OK. A legitimate issue. I am used to getting my way. But I've never bullied my staff or set myself up in an indulgent estate. My parents tried to kidnap my inheritance, but I hired better attorneys. At twelve I bartered my freedom and packed the Ma and Pa yacht clubbers off to the south of France with an annuity—*after* they assigned parental rights to my aunt."

That shut us up.

Carla cleared her throat and smoothed her skirt. “Patton. Your friend. She’s not here to authenticate her photographs, so they might be suspect. I hope it won’t come to it, but I will go public and verify Gordon’s footage if Peter thinks it’s necessary.”

Ian snorted and shifted in his seat. The crowd pointed as a black SUV shadowed by a state trooper cruiser inched its way to the front doors, and TV crews jostled cameras onto their shoulders and shoved their way toward the arrivals.

Peter, Ian, and I climbed down into the parking lot. Ian snatched his pack and opened his hand for his phone, but Peter grabbed his elbow. “We’re here because the governor is talking about wolves—rescinding his wolf week proclamation. Each news team is allowed one question. We’ll talk strategy as we walk.” Ian grabbed his phone and marched away. Peter reached into his pocket and handed me another phone. “Let’s retire your ancient one. Here’s a smaaartphone for a smart you,” he said. He shuffled after Ian.

I zipped the phone into a seldom-used pocket, wedging it between balled up fish line and sheets of emergency toilet paper.

CHAPTER 37

I hauled myself into the front seat opposite Carla. She offered me a can of cranberry juice, frigid from an unseen cooler or, more likely, a built-in refrigerator. "Peter and Ian can follow press ethics, the high road. Work on a balanced story. All that."

I swallowed juice. "And that leaves us…?"

"Nothing illegal. Been there. Done that." She grinned an immaculate, even-toothed smile. Evan and I had gone into debt to put that kind of orthodontic perfection on Kate. Carla waved her arms in energetic circles. "Great Nations plans to morph Maine's forest into something that's not forest. Its corporate buddies are salivating, waiting to see if undoing the forest drives up stock prices and profits."

"Wild Pines Resort," I said.

Carla chuckled. "Yes, but wolves knock the boys out of the game. I want them knocked out of the ball park." She wiped condensation from the can onto her leather seat. I pressed my cold can to my still throbbing leg.

On a nod from the state trooper, all four doors of the black SUV opened, and the governor, the senate president, and our wildlife commissioner, Ryan Robertson, stepped into the sun, squinting and adjusting ties. Mike Leavitt waved them up the stairs, grabbed the governor's elbow, and guided the dignitaries into his lair.

Carla flipped curls away from one ear and inserted a familiar earpiece. "Gordon set me up with gadgets."

"Where *is* Gordon?" I asked.

"Don't know. I hired him to import wolves and protect them until they had pups. He's done that and now he's gone."

She leaned into the truck's control panel and played with some dials. I cringed at the booming sound of scraping chairs and people calling out to each other.

"Sorry. I'll turn it down until the governor speaks." She pointed to the blinking lights. "We can hear the lobby, the main conference room, and some of the parking lot. I asked the crew not to wire the men's room, but I'll bet it's hooked up if Gordon had anything to do with it."

"MAST's new building is wired? That's your idea of legal?"

Carla clapped her hands with delight. "I own the building. My contractors. My wiring."

"I'm lost," I said.

"Mike Leavitt's going to announce his education center was a donation from an anonymous benefactor." She bowed from her waist toward me. "A donor who insisted on a contract with conditions, anonymity, and a five-year lease before MAST receives title to the building." She giggled. "Here's the good part. MAST must host ten years of the benefactor's wildlife displays."

She bounced in her seat, oddly excited. “The first show goes up in November.”

“Wolves?” I asked.

“Wolves, lynx, coyotes, foxes, bobcat, eagles. My negotiating attorneys didn’t reveal the full title. Maybe I’ll call it ‘Precious Predators.’”

“Where did you get this crazy scheme?”

“I infiltrated Great Nations’ headquarters,” she chirped. “Took notes on how to buy my way in. GNF buys its way in everywhere it goes, so I wanted to learn from a pro.”

“Monson,” I hissed as if I were trying to avoid a recording device. “I saw someone named John Tario die a grisly death. Gordon probably had a hand in it. Maybe he didn’t mean to kill anyone, but I’m sure he won’t be turning himself in from remorse. My best friend was killed over *your* wolves. Murdered! This is no game.”

“I know that,” she snapped, yanking a handful of curls to the back of her neck. “I belong to four wolf-hate groups that tell me how to use sniper rifles to shoot ticks off flying ducks. Of course the rifles aren’t for ducks.” She folded her arms over the steering wheel and dropped her head on them. “OK. OK. I flew to Maine when I was notified about the poison. Before I hired Gordon I had him investigated. I knew he might be a risk.”

“Might? Might? What risk did you dig up?” I asked.

Her voice echoed through folded arms. “Not much, and my investigators said that wasn’t good. He went to Vietnam as an intelligence officer and disappeared for two years. No record of promotion, only his discharge. No work record, bank accounts, driver's license. Just some rantings on Laotian refugee sites."

I leaned across the center console into her space but sat on my hands so they wouldn't go after her. "And Shannon? Shannon? You didn't assess her risk? Just happy to watch surveillance videos and plan how she'd be useful? You were happy to have someone stumble on wolves as if they'd magically appeared in Maine?"

Carla jerked upright. Her green eyes snapped with anger. I wasn't falling into line.

"I get that wolves might finally demolish the good-old-boys club that runs the woods," I said. "I get that better than most people. I've lived on scraps tossed from their clubhouse for years." I fingered the door handle, contemplating escape. "You're in over your head. Clever, but too inexperienced to see the big picture. You dropped hungry wolves into a landscape surrounded by thousands of people who see them as a threat."

We heard Mike Leavitt rap the microphone for a sound check, and then he thanked their "far-sighted benefactor" for a gift even he couldn't "stuff down the chimney." Carla rubbed her hands together as if she anticipated a gourmet meal. I hunched in my seat, fingers twitching on the door handle even though my ears wanted to stay in the van.

I imagined Mike nodding to his VIPs. "I am surrounded by leadership we—you— elected," he said. "Leadership pledged to secure our sporting heritage. In our audience sit another thirty-six legislators who are A-rated MAST lawmakers. I say a standing ovation is in order." Carla tapped one hand on the steering wheel and stared at me throughout the thunderous applause. More cheers as Mike ushered Governor Arthur Lord to the podium.

"As governor I owe you all an apology. I'll get to it. First let me bring on Commissioner Robertson to read out what's been our official wolf position since day one."

Paper crackled into speakers and I recognized Commissioner Robertson's squeaky voice. When we'd needed a lion, the governor had appointed a mouse. "The Maine governor's office is not in favor of wolf reintroduction," he read. "Until there is a clear public mandate and authorization as required by the legislature, the department will not promote the reintroduction of wolves into the state of Maine."

Lord's voice resumed and boomed. "That covers it. On my watch, wolves will *never* return to Maine. Here's your apology. Wolf Awareness Week was a mistake my office accepts. I have recalled the proclamation to rectify my mistake. I'm with you. And ... and I understand the predator derby scheduled for this weekend has been postponed. I've asked Mike to sign me up when it comes 'round again." He shouted his last words. "I am locked and loaded for the derby. Count. Me. In!"

I dialed down the governor's cheering squad. "Predator derby?"

"Postponed," said Carla. "The Montana outfitter they hired to stage it never showed up."

"No. I mean a predator derby. What is it?"

"A competition like other derbies out west. Hunters get points. After two days the hunter with the most points from killing the most predators takes home a new ATV." She raised the volume as the governor invited questions.

Shannon's mysterious dangerous-time-in-the-woods message to Bart and Marta wasn't a mystery any more. Most hunters I knew would hang their heads in shame at the idea of a predator derby. My father entertained us with loser stories, bragging about being outwitted by hungrier "varmints." He was especially proud of a bobcat that snatched dead ducks off the hood of his truck.

"Governor." Ian must have stood under a secret microphone, because I heard him draw a ragged breath and blow it out as whistling air. It was his moment and he knew it. "This week the *Bangor Weekly* will run a series documenting the wolf's return to Maine. Not just one wolf. A pack of wolves with pups born this spring. We understand the federal Endangered Species Act will determine how this species will be protected. How will you and state officials comply with the provisions of this act? How will you move to support—"

We couldn't hear the rest of his question. The room erupted. Carla and I flinched as thwacks and thumps crackled through to us. I thought chairs might be hitting the wall.

Ian yelled, "Shit storm! Duck and run!"

In the parking lot, TV crews stopped dismantling equipment and elbowed their way back through the front doors. An exit door in a portable construction trailer at the rear entrance cracked open to allow the black tip of a trooper hat to tilt left and right. Governor Lord, Commissioner Robertson, Mike Leavitt, and a third man tiptoed into the shadow of the building. I recognized the sharp pleats on Calvin Harworth's trousers even before the sun caught his carefully creamed hair. The trooper stalked toward his SUV.

"Can you pick them up?" I asked. "Record what they say?"

Carla spun dials and hummed operatic bits from "The Moldau."

Mike Leavitt's voice was hard and unforgiving. "Harworth, I thought you said Great Nations had this contained. That you'd close off the area and track down the rumors or—worst case—eliminate any wolf you found."

Governor Lord turned on his commissioner. "Robertson. At what point were you going to brief me that we already had wolves? Before or after I made a flaming asshole of myself?"

Ryan Robertson stammered and hopped back as if he'd found hot sand under his feet.

"Don't bother," the governor snarled. "Your resignation. On my desk by five today."

"Gentlemen." Harworth's frosty voice cut the tension. I saw him raise his hand and wave the SUV to the front of the building. Even state troopers obeyed Harworth. "Gentlemen. It's not too late."

Except for heavy breathing and the faint sounds of mayhem, silence. If I'd been the governor's advisor, I'd have shoved him into his car and told him he didn't want to hear anything about the conversation to come. Like boys hatching a panty raid, they drew closer in the building's shadow.

"You're smiling," said Carla. "Why?"

"Because someone is about to make a mistake," I said. "On tape."

Harworth droned on as if he were bored with a class he had to teach. "It will take days to sort out the *Bangor Weekly*'s claims no matter what they print or post. Days or weeks before the feds send out a field team. Weeks or months before the Interior Department and its Fish and Wildlife Service craft a management strategy. Federal agencies crawl more slowly than glaciers." He sighed. "I can have my Idaho team on the ground tomorrow."

I saw him turn toward Lord. "When we're done there will be no trace of wolves, Governor. No rotting carcasses. No bones. No graves."

"How can he guarantee exterminating an entire pack?" I asked no one in particular.

Carla sniffed. "Aside from poison at the den, and they've left the den, the only sure method of dealing with an entire pack is on open snow. From the air."

Of course she'd know that. I doubted she was disturbed by her wolf captives biting the ground and themselves, frantic in rotor wash that flattened them in the snow.

I heard a zipper and hoped no one would relieve himself on tape even if the embarrassment factor would be useful. More zipping as Harworth wrestled with his crisp new jacket. "I have two requests."

Governor Lord's voice was low. "Go ahead."

"First, to protect us all, no questions about methods. There's no way to terminate a wolf that seems to be widely socially acceptable. And secondly, while it may seem premature, I want to be perfectly candid with you, Governor."

Lord crossed his arms. "Go ahead."

"Great Nations Forest will expect an expedited permit process for our Wild Pines project."

Robertson broke in. "Governor, I don't think we have control over that. There's the public hearing process and ..."

Harworth raised both hands for silence. I felt his sneer all the way across the parking lot. He had to know more about the rabbit warren of tunnels into and out of everyone's pockets than Robertson. "We'll discuss that, Commissioner. You might start by requiring Great Nations to pay for increased staff support to manage our sizable permit application. We will complain, of course. After a decent amount of time, we will provide you the funds you request, and we will also suggest the consultants your agency might hire to guide regulatory staff in the decision-making process."

Carla gasped. "Is this guy for real? He's like a bad movie."

I turned up the volume.

The governor groaned. "Wolves. They'd have to leave tracks. Take a crap. Jesus, Robertson, where the hell are your game wardens? I don't understand how a pack of wolves could have tiptoed across the border without anyone getting a whiff of them."

Secure behind her black windows, Carla executed another low bow over the steering wheel. Her dimples crinkled and she aimed a mischievous smile at me. "Governor. You're welcome," she said.

I wanted to grab her shoulders and deliver a rugged shake.

Lord looked anxiously up and down the parking lot. "I've got to get back to the statehouse. Robertson, I still want you in my office later. Mike, I need a favor. Call my press secretary. Brief him and have him meet me in fifteen minutes. Feed him some quotable lines that get me out of this mess—something soft and fuzzy about respecting wildlife. Calvin, I accept Great Nations' assistance and your conditions, and I'll leave you to it. Before you eradicate the wolves, I suggest you tighten your gate procedures to keep out reporters and riff-raff." He snapped his shirt cuffs into place and tightened his tie. "Now, gentlemen, let's get to work. Kill us some wolves. Exterminate the vermin while we've got God, time, and ammunition on our side."

The governor stalked toward his SUV, signaling the trooper to drive toward him. Harworth and Leavitt turned their backs on the commissioner and slipped into the building. Ryan Robertson pulled out a cigarette and lit up, leaning against the building. The front doors burst open. Knots of cursing, gesturing people flooded the parking lot and formed larger groups of cursing people yelling into TV microphones. Ian and Peter were missing. I wanted out of Carla Monson's truck.

Carla pulled at her earpiece and dropped it in her lap.

I felt like my whole body weighed eight hundred pounds and was part of the truck seat. How many hunters would it take to kill a few wolves? "You didn't anticipate this next part of the wolf story, did you? Because lots of these people are headed home to load up and hunt wolves."

"Actually, Patton, I did," she said. "We're ready for them."

CHAPTER 38

"We?" I said. Carla pressed her empty can against the steering wheel where it slowly collapsed.

"OK. History. When I was thirteen, a hunter murdered my aunt, the woman who was my guardian and chosen mother. That flattened me, but it freed me up 'cause I had money and no one cared that I was unsupervised. I applied for a passport to join my parents, who had no interest in seeing me; got delivered to the airport, where I escaped social services; and took a taxi into Boston and contacted my attorneys.

"I bought a hundred thousand acres and made hunting illegal. I built a tent platform where I could scream or do yoga—some days both at the same time—but I could feel machine noise through my mat. Next door, Great Nations was stripping lands I'd tried to buy. Its attorneys refused to talk to my attorneys. I was a bug not worth squashing."

"You're how old?" I asked.

"I know what *that* means. I was twelve when I got my millions and joined a rich kids' support group. The Baby Billionaires recruited me and they trained me. We do philanthropy as a team, and on this the Babies are all in with me."

I wished for a fresh cold can to press on my aching leg. My brain ached, too. What *was* Monson? Prodigy? Aberration? Spoiled rich kid? All that?

She leaned toward me confidentially. "I did surveillance on the enemy by transferring to a private school in Boise that said it had community internships. Who pays attention to a kid volunteer carrying mail or pestering techies for computer lessons? I got way inside Great Nations, where they seduce towns, politicians, governors, and groups that should know better. I mean, by now don't most people know the toy on the outside of the cereal box looks nothing like the toy inside?

"What they spend to win over the little people is nothing compared to the millions they score. They study the little people's desires so they can come to town, offer bribes, and make friends. Great Nations launders the benefits—the bribes—through a charity. Money goes to a hospital, a sewer project, sports programs, dogsled races. Soon the *nice* corporation owns everyone it needs to get its project approved, and the little people wake up as caretakers, gardeners, and maids."

When she leaned back in her seat and flipped curls away from her cheeks, I saw very old green eyes above her dimples and a manifesto I wanted to cut short. "And the wolves?" I asked.

"Great Nations was cutting the woods around me and I was swamped with panicked deer. Then I found logging crews making suspicious roads, so I used my old computer passwords to find the Wild Pines project, freaked big time, and called in my friends. A

Vermont Baby Billionaire sent me the thing that sealed the deal, a Great Nations newsletter with the best headline: 'Wolves Could Destroy Maine's Forest Industry.'

"That sounded good to me. A Brazilian Baby sent me Gordon Samuels, and I hired him to prepare my land and find wolves. I created a foundation and handed out grants to every chamber of commerce, school, hospital, county office, and club within a hundred miles of my land, and they signed contracts that make them partners in the wolves' future, even if they don't know it yet. And the big wow: the Babies and I built MAST a new building, and we're on track to reduce their chokehold on what goes down in Maine."

She filled her cheeks and blew out air as if she'd just run a race. "I think Gordon filled you in on the rest."

I pressed my back against the padded door and felt the handle in my back, pushing on it harder just to feel I had options outside the truck. "What about the ATV vigilantes guarding your property?" I asked.

She grinned and bounced happily in her seat. "In Africa it's a standard game reserve tactic. Hire badly paid locals who normally slaughter wildlife and pay them more to switch sides."

I had an eerie sense that Shannon would have thrown her arms around Carla Monson and hugged her. I wouldn't do that. The media horde was coiling cables and wrapping up its coverage, so I was running out of time for what I planned.

"Quickly," I said. "The rest of it."

Carla ticked off the future, listing a strategy for each raised finger while I lost count. To the east, grants to Baxter State Park for biologists and more park rangers. To the north on Penobscot Nation tribal lands, a Wolf Heritage Center to attract millions of tourist dollars. Local schools teaching her foundation's ecology curriculum in return for college scholarships. MAST weaker and compromised for accepting anti-hunter funding. Six wolf packs in fifteen years. No Bogside Bar. No Wild Pines.

My brain glazed over. Carla was like an invading country whose spy network had taken down the opposing army while it slept. She'd stolen GNF's buy-them-all strategy. I had a cringing moment remembering my rants against big money controlling big woods. What happened when big money was on our side?

As I expected, she'd missed the messy stuff—politics and the intrigue it spawned. I could do politics. I could sabotage Governor Lord, Ryan Robertson, and Mike Leavitt—set them up so most folks would avoid them like the plague. If we were lucky, they might even do jail time. I sighed. There was the *we* I hadn't signed up for.

"Your system broadcasts as well as records?" I asked.

"In the parking lot and conference center, and I can send stuff anywhere in the world from my seat."

"All right," I said, opening the door. "Don't take it personally but I won't help *you*. I *will* help the wolves." She chewed lipstick off her lower lip, disappointed I wouldn't be getting with her program.

"One more question. Robert Atkins knows about your ATV squad. Have you contacted him? Just nod. Don't speak. Please don't speak."

Carla couldn't just nod. "He's considering my offer to manage security but thinks I should be in daycare. He says he'll only do it on his time off for no pay, and he said my squad lacked discipline so I should have someone his nation could trust."

Wonderful, I thought. *How could we share eggs without his bringing up Monson's offer?*

"OK," I said. "Will you do as I ask?"

She shook her head. Curls tapped each ear for added emphasis. I climbed out.

"Yes. Yes. OK. OK. Your way," she said.

When I leaned into the truck, my elbows squeezed leather-scented air from the passenger seat. "Don't worry. People used to pay me for this advice and then ignore it. Discuss your wolf invasion plans with only your philanthropy partners, not the *Bangor Weekly* or any other public oracle. Any campaign narrowed down to one personality gets instantly vulnerable. Keep this about woods and wolves. I assume you've seen the *Wizard of Oz*. You know, when the man pulling the levers behind the curtain tells Dorothy, 'Pay no attention to the man behind the curtain'? That's you. Very young woman who should be hiding behind the curtain.

"Be squeaky clean from now on. Run background checks on all your staff—especially your ATV crew. Retire anyone with a criminal record, even a parking ticket."

"You're not going to *do* anything?"

"I get to take down our fearless leaders so they won't be trusted. You want to write any of this down?"

Carla screwed up her unlined face but reached for a small screen and held her fingers over its keypad.

"When I drop my pack by MAST's front door, broadcast the conversation you just recorded. Crank up the speakers so the highway hears it. When it ends, rewind the governor's last words. Repeat the wolf-killing part multiple times. Then find your people. I'm sure you have people."

Carla nodded without looking up. A slow grin spread from her left dimple to her right dimple.

"Get the wolf killing conversation up online. Just the audio. Add no text or visuals. Let Peter have the full story. Send it out everywhere: networks, Internet. Get the Babies on it."

Carla's fingers were still tapping when I slapped her hood as a good luck gesture. I'd been rough on her, but I thought she could take it. I hoped it wasn't jealousy over what I could do with millions I didn't have.

Weaving my way through the dispersing crowd who seemed unaware of my "Don't Shoot" vest, I thought Ian and Kate would be proud. I was about to drop important men into an electronic arena that savored the red meat of exposed people almost as much as the Roman mob appreciated lions mauling Christians. Maybe more. The Romans didn't have instant replay or YouTube. The delivery truck was gone. I assumed the newsman and the newsboy were on the road, putting distance between themselves and anyone who might slow them before they broke the story.

I intercepted two TV vans and the public radio reporter by yelling, "Get out. Hook up. Large story."

A reporter trailed me. "Where have you been? Got something good? What are you wearing? Don't shoot what? Conover? Conover!"

I saw Mike Leavitt thump through the lobby and fill the door with his bulk, so I waved from the top step and turned toward the parking lot. Pock's black nose twitched from my Subaru window and I heard his howling-for-dinner voice. I closed my eyes and saw Katu, nose to the ground on the scent of his next meal. Cameras leaned toward me. Reporters whispered, "Get a close-up of that vest."

Everyone was hungry. Good. I faced the crowd and dropped my pack. Loud speakers on the side of the building crackled into sound.

The wolf-killing plot boomed over the parking lot like a stuck record, and people formed angry groups and then swayed away to find more angry groups. They looked like schools of fish caught in currents they couldn't fight. A few men emptied gun racks in their trucks and shot out the speakers.

Mike Leavitt climbed down the steps and sputtered in my face. "If we have to save deer to feed wolves we'll be regulated right out of a hunting season. The sons of bitches will eat their way through a herd that's already a disaster."

I tried to control my urge to hop up and down. Freedom to say what I'd never had permission to say felt like the early stages of champagne—bubbles up the nose and feet off the ground. I looked into the cameras. *Here we go, Shannon. You're up here with me. Done with compromise, right? Clap loud, OK?*

"We expect people in India to live with endangered tigers," I said. "Why can't we learn to live with wolves? They need large chunks of forest and we've got nine million acres of that." I stepped down into the face of a man shouting that giving up one deer or moose to a wolf was against his religion, against his right to bear arms, and, for all I knew, against the washing instructions in his too tight underwear.

Gently I lifted his hat and squinted into his eyes. "I understand you don't want to share your game with wolves or coyotes or bears or ravens or eagles or foxes or anything else that makes meals off them, but the law is clear. You have to share. Maine's wildlife is not a carnival shooting arcade managed for an exclusive minority." I replaced his hat. "Didn't your mother teach you to share?"

"Patton," called my favorite public broadcasting reporter, "will you comment on the plot to assassinate wolves?"

I climbed back up the stairs, shaking the giddy feeling from my hands, Gordon's voice strangely loud in my ears. *You've been watered down to a pathetic squeak instead of righteous thunder ...*

I opened my arms wide, thinking I could do righteous thunder, and it helped that I knew real conservation started in the human heart, not out where animals actually lived. I wasn't sure about the hearts in the MAST parking lot, but I was pretty sure about the hearts that listened to public radio.

"Maybe it's time for Maine people to take ownership of what we already own," I said. "Maybe we didn't know *our* wildlife belongs to all of us. It does. It's a law. Salamanders to moose. Ours to enjoy. Ours to protect. Somehow a powerful club of business interests swamped the integrity of our wildlife defenders. They overwhelmed professionals we hired to guard animals that can't protect themselves. This club seduced a chunk of Maine's sportsmen into caring more about roads that speed them to easy kills than how animals might survive a forest diced and sliced by those roads.

"Today you heard powerful club members plot a wolf-killing spree. Don't trust these men. Under their supervision deer die because they have no winter shelter. Trout and salmon suffer from clear cutting and road building that ruin ponds and streams. And under the lie of something this club calls conservation, they've found new ways to bulldoze the backcountry into condos. The hunger to turn forest into cash is infinite, but the places our wild animals live, feed, and shelter shrink every day."

I saw a few women step away from their husbands and uncross their angry arms. Uncrossed female arms are a good sign, so I sucked in a deep breath and kept at it. "This club's greed scares me. I hope it terrifies you. We'd better show up and outnumber them—because we do. We outnumber them by hundreds of thousands of people who care about Maine's wild animals. So starting today, let's expose this club for what it is not.

"It is *not* the future of Maine's woods, waters, and wildlife—*all* the wildlife that belongs here, including animals we've exterminated out of greed and fear. If we welcome the wolf, despite the challenges that arrive with it, then we start to put this club out of business. So, people of Maine. Will you step up? Let's welcome the wolf—welcome the wolf home."

Of course there was no applause. Mike Leavitt's face was so swollen red with fury his cheeks made slits of his eyes. I imagined Shannon cheering wildly in the rain and wind as she ripped survey tape from trees.

Someone wearing full camouflage yelled, "You have anything to do with spilling the governor's private conversation?"

I picked up my rumpled daypack and raised my arms. "Do I look wired for that?"

CHAPTER 39

Three hours later, when I pulled over by Antler Camp's mailbox and stretched my arm toward a stack of bills, Anderson Barter pulled his cruiser from Motor Mark's dark driveway and flicked his light on high beam. I swerved to avoid him and gunned my car down the driveway. Halfway down the hill, slick gravel grabbed my tires and skated me toward the lake, but the dock's raised edge parked me roughly and delivered a dose of reality. I'd just inherited Shannon's intent to go public with wolves, and Shannon was dead.

I inhaled five deep breaths and blew them out, feeling around for a can of mace stashed under my seat. Standing in the driveway, flicking the mace lid open and closed, I heard Anderson gun his motor and squeal away. I checked my watch. With a few hours' sleep I could make the Stratton Diner for lunch and maybe snag Sam if he lurked in the neighborhood; then I'd make Phil's trailer by late afternoon. I was about to duct tape the spreading crack on my windshield when my phone rang. "Yes, Peter," I said, holding my phone together with one hand while I grunted leg lifts into the dark. I needed blood flow.

"You're not using the phone I gave you."

I didn't answer.

"If you had, you'd know, by mistake, I swapped your new phone with Ian's. You've got Ian's."

"That's great!" I said and I meant it. I celebrated with a halfhearted amateur karate kick aimed skyward.

"OK. OK. He's suffering. He tells me you've split up. He's on an all-nighter with Anita and hopping mad about the phone screw-up, but says they're close to two possible den locations. He saw you on the news and said to tell you you'd blown your cover."

"Peter, imagine netting all these bad boys at once. What are the odds we could ever do that again?"

Peter snorted. "Monson told me she adores you even though you were rough on her. We're going to need the next generation, you know. What are you *doing*? Running uphill?"

"I'm walking Pock around the outside of my mother's nursing home. Family emergency." Kate would not approve of my filing a false flight plan.

I could hear his slow breathing—a rasp on each exhale. "I'm sorry if this is a bad time, but I need you to rendezvous with Ian tomorrow and help him find the den. We'd like to run our own pictures this week."

"Tell Ian I'll try for Monday. Sorry, but I need to sort out what's going on. Tell him to leave me messages on his smaaartphone—the one that's now *my* smaaartphone."

"You know how to work it?"

"It's still a phone," I said, hanging up.

Ian wouldn't wait for Monday or for me, so I gave myself permission to go my own way. I grabbed Pock's collar, dragged him inside, and set my clock for a few hours of sleep. As I bent to untie my boots, Pock clawed open the camp door and bolted uphill toward Motor Mark's.

Thinking Anderson might have relocated to nearby surveillance, I stuffed dog biscuits in my pockets, crammed a headlamp on my head, and grabbed my emergency daypack from my car.

My neighbor's barn was a fogged silhouette when I reached the pasture, breathing hard and trying to call Pock. I bent, hands on knees, struggling for breath, and almost missed the bloody trail. I refocused my light. Brown blood. Not fresh and not Pock's. The drag trail toward the barn was recent—crushed grass struggled to stand tall again. I followed the trail uphill but stopped at the edge of the field, struck by the mystery of a large, quiet structure that appeared empty. Only days ago I'd told Millie about the wooden horse and its hidden attackers—the slaughtered town that ignored Cassandra's warnings.

To me, the comparison was as fresh as the drag marks in the grass. It could have been the shifting fog, but I felt the barn breathing. I passed my eyes over every inch of what I could see. I was the only one who could heed or ignore the warning rising in my throat.

I imagined the barn's insides. Last winter I'd slipped inside and found an exact copy of my family's barn. A hayloft filled half of the second floor so bales could be dropped to stalls below. In the open two-story space, I'd leaned against a wire pen that was still so strong my weight didn't sag it. I couldn't remember anything that could hurt me or my dog.

Wrapped in fog, the field seemed silent, but then something had bled out on the path and been dragged across the field. I swung my beam uphill over Pock's tracks. Barely visible dents in dew, they disappeared behind the barn. I had a flash of how confused a fish might feel looking up through a distorted film trying to decide if it should leap for something dragged over the surface—a fly tossed in its pool, or, in my case, something dragged up my path to the field. The barn appeared and reappeared in tattered fog. Not willing to bite, I retreated to the trees, extinguished my light, and crouched.

Pock padded around the barn's far wall. His nose greedily inhaled ground, but his body cowered inches over the dirt, tail shoved between his back legs. He looked like hungry fear.

"Pock," I yelled. "Zip, zip!" His head came up but not toward me. Staggering back he collapsed, front legs first, fighting what looked like a heavy load on his back, yowling wet gurgles until he silently dropped. I ran. I knelt over my dog just as the impact rocked me sideways with an oddly familiar thwacking sound. Gordon's website. The dart parting air as it found and dropped each Alaskan wolf.

I had time for two thoughts. *This stuff acts faster than any recreational drug I took in college. I'm drooling.*

CHAPTER 40

How had blood, hay, and perfume found their way into my bed? It took effort to heave breath into my chest. Blood, hay, and perfume—but not my bed. My hands scrabbled over crooked boards and my fingers crawled into splintered spaces. Every cell screamed. *Don't do it. Don't look!*

Then sound. Heavy rain. Not cozy cabin rain. High, angry, drumming torrents on metal. And near my head I heard musical metal and Pock moaning. Looking was required. Looking for Pock. I opened one eye to dawn dinginess and high walls swirling behind confused geometric patterns. I tried to focus. I was sprawled next to a wire fence. Someone squatted nearby. I closed my eyes and squirmed away from the smile.

I closed my eyes, smelled death, and willed my lids open to see bones inches from my nose. They were cracked into a collage of brown marrow, caked blood, and white bone. I threw up on them and pushed back against the fence. *Breath*e, I thought. *Breathe.* I recognized the perfume as Pock's recent good smell—a spice I didn't recognize. After more clinking metal, I understood. Bracelets. Victoria Brinkman. Vicki.

I moaned. So much for my ability to notice universal truths. Dawn offered no protection from a determined attacker, and a lone gun-toting woman—not a man—had shot me. My eyes felt filmy. When I thumped my head on the floor to clear my vision, shadows leaped and slithered between vertical posts across the pen.

A pen. I was in a pen. *Inside* a pen. Pock and Vicki were *outside* a pen. She hummed. Tied near the front door, Pock whimpered and scratched the floor. Inside the pen shadows leaped, crawled, slithered, and scattered decades of dust into the air. Wolves.

I tried to stand and melted to the floor. The wolves hunched together, hair erect on shoulders and ears, teeth bared—a frozen tableau of fear aimed at me. I wondered how my fear looked to them.

"They don't like quick movements," Vicki said.

I slowly stretched my legs to assess damage. All my toes wiggled, but the pain shooting up my right leg spilled nausea into my stomach and closed my throat. My one pair of good pants was crisscrossed with jagged holes oozing blood. Holes where my skin was slashed looked like a gory checkerboard.

"Barbed wire chews skin." Vicki again.

I couldn't think of anything to say. There were a million things I wanted to ask, but I didn't think any of it mattered since she planned to kill me. *That's weirdly calm*, I thought. *Well, she is. Going to kill me. I was right. Shannon's killer and the wolves—found together. I was right about it, but I probably won't get credit for it.*

"All right," she said. "I'm off on business. When I get back tomorrow morning, I expect you'll resemble the bones you barfed on."

"You. *You* were in *my* home."

"Just researching your weight so you didn't overdose. The vet bottle in the bathroom had your dog's info. I had to guess your weight from jeans and that wasn't easy. Your labels are years faded."

I found I could crawl, but each time I moved, the leaping, writhing shadows bunched together as a bristling pack. All I could think about was Marta gaily reciting the value of each tearing, chewing, shearing, grinding wolf tooth. I held my breath and rolled on my side to face Vicki. She couldn't know how the black mascara and eyeliner rimming her eyes resembled Katu—a Katu without curiosity.

Behind me I heard the wolves start to pace again. One gloved hand waved a hypodermic needle as Vicki raised the other to slide bracelets inside the cuffs of a black denim jacket she wore over matching overalls. A tight black ski cap covered her hair. I had a crazy thought that Vicki would be a woman who hated how hats flatten hair.

"Pock, lie down," I said. "Good boy. *Good boy*." He wobbled into a crouch and dropped to the floor. One wolf barked a sharp, short bark.

"They hate dogs," said Vicki.

"Your perfume on *my* dog."

"Last Friday while I readied your accommodations, he came here to eat hot dogs I'd sprinkled up the trail. One day, four dozen hot dogs, and he was mine. Today he delivered you to the barn when I wanted you." She dropped the needle into a thick rubber pouch. "I shot you with wake-up juice. I need you both fresh. I'm counting on your pet to keep them riled up and edgy. If you smell like him, maybe they'll eat you as a poor substitute."

"I was under the impression wolves didn't kill people."

"They don't. Not really. Pets are the killers. Each month a pit bull kills someone somewhere. Badly behaved wolf hybrids wreak some havoc, but they aren't real wolves. It's the exceptions I'm counting on."

"Exceptions?"

"Two wolf handlers were recently mauled and killed inside enclosures. In both cases the wolves were captured, stressed-out wild wolves." She pointed to my leg. "And the handlers had fresh wounds that invited attack."

"This seems like a lot of trouble, Vicki. Why don't you just drop a tree on me like you did Shannon?"

Eyes twinkling, she reached for an upside-down milk crate, knocked off its dust, and sat facing me. "OK. We'll chat. This has been—of necessity—a lonely process."

"Shannon," I whispered. "Shannon?" Cold, exhaustion, drugs skipping in my blood, fear, or all of it stewing together, threatened the shakes. I pressed my fist through a hole in my pants and found a spongy spot to push. Pain shot up my leg faster than I could suck air, but there was no way I'd let Vicki enjoy my chattering teeth.

She looked at her watch. "Not a long chat. Shannon was trouble, always pushing. More trees. More old trees. More limits on harvesting. More land for lynx. More land for wolves. More. More. More. When her boss wouldn't listen, she started on me. After she met up with the howling people and started looking for wolves, it was only a matter of time before she found something. She knew wildlife and she knew the woods. I'll give her that. When she said she was on the trail of wolves, I believed her and stayed right on her."

"She'd never tell you," I said. "Never."

Vicki slid an escaping overall strap back up over her shoulders. "Sam was sleeping in his car behind the gatehouse when Shannon called her friends about finding the den. Apparently their phone reception was so bad her yelling woke him, and, like always, we swapped whiskey for information." She crossed her legs with a satisfied sigh. "I tracked her from our satellite mapping system. I could even see reflective straps on her pack, so I always knew what she was up to, and later on I knew where the wolf search should start."

After I'd left the MAST parking lot and before it grew dark, Vicki had probably zoomed in on my car heading north. I was followed without being followed. "Why not have Shannon fired?" I asked.

"Have her become a wolf celebrity? Unacceptable."

"Did you mean to kill her?"

"No, of course not. That's not who I am." She was quiet for long seconds and then sat stiffly upright and roughly pulled her hat low over her ears. "Maybe that's who I used to be ... because ... here I am. Shannon might have been the last person to shut me off without giving me a chance. It sounds so clichéd to say she was the last straw and I snapped on it, but, yes ... she could have been that last straw.

"I don't have poor-me ghetto credentials, but you try potato-digging servitude with six brothers and a father who don't think you're worth notice or conversation or college or even a library card. Everyone's acted out some version of *no*, and *no*, and more *no* until Shannon's *no*. And now everything feels like ... *yes*."

She sighed and lifted her coat cuffs to drop bracelets on her white wrist. "I followed her behind Monson's gate to offer her an alternative, but she sneered at me and slammed the trust. She'd found the den and photographed the cub. She was going to self-destruct and call the feds. Make the wolves public so she could stop Wild Pines and *saaaave* the planet."

I put my hands over my ears. "I don't want the rest of it."

Vicki leaned so close to the fence her lips created a hum off the wire as she raised her voice. "When she started to crawl back in the den, I pulled the thermos out of her pack and knocked her out. The tree looked like a logical natural hazard, so I rigged a rope and dropped it on her where she lay."

Grabbing a handful of hay, I balled it tightly in my sweating palms, anything to master the obscenities I wanted to scream. "She woke up, you know." I leaned closer on my side of the fence. Only a wire strand separated our lips. I wanted to spit the words. "She thrashed with a limb in her throat until she died."

For almost a minute Vicki blinked hard and swallowed hard, but she didn't look away as she nodded and rocked back on the crate, nodded and rocked like people do when they're holding something inside. At least she'd gone quiet.

I didn't think a rational approach would save me, but I'd been trained to ask questions during impossible negotiations. "I don't get it, Vicki. Why bother? So what if one project gets sidelined by an inconvenient animal?"

She threw her arms in the air and bounced on the crate. "I can't believe you don't get it, Conover. *You* who spouts off about nature and money. Money is the only tool we have to make sure any forest makes it to the future."

The blood on my leg was drying. I could feel scab crust gluing itself to my pants. Maybe I wouldn't smell like fresh blood for long.

"The trust works because we use easement contracts to funnel foundation millions to landowners who agree to save some of the forest in return for using the rest of it the way they want to. Your kind—the squeaky-clean, enviro types—you sneer at us. You complain we're in bed with forest rapists. *You* make our funders nervous. I lost a five-million-dollar grant when the Ocean Foundation decided it couldn't trust us."

I snorted and wiped my nose on my sleeve. I don't remember sneering but I must have.

"Don't sneer at me, Ms. Conover. Congress isn't going to fund more national forests or parks. The only way to save your precious woods is do the deal. So what if they raze every goddamn tree? It all grows back. If we buy owners' rights to build Walmarts anywhere and everywhere, we get to tie up big chunks of woods as woods. So Great Nations gets some chunks they think will turn a profit as choice real estate. Really? You think that will work? I don't think Anderson Barter, his sales team, or city buyers have any idea that black flies start sucking blood in May and aren't full until November."

In my father's real estate office, I'd seen no evidence that ignorance doomed a closing, not when people dreamed of owning a piece of Maine. GNF's lots and condos would sell ... eventually.

Vicki kicked the milk crate toward Pock. Somersaulting on the edge of his leash, he lunged toward me, only to be jerked back toward the wall.

She paced outside my prison. "And what's more, if I don't raise money, I don't make the deals. If I don't make the deals, I don't get to be the first woman to head up an environmental organization with millions in assets. You know all about the green glass ceiling, don't you? A glass ceiling is just another *no*. I'll bet you've bumped your head on that *no* for years. The great outdoors isn't any different than any other place where the men in charge say, 'No, you don't get to run the place.'"

"Vicki. No one's going to blame you if wolves stop Wild Pines."

She zipped her duffel bag. "Maybe. Maybe. But I'm an opportunist. What I've got here is the opportunity to eliminate an animal that threatens my future with Great Nations, *and* I get to discredit the state's prominent green do-gooder." She pulled off her hat and shook her hair into place. "So. *You* imported them illegally. *You* are hosting and hiding them right next door before *you* release them. Of course, *you* could tell reporters you'd seen wolves. *You* were holding them in your backyard. Every group *you've* ever worked for will be tainted, and we'll be back on top in the foundation money game because everyone will assume your green friends helped *you* get the beasts to Maine."

"Vicki. I quit. I quit that work. I'm not a player."

"Oh, really?" Hands on hips, it was her turn to sneer. "Yesterday the press stampeded at you when you curved your little finger. And your speech. Perfect. 'Welcome the wolf.' Won't that look good in your obituary."

I looped my fingers over a wire segment and struggled to haul myself upright on one foot. I felt scabs pop and blood trickle down my right leg. Again, she shoved her bracelets under her sleeves. The contrast of overall Vicki with cashmere Vicki was schizophrenic. *Yes, Ian. Never underestimate female situational cross-dressers.*

"I have a date with a Montana cowboy," she crowed. She kicked my headlamp toward Pock.

I slumped down facing the wolves, who'd decided to sit touching each other while humans occupied the far end of the barn. The rain had softened to a dripping reminder that we shared the same roof. When I lowered my eyes, their hair relaxed ever so slightly. Good information. Avoid the direct stare. I'd already figured out Hmong. Within three or four yards of him, the other wolves cowered, heads and tails submissively low. I counted.

"Not curious how the wolves ended up next door?" called Vicki as she stopped to unclip her overalls and leave them discarded on the dirt floor. "I paid MAST's Montana outfitter twice what he'd earn running their shooting spree—hired him away from Mike Leavitt's predator derby follies when he said he could capture the pack, and he did. He even brought me some of that poison they use out west. For backup if I need it. If there were to be a careless mishap with the poison *you* used to punish Great Nations for going after *your* wolves, that would be tragic, wouldn't it?" She turned toward the door.

I leaned sideways to unsettle the crouching pack, not sure I'd counted correctly. "I'm curious about the radio collar. What did you do with it after Sam gave it to you?" I asked.

Her laugh sounded appreciative to me. "Oh, you got that part? I downloaded what I needed and marked up a map with the brutes' favorite routes. Then I gave the map to my cowboy friend."

"I hope you haven't paid him yet," I said. "You're missing some wolves."

Vicki stepped to the cage and frowned at the wolves that were again leaping and digging. She whacked the pen with her open palm. Terrified wolves circled in the center of the pen, urine and feces dropping from them as they sought escape.

"Disgusting," she muttered and slammed out the barn door. When she dropped the wooden cross bar in place to seal the door, the wolves, Pock, and I all jumped at the same time.

CHAPTER 41

I looked up at bird-dropping-stained windows in the barn's hayloft. I had mid-morning gray light, steady rain, two parent wolves, and three wolf youngsters. Their older brother and sister, Katu and Alak were missing. Black-rimmed eyes widening on me, Hmong helped me search the barn, turning his head as I turned mine.

Our side of the barn was two open stories of dusty air capped by the metal roof. Around us, three freestanding walls of double chicken wire were stretched into place by a rugged framework of crisscrossed lumber. Behind the wolves, the pen's far wall was nailed into the barn's siding. Outside my wall, tied to a thick iron ring, Pock lay only a few feet from the barred front door. At the other end of the barn, also outside the wire, stalls and small pens disappeared in shadows.

I scrabbled sideways to get a better view of the hayloft. I already knew that outside its door, a raised dirt ramp let trucks drive in and out of the second story. Mimicking my explorations, Hmong lifted his nose and sniffed air above his head. I thought the second-floor door had to be open because spider webs waved in a breeze we didn't have, and white mounds of swallow guano on the beams advertised outside access.

I could easily see the ancient block-and-tackle apparatus suspended from the loft ceiling, a thick rope dangling from two pulleys. As children, when this contraption in our barn wasn't unloading hay, we'd used the rope to swing out the door into the sun and then back into the barn's dark corners.

The idea of an open door somewhere made my heart thump faster until I narrowed my eyes to squint at the pen's ceiling. Like decorative silver icing, coils of barbed wire covered the top of our prison. Deceptively simple, barbed wire inflicts damage with struggle. The more one resists, the more it bites the body. I must have been almost comatose when Vicki dragged me over barbed wire.

Our pen was almost half the size of a basketball court. Crumbling hay bales littered the no-man's land between the wolves' side of the court and mine. Halfway between the wolf side and my human side, a small wood-framed door hung in the fence, its padlock looking rusted but sturdy. To my right, a sagging stack of rotting bales tilted against the far wire wall, sheets of ripped plastic tarp draping their moldy tops and glistening in gray light. When leaking rain smacked the plastic, my dry throat tried to swallow but couldn't.

The wolves were restless. I recognized Mekong for the fierce prowl that kept her body between me and her pups. Despite her warning bark, the pups crawled to the pen door, rolled on their sides, and strained against the wire. In one bound Hmong straddled them and savagely head-butted each, his lips curled back over white fangs.

Instant sweat beaded my upper lip. *Canines are the ripping teeth. Right, Marta?*

I squinted through the fence and found what tantalized the pups. A battered deer leaned against the pen, her tongue sagging low and her collapsed chest dented with tire tracks. Clever Vicki to tease them with roadkill they couldn't have and help them think about what they could have in the cage. Fangs bared, Mekong crawled toward her family. She grabbed the nearest pup and yanked it from under Hmong's snarl, nudging its head to the fence, where it could lap blood on the floor. The wolves were thirsty too.

I wondered what Vicki had done with my pack. I longed for bandages, clean sweatpants, granola bars, water bottles, and painkillers. Pock's collapsible water bowl would have been handy. Rain splashed near my feet. When I looked at the stacked hay and ripped plastic, Hmong cocked his head as if he recognized intelligent planning. Turning on my back and pushing with my good left leg, I used my arms like lobsters use claws, scrabbling backward toward the bales. I panted involuntary moans. Each lurch toward hay was a fresh knife twisted into my wound.

I reached up and pulled at the shredded tarp, ducking a flying object that thudded toward me—the pole end of a pitchfork missing its sharp tines. I had a moment of regret, thinking I wouldn't have the opportunity to skewer Vicki into a cashmere shish kabob. Held against my right leg like a splint, the pole eased my pain. I was grateful for any new tool.

Tarp in my teeth, I inched backward toward a center-court bale. I punched a hole in a sagging bale, ripped away a section of tarp, and shaped the plastic into a bowl. Ignoring snarls and growls, I used the pole to push the improvised water bowl under the largest leak, and then I scuttled back to rip another bowl at my end of the pen. All five wolves sniffed the air as they watched bowls fill. After circling the bale, Hmong drank first, unblinking eyes on my lowered eyes.

Pock lifted his head toward the lapping sounds while I hummed a soothing message. "Pock, Pock, you love my socks. When we get home they're yours alone." He looked at me with filmed, dull eyes, no sign he'd shared my bed and chewed my socks. Vicki's doses were an inexact science.

I rolled over to drink from my bowl. Something shifted in my pocket. Duct tape. Vicki had taken my pack but missed my pockets. I braced my back against my side of the fence, spread my legs wide, and arranged my emergency supplies. I felt rich: duct tape, toilet paper, fish line, nail scissors and file, a tube of lip balm, chocolate bars, dog biscuits, a wooden pole, shreds of tarp, and mace. What were the odds I could blind five wolves anyway? They hadn't shown me any reason to act defensively. I set the mace aside for Vicki.

I removed my fleece jacket, thinking that I might rip out the lining for another use. My hand slid over the passport pocket and found Ian's phone. Well, I wasn't so smart. I could have been in the hospital getting cleaned up. I could have sent a posse after Vicki or called Moz and told him I was scared and ready for help. The screen filled with a picture of my outhouse, door propped open, Ian on the seat taking his own picture. At least he was smiling. Of course there was no signal strong enough for an actual phone call, not inside a remote barn guarded by a metal roof and tall maples.

I was strangely relieved. Five sets of gold eyes glowed at me from across the pen. Mekong lay in front of her children, panting despite the barn's damp chill. Hmong sat alert and watchful, hungry eyes on Pock.

"I could have blown it, folks," I said evenly, careful to lower my head and avoid direct eye contact. Hmong cocked his ears. Mekong flattened hers and growled a warning toward her pups, who skittered toward the far wall, snapping and bumping each other.

"I might have called for reinforcements without considering your future. Apologies. Fear. Pain. That kind of thing." I unwrapped a chocolate bar and reverently arranged each brown segment on my good thigh. Each square I sucked dissolved into brown calories I visualized flooding my body. I warmed bits of lip balm between my fingers and worked them into the most painful tufts of flesh. I pulled a piece of plastic around me like a cape and wiggled my butt to secure its edges under me. The rain was slowing and on the way to clearing; the temperature was diving.

"We need a plan that gets us *all* out of here. This should be your last cage experience. Even with a signal, I can't think of anyone official to call who'd release you. Maybe Moz, but not the warden part of him. Who knows where Gordon is, but we'd hate to disappoint him at this point. Right?" Hmong padded to center court, nose up, snuffling great gulps of air. Almost eating air. My chocolate? Lip balm? Blood? So far he'd stayed on his side, executing only defensive moves.

Individual hairs in the thick ruff below Hmong's ears vibrated with meaning. I'd been dropped into a foreign country without a translator. I opened the phone, thumbed my way through Ian's downloads and found a chart with all the wolf communication I'd ever want to know: ears, mouth, tail, paws, guard hairs, postures, urination strategies, and ... muzzle licking. The pups crowded low around their mother's mouth, pushing her muzzle.

I checked the chart. Pups' licking behavior made an adult wolf regurgitate food for them. Mekong's pups were almost full grown; only their thinner chests and clumsy paws—like children wearing adult shoes for the first time—signaled their youth. Maybe stress had them regressing. Patiently Mekong allowed the slobbering, and then she bent and retched thin liquid.

Hmong stared at Pock, lips slightly parted in anticipation. Food was on everyone's minds. How could I keep five wolves at bay with a pitchfork pole? I scrolled through the phone's sound library, thinking noise might be a defense. Ian was partial to Indie bands. I wasn't sure what the wolves might like.

I found the recorded howls. They'd already terrified my dog and enraged a bull moose. This was Hmong's territory, except for the small patch where I huddled. What would the cry of a strange wolf do? Cause retreat? Attack? I closed my eyes and sent myself back to the log overlooking the river, where Bart, bathed in a green glow, scanned the river and Marta patted my knee.

I was sure I was in a hot shower with a rough washcloth on my nose, so it took a few sleepy seconds to realize I'd slid sideways onto the floor and I had wolf tongue on my face. Another second to know I shouldn't move. Was Hmong after salt? I didn't remember crying. Mentally I explored the rest of my body and found no new pain, only hairs on my forehead lifting lightly with each panted breath.

I don't remember twitching either, but I must have pressed the phone in my hand. One long, slow howl rose from between my fingers. Hmong growled against my cheek. I felt at least twenty of his forty-something teeth. I jerked my thumb over the phone's surface for silence. The pressure of his teeth eased away from my cheek. I heard careful, padding footfalls around me. Then over me. He straddled my curled body the way he'd straddled his unruly children. Belly hair scraped the top of my tarp. I felt him staring over me at my dog. *Is the animal I smell near you available for food?*

He's my best friend.

He's part of your pack?

You could say that. Mess with him and you'll have to mess with me.

Pock whined. Hmong answered. Low and deep from inside his stomach, the growl clawed its way through his throat, hissing and gurgling through his teeth. I concentrated on muscle control, regular breathing, and shut eyes. The wolf padded around me, vaulting me lightly where I'd slumped near the fence. Two powerful blows bounced my head against the barn floor. Head butts.

I yelped. "Ouch, damn it! Cut it out!"

Hmong lifted his leg to wet my section of fence and, stiff-legged, fairly bounced back to his side of the court. Straddled. Head-butted. My territory annexed by pee—but I was alive. Pock was the anticipated meal and he trembled by the barn wall. How would all of us get out without some of us killing each other?

Maybe one of us had a chance. If I freed Pock and he found an open door, I thought he'd head back to his food bowl. I sat up and slithered the tarp off my shoulders, rearranging my tools. My fingers ached. I needed them to behave, but some of them resembled gnarled, deformed witch digits from children's scary storybooks.

My fingers had terrified my husband. When I reached for Evan across the sheets, I could almost feel his private parts freeze under the covers.

"There's an arthritis treatment that restores your hands to what they were, right?" he'd asked, rolling away and offering me his back.

In the dark, I struggled with my wedding ring, then I spent the night in the bathroom, greasing my finger until the ring pinged musically to the tile floor. Nothing was going to restore the marriage, not after he'd welcomed smooth hands under different sheets.

You just never know when something will come in handy, I thought. My crooked fingers seemed ideally bent to navigate the chicken wire's curves. I dropped my nail scissors outside the fence and then crumbled dog biscuits through the mesh. The wolves padded and paced, sniffing food. I folded my right hand into a narrow wedge and scraped it through the fence to the scissors. I blew biscuit crumbs toward Pock and whispered, "Come. Zip, zip. Good dog. Let's see how close you can get. Look at me—not the bad stuff." Pock inched closer, his nose in crumbs. The leash tensed off the floor.

I fingered the scissors and nicked the leash just as Hmong's hoarse bark at my shoulder sent Pock airborne. Either the slashed leash or the wolf's threat set Pock free. Torn leash tangling his legs, he clawed the barred barn door. The pack clustered at the pen door—four wolf lengths from his feverish digging. Mekong thrust her muzzle through the mesh, curling long, lingering snarls in his direction. Hmong paced behind her. The pups studied their dog cousin, heads cocked at different angles, confused by something that was and was not a wolf. By freeing Pock, I'd only made him more irresistible to the pack. His desperate whines cut me more than barbed wire ever could.

"Pock," I yelled. "Out. Out!" He leaped away into stall shadows on the far side of the barn. I collapsed in a limp heap, suddenly lonelier than I'd ever been.

It was time to go. Scanning the windows to check on afternoon light, I studied the pen's ceiling, thinking it was about eight hay bales away. Four bales were already stacked against the wall. For my leg to hold weight I needed a splint. For padding I rolled tarp fragments around the pitchfork pole, then angled the bulky splint vertically from my ankle up into my crotch and duct taped the mess around my right leg. Instantly, spasms eased to a dull ache.

I pulled myself up on the wire and limped to the pile. I shoved at bales until each had a narrow ledge to hold my weight. I figured I needed to drag four more bales up the stack to complete my hay ladder and reach the ceiling.

The barn was losing light by the time I'd dragged all the bales into my hay tower. It helped that each rotting surface stuck to its neighbor like a moist layer cake. Five wolves lay hypnotized in the middle of the pen, watching me as if they were reality show judges. Before hoisting the final bale, I hobbled to refill my pockets with my treasures. The wolves shrank to their end of the court, but I wasn't fooled. I'd seen Hmong bound at least fifteen feet to straddle his pups. I could imagine his teeth in my ankle as I made an assault on the ceiling.

After a sweaty crawl up tottering bales, I was too tired to care that thick clamps gripped the pen's ceiling to the pen's walls, and the escape attempt was over. I didn't have any more tears. Squeaking, one bat flicked overhead toward a fall hunt. I'd lost the day and lost Pock. I crumpled on the sagging hay, shoulders wedged into the ceiling, torn leg screaming. Cold, tangy air teased through the open loft door. Against the rising moon, more bats flew out the door. Hay, bats, moon, blood, wolves, poison, murder, a witch in black cashmere—happy early Halloween.

The hay vibrated with Hmong's and Mekong's paws testing the lowest bales. As I couldn't go up and had no desire to climb down, I huddled in my tower waiting for Vicki. I hadn't forgotten her cowboy's 1080 gift, but she'd have to immobilize me before she could poison me. All I could think about was a hot bath, my bed by the woodstove, macaroni and cheese—and the mace in my pocket.

Drooping like an injured wing, my splint-heavy leg wanted to drag me off the ladder. I wound both hands through the mesh and hauled myself into a crouch. I didn't flinch when Pock's cold nose nudged my fingers. It was the right time for someone to find me. I heard his tail sweep the floor in happy circles. Dust and hay rained down on me. "Good boy. Good dog. *Extra,* extra good dog," I whispered. My best friend—not gone home for dinner, just up the back stairs to safety.

Moonlit shadows enlarged his shadow on the barn wall, his wagging tail a monstrous clock hand ticking time. Moonlit barbed wire glittered overhead like an evil frost. Someone had tossed old tires on top for extra weight, but my fingers found a gap between fence and ceiling wire. Pock flopped to the floor and licked my hand. I rubbed his muzzle and chest and under his paws found the loft's wide pulley rope. I clutched it like I'd been under water with one breath left and I tugged. Overhead the pulley creaked, and behind Pock the rope's free end slid away, unconnected to anything I could use for leverage. My end was too thick to weave through the ceiling's mesh.

The overhead pulley system glinted in half light. After a lifetime without pulleys, last week had been full of them. Engunn's boastful Z-drag. Ian hauling my canoe over the dam, and the Mahoneys' pulleys and tarps hiding their campsite. Yes. I could pull the ceiling off my head, but I'd need fish line, duct tape, and my dog to do it.

The final ceiling assault was a miraculous blend of my pockets and my dog's habit of doing the right thing after I'd given up hope he'd behave. I wove fish line into a spider's web of knots and tied one end of the web to the pulley rope and the other end to the pen ceiling above me. I wrapped duct tape around the entire mess, hoping nothing would slip. I'd connected the cage ceiling to the pulley system. I needed Pock to do the rest.

Coaxing Pock into grabbing the rope's free end used up an entire night of useless commands as he ran wildly between the open door and my begging form. Our panic energized the wolves into frantic backflips off the hay tower. Each time Hmong and Mekong charged, I felt more bales shift away from the wall. I didn't need to remember "The Three Little Pigs" to know straw structures were doomed.

Returning bats flew in the loft door and fluttered out in fright. Sobbing and clinging to the fence with one hand, I offered Pock the last biscuit. "When Vicki comes I need you to run home. No hot dogs this time." I felt Pock's muzzle in my hand. His soft lips wiped my fingers for final crumbs. "I love you, but don't think this lets you off the hook for chewing my heating pad. We could have been electrocuted. Time for you to go, boy. Pock. Out. Out! Go play. Go PLAY!"

Pock lunged for the free end of the rope and tugged it mischievously toward the barn door. He wanted tug of war. My end of the rope, taped and woven into the ceiling wire, lifted into the creaking pulley. Pock growled and jerked the rope, gaining inches. I ripped the tape off my splint and shoved the pole into the wire over my head. Pock pulled. I pushed. The rope inched into overhead machinery. The pen's ceiling clamps creaked and popped. I only needed space enough to slither away from my hay ladder.

When Hmong leaped to the top bale as I rolled into the loft, agonized hot breath blew by my ankle as the ladder melted and he tumbled to the floor.

CHAPTER 42

Outside the barn I leaned against the loft door and balled up tape on one end of my pole to fashion a padded crutch. A thin snow had ended the rain, and the world smelled cold and clean. I smelled like crushed chocolate and sweat. I watched the moon's face age gray with approaching dawn and looked left toward Mark's house, where, down the road, his white attic angled up over the maples. In front of me, hay-field stubble glinted in frost sculptures, and behind the field, unbroken forest skirted the lake and stretched north. In the east, dawn struggled with the last storm clouds, and the path to Antler Camp slashed a dark, tempting gash toward home.

Pock rolled grimly in the snow, determined to clean every part of his body. September snow meant an early, hard winter. How would I shovel the roof on one good leg? I was still warm from my escape, but that would fade when cold and reality set in.

Hunger rumbled deep inside where I dreaded Vicki's return, so I sucked small snowballs and waved Ian's phone to find a weak signal. No one picked up. I left messages for Moz, Ken, and Peter. My frozen fingers tapped twig-like at the keypad until I'd left identical messages. "V. Brinkman coming to kill me & wolves.

Mark's barn. Bring trucks. Lights. Chaos. DO NOT CALL 911. Help free wolves." I sounded screechy. "Am sane."

Where was everyone and why didn't they sleep with their phones? Calling 911 would condemn the pack to a zoo or wolf park. I'd been to a wolf park—schoolchildren on bleachers, wolves pacing a double-thick fence, haunted eyes sweeping the crowd without seeing it. The thought of Mekong and Hmong howling before cheering bleachers was just what I needed to push me over the criminal edge into not caring about jail. Somehow, despite a screaming leg, a body wracked with shivers, urgent hunger, and the threat of Vicki, I felt strangely good.

Good, except for the weight of Gordon's gold wolf lenses glittering at me. *OK Gordon, as you know, I was probably done sitting in rooms with people who never intended to change, but this should really finish it.* I stomped snow with one good leg and waved my homemade crutch at the sky.

"I know. I know!" I yelled. "Another stream, river, mountain, forest; I know they won't be done with it until it's gone. Capitalized. In the bank. I know. I get it! I'm just pissed off that today it's come down to me. The dark forces will have revenge, Gordon. They'll want more than a chunk of my ass." Pock cocked his head, unsure if my outburst was for him, but I aimed for Gordon. "You'll be laughing at me from some steamy bar when they come after me. I just know it!"

I snapped a picture of Pock and proudly sent it to Kate. *Phone progress. Love U. Up early w/ Pock. Remember always, love U more than choc chip cookies. Always.* A wave of despair lapped just behind my ears on its way to drown my brain. Even my good left knee felt more like seaweed than cartilage. I scanned incoming messages. One from Moz. Two from Peter. Five from Ian, who'd called his own phone to reach me.

Moz's voice bounced with effort. Was he running? "Ian. I am looking for Patton. You both are to avoid Victoria Brinkman. Call the police if you see her. Tell Patton that Sam gave Vicki the collar." There was a pause and truck ignition. "I am now leaving Brinkman's apartment. I found trophies. At the University of Maine, Vicki was the Woodsman Club's award-winning female logger. She dropped the tree on Shannon. On her wall are tracking-collar maps. Contact me when you have reached Patton with this message."

Timing, I thought. So much about life is timing. I wondered if it was too late to take him up on his offer to come get me if I ever found fear or fear found me.

Peter's voice carried more urgency, but he left the same surprise-Vicki's-an-ace-logger message. To collect Ian's number, I opened his last message.

"Where are you and, goddamn it, where's my phone?" he whined. "I'm going to lose the signal anyway soon. I'm past the gate. Anita found two likely den sites and I'm on my way. Yes, Mom, I'm warm and wearing other people's clothes. Sorry you'll miss me grubbing around in leaves and shit. Text me so I know you're still a threat."

I smiled and sent him some directed thought, stomping my crutch for emphasis. *Go get 'em, Ian. Yes, sorry to miss your hands in dirt, but busy here keeping Vicki occupied so you'll have a clear shot.*

Trees bloomed from fuzzy dark shapes into limbs and trunks in the gathering light. No sign of friends, and I thought I'd run out of time to call 911. Adjusting the crutch-pole under my armpit, I thumped back into the loft. I dragged a tire off the pen ceiling and tied it to the free end of the loft rope. I wasn't sure how I'd use the tire, but the weight of the rubber on the weight of the rope seemed like the start of a plan if mace failed.

I slid down the glazed ramp and hobbled toward the front door. I couldn't feel my leg and that was good, but I couldn't feel other essential body parts either. Without warm clothes, food, and rest, my time upright was limited.

Pock sat stubbornly in the field, ears flat with disapproval, head swiveling toward Antler Camp, white buoy clamped in his teeth. He'd probably dropped it outside the barn when he ate Vicki's hot dogs. I needed a safe place to stash him while I released the wolf family. To the right of the barn's front door, a rusted Cadillac sagged into a vicious rose patch. After barbed wire, what were thorns? I unwrapped the last chocolate bar and lured Pock and his buoy into the car. Wolves were a much bigger problem than chocolate would ever be for my dog.

I shouldered up the massive bar that secured the barn's front door and heaved it aside—the weight a warning that Vicki was strong beyond her slender stature. Inside the pen—rustling and movement in the dark. I fumbled on the floor for my pack and then my headlamp. Mekong was a snarl with a rigid crooked tail, ruff hairs vertical with rage. Inches from the gate, Hmong also glared his challenge. Every tooth dripped saliva.

I bent my head to avoid direct eye contact and attempted a tiptoe toward the gate, but growls punctuated each crutch thump. I aimed the pole at the padlock and slammed the lock. Nuts and metal bits sprayed the pen floor. The gate swung toward the wolves. No one moved, flinched, cowered, or pounced.

Heart hammering, I closed the gate. Not ready. Not yet. I peeled a strip of tape from my crutch and reattached the gate. I needed the wolves to flee the barn and wasn't sure if the dead deer would distract them. Grateful for a tiny doe, I grabbed a rigid hoof and limped into the field, dragging her. I prayed the pack wouldn't see or hear Pock. The Cadillac's windows were cloudy with his breath, but to weaken my dog smell, I reached for snow to clean my hands.

Under my fingers large tracks melted into a fresh trail. I scanned the field, adding my headlamp beam to the gray light and found matted trails circling the barn. One shivering, mournful howl rolled from the maple trees. It was hard to separate the gray wolf from the gray tree trunks, but when Katu's black bandit stripes moved across his heaving chest, I was thrilled to see him.

Yips, yelps, and short convulsive howls burst from the open barn door. At the end of the dirt driveway, headlights lit the visible sliver of Mike's attic wall. Vicki. I hoped she'd walk through the field to avoid leaving tire evidence. Katu's ears flicked forward at me. We had seconds. I hobbled into the barn. Caught in mid-howl, the wolves froze.

"All right, team," I said, fumbling with the tape on the door. "Family's come to pick you up. Everyone ready to go? Be swift out there. Know your poison and your traps. Have lots of pups. It's OK to eat miniature pets but no retrievers. Show up for Bart and Marta and please—" The words caught as I leaned my face into the mesh. "I am so sorry I thought you could be tools or strategies or policies. Go. Go be wolves."

I yanked the gate and dropped to the ground, body curled in fetal, bear-attack position, injured leg twitching. I tried to count small gusts of wolf air that blew by me. Against all rational behavior, I lowered my arms. Mekong's yellow dagger eyes calmly explored mine. She swung her head toward the barn door, where one pup hung over the sill, waiting.

I grinned. *You're welcome.*

Don't mess with us again.

I hope someday I get to see you running wild in the woods.

Don't count on it.

She sprang at the door and butted her child out of sight. I stumbled into the field to watch a yowling, wagging, licking family reunion over the deer carcass. Youngsters jumped over Hmong.

Mekong licked Katu and rolled him in the snow. Everyone tried to tug the deer in different directions. I aimed Ian's phone at the pack and clicked pictures while I searched Mark's farm road for Vicki. Maybe pictures would help someone recreate the scene if I couldn't.

All six wolves snapped to rigid attention in a hair-raised wedge, adults shoving youngsters to safety in the rear, so I limped a tight circle to look the way they looked—toward Antler Camp. At the edge of the field, dart rifle slung over her shoulder, Vicki vaulted off the seat of my ancient tractor. *My* tractor from *my* barn, clearly part of her plan to prove I'd captured and held the wolves.

"Shit! Shit! Shit!" she screamed.

I backed toward the hayloft.

Behind the Cadillac she raised her arm to aim at the wolves. "Shit! Shit! Holy shit! Conover! What have you done?"

Actually done *something, Vicki. Got my ass off the chair, crossed the line, left the building. Actually done something.*

She lowered her rifle as Hmong melted into the woods, dragging the deer between his legs. His family was already tail shadows waving in the trees. On a straight line north, they'd cover the miles to Bluffer Brook by midnight.

Braced across the hood of the car, Vicki bent to sight me through her scope. I was an ideal, crippled target flailing up the ramp. The loft was not my first choice of last stand locations. I'd hoped to spring at Vicki and mace her as she stepped over the raised sill of the first-floor door.

"You have a date with 1080, dearie," she yelled. "And there's enough wolf hair and crap in the barn for the feds to nail you for messing with one of their pampered species."

I dropped to the ground and rolled sideways, hoping to fall off the far side of the ramp out of sight. Coated with gravel, I teetered at the edge of the drop and closed my eyes. Vicki's laugh slid into a scream. I opened my eyes to see her gun arm jerk up as Pock slammed his buoy into the Cadillac's window. Against the glass it exploded like a giant white bullet shot through mist. Vicki fell behind the car. A dart whistled over my ear.

"Good boy, Pock," I panted, leaning on the crutch and gaining the hayloft door. "Extra good boy."

Bats swirled in the gathering light, chirping as they fluttered into ceiling cracks. I had one chance to disable Vicki—one chance and no place to hide in the loft, so my attack had to be on her turf. I leaned against the barn door and shoved it open. More returning bats swooped around my head. I tossed my crutch outside the door and ducked inside, pulling the rope and tires into the last patch of darkness. It took less than a minute for the rifle barrel to arrive at the door and scrape the sill, its black tip sliding in and out, testing the barn's atmosphere as a snake tongue tests air for prey.

"I don't think I have anything you want, so I suppose some kind of a deal is out," said Vicki. "I let you live. You take the blame for the wolves. For you ... that would be more fame than blame. I give you something you've wanted for years."

Not the purple parka, I thought. *Don't want that. Your job? Yes, your job. Good salary. Paid time to travel woods roads. Health insurance. Of course there'd be changes. Limited harvesting on easement lands. More large trees. No Bogside Bars, paved golf cart trails, sludge fields, wind towers on wild mountains.*

She chuckled as if she'd read my mind and kicked my crutch away from the door. "Right. Message received. I don't have much of what you want except what I've risked to keep. As if I'd give that up."

Vicki retreated a few steps, squinting in the door from a safe distance. Blinded with growing light, she couldn't see into the barn's dark interior. She ducked a bat, waving the rifle at its confused flight path. She ducked another and lowered the gun to reach into her hair as if the bat had messed it badly.

*Come on, bats! More bat*s. I was the bat cheering section.

Impatient to roost, a swarm swooped from the sky and aimed its black, undulating shape up the ramp. Vicki dropped the gun and waved her arms frantically over her head. Flying through the air on my tire swing, feet aimed out the barn door, I slammed her side, felt ribs crunch, and watched her sail over the ramp.

I swung back inside the barn and dropped to the floor. I felt my pockets for mace. Tossing my crutch away to decoy Vicki might have been a mistake. Adrenaline, cold, and pain had me helpless on the floor. Dots swirled behind my eyelids. I struggled for focus. I had hay up my nose and hay down my throat. I heard bats settle while I waited for the thwack of the next dart.

My memory is as spotty as the dots that took my vision. My tractor coughed into gear. There was more "Shit! Shit! Shit!" from Vicki but that faded. Someone knelt on the barn floor chanting unfamiliar words that flooded me with narcotic relief. Fingers gently worked their way under my hair and around my scalp, sliding down my neck to press my shoulders and lift each one slightly off the floor and replace it. Open hands explored my spine, pausing on each rib, and then they started down my thighs, searching each muscle until they found the barbed wire wounds. The chants became soft moans, and I wondered what I was wearing for underwear. With my nose pressed to the floor I had no desire to move even if I could have moved.

"I must examine your pain," Moz said. "Please trust me while I search. I know you are cold. Too cold. Heat will be next."

I should have opened my eyes when he rolled me over and undressed me on the barn floor, but I think I knew watching would only make it weird.

Of course, he knew that, and pressed his thumbs down over my eyelids and whispered, "No thoughts. Just feel as you return." He hugged me into something scratchy and warm that smelled like skunk traps and strange tea and then climbed in beside me. I felt really alive.

CHAPTER 43

I remembered Millie. Smelling Millie. She'd stripped down to flour-smelling skin and crawled inside the warden service blanket, replacing Moz, whom I don't remember all that well. "I think he was almost naked, too," I said. "His muscles smelled good."

"Well then, lucky you," Millie whispered. She wiped hair from my face and kneaded my back into warmth. "But now you have me since he's gone after that woman."

My eyes were open by the time Millie waved the ambulance up the ramp into the barn and checked to make sure Anderson Barter wasn't on it. She held me as I flinched away from the medic. "You'll probably be needle phobic for life," she said.

The world went black.

The day she'd tried to kill me, Vicki ended up in the emergency room of the Greenwood hospital. The night nurse closed my door and checked my IV line. "They're still stitching her up. She looks chewed. Why would anyone try and outrun Robert Atkins? I'd lie down and put all four paws in the air. First, because he was going to catch me no matter what I did, and second ..." She lifted my pulse monitor. "Well, well. *You* seem to know, deah."

After I left the hospital, Ken lugged in a month of wood before he flew to Idaho to join an undercover operation investigating illegal 1080. "I'll drive down to Boise and check out Great Nations' home turf," he said. "I've been invited on this year's wolf hunt. Some budget crisis got wolves kicked off Idaho's endangered species list. Don't ask me. I don't get the politics, but last year hunters killed almost half the population as near as anyone can figure out. We can each kill five apiece—ten if I trap five and shoot five."

Millie's foot darted out for a lethal kick, but he ducked and leaned over my bed. "Sorry. It's just that wolves are a mess everywhere. I'm not going to shoot one, but I might tag along to see what's what.

"Harworth won't be there. He's mostly in Maine trying to get an incidental take permit. When—and I say *when* so you'll be real about this—when GNF gets a permit that allows them to kill or disrupt a certain number of wolves, he plans on building his resort. Interior told him he'd need at least four breeding packs before they'd consider his application."

He played with his pocket calculator. "Allowing for pup and adult mortality, Harworth's got about twenty to thirty years before he can use the fancy roads he's put in. I'm ordering you to relax, Patton. If it looks like a wolf, hunts like a wolf, and breeds like a wolf, it stays. That gives you a decade or so to engineer a better future for these parts."

He chuckled his way out the door, but I knew he'd issued an invitation I wasn't sure I could accept. Who sends a party invitation to just one person? Beating back the FOD's was going to take a large, lively crew of volunteers and I was living alone with a dog and two more years of canned food.

The tourism office still called Maine's forest a "vast expanse of green." Maybe I could start with them and then figure out who else needed a stump field education. Talking at folks was never going to work. People should stand with one foot in a real forest (maybe on Monson's land) and the other foot in what used to be a forest. They needed to hear the swoop of birds' wings and the rustle of small creatures tunneling through brush and then lean the other way and hear only, well, nothing but insects buzzing over severed limbs.

The district attorney told me it would be tough to connect Vicki to Shannon's death on my word alone. He's charged her with my attempted murder and "likes her" for John Tario's because Moz found a vial of 1080 in her pocket. Interior's U.S. Fish and Wildlife Service charged her with transporting wolves across international borders and eight other endangered species crimes, a magic move Shannon would have preferred over a neat legal resolution.

In a press conference, the feds cited Vicki's prints on a reinforced cage, her tranquilizer rifle, dart boxes in her car, and wolf locating maps on her walls. They produced a tracking collar found in her desk and a Great Nations employee who swore that Vicki was desperate to get the collar after he'd found it in the woods. Sam's face looked just as cringing and red in the news as it did behind the gate.

Millie brought me casseroles, cookies, and a Great Nations newsletter. I dropped the charity bike race article into the fire and watched Engunn's green Lycra melt into what could only be Idaho's Sawtooth Mountains. Who needs craggy peaks and a paycheck when I have Millie recruited for the next fall's "no balls" trip? The food will be fabulous.

Peter's board of directors closed the print side of the paper, and the irony of my Value Nature blog wasn't lost on either of us. He stopped by camp and left me his *Bangor Weekly* gas card to use up and told me to keep writing. The digital edition would pay.

"They'll pay," he said. "Not much, but they'll pay." In gaslight, his sagging skin looked terminal, but his eyes burned with hope. "Ian's taking me out west as a researcher. I've never been to New Mexico. It's time I accepted help and some adventure. The kid owes me."

"Make sure he wears rattlesnake-proof boots," I said.

Peter left me his aftershave-scented blueberry parka, and while Pock snored on my good foot I used it as a pillow and worked up a post on Maine's most enduring economic sector. Rebuttals and testimonials almost crashed the site, and advertising doubled. It's not my fault wildlife churns out over a billion a year for Maine. The new online editor was ecstatic.

Before Ian left for the desert, he stitched my old guide patch, still gritty from Grants beach, onto a new, screaming-red L.L.Bean jacket. He loaded the pockets with toilet paper, mace, chocolate bars, and my fingerless gloves.

I pushed my father's fur hat on his head and wished him luck. I also slipped a copy of Thoreau's *The Maine Woods* into his pack, mostly to irritate him. I folded the page where Thoreau confesses he'd found Maine's most intelligent residents deep in the forest. Maybe Ian would remember Rachael, Ken, Millie, Moz, Anita, Bart, Marta—and me—and shove up his sunglasses and smile.

Activists in New Mexico promised him a good salary if he'd expose dark forces killing endangered jaguars, but I understand the big cats aren't nearly as friendly as wolves. He left Maine a hero. A self-snapped photo in front of the den, fingers split in a peace sign over the pup's carcass and the massive stump he moved to get at it, went viral around the globe.

The press missed Ian's best story. Pinned to my camp wall are his sketches of wading herons, stump fields shaded to look like cemeteries, snarling skidders, ducks leaning into the wind, and his own fingers deep in wolf pup fur.

Rachael Kenneth accepted the help of a Carla Monson ATV ranger, a retired attorney hired to put the inn on the National Registry of Historic Places. She put up a "For Sale" sign, hoping her tax-exempt status arrived before a buyer was fool enough to take on "too much work and too much rot."

Except for Katu's sister, the wolves have disappeared. Alak's buckshot-riddled, gutted body hung off the bridge near Grants two days after I freed the wolves. The pack roamed across my pill-fogged brain for days, fading in and out of Carla Monson's forest, loping through Baxter State Park's roadless mountains, noses down on moose trails north into Penobscot lands. Only one Carla Monson border was vulnerable to possible wolf crime, and so many ATV rangers patrolled it even a low-slung weasel would turn and slink home.

Carla either took my advice or listened to her Baby Billionaires. She's as absent as the wolves. Her foundation office emailed me an invitation to the grand opening of a "Precious Predators" exhibit sponsored by the Maine Association of Sportsmen and Trappers. Mike Leavitt's not smiling in the publicity shot.

Last month *Forbes* magazine awarded her "Don't Shoot" clothing line first place in a contest called "Marketing Social Justice." The cover featured women wearing orange burkas as they occupied an all-male parliament building. Carla had to be there under a burka, so I taped the picture to my refrigerator.

Great Nations Forest LLC posted Ian's and my photos with eviction notices at all five gates, but I can get around that. Bart and Marta have a new project designing technology for wildlife forensic investigators. They drive a company-owned motor home with huge, dirt-hugging tires. "You'll fit in the closet," they hummed on the phone. I felt like humming back.

I never figured out why Shannon distrusted Phil, but if she didn't take his offer of a better job, I trusted her instincts. She probably knew that choosing wolves and betraying Great Nations wouldn't help her résumé or repay her loans, but it would feed her soul.

Kate and her roommate came to clean house, change my sheets, and Kate left me her will. Scrawled but detailed and witnessed, she'd cut her father off from inheriting her unused gift cards. "No-shows don't get the good stuff," she'd said. "I want you to have it all." When I was up and around, I'd have to deal with the resilient residue of our losing Evan.

The young women wired a hookup to Motor Mark's signal. I said I didn't need it, but they insisted. "We stopped at Sea View to see your mom," Kate said. "Gran-gran talked us into putting you on a dating site. Says the nurses are always telling romantic stories. She helped us with your profile, and you'll like this: she said we had to list your religion as Church of Nature. She's off hospice and on multiple desserts." Kate leaned in to squeeze Pock and me in a hug that smelled like baby powder and mint tea. "Your account's called flyfishfemme. Have fun, Mummy!"

In my zip code corner of the world, *flyfishfemme* attracts gun rights evangelists and militia wannabes. Church of Nature turns out to be code for closet nudists. Fending off suitors from divergent camps helped pass the healing time.

From her poster above my bed, Shannon's always laughing. *Good lord, Patton. These people are creepy! How on earth do they plan to "satisfy" you on a first date? Who even brings up satisfaction on a first date unless they're talking wine or cookies?*

I received a bug-splattered, beer-stained paperback copy of *The Monkey Wrench Gang* in the mail. No message, and postmarked from Santarém, a steamy Brazilian city hacked from jungle. The book's hero is an irreverent vet bent on saving wild deserts, and apparently, it's the classic hymn to lawbreaking on behalf of the natural world. Trust Gordon to sink his teeth into my most sensitive tissues.

Moz seems to have firm control over a business called North Woods Security Systems. He allows no press coverage, photos, or incidents, so no one knows what it does, but I can guess. Commissioner Robertson's attempt to fire the Warden Atkins part of Moz fizzled after a visit from the chief of the Penobscot Nation. Most days I hobbled up to my mailbox hoping for a paper-bag puzzle, but all I received was a map with a date scrawled on it.

The first November week I could limp without crutches found me on a ledge next to a freezing river—sitting where Moz's map said I should be. September's freak snow had been a good predictor of an early winter. Chunks of ice careened around the river, behaving, I hoped, like my white blood cells on active duty, and my arm ached from shots sent to destroy barbed wire germs erecting scabs on top of scabs. Pock's head twitched on my leg brace as he ran in his sleep.

I eased his head onto my pack and stood to hobble up and down my slice of rock. All around me tall trees stood like silent statues, their green needles slowly losing color to fading light. Shaggy and suddenly dark, they looked like they'd closed ranks to defend us. A pileated woodpecker's sharp cries sent something small and furry scurrying across the rock inches from my feet. Pock's nose only twitched a bit in sleep. I was so glad to be outside that even small patches of gray lichen clinging to rocks seemed more interesting and alive than anything I'd seen from my bed.

I opened a bag of Road Kill croissants and breathed chocolate the way people sniff paper-bag air to recover equilibrium. I settled my headlamp around my wool hat, not sure I'd need it. As it rose, the moon appeared to pour rich, white cream into the river.

Pock sat up and arched his back, sniffing at ice chips nudging his paws. He thrust his nose into the wind and then crawled behind my legs. In the middle of the river, white beams shivered as thin shapes sliced the current—four oversized war canoes so low in the water, paddlers' waists looked disappeared into dark liquid. They came at us from Canada, surging forward on explosive strokes, cargo spaces crammed with tarped shapes.

A few boat lengths from my rock—close enough to see black paint on chiseled, high cheekbones—each canoe tipped slightly, shuddered in the pull of downstream current, and disappeared. The last canoe aimed for our rock. Pock wagged his whole body and crouched for a happy leap. I lunged for his collar. We collapsed together, feet in the river, bodies jumbled on the ledge. The last visible paddler raised a blade in quick salute. On it painted coyotes danced away into the river's shadows.

"Shhhhhh. Shhhhhh," I whispered to Pock. I didn't expect anyone to howl, not my trembling dog, the kidnapped animals, the paddlers determined to heal their lands, and—of course—not Moz. I knew I wasn't breathing, hypnotized by white light on heaving shoulders, wolves silent and crouched in dark crates, and a front-row seat to an ancient wrong secretly set right. *Home,* I thought. *Home.*

I don't regret giving up the statehouse and the sad state of my career. Engaging the Forces of Darkness on natural turf feels like weather in my face. I'd rather have weather in my face than a microphone under my lower lip any day.

For the most part, when animals aren't chasing or threatening me, they're on my side and I'm on their side. I couldn't have subdued Vicki without the wolves' warning, Pock's Cadillac attack, or the bats' assault on my attacker's perfect hair. And without my stepping up, the wolves might be entertaining school field trips instead of rolling in wet sand, head-butting unruly pups, howling just to howl, or going nose to nose with a moose in a bloody ancient dance I'm sure we'll never really understand.

My best friend licked my hand and wagged his damp tail. I stomped my feet and felt ice water soak my socks. Then I switched on my headlamp and aimed the small beam up a dark trail into dark woods.

ACKNOWLEDGEMENTS

Deadly Trespass could not have happened without the support of people who believed, people who answered my calls for help, and those who taught, guided, instructed, and said, "Don't you dare give up." Thank you, all.

I owe a huge debt to my Stonecoast Writers' Conference classmate and my writing "buddy," author Meredith Rutter, (aka Meredith Marple, "*The Year Mrs. Cooper Got Out More*"). She not only catches every tiny error, she also listens to my dreams so that her praise and criticism always honors my journey. And my appreciation to our conference instructor, author Lily King ("*Euphoria*"). Your "character, character, character" message got though.

Thank you to biologist Peggy Struhsacker for reading a first draft and using her wolf expertise to give me professional feedback. I am indebted to wildlife biologist Ron Joseph for his 33 years defending the wild world and letting me know a pre-publication draft read accurately as "almost non-fiction." Maine biologists

Mark McCollough, Wally Jakubas, and Bill Noble took my calls and questions early in the process.

Thank you, brother Rupert for giving me author Rick Bass's *Nine Mile Wolves*, and thank you, Rick, for your mentoring at the Bread Loaf Orion Environmental Writers' Conference.

I am grateful for the clear-eyed research and wild world eloquence I found in *The Wolf Almanac* by Robert H. Busch; *The Great American Wolf* by Bruce Hampton; *Vicious, Wolves and Men in America*, by Jon T. Coleman; *Return of the Wolf, Reflections on the Future of Wolves in the Northeast* by Bill McKibben, John Theberge, Kristin DeBoer, Rick Bass, and editor Rick Elder; *Of Wolves and Men* by Barry Lopez; and (the bible of wolf biology), *The Wolf, The Ecology and Behavior of an Endangered Species*, by L. David Mech.

Good friend Linda Koski's work to painstakingly proof early drafts was a special gift. My first "beta" readers gave me support and courage: Norma Dryfus asking permission to send loved pages to NY friends, and eclectic, literary Mike Welebit, on the eve of a Middle East job, staying up too late, getting pulled into the story, and telling me the wolf chapter was "pure literature."

Thank you to agent Paula Munier, who, after reading my manuscript, left me messages on cell, land line, and on line saying she "loved it." You gave me invaluable gifts of professional content editing and advice.

A special thanks to four friends who became my mantra when I first sat down to write and burst into tears. Chanting their names ("Dorcas, Gretchen, Sally, Jean"), kept me unafraid and typing. And Dr. Sally Stockwell, thank you for listening to chapters over the phone, telling me I had bull frogs wrong, and laughing in all the right places when I'd been alone too long.

And gratitude to Kwill Publishing's Cate Baum who has been a stunning editor, a truth teller to her authors, and a mentor of hope to me. When I said I had no idea how the unpublished manuscript could win awards and not find a traditional publisher, she said, "Oh, I know why," and rolled up her sleeves to make *Deadly Trespass* happen.

And finally to Phyllis Austin, Maine's ace outdoor reporter and lover of all things wild who left us in 2016. Phyllis, this work may be officially fiction, but wherever you are, you know it's not. Because I saw how you dug out every scrap of truth and then verified it until it shone clearly in badly needed light, I learned that truth is not something relative, it's just hidden...and waiting. Thank you, Phyllis.

QUESTIONS FOR BOOK CLUBS AND READERS

1. When did you know the narrator was a woman? What gave her gender away? Did it matter if you didn't know right away? Why did the author make this choice?

2. The author, Sandy Neily, said, "The hardest part, after working for decades in conservation, was learning how to write a story that wasn't preachy, that might just be compelling entertainment. It was hard work to harness larger themes so the story and characters came first." How'd she do?

3. What is Patton's relationship is to the natural world? What events disclose or deepen this relationship? Does Patton grow or change during the novel?

4. Patton's game warden friend, Moz, leads a conflicted life between his Penobscot Nation roots and his game warden profession. Have you had to navigate a conflict like this? What are your coping solutions?

5. The author does not bring Patton and Moz together despite their attraction. Why?

6. *Deadly Trespass* takes places in a hunting and fishing world that may not be familiar to some readers. Did the story's treatment of this world challenge or surprise you in some way?

7. If you are more familiar with this sporting world, did the author help or hurt people's understanding of it?

8. Pock may be a dog, but he's an important character. What does he add to the story beyond moving the plot forward?

9. The intern reporter, Ian, is a foil and contrast for Patton. What are the urban and rural tensions? The tensions between technology and a more primitive world?

10. Some early readers thought Patton might not be "likeable" enough, but the author decided to keep most of her protagonist's rough edges. Why do you think she made that choice?

11. Do you have a special "wild" or wild-feeling place that is at risk? What forces are at work there?

12. Patton accepts her law-breaking role as she frees the wolves. Can you imagine a situation where you would step outside the law to defend something?

13. Do you agree or disagree with Patton when she says, "...wild animal health depends on our setting up the outdoors as a zoo—a zoo without bars. I know it's a contradiction, but today no animal can be free until we accept responsibility for its freedom. I don't care if you crate it up and ship it to Yellowstone, dismantle dams so fish can swim upriver, or pass laws that stop people

hunting species into extinction. Human hands are all over wild, but then we have to step back and let wild ones be what they are..."

For fun or just extra credit, what would you do if someone sent you a belly fat book? I'd love to know, so please email me! And I'm happy to arrange Skype Book Club visits.

Go to http://www.authorsandraneily.com

LEAVE A REVIEW

If you enjoyed this book, why not leave a review on Amazon?

You can also leave a review on Goodreads.

Thanks! Sandy

Made in the USA
Middletown, DE
03 December 2018